LETTERS
FROM THE
PRESIDENT

LETTERS FROM THE PRESIDENT

John Little

ALLEN & UNWIN

First published in 1995 by
Allen & Unwin Australia Pty Ltd
9 Atchison Street, St Leonards, NSW 2065 Australia

National Library of Australia
Cataloguing-in-Publication entry:

Little, John, 1942– .
  Letters from the President.

  ISBN 1 86373 919 X

  I. Title.

A823.3

Set in 10/11.5 pt Times by DOCUPRO, Sydney
Printed by Australian Print Group, Maryborough, Victoria

10 9 8 7 6 5 4 3 2 1

FOR ANNA

One

The ferry appeared in the distance as a shapeless smudge, ploughing steadily through early morning water the colour of lead. As it grew larger Laura Bailey began to make out details: old-fashioned superstructure, an elegant counter stern, a hint of blue paint, woodwork gouged by years of hard work. Behind the windows of the wheelhouse she glimpsed a bristled face with a black cap jammed on top, wisps of white hair escaping out the sides. The skipper looked as worn as his command.

Thirty yards from the wharf the thud of the exhaust slowed. Laura saw a flash of spokes through the windshield, a hand reaching for a lever. The bow swung and the vessel glided alongside. At close quarters now, she could hear the clatter of the diesel revving deep inside the hull, shaking the timbers and rattling the windows as the screw fought forward momentum. The whole quivering mass slowed and stopped, with the sponson just kissing the piles. Stepping leisurely down from the wheelhouse, the skipper walked to the stern, dropped a loop of line over a bollard and stood aside to allow his passengers to disembark. When the last of them had said their singsong, 'Bye, see-ya-later-on,' he looked up to where Laura stood waiting, grinned and swept his arm aside in an exaggerated gesture of welcome.

Automatically she grinned back, showing no sign of the turmoil she felt. She stepped down onto the ferry.

'And where can I take you today?'

'I'd like to go to Coaster's Retreat.' Her American accent was a grating contrast to the flat Australian drawl.

The skipper doffed his cap in mock politeness. 'Yes ma'am. Leaving right away. Which jetty would you like to get off?'

'I was hoping you might be able to help me with that. I'm looking for a gentleman called Bing Connick. Do you know of him?'

'Sure. Everyone knows Bing. Must be a friend of yours, hey?'

She smiled. 'Well actually no, we've never met. But I'd be grateful if you could let me off at the right place.'

'No trouble.'

The skipper deftly flipped off the mooring line and with three blasts of the horn guided the ferry astern. Plunging the throttle forward he churned up mud and foam before gathering way and heading downriver. Once on course he glanced back at his solitary passenger. 'Like to step up into the wheelhouse and I'll give you the tour?'

Laura smiled at the Australian informality. 'Thank you, that would be marvellous.' She climbed three steps and stood beside him, looking out at the riverbank slipping by. It was typical Sydney bushland. Pink angophoras, she-oak and ti-tree. Now and then she spied a glimpse of a house, often little more than a shack with a jetty and pontoon in front.

'What sort of people live out along the river?' she asked.

'Not many have regular jobs. They're mostly artists, writers, fishermen, that sort of thing. Bing's pretty typical. He turned up about ten years ago. He reckons it's paradise.'

A few ruffles on the water signalled the beginnings of the sea breeze. The skipper pointed through the window at a jetty jutting out into the river, a battered-looking aluminium boat tied to it. 'That's Bing's place now.

You'd better step up to the stern and get ready to hop off. I suppose he's expecting you?'

She smiled, more to herself than her guide. 'No. This is a surprise.'

The skipper guided them alongside. Laura stepped ashore and turned to wave, receiving a raise of the hand in return. For a moment as she watched the ferry recede into the distance, she thought of calling it back. Her arrival at this rocking pontoon was the end of a journey which had begun two days earlier in the United States. In the familiar comfort of the Jumbo droning over the Pacific, her quest had seemed logical and right. She was not used to self-doubt, but now that she was here, about to confront a man she had never met, with a proposal which would probably seem quite insane, she was not so sure. She turned towards the land. A bearded figure, barefoot, wearing ragged shorts and a threadbare Hawaiian shirt with all the buttons undone to reveal a brown chest, was walking down the jetty towards her. He was carrying a knife.

For a second Laura had a moment of panic. What did she know about Connick anyway? Why does a successful, respected professional toss everything in to bury himself in a backwater like this? Perhaps he was mad. No one knew she was here. What if . . .? But then rationality reasserted itself.

The man waved his knife. 'Excuse the gore.' Laura noticed his hands were bloodstained and a blob of gut glistened on the instep of one foot. 'Bing Connick. Welcome to Coaster's Retreat.' The words were polite, but there was no welcoming smile accompanying them. The sun came out from behind a cloud and suddenly, as if someone had turned a switch, the buzzing of cicadas filled the air. She had the feeling that she was an intruder in an alien place. Connick was waiting.

'My name's Laura Bailey.'

He said nothing. She went on rapidly to fill up the silence. 'From Nebraska.' She rushed on. 'I should explain.' But how could she explain to this sunburned man here on an isolated river in Australia the lifetime of love and anguish that had led her here?

Still he said nothing. In Laura's experience there were certain rules of conversation. You did not just leave people hanging. Connick looked at her, refusing to help. Rude bastard, she thought. She was about to say something cutting when he spoke. 'Perhaps you'd better start at the beginning.'

She looked about. 'Do you think we could sit down somewhere?'

He stared hard at her. Grey eyes in a brown face. For a moment she thought he would turn and leave her standing there, then he shrugged. 'OK, follow me.'

Connick picked a keeper net out of the water with half a dozen fish in it and led her up a short path to a weatherboard house hidden in the trees. On the verandah were a couple of rods and a tackle box. Odds and ends of tools. Beyond, Laura could see a clean, airy interior, cheap furniture, polished wooden floors with a couple of Middle Eastern rugs scattered on them and a few prints and posters on the walls.

He gestured towards a sagging couch on the verandah. 'Make yourself comfortable while I put these fish in the fridge. Coffee?'

'Please, white and no sugar.' He hasn't even asked who I am, she thought. Maybe living here has killed his curiosity. Another thought occurred to her. Perhaps he's lost his talent entirely.

In a few minutes Connick returned and handed Laura a steaming mug. He sat down in a creaking cane chair and waited. She said, 'The ferry skipper told me you reckon this is paradise.'

The corners of his mouth turned up slightly in either a grin or a grimace. It was hard to tell.

'Bob Ross? He's right, it is paradise. This is one of the last peaceful places left on earth. It's America twenty years ago, without the crime, the pollution and the rat-race. Great climate, great people, plenty of space. It suits me fine.'

4

'How do you spend your time?' Laura asked.

'A bit of fishing. Sail a bit. Grow a few vegetables. Have a drink with the neighbours. That's about it.' He gave her that look. Again, neither friendly nor unfriendly. 'And you?'

'I run a ranch.'

Connick said nothing. 'Do you find that hard to believe?' she asked challengingly and was annoyed again by his ability to put her off balance.

He said, 'I guess you haven't come here to talk about ranching. You'd better tell me what it's all about.'

This man doesn't like me, she thought. He's like some sort of hillbilly, suspicious of strangers. She wondered again if she had made a mistake. She put the mug down. 'Can you remember what it was like, Mr Connick, to be young and in love?'

'Love?' he repeated thoughtfully. 'No, I'm afraid I can't remember much about love.'

'I want to tell you a love story. A twenty-year-old American girl and an airman. He's twenty-three. It's during the Vietnam War. You do know the war?'

'Oh yes. I spent a lot of time in Vietnam. Too much time.'

'Well he was posted there. His name was Dan. He and his fiancée had their whole future planned. He would do his tour, come home and they'd be married.'

'His fiancée? Old-fashioned word. What happened?'

'He never came back. His plane was shot down. After the war ended there were no remains, no name tags, nothing. He just disappeared.'

'An MIA.'

'Yes, missing in action.'

Connick's attention focused on a pair of brilliant red, green and blue lorikeets which fluttered down to the rail and began picking at some seed he had scattered there. He could not help noting the familiarity of the situation. Much of his professional life had been spent listening to stories like this. The journalist still in him could see it now; grainy photographs of the young lovers from two

5

decades ago, some description of the war in Vietnam, the core interview with the surviving lover, a few tearful quotes. He would have turned it into a nice thousand-word feature. He had written many such stories and in the end had grown unutterably weary of them. He became aware that she was waiting for him to say something.

'What happened to his girlfriend?'

'I waited and waited for some word. The worst part about it was that there was nothing conclusive. I didn't know if he was alive or dead. He was just missing. I sometimes think it would have been better to have learned that he was dead instead of nothing. As it was, my life just sort of marked time.'

Connick mumbled something which she took to be sympathetic.

'By 1972 I could tell that the war was coming to an end. I was still clinging to the idea that he might come back. He was shot down in '67. In '73 the war ended and all the POWs came home. When he wasn't among them I made a decision. I decided to get on with my life. There was a man who'd been courting me. I got married and tried to forget all about him.'

'But you couldn't.' It was a statement, not a question.

'I thought marriage would cure me, but it didn't. All the time there was this unanswered question about Dan. It should have worn off with time, but instead it got worse. It's become something I just can't shake. I keep asking myself, is he sitting in some damn jungle prison rotting away? Or is he living in a village wearing black pyjamas and a conical hat, tilling rice? I can't let it go.'

'Have you asked the State Department for information?'

'I've asked everyone I can think of. All they can tell me is where and when he was shot down and that he's missing. They're working on it they say. Goddamn bureaucracy. They're hopeless.'

Connick was about to ask another question. Suddenly he was disgusted at his interest. 'Let me tell you something about MIAs,' he said, more harshly than he meant to. 'There's been hundreds of stories of sightings. I've chased a few of them and they've come to nothing. There's an entire industry in South-East Asia preying on the relatives of missing Americans. Show them a fake photograph, phony dog tags, promise them a reunion, take their money and run. No one's ever seen one. I don't know what you've got in mind, but I'll tell you this for free. Your boyfriend is dead. He either died when he crashed or he died afterwards, but he's dead Mrs Bailey. Face it.' With an effort he softened his tone. 'Why are you telling me all this?'

'I'm quite well off. I could never have done anything while I was married, but now . . . I've come here to make you an offer. I want you to help me answer the question once and for all. I want you to find out what happened to Dan. I'd pay you well.'

'Money's a very low priority for me, Mrs Bailey.'

Laura looked around her at the weatherboard cladding obviously in need of paint, Connick's ragged clothes, the sagging verandah furniture. 'Oh really? If I'm not mistaken you could do with a few dollars.'

'I get by.'

'And what about the story?' She looked at him squarely, feeling at last she was getting his measure. 'You know a good story when you see one don't you?'

Off in the bush a kookaburra gave out a raucous cackle. As if it was a trigger Connick laughed harshly. 'If you've come all this way to try and interest me in an MIA story I'm afraid you've wasted your time. I haven't written a story in ten years and I hope never to write another.'

'You used to be a good journalist. Some say great. I didn't often agree with you but I read your stuff for years.'

'That part of my life is over.' He waved his arm in a sweep encompassing the birds, the river, the house. 'This is my life now.'

'Why don't you give it some thought?'

Connick studied her in silence. Wide-set blue eyes,

7

straight blonde hair which she allowed to fall naturally to just above her shoulders. A little out of her depth, but underneath he could sense her resolve. She was right. Although he lived simply, his investments had been eroded by inflation. He could do with the money. But an MIA story? That particular wild-goose chase had been the downfall of half a dozen journalists he could name. Despite himself he toyed with an idea, just for the hell of it. Forget finding a long-lost American. This woman, with her twenty-year fixation could be a story herself. A magnificent obsession. It might be worth a few dollars to one of the glossies.

He got up, walked over to the rail, picked up some seed and held it out at arm's length. Two lorikeets fluttered over to him, landed on his wrist and began eating out of his hand. Then another pair perched on his shoulder. In a few moments there were a dozen of the little birds all over him. He turned back to her and with a chorus of angry chittering they rose up in a rainbow cloud.

'How tough are you, Mrs Bailey?'

She looked at him evenly. 'Tough enough. Why?'

'There's a reasonable chance that poking around in Asia looking for MIAs could be dangerous. I just wonder if you could handle it.'

Laura got to her feet, stepped close to him and deftly grasped his wrist and forearm. She swivelled her hips and flipped him over so that he landed flat on the ground on his back.

The breath whooshed out of Connick's lungs with the impact. He looked up in surprise. She was standing in a loose stance with a slight smile on her face.

'Jesus Christ. You've been watching too many movies.'

'My daddy taught me that. Taught me how to throw a steer or a man, whichever gave me trouble.'

'So, you've learnt a few moves. I'm talking about a different sort of toughness.'

'You don't have to worry about me. I'm tough enough.'

Connick got to his feet and smiled. 'All right. I'll tell you what, let me think about it. Where are you staying?'

Laura named a motel ten miles away from the ferry wharf. It was a lot more downmarket than she was used to but was the only accommodation she had been able to find within reasonable distance.

'Give me a day. I'll come by the day after tomorrow and we'll talk some more.'

Laura Bailey gazed at him coolly. 'That would be fine, Mr Connick.'

'Call me Bing.'

'Well thank you! It's Laura.'

By the time Laura boarded the ferry for the trip back from Coaster's Retreat the sea breeze had set in, flicking up little whitecaps and joggling the pontoons along the river bank. There were a dozen or so passengers on board. Bob Ross, after giving her a nod of recognition, spent the journey chatting with two women. Laura was glad to be left to herself. She wanted to think about the meeting which had just taken place. Bing Connick was unsettling. She thought of herself as a straightforward person and she expected most other people to be the same. She wondered what made him so prickly.

After the ferry pulled into the wharf she drove her hired car back to the motel. The rooms were built of painted concrete blocks and decorated with drab brown furniture. The carpet was a hideous floral design installed more for its ability to hide stains than for any aesthetic reason. She noted with amusement the small door set into the wall for breakfast to be passed through in the morning. There was a tray with teabags, a miniature jar of instant coffee and some satchels of sugar on a bench. In the refrigerator the manager had placed a small bottle of milk. The motel was like Australia, she thought, quaint and a little bit behind the times.

She walked into the bathroom and noted the cheap

plastic fittings and the strip of paper sealing the toilet lid with a message assuring her that it was clean and sterilised. Looking around, she noticed that the wash-basin had a grimy ring around it. The bath too looked as if it had not been cleaned for ages. With a grimace she went outside and marched down along the row of cell-like doors to the office. As she stepped in she could hear the sound of a television set in a back room somewhere. She gave the bell on the counter two sharp smacks with the flat of her hand and a few moments later the proprietor appeared. A slight man with a weedy little moustache and thinning hair, he was wearing shorts and rubber thongs and a shirt which looked as if it had been slept in.

'Mrs Bailey, room 8. The bathroom's filthy.'

The man blinked dully. 'Filthy? It can't be, it's cleaned every day.'

'That bathroom hasn't been properly cleaned in weeks, let alone every day. I'd like you to fix it please. Now.'

The owner stared at her with dislike. 'I'd like to help, but the cleaner's left for the day. I'll have her see to it tomorrow.'

'I can't wait until tomorrow. I want to use the bathroom now and I'm not going back to that room until it's clean.'

'Lady, it's not possible,' he said in exasperation.

'Isn't it? Surely the program can't be that riveting.'

The man held her gaze for a moment then dropped his eyes. It was not through any desire to give service that he capitulated. There was something about Laura's demeanour that made him realise there would be no point in arguing further. Silently cursing the fates that had sent this harridan to him he went back inside and fetched cleaning equipment. Laura was tactful enough not to watch as he got down on his hands and knees and scrubbed the bathroom until it gleamed. As he was packing up she looked over the results.

'That's fantastic,' she smiled. 'Thank you. I'm sure I'm going to have a wonderful stay here.'

She closed the door. 'Bloody ballbreaker,' he muttered. But not so loud that she might hear.

Laura made tea, then turned on the television to be confronted by a game show. An excitable man kept up a barrage of talk while he spun a wheel. It stopped and an overweight woman shrieked with delight, enveloping him in an exuberant hug. She switched channels. A young woman was talking with exaggerated brightness to a person dressed in a bear suit while an audience of four-year-olds listened attentively. Sighing, she turned down the sound, opened her purse and took out a photograph.

Dan was wearing his uniform. He gazed confidently at the camera, clean-cut and sure of himself. The definition was good enough to see the smattering of freckles across his nose which gave him a little-boyish quality. Although it was a black and white print, she could picture the precise shade of his striking red hair, the way he held himself, everything about him.

The TV program had changed. The Three Stooges mouthed at the camera with silent lunacy. The middle one turned and poked the one next to him in the eyes, then did the same thing to the man on the other side. She remembered a weekend they had lain in bed naked, arguing with mock ferocity about which one was Curly and which was Moe. At some stage Dan kissed her and she had whispered to him to wait while she turned over onto her knees so he could slide into her from behind. She had felt wanton and deliciously sluttish and she didn't care. She was so in love she would do anything.

Laura held the photograph against her breast and closed her eyes. They had loved everywhere. In his car, on the beach, standing up in a stairwell, once in a canoe. For a few vivid months she had gorged on love, then he went to war. She blinked and with an effort dragged her mind back to the present. For a moment today Bing Connick had almost convinced her she was being foolish. Now, her resolve was back again. She ordered a room service meal and propped the photograph against a water glass where she could see it while she ate.

Two

When Laura left, Bing watched the ferry disappear around a bend in the river then got into his battered runabout and headed in the opposite direction. He stayed close to the shore, the aluminium hull clanging noisily as it pounded the wavelets. Every now and then he waved at people as he passed but he did not stop, he was heading for a pontoon half a mile away where Brett Davey lived.

A successful artist who could easily have afforded a lavish home in one of Sydney's expensive suburbs, Brett preferred a weatherboard house on the river where he lived with his wife and a large brood of children with coffee-coloured skin. Brett's wife Kath was Aboriginal. They had met when he was in the Northern Territory attempting to capture on canvas the incredible landscape of red, ochre and blue.

Brett was seeking permission to enter tribal lands up near the Gulf of Carpentaria. He had to negotiate with the local Land Council and Kath had been the liaison officer. Tall and slim, with the wide mouth and flat nose of her people, she wore her jet black hair swept back dramatically from her forehead, only partly tamed by a headband. Hers was an unconventional beauty and there had been an immediate attraction between her and the bearded artist whose attitude to life was in many ways more Aboriginal than white.

At that time Brett was living a nomad existence, travelling and sleeping in an old Volkswagen Kombi van. He was passionate about the red centre and the people who inhabited its sparse wastes. Travelling from camp to camp, living with the Aboriginal people, eating their food and taking part in their ceremonies, he stayed in the territory for six months until he had completed enough pictures for an exhibition. When he returned to Sydney Kath went with him.

Brett was Bing's closest friend. He was the only one who knew why he had chosen to bury himself in his shack on the river and the only man he felt completely comfortable with. The two of them shared a dislike of convention and a love of messing about in boats.

Bing tied up and walked up to Brett's house. It was hard to tell where the bush ended and the dwelling began. Bougainvillea and jasmine covered its sides and gum trees spread their great branches over it. Bing shouted a greeting through the door and looked inside on a confusion of toys, bicycles, half-completed sculptures and paintings. Mobiles tinkled in the breeze and the sounds of Bob Dylan wafted from within.

He heard an answering shout and Brett came to the door. He was wearing a sarong and both it and his bare chest were splattered with paint.

'Sorry, I've caught you at the moment of creation.'

'Bugger creation, mate. How about a beer?'

Each clutching a can of VB, they sat down on the verandah looking out over the river. A sailboat was heading upstream, tacking from bank to bank. They watched it in silence for a moment or two. 'Lovely cut on the main,' commented Brett.

Bing mumbled agreement, then said, 'I had a visitor today, an American woman. Just turned up out of the blue with a proposition.'

'Oh yeah. What sort of proposition?'

'She wants me to go looking for an MIA.'

'Where? In Vietnam?'

'I guess so. He was shot down there in '67.'

'Sounds like fun. You going to do it?'

'Well I started out saying no, but it ended up maybe. She's a pretty unusual woman.'

Brett gave him a knowing look. 'Oh yeah?'

'She threw me on the ground with some sort of jujitsu hold.'

'Christ what did you do, make a pass at her?'

'I told her she wouldn't be tough enough for Asia. It was her way of demonstrating that I was wrong.'

'Sounds like quite a lady.'

'She's ballsy all right. The question I'm asking myself is, am *I* tough enough? I really don't know if I'm ready to go back.'

Brett turned and looked at his friend. 'Well I guess only you can decide that but, if you like I can put in my two cents worth.'

Bing took a sip of his beer. 'I'm listening.'

'All right. I know why you came here, but I reckon you're going to have to confront the past sometime and it seems to me the opportunity's just come knocking at your door. If you don't go back to Asia now you might never get another chance.'

A hundred yards away a pelican ducked its head under the surface then tilted its beak skywards. The neck pouch was back-lit by the sun and they watched the silhouette of a mullet slide down into its throat.

'God, look at that. I've got to put that in a picture one day.' Brett turned his attention back on Bing. 'Like I said, I can't decide for you old mate, but I can tell you how it is with me. I love the river, but as much as I like being here, every now and then I've got to get out into the big wide world and see what it's like. Even if it only makes me appreciate this more when I come back. Of course I haven't been through what you have, but you can't just bury yourself here for the rest of your life.'

'Can't I? I've been enjoying it pretty well so far.'

Brett's attention shifted from the pelican back to the

sailboat. 'He'd do a lot better if he trimmed that headsail a bit.'

Bing studied the boat. 'Yeah, the leach needs tightening too.'

The two friends continued comfortably to discuss the shortcomings of the sailboat until it disappeared from sight. Bing drained the last drop from his can and crushed it with one hand.

'I'd better be getting back. Leave you to it.'

'OK.' said Brett. 'I'll see you.'

Bing got into the boat and cast off. 'Thanks.'

Laura was sitting in the sun outside her room reading a local newspaper when Bing Connick arrived. He had put on a pair of clean jeans and shoes for the occasion and his shirt was buttoned up. He sat down beside her and said, 'Are they looking after you here?'

She smiled. 'We had a few problems at first, but I think we understand each other now.'

'It's a bit of a backwater.'

'Yes, but I can see why you like it. I kind of like backwaters myself. Have you made a decision?'

'Yes. In principle I'm prepared to help you, but we need to talk about the details.'

'Go ahead.'

'You pay all expenses and in return I get all story rights, regardless of what we find. If anything.'

'That's fine.'

'One other thing. I wasn't kidding when I said it could be dangerous. I'm too old to indulge in heroics. If I want to call a halt you accept the decision. No arguments.'

Laura shook her head. 'No deal. I'm used to giving orders, not following them. Especially when I'm paying the bills. I'll listen to your advice, but I won't promise to follow it blindly.'

She stared at him without blinking while he thought about it. After a few moments he said, 'OK, but I'll tell you now that the chances of even finding out what happened are pretty slim. The chances of discovering that he's alive are non-existent.'

'So you say. But I still want to try. Where do we start?'

'I've been thinking about that. Thailand.'

'Thailand? I would have thought Vietnam.'

'There's someone I want to see in Bangkok first. He knows more about MIAs than anyone I know.'

Laura turned and held out her hand. 'Bing, we've got a deal.'

Bing took her hand. It was dry and firm. He looked her in the eyes. 'Deal.'

Three

Hunter McCormack signalled lazily to the waitress. The girl reluctantly slid herself down from the stool where she had been talking with the barman and walked over to his table, dragging her sandals with each step. She could have been aged anywhere between twelve and twenty-five. The bar was a bare room with open sides giving onto Patpong Road. Cheap plastic-covered tables, tiled floor, girlie pictures peeling on the walls. It was mid-afternoon and the daily thunderstorm was raining down in sheets outside. Along one side wall a flight of stairs led upwards. At the bottom of the stairs crudely lettered posters proclaimed, 'LIVE SEX EVERY NIGHT' and 'BANGKOK'S MOST BEAUTIFUL GIRLS UPSTAIRS'. A scattering of framed pictures showed innocent-faced Thai girls in G-strings, caught in the photographer's flash, pouting and posing hipshot at an unseen audience. The action would not begin until well into the evening, when the tourists came flocking in. The only people in the bar now were a couple of deaf-mute prostitutes seated on either side of a young, long-haired European. They were attempting to proposition him through explicit sign language.

McCormack looked the young waitress up and down, taking his time. She slouched, one hand on her hip, in an exaggerated waiting pose. She was one of hundreds constantly drifting into the capital from the provinces chasing an elusive dream of riches. She was uneducated and naive and within a year she would probably be another worker in the sex trade.

'Another Tiger,' he said, gesturing at the empty beer bottle in front of him. The girl shrugged, shot him a look and slouched away. McCormack sighed. She knew nothing about the world and she was already world weary. Others might anguish over the minor tragedy, but Hunter McCormack had never been troubled by compassion. He was the perfect professional, taking pleasure in the objective observation of the human condition. Here in Bangkok there were enough foibles to amuse him for the rest of his life. He lifted the bottle to his mouth and swallowed with pleasure.

He'd met Bing when they were both covering the Vietnam War. When it ended Bing and most of the other correspondents moved on. But McCormack had been seduced by Asia. In love with its deviousness, its heat and corruption, he moved to Bangkok and made a living stringing for newspapers in America and Europe. The telephone call had arrived a few days ago. Bing Connick was coming to town and wanted to talk to him about MIAs.

The barman pressed the CD play button and 'Like a Virgin' emerged scratchily from the speakers. There was a movement in the street outside and Bing came ducking through the rain, an umbrella shielding a good-looking European woman. Spying McCormack, he led the way over to his table. McCormack rose and extended a hand. 'And so the prodigal returns.'

'How are you Hunter? I see your working environment hasn't changed.'

'I'm too old to change, Bing. The Glitter Bar suits me. The girls know there's no point bothering me, at least during daylight hours. It's a good place to do business.'

'And how is business?'

'The Khmers can be relied upon to keep up the slaughter in Cambodia, Burma's fighting the Karens, Vietnam's becoming a good story again. Never better.'

One of the deaf-mutes held out thumb and forefinger forming an O. She poked the forefinger of her other hand into the ring and moved it in and out. The other girl held onto the young European and nodded vigorously. He shook his head and the pair of them broke into hilarious, silent laughter.

McCormack indicated the trio. 'Thailand's an absolute smorgasbord. Take your pick. The sex trade, AIDS, drugs, pirates. They're ripping out the rainforest and buggering the environment as fast as they can. Bangkok's so choked with traffic they have gridlock that lasts half a day. Environment stories, pollution stories, you name it. Wonderful stuff.'

Laura was looking at McCormack with a mixture of amusement and distaste. He was fiftyish, dressed in fawn slacks and a safari jacket of the type war correspondents used to wear but which had a curiously dated look in the nineties. McCormack's dress, like his cynical view of the world, never changed. Bing introduced them.

'And what brings you to Bangkok, Laura? You're not a journalist are you?'

Bing said, 'Laura's the one interested in MIAs.'

McCormack chuckled with pleasure. 'You've come to the right place for MIAs. Only last week I had a guy trying to flog me a photograph of three Americans supposed to have been taken in Laos. It was the usual thing. Dressed in peasant gear holding hoes, genuine looking dog tags. Quite a nice job.'

'And did you follow it up?' said Laura.

'Good God no.'

'Why not? How do you know the photograph wasn't genuine?'

'My dear Mrs Bailey, there have been dozens of photographs just like it and they're never genuine. It'd be more than my reputation was worth to waste my time with it.'

'But do you believe all of the Americans who were unaccounted for after the war are dead?'

'That's what the Vietnamese tell us.'

'Yes, but do you believe them?'

'This is Asia, it's best not to believe anything in Asia.'

'You've got to believe in something.'

'I believe in what I can see. I believe that young fellow over there is going to walk out the door soon with those two hookers. I believe he's got a good chance of catching the clap, maybe something worse. I believe they'll be back here tonight working their double act. I believe maybe they'll be dead of AIDS in five years. But live Americans? I'll believe that when one comes walking out of the jungle.'

Laura realised that she was being mocked. What would be the point of talking to this man about a love affair more than twenty years ago? About the nagging ache which had never gone away? The need to lay her obsession to rest? Sitting in this sleazy bar she felt she was wasting her time. She was about to retort when Bing spoke.

'Hunter's trying to be obnoxious. He knows more about MIAs than anyone. It's just not in his nature to be helpful.'

McCormack raised his hands in protest. 'I hate to see people waste their time, that's all. But seeing as you're here, ask me anything. I'll be helpful.'

Laura said, 'How would I go about finding out what happened to an American who went missing in action?'

'Well you could ask the Viets themselves. Now they've won the war for the greater glory of communism they've fallen in love with the market economy. But the US wants the MIA question cleared up before they'll do business.'

'So if I asked for specific information would they tell me what they knew?'

'Not necessarily. If he's alive they're certainly not going to say so and if he was captured and died they won't let on either. They'll tell you no more than suits them.'

McCormack took a swallow of his beer and continued. 'Look, there's a whole MIA industry here. There's a bunch of mad vets trying to raise funds right now to go into Laos and look for POWs. A goddamn search and destroy mission.' He snorted in disgust. 'There are all sorts of experts, some of them genuine, most of them no more than con men. This man you're interested in, what did he do in the war?'

'He was an electronic weapons expert. He flew F101s. Something to do with jamming enemy weapons systems.'

'A backseater eh? Well that's interesting. That may make a difference.'

'Why?'

'Relax for a while,' McCormack said. 'I've asked someone along for you to meet.'

Outside the rain had stopped. People were beginning to drift into the Glitter Bar, although in daylight there was nothing glittering about the surroundings or the clientele. A group of four girls, looking as though they had just woken up, sat down at a table where they sipped from bottles of 7–Up, singing along with the piped music. 'Like a vir-gin,' they mouthed together like schoolgirls. In a few hours time they would be upstairs 'exotic dancing' with bananas and bottles and razor blades for a leering audience of drunken men. Between acts they would circulate hoping to find a customer to take them home. Two Europeans came in, nodded to McCormack and began to drink beer at a nearby table. Three Japanese tourists eyed off the girls but it was still too early for work and they took no notice.

Despite the fans thunking overhead, Laura felt hot and enervated. McCormack gestured to the women. 'Hey Bing, remember the ladies in the Carevelle? You could put them on room service. Now that was civilised.' He coughed with merriment and Laura heard the phlegm rattle in his lungs. She looked over to the table with the deaf-mutes. One of them held an imaginary penis in her hands and made bobbing motions with her head up and down. The young European man laughed. McCormack began discussing a mutual friend in Saigon. Interrupting the conversation in front of her she said to Bing, 'Look, what are we waiting here for? I can't believe that this is going to help. I think we should go.'

Bing said, 'Why? Is something wrong?'

'Wrong?' She took a deliberate look about her. 'This place. It's . . . vile.'

'This isn't a cattlemen's meeting in Nebraska. We're not discussing the price of beef here. If you're serious about what we're doing, I suggest you stick around for a while.'

'Well *you* might feel at home here,' Laura said. 'But I don't.'

McCormack watched the exchange with a slight smile on his face. He glanced towards the street. 'Just relax, Mrs Bailey. You might be about to learn something.'

He got up and went across to a man who had just entered. After several minutes the two walked over and sat down. McCormack introduced the new arrival. 'This is Dean Buggins.'

The man nodded, but did not shake hands. Wary. Spare as a coolie. A haunted face with sunken cheeks and bulging eyes, the dominating feature, a beak of a nose. He shook out a cigarette and placed it in his mouth, lighting it with a Zippo lighter. Laura noticed that his hands shook and there was a nervous tic in his eye. McCormack went on, 'Dean's an MIA expert, aren't you Deano? He's got a bee in his bonnet about them but the trouble is no one will listen.'

Laura was becoming used to McCormack's style by now. Apparently he used the mocking approach with everyone. He indicated Buggins. 'When I told Dean just now that your man was a backseater he was fascinated, weren't you old buddy? You see Dean here has a whole bunch of stuff rattling around in his head about the backseat boys, which he's been trying to tell people for years. You'll find it fascinating.'

Buggins ordered himself a beer and stared intently at the three of them, as though making up his mind whether to talk. Bing said, 'Anything you can tell us, we'll listen.'

Buggins was silent. Bing wondered if he was about to walk out. Eventually, after a long moment he said, 'You'd know what the NSA is, Bing?'

'Sure, the National Security Agency.'

'I spent thirty years with the Agency, some of them in Vietnam as a codebreaker and analyst. You were there so you're probably aware that we used to listen in to the North Vietnamese.'

Bing nodded.

'We had ground posts and spy planes picking up their radio transmissions. Most of the stuff I dealt with was about troop movements along the Ho Chi Minh Trail. In 1968 we broke a code which allowed us to intercept very high-level communiques. Did you learn any Vietnamese when you were there?'

'Yes, some.'

'Do you know what the word "my" means?'

'Americans.'

'That's right. Well these messages concerned the transportation of my, Americans, or "giac lai my", bandit American pilots, by the ban. Do you know what "ban" means?'

'No.'

'It's Vietnamese for friends. It's the name they gave the Soviet advisers who were stationed in North Vietnam. In each case they were taken to areas where we knew there were Soviets.'

'The implication being what?'

'That the Soviets wanted to interrogate them.'

'And why would they want to do that?'

'The backseaters operated a jamming device called the Wild Weasel. It made North Vietnam's ground-to-air missiles go haywire. These missiles were the same ones that the Warsaw Pact countries relied on to repel NATO air attacks. The Soviets had to find out what was going wrong.'

Buggins spoke with authority, but without passion, like a lecturer who has given the same lesson many times Before continuing he dragged hungrily on his cigarette, grimacing with the effort to suck in a great lungful of smoke.

'The North Viets developed a method of shooting down the planes by flak-trapping them. Large anti-aircraft guns would divert them towards smaller weapons which could bring them down without totally destroying them. When those backseat boys came parachuting down it was like manna from Lenin. They were electronics experts, air-defence experts, some were in the space program. They had all that invaluable information in their heads. Of course the Soviets wanted to interrogate them.'

Another lungful. His smoking was a form of punctuation.

'I remember the peace talks and the repatriation of POWs,' Bing said. 'None of them ever said they'd been interrogated by Russians.'

'That's right. And I can tell you why. If they refused to cooperate they were killed.'

'And if they did cooperate?'

'If they did they went on.'

'Went on where?'

'To Russia.'

Buggins had forgotten his beer. He ground his cigarette into the ashtray and immediately lit another. The bar was filling up rapidly and the room was loud with conversation. The two deaf-mutes had finally succeeded in their campaign and led their young conquest out the door, one on each arm. McCormack, apparently uninterested in what Buggins was saying, smiled like a man who has just won a bet. 'What did I tell you?' he said. Buggins took no notice. He continued to deliver his lecture.

'Towards the end of 1972 when the Paris Peace Talks were about to take place I made a list of all the men missing or captured. There were about a thousand. Of these about fifty were people with special talents. I designated these MB or Moscow-bound.'

Bing interrupted. 'How did you know that they were Moscow-bound?'

'Well at that stage it was just a logical deduction. But in late 1977 and early '78 I was analysing flights in and out of the civilian airport at Hanoi. I came across references to special flights from areas where we knew American prisoners had been held. There were four different types of flight. Special flight A referred to high-level military passengers, B referred to high-level political passengers, C was a planeload of international diplomats and D was the last category. The D flights would always originate in a POW area, fly to another POW area or Soviet interrogation centre and back, or to Hanoi and out of the country.

'When I started checking into the D flights I found that the men would get off at Gia Lam airport, go to a special holding area and then within hours a Russian airliner would take off for Moscow.'

'That was four years after the war ended,' Bing said.

'That's right. When I saw the pattern I talked to other NSA personnel working on Soviet intelligence. They backtracked through their intercepts and found that the same thing was happening from the late sixties on.'

Bing looked thoughtfully at Buggins. 'It's just speculation. Do you have any proof that these men went to Moscow?'

Buggins flared at the challenge. Suddenly he was no longer a man repeating the same speech for the umpteenth time. Bing glimpsed the passion which drove him.

'It's not speculation. It's a given. Some of them must have gone on. For any intelligence analyst to think otherwise would be an act of gross incompetence.' Buggins stared angrily at Bing, desperate to be believed. 'You're a journalist. You were there. Can't you see it?'

'I *was* a journalist, not any more.'

Buggins had stopped speaking. He looked at McCormack as if for support but he was watching the interplay of bar customers with the professional interest of a critic at a new production of an old play.

'Aren't NSA personnel sworn to secrecy for life?' Bing said.

'That's right. My government has broken trust with the American people. Someone's got to speak out.'

'What do you mean broken trust?'

Buggins gripped the edges of the table with both hands and stared beseechingly at the three people seated opposite. 'Don't you see? The American government has turned its back on these people. The President himself knows that some of them went to Russia.'

'How would the President know about these MBs?' Bing asked.

'During the Vietnam War, President Blanchard was the Director of the CIA. The intercepts, my analysis about the MBs, it all ended up on his desk. He must have known. I've been to the States and lobbied Congressmen, I tried to testify before the committee inquiring into MIAs. They treated me as though I was crazy. So I came back here. I've told this to McCormack and a few others, but they're not interested. The MIAs aren't a story. No one believes in them any more. I'm probably wasting my time telling you.'

Buggins got up in disgust. For a moment he seemed about to walk out, then he headed towards the men's room. 'He looks a little unhinged to me,' Bing said to McCormack. 'What do you think of the story?'

'He's unhinged all right. Mad as a cut snake. And bitter as buggery. He had an impeccable record in the NSA. Lots of commendations, but his MIA theories went nowhere. He's been treated like some kind of loony. Maybe the story is true. Maybe there are dozens of Yanks living in Siberia or somewhere, but who would ever know? And how would you ever prove it?'

Buggins returned and sat down but he had apparently said all he was going to on the subject of MIAs. He made no move to resume speaking.

Laura had been quiet throughout Buggins' narrative.

He had summoned up a disturbing vision for her, of Dan's plane, damaged by artillery fire, smoke billowing into the cockpit, Dan plunging sickeningly towards the ground, grabbing desperately for the ejection seat control and parachuting down to what? Torture, pain and possibly death. Now she spoke. 'I know how you feel, Dean, my fiancé was one of those MIAs. Was, is, I don't know if he's alive or dead. But that's just it, I don't know. The government thinks the MIAs are disposable, just something to be left behind, along with the jeeps and tanks and guns. They say why can't you just get on with your life? It was all so long ago. Let it be. But I'm like you, I can't just let it be.'

Buggins regarded her with new interest. 'I'll help you if I can,' he said.

'You said you had a list of people you thought were Moscow bound.'

'That's right.'

'Could I see it?'

'Sure.'

'When?'

'Not tonight. I keep it in a safe place. I'd have to fetch it.'

'Tomorrow?'

'All right, tomorrow.'

Buggins seemed deflated. The passion spent. Despite Laura's expression of interest it seemed that he had nothing else to say. He sat quietly smoking and watching the interplay of customers in the bar. Laura suddenly realised that she was starving.

'Would you like to join us for dinner, Dean?'

Buggins shook his head. 'Thanks, I've got to get home.'

'Mr McCormack?'

'No thanks. A bit of business to do.'

Outside, the rain had stopped and people were setting up stalls in the centre of the street selling clothing, electrical goods, watches, souvenirs. On an impulse

Laura leaned forward and gave Buggins a peck on the cheek. 'Thanks Dean. You're a nice man.'

Buggins flushed. 'Where are you staying?'

'The Oriental.'

'I'll call you.'

Laura and Bing walked down Patpong Road into the main street to find a taxi. Buggins, lighting another cigarette, turned and headed in the opposite direction.

Threading his way through the crowded streets Dean Buggins was oblivious to his surroundings. He was replaying in his mind the conversation he had just had. Connick, like every journalist he had met, had seemed sceptical, but the woman was obviously intrigued by his theories. It had been a long time since anyone took him so seriously.

Buggins had not always been the driven creature that he was now. He remembered vividly the precise day his interest in the MIAs had turned to obsession, an obsession which destroyed the things he loved most in the world. The tragedy was that he knew it was happening but was powerless to stop it. He had retired from the service and was living with his wife and two daughters in a small town in the mountains of Montana. He got himself a stress-free job managing a hardware store for a living. The town was so remote that it didn't even receive network television. He was looking forward to his little slice of the American dream, having a pleasant life watching his children grow up. Then in 1985 cable television brought national news to the wilds of Montana and Dean Buggins' life changed forever.

He was seated on the lounge with his wife Anne and the girls were playing in their room when a report came on about the first excavation of a crash site in Laos. Voicing over shaky hand-held shots of the wreckage of an AC-130A Spectre gunship, the reporter said that the remains of the entire crew had been found.

Buggins leaped to his feet and kicked the couch. 'That's a damn lie,' he shouted.

Anne stared at him in amazement. He strode around the room in a fury. 'What's the matter? What is it?' she said.

'I remember that crash. Just after it went down I decoded some intelligence which said that five of the crew bailed out and were captured alive. They were alive goddamn it. They were alive!'

His wife had never seen him like this. She watched with apprehension as he raged around the room then grabbed the telephone. 'I'm calling Simpson.' Carl Simpson was an old friend from NSA days who he had not talked to since his retirement. When he got through to him in California he asked if he had happened to see the news item. Simpson had not but he clearly remembered the crash. He had intercepted messages from another source which confirmed Buggins' intelligence. That call was the first of many to former colleagues, each one only making him more and more distressed. As he spoke to them he learned little by little what had been happening while he had been living in Montana. In recent years the government had reclassified more than two thousand MIAs in Vietnam and Laos as 'presumed dead', yet when he last heard hundreds of them had been classified alive.

Anne had been married to Dean for eighteen years. It hadn't been easy being a serviceman's wife, never settling for long in one place, trying to bring up two children in a succession of military homes in far-flung parts of the world. She had looked forward to some normality in Montana. Her world was suddenly about to be turned on its head.

At first she thought that Dean's obsession would be short-lived. She resolved to hold her peace until it had run its course, but the more Dean looked into the fate of the MIAs the more the isssue began to possess him.

Late one night when he finished yet another phone call which left him indignant and trembling, Anne quietly took his hands in hers and said, 'Dean, the past is past. The MIAs have nothing to do with you any more. Can't

29

you forget them and let's you and I and the girls get on with our lives?'

Dean loved her. He knew that his behaviour was placing strains on his family, yet he could not shake off the conviction that he had to do something. He had spent his working life giving unquestioning loyalty to a government which lied to its own people. He pulled her close and hugged her. 'I'm sorry Anne. I know it's hard on you. All I can say is I'll try.'

For a time he did try. He started putting in longer hours at the store and avoided watching the news. Then one day he received a telephone call from the parents of an MIA who had been shot down in Laos. They had been referred to him from a veterans' organisation and he had been moved almost to tears by their pathetic need to find out whatever scrap of information he might be able to give them about their son.

He had told them what he knew and from then on the obsession had proven impossible to shake. He began corresponding with the relatives of other MIAs, he wrote letters to Congress, he hounded former colleagues about specific cases.

His work began to suffer. Even when he lost his job he could not help himself. The final straw came when, in frustration at government inertia, he went public. When he joined the NSA he had signed an oath never to reveal its secrets. Now he felt he could no longer keep that oath. For weeks he agonised. He slept little and he became a silent stranger to his family. Anne was convinced he was having a nervous breakdown but when she tried to talk to him about seeking help he withdrew further. She knew that whatever was torturing him he was beyond her help. He would have to work it out for himself. She went on with her daily routine, looking after the girls, cooking meals, trying to cope on their pension, determined to wait out the crisis. Finally Dean called a newspaper reporter in Washington and poured out to him the whole story; the intercepted signals, his theories about the MBs and his conviction that somewhere some MIAs were still alive.

It made ten paragraphs on page five. In Washington the story created hardly a ripple, but in the little town in Montana the Buggins family became a curiosity. When Anne went shopping people stared and whispered. At school the girls were taunted for having a daddy who was a nut case.

In the grip of forces he could not fight he left the family and went to Bangkok. Ostensibly it was just for a short investigative visit, but he and Anne both knew he would not be coming back. Two years later they divorced.

Dean Buggins turned off the busy commercial streets into the quieter residential quarter where he had his apartment. He mounted the stairs, let himself in with his key and turned on the light. There was a note from Somi on the table telling him that she would not be home tonight. She had gone to visit her sister who was ill.

Buggins had just put the note down when there was a knock at the door.

'Who is it?' he said.

An American voice said, 'Dean Buggins? I have a message for you.'

Probably another MIA enquiry, he thought to himself.

He opened the door to see not one but two men, both in shadow.

'Mr Buggins we've come a long way to see you. May we come in?'

Buggins stepped aside wearily. He could never say no to people in need.

Four

Laura and Bing were dining in the hotel's riverside restaurant. To get to it they had crossed the Chao Phrya River in the hotel's launch. The rain had stopped and they sat on the terrace enjoying the tropical evening as they looked across the water at the bustle of a Bangkok night.

The waiter brought green chicken curry garnished with fresh coriander, spicy fish and steamed rice. It was a long time since Bing had enjoyed the subtleties of Asian food. Laura had never tasted anything like it and she delighted in the delicate sensations on her palate.

They said little while they ate. When the waiter cleared away the plates and brought delicately scented jasmine tea, Laura asked Bing what he had thought of Buggins.

'These intelligence analysts are a pretty strange lot. They sit all day locked away in rooms decoding messages and trying to interpret them. It's like reading the tea-leaves. It's easy to see how they could go a little crazy. But what he said about the missiles makes sense. When I was there I remember how the SAMs were never as effective as we thought they'd be. The jamming technology was top secret of course, but we knew our guys were using something.'

'What about POWs being Moscow-bound?'

'Let me put it this way, if I wrote up that story without supporting evidence it'd go straight on the spike and my editor would want to know if I'd lost my mind.'

'I'd like to see the list,' Laura said. 'If Dan's name was on it wouldn't you want to follow it up further?'

'Perhaps, but I don't see how.'

They were ill at ease, like two negotiators cautiously feeling each other out. Laura glanced at the winking lights across the river and back again. She decided to change the subject. 'You must have missed Asia after spending so much time here.'

'A lot's changed.'

Another person might have sensed his reticence, but it escaped Laura. She was direct herself and she found it difficult sometimes to grasp that others did not approach life in quite the same way. 'Was it the war that made you give up journalism?'

'The war was part of it. You couldn't report Vietnam and not be affected by it.'

'But wars are part of the business, aren't they?'

'Yes and most wars you manage to keep detached from, but in Vietnam I got involved.'

'You mean politically? I know most reporters were against the US presence.'

Bing was becoming irritated by her questions. 'They were against it because it was wrong,' he said.

'Really? I supported our involvement. I still think we were right to be there. We should have hit them harder from the beginning instead of pussyfooting around.'

'Yes I've heard that opinion often. Mostly from people who were never there.'

'Don't you believe in fighting for what's right?'

'Let me tell you what that war was like. It was sold to the American people as a fight for democracy, which is a noble-sounding idea. When you got close to it there was nothing noble about it. I remember a village which we destroyed in order to save it from the communists. We pounded the hell out of it. At a certain point the villagers put down their hoes, walked out of the paddies and put their belongings on bicycles and carts and buffaloes and headed off down the road while the soldiers fought over their homes. I was there when they came back. The women sat down on their heels in the wreckage and rocked back and forth with a sort of howling. It was the most moving thing I have ever witnessed. The men didn't cry, they just seemed resigned. I realised then that they didn't care if they were communist or capitalist, the war actually had nothing to do with them. They just wanted to be left alone to plant their rice, bring up their children and get on with their lives. It was from that point on that I became opposed to our involvement.'

Bing had become intense as he spoke. Laura replied with equal force. 'We had to fight. You can't just let people walk all over you and take what they want. People or countries, it's the same.'

'Yes I've heard those arguments too,' Bing replied. 'Fight the good fight for freedom and democracy.'

'No, I'm talking about helping friends when they're in trouble.'

'I'll tell you how America helped its friends. Towards the end they lied to us about everything. About the body counts, about our own casualties, about the way the war was going.' He caught her eyes and stared. 'And if Buggins is right they lied about the MIAs too.'

Laura flushed with anger. 'So you'd say that Dan was wrong to go and fight?'

'Since you ask, yes.'

'You believe he was risking his life for a lie, is that it?'

'I can see why you wouldn't agree.'

'Well why the hell did you agree to look for him?'

'It's a story.'

'Is that all this is to you, just a story?'

'Look, he was *your* boyfriend, not mine. I'll help you search for him but don't ask me be personally involved.'

'Why not? You just told me you got involved in Vietnam. Are you afraid you might feel something? Is that it?'

Bing slapped the table with exasperation. 'Jesus, Laura! You don't let up do you?'

'I'm sorry. I'm not attacking you, believe me. I'm just trying to understand you that's all. I'm not used to people who are so . . . insulated.'

'Well I'm afraid that's how I am. You'd better get used to it.'

Bing waved the waiter over with a curt gesture and asked for his check. They caught the launch back across the river in silence. When they got back to the hotel Laura said a brief goodnight and left him in the lobby.

When Laura got to her room she washed her face and put on the robe with the hotel monogram which had been laid out on the bed for her. She sat down and looked out over the river. Even at this time of night it was busy with traffic. A string of deep-laden barges, their midsections practically awash, slid past. A long narrow boat with an automobile engine mounted at the stern on a swivel roared along at speed. Laura's mind was racing. She tried to think of home and friends, but Bing Connick and the unpleasant scene at dinner kept intruding. There was something contradictory about him. He had been ornery and obnoxious on his high horse about Vietnam, playing the case-hardened correspondent, but earlier he had listened sympathetically to poor, driven Buggins and, unlike McCormack, he didn't dismiss what he said out of hand. Underneath the shell, there was something injured about Connick. He had a barrier around him which she thought few people would ever penetrate.

Sighing, Laura snuggled deep into the blankets. Her racing thoughts finally stilled and she slipped into deep sleep.

Five

When Laura left, Bing went to the bar and ordered a
Scotch on the rocks. The decor of white cane furniture
and potted palms was self-consciously tropical. In one
corner a trio of piano, bass and drums was playing muted
jazz. The after-dinner crowd were well dressed and
mostly European. It was a long time since he had sat like
this in the bar of an international hotel with good booze
and sophisticated music.

The pianist had a nice touch. A little of the discor-
dancy of Thelonious Monk, but just enough to make the
music interesting, not inaccessible. Bing nursed his
Scotch. He would have to try not to fly off the handle
at Laura, but her directness would take some getting used
to. Her questions about Vietnam had aroused memories
he had spent years trying to forget . . .

The soldiers moved slowly through thick jungle, the rain
coming down solid, drumming on the leaves, penetrating
everything. The earth was slippery underfoot. Bing and
Dave Lindley had been with C Company for two days,
following them as they went on patrol. So far things had
been uneventful and they didn't know whether to be
grateful that they hadn't come under fire or disappointed
at the lack of copy.

36

Dave was a tall, gangling Australian, all arms and legs, with a long nose which bent slightly to one side. He had been in Vietnam as long as Bing and had experienced just about everything a war zone could throw at him. Bing liked working with him. He handled danger with laconic competence. And he was a fine photographer, with an instinctive knack for capturing the precise moment which defines a scene. The two of them had a good relationship both on a professional and personal level.

The sound of automatic fire did not come suddenly so much as it insinuated itself through the downpour. A young soldier walking ten paces from them, his M16 at the alert, grew a red flower in his chest and sank to the ground with a look of surprise. Bing and Dave threw themselves flat in the mud and the leaves ripped to shreds around them. Bing could see Dave lifting the Nikon up to his eye and his left hand twisting the focus ring. The motor drive whirred with high-pitched, robotic urgency. Another soldier was lying ten feet away, too shocked to shoot back. Out of instinct Dave swung the camera on him a second before a burst of fire raked the leaves and hit him in the throat. Scarlet arterial blood spurted onto the ground and quickly diluted in the mud. The soldier died with a choking sound.

They were pinned down flat waiting to be killed. A few yards away a soldier broke and ran, the bullets catching him in mid-stride. He saw Dave squeeze off three or four frames before another burst of fire sent him burrowing into the mud again. Bing said, 'You've got your pics Dave, keep your head down.'

Muttering into the ground Dave said, 'I hope the bloody lens isn't fogged up. Bloody rain.'

Somewhere nearby they could hear the patrol commander radioing for helicopter assistance. 'Christ, I hope they come soon or we're in deep shit,' Bing said.

'You mean we're not already?'

Some of the Americans had recovered from their shock and began to return fire. A hand-grenade exploded and

Bing took a chance and lifted his head to take a look. There was little to be seen: half a dozen soldiers lying on their bellies firing into the jungle, the two dead men and a wall of dripping leaves. Somewhere in there were the Viet Cong, but they were invisible. He wondered who the dead soldiers were. He would have to get their names and biographical details when they got back to the camp.

Ten minutes later there was a clattering at treetop level and the choppers raked the invisible VC with rocket fire. The firing ceased for a few moments and the patrol broke and ran for a village five hundred yards away where the helicopters could land.

When they could see where they were heading, Bing and Dave went on ahead and were waiting as the Americans came walking out of the trees carrying their dead and wounded. Dave clicked off several more shots of the scene, with the villagers looking on in the background. As always, the Vietnamese peasants stared at them without expression. Bing could detect neither friendliness nor hatred on their faces. It was as if they were indifferent to what was happening.

This inaccesibility was one of the great frustrations of his job. Covering the fighting was merely a matter of observing what happened and staying alive. Divining what the Vietnamse people actually thought about the war was a lot harder. Many correspondents didn't even bother, but Bing attempted to talk with ordinary men and women as often as possible. He would like to interview these villagers now, but he did not have his interpreter with him and his Vietnamese was not up to the job. If he got the American interpreter to help he knew he would not get honest answers.

Bing and Dave shared a ride back to the camp with a wounded soldier. He looked as though he'd been doused with blood. It didn't seem possible that so much of it could come from one human being and he could still be alive. An army doctor had staunched the wounds and put a drip into his vein but his face was a pale death mask. Only the slight rise and fall of his chest showed that he was still alive. Bing tapped Dave on the arm and nodded towards the man. Dave lifted the camera and took a series of snaps. As he lowered it he said quietly, 'Poor bugger, he'll be lucky to make it.'

It had taken them half a day to walk into the ambush, but they were back in camp in eight minutes. They were sitting in the mess tent having coffee when the company commander came up and joined them. 'Jacobsen didn't make it.'

'The guy in the helicopter?' Bing said.

'Yeah.'

Bing said, 'So that makes three.'

'Yeah, three of ours for God knows how many of theirs. Maybe none, maybe half a dozen. The gunships must have got a few.'

'Yes, you'd imagine so.'

'Did you get a story?' the commander asked.

'Yes, it's a good story. It'll get a good run.'

'Then the day hasn't been entirely wasted.'

Bing looked at the commander. He looked like a man spoiling for an argument. 'Can I get you a coffee, Major?'

'No thanks, I don't feel like coffee.' He toyed with the sugar bowl and said savagely, 'Do you ever wonder what the fuck it's all about?'

Bing said, 'All the time.'

The commander shook his head, staring at the bowl. 'They were three good boys. They didn't like being here but they didn't complain like a lot of them. They went out and did their job. This morning they were alive and this afternoon they're dead and we're sitting around here drinking coffee.'

'That's the way it goes,' Bing said.

'I mean I lose three men and for what? Just what the fuck did we achieve out there today?'

'Not a real lot I guess,' said Bing.

'You're right,' said the commander. 'You're absolutely right. Shit! What a way to fight a war.'

Neither Bing nor Dave spoke. There was nothing to

say. 'We're going out again tomorrow,' the commander continued. 'Want to come?'

Bing looked at Dave. Neither of them wanted to push their luck further. 'Thanks, I think we'll pass.'

Shrugging, the commander left to call up a helicopter to take them back to Saigon. A little while later he walked them out and watched them climb aboard. Just before the rotor started slowly scything the air he said, 'Have a beer for me you guys.'

Bing raised his hand and said, 'Take care,' as if sudden death was something he could avoid.

Back in the capital Bing went home to his third-floor apartment, cleaned up and began writing his story. The private Dave had photographed at the moment of death was twenty-one, came from a small town in the Midwest and had been due to go on R and R in three days. He was just finishing up when there was a knock on the door and Dave walked in carrying a large envelope. Without a word he slid out the prints he had developed and put them on Bing's table.

Bing picked up the first one and whistled. Dave had captured the terror in the young American's eyes at the very moment the rounds caught him. Looking at the picture you could almost smell the fear and feel the mud soaking into your clothes. He shuffled through the other pictures. The wounded man with the drip in his arm was silhouetted against the open door of the helicopter. The contrast gave the picture a stark, raw quality. They were all good but none of them had the magic of the first one. Bing tapped it and said, 'It's a great picture, Dave, you could win a prize with that one.'

Dave picked it up. 'Not bad.'

'Jesus, you Aussies,' said Bing, laughing. 'What does it take to get you excited?'

'A cold VB, a warm woman and a sundrenched beach, mate. When all this is over come to Australia and I'll show you what I mean. It's God's country.'

'I might just take you up on that. Listen. I've got to

get this stuff away. What say we meet at the Caravelle in an hour for a drink?'

Dave nodded. 'OK mate, I'll see you there.'

The top floor of the Caravelle Hotel was loud, smoke-hazed and boozy. The noise hit Bing like a gut shot when he walked in the door and headed towards the bar where Dave and two other correspondents were drinking. There was a row of plastic tables and chairs next to the windows looking out over the city, occupied mainly by other newsmen and women whom Bing knew. The centre of the room was cleared for dancing although at this time of the evening it was empty. Along one wall a dozen girls roosted like birds, their bright, predatory eyes missing nothing.

The men at the bar made room for Bing as he approached. An English newspaperman with a florid complexion and a network of veins showing in his nose asked Bing where he'd been. 'We didn't see you at the four o'clock conference.'

'Hello Donald. No, Dave and I had other things to do today. Any surprises?'

'What do you think? They gave us a load of bullshit about that skirmish yesterday down near the delta. Three hundred VC killed, only light casualties by the ARVN. Can we see the bodies? I say. So sorry, they say. There's no way of independently checking. How can we believe you? I say. They shrug their shoulders. They know it's bullshit. They know we know it's bullshit. They don't even pretend it's true any more. The whole bloody thing was useless. I don't know why I bother.'

'I know what you mean. I don't go to too many press conferences these days.'

'I know, but one feels one has to go through the motions sometimes.'

The third correspondent was an American wire-service man. 'We've been taking bets on how long it'll be before America loses the war,' he broke in. 'I say six months, what do you think Bing?'

'I don't know. Maybe not that long.'

'Anyway,' said the Englishman, 'I'm going home. I got the telex today. A nice job on the foreign desk, regular hours, maybe a little woman and a house in the suburbs. No more bloody bang bang for me.'

'Lucky bastard,' said the American. 'No way I'm getting out of here 'till General Giap marches through the palace gates.' He turned to Bing. 'What about you, Bing, you've been here five years, you must be sick of it by now?'

'No as a matter of fact I'm not. I like it here. The place suits me.'

'What on earth can you find to like about it? You can't eat the food, you can't understand the people, it's too damn hot. Oh what I'd give for a New York winter. The only thing it's got going for it is the story.'

'Well as it happens I quite like the food and I like the people too.'

'What's to like?' said the American. 'Tell me honestly what can you possibly have in common with a man who's spent his entire life walking around behind a bloody buffalo in a pool full of water?'

'You should talk to a few of them, you might surprise yourself.' As soon as he said it Bing was aware of how self-righteous he sounded.

The American and the Englishman exchanged glances. Connick could be a real prick sometimes. He was known for having more contacts among ordinary Vietnamese than any other correspondent. Unlike most of them he actually seemed to enjoy squatting in the dust and talking about harvests and family trivia. His reporting was undeniably insightful, but most of his rivals thought the end result was hardly worth the discomfort involved.

Dave broke in. 'When this is over I'm going to take him back to Australia. Cool out for a while and enjoy the good life. There's no bloody wars there mate.'

'Ah you'll never get this guy out of Asia,' said the American. 'He's starting to get slanty eyes himself.'

The volume of the music inched up a notch and some of the girls began to dance together, casting sideways looks towards the men at the bar. The American nudged his companion and said, 'What about one for the road before you go home?'

The Englishman laughed. 'Christ, I'm so full of penicillin if I had another shot I'd start leaking.'

Bing turned away from them and glanced towards the door. He was waiting for his interpreter to brief him on an assignment next day. Nguyen was just entering, accompanied by a tall Vietnamese woman wearing traditional clothing. She was immaculate and aloof. Even more noticeably because of the sleazy surroundings.

Nguyen came up and greeted Bing. He turned to the woman beside him and said, 'Bing Connick, I'd like you to meet my sister Phuong.' She held out her hand and he took it. It was cool, firm and dry. 'How do you do?' As she spoke she looked directly into his eyes for a moment before turning gravely away. Bing had the sense of being carefully appraised and of somehow not quite measuring up. He mumbled a greeting and asked if she would like something to drink. She accepted a lemonade and he said, 'Please excuse us for a moment, I have to discuss some work with Nguyen.'

Bing and Nguyen drew aside from the others and he began his briefing. As he spoke he could see Phuong listening with polite detachment to his colleagues. Their demeanour had changed. They no longer slouched against the bar, but had straightened up to face her and were talking animatedly. He heard the American guffaw loudly and Phuong gave a slight smile. The Englishman asked her a question and laughed at her reply as if she had said something hilarious. She was standing two paces away, very straight, glossy black hair falling below her shoulders, wearing a white blouse with a high neckline and a long black skirt split at the side. When she moved slightly the skirt parted for a second and Bing caught a glimpse of pale skin.

Having concluded their business, Bing and Nguyen returned to the main group. The American said, 'We were just telling Phuong here that she should join us for dinner. We're going to André's. Best French cooking in Saigon.'

Phuong smiled. 'Thank you, I'm afraid I can't tonight. I have an engagement already.'

'Aw c'mon, Phuong. Nguyen, tell her to come. You too,' he added as an afterthought.

'No I'm afraid we have family matters to attend to,' Phuong replied. 'We must go.'

Bing tried not to join the others in staring at her as she walked out. When she had disappeared the Englishman said, 'That is one beautiful woman. I'd stay another year if I could have that.'

'You won't find any like that in Fleet Street,' said the American. He indicated the girls on the dance floor. 'Better grab some while you can.'

Bing downed his drink and left them to pursue their further adventures. He walked out of the Caravelle into a gaggle of cyclo drivers all haggling for his custom. He chose one and they set off towards his apartment. Sitting back behind the driver he watched the life of the streets move past. The food stalls were crowded with customers and the street-front shops were busy with people bargaining. Day or night, commerce never stopped. The war had brought prosperity to entrepreneurs who sold black-market goods stolen from the Americans, or catered to the needs of fighting men spending their dollars with the reckless knowledge that they might not be alive tomorrow.

Normally he would have used the ride to clear his mind but he could not get Phuong out of his thoughts. He was intrigued by her remoteness. He had known her brother for a year but this was the first time he had met any of his family. Normally Nguyen would never bring a family member with him to a business meeting, no matter how casual. Like many things in Asia he thought there was a meaning behind the seemingly innocuous encounter. He assumed it was a sign that he was accepted and trusted.

Next day Bing asked Nguyen if he would mind if he

invited his sister out socially. Nguyen offered no objection and a few days later he asked Phuong to accompany him to a cocktail party. She politely declined.

Was it coincidence then, that a week later he walked into a market near his home and encountered Phuong buying coffee at the same stall he always used? At the time he thought so, but after the events which followed he would torture himself with doubts, for it could just as easily have been part of some carefully orchestrated plan in which he had no more control over his role than a marionette has over the puppeteer. Waiting his turn at the counter he imagined he saw something familiar about the back of the woman in front of him. But Saigon was full of slim women with jet-black hair. The transaction finished and Phuong turned around with a slight gasp of surprise. Bing's face split into a broad grin of recognition. 'Phuong. Fancy meeting you here! Do you live nearby?'

She smiled her enigmatic smile and told him her address, just three blocks away. Bing said, 'I'm heading that way myself, let me walk with you.'

Phuong nodded and thanked him. With his tin of coffee in hand he set off beside her. The street was busy with evening commerce. The food stalls were crowded, the air buzzed with traffic noise and the cadence of the hawkers promoting their wares. An old beggar with one leg hobbled towards him and Bing gave him some coins. The man nodded and limped away, his wooden leg tapping the pavement. Bing turned to Phuong. 'Do you live alone?'

'No I live with my sister.'

'And are you eating with her tonight?'

'No, she has gone to the cinema. Tonight I cook for myself.'

Their route led them past an upstairs restaurant that Bing knew well. As they approached the entrance he said, 'Why don't you forget cooking and come and eat with me?'

She considered this for a moment, then said, 'Very

well. Thank you.' It was said without coquettishness and it left Bing feeling as if a rare gift had been bestowed upon him. They climbed the stairs away from the noise and petrol fumes. The restaurant was half full of diners eating and conversing noisily. The kitchen was open to the dining room and they could see the woks flaring over the gas range and smell the ubiquitous smell of nuoc nam, the fish sauce which seemed to accompany every Vietnamese dish. Bing showed Phuong to a table beside the window which looked out over the street. Wire mesh had been placed outside the glass to prevent bombs being thrown. The waiter, a chubby little Vietnamese wearing a stained white apron and a permanent smile, came up and welcomed Bing in French. 'Ah Mr Connick, how are you? We have a special tonight, chilli crab. What do you think?'

Normally Bing would have accepted the suggestion, but he knew that it was impossible to eat chilli crab elegantly. The only way to handle it was to attack it with hands and fingers and usually the diner ended up with red chilli sauce everywhere. Like a schoolboy on an important date, he wanted to make a good impression. They ordered two dishes, ca hap or steamed fish, which was prepared with garlic, ginger, coriander and nuoc nam, and ga xao xa ot, or chicken with lemon grass.

Bing knew the food would be good. Nevertheless when it arrived he waited with apprehension as Phuong tasted it. She gave a murmer of approval and he grinned with relief. 'A good choice,' she said. 'You seem to know about Vietnamese food.'

'I've been here five years. I hardly ever eat American food any more, it seems bland and boring after this.'

They ate for a time, confining their comments to the food, then Phuong put down her chopsticks and said, 'My brother tells me you are different to most Americans here.'

'Oh, in what way?'

'You are interested in what the Vietnamese think. You don't just go to press conferences all the time.'

'Well we're supposed to be here because the Vietnamese want us to help them. That's what the politicians are always saying. It seems to me that if we're going to do our job properly we should ask the people themselves their feelings.'

'And what do they tell you?'

'Different things. Sometimes they tell me what they think I want to hear, or what the local VC commander would want them to say. It's my job to try to work out the truth. The more I talk about the rights and wrongs of the war the more I understand that there's no simple answer. It's not like the Americans paint it; we're not really here because all Vietnamese want us to save them from the communists, but the people back home who are protesting every day haven't got it completely right either. It's complicated, I'm still learning.'

Bing could not tell what effect, if any, his words had on Phuong. He was afraid he sounded pompous. He should lighten up, say something amusing, but there was something about her demeanour: a patient, waiting interest, that made him go on. 'I sometimes feel that I'd like to stay here forever.'

As soon as he said it he was aware how bizarre it must sound. It was not the sort of statement you made to someone you hardly knew. He grinned apologetically and plied his chopsticks to cover his confusion.

'Perhaps you will.'

'I don't think so. The war will end soon and I'll probably go back to America.' Bing paused and said, 'Tell me about yourself Phuong.'

'My family are from Saigon. My father is a professor at the university. He teaches economics. My sister is studying and of course you know about Nguyen.'

'What sort of work do you do?'

'I work at the American Embassy as a secretary.'

'How do you get on with the Americans?'

But to this question as to many others later, Phuong did not reply. Instead she smiled slightly and looked towards the waiter approaching. 'The tea is coming, we should clear a place.'

They were in the restaurant for an hour, but at the end of it he felt he knew little more about her. His conversation had left him with impressions but nothing concrete. Despite her education and her job at the embassy, she appeared to have little interest in politics or the war. She confessed that she enjoyed American films but, unlike any other Vietnamese woman Bing had been involved with, she appeared to have no desire to visit the US. On that first date, if such a formal encounter could be called a date, they conversed easily enough but Phuong gave no sign that she was interested in Bing as anything other than a friend of her brother. Her reticence only made her more enticing. There was something elusive about her. She was serene, controlled, enigmatic and unreachable.

When they had finished eating Bing paid the bill and they walked downstairs to the street. He offered to see Phuong home but she smiled and declined. She walked off into the crowd and even after she had disappeared he stood watching after her for a long time. He knew he was smitten.

Bing's usual relationships with women tended to be brief and bawdy. With Phuong he found himself embarking upon a patient and decorous courtship, devoid of the flirtations he was used to. In Saigon sex was one of the easiest commodities to find. As easy as black-market consumer goods or drugs. But it was not the thought of sex which fuelled Bing's infatuation. It was as if he had discovered something precious which he had to possess no matter what the cost.

They had known each other for three months when Bing went away to spend time with another American patrol, engaged in search and destroy operations in Phuoc Tuoy Province. It was a useful few days. A teenage private trod on a booby trap which hammered bamboo stakes into his feet and calves. One day they entered a village and discovered the entrance to a tunnel system

48

storing food and weapons. On two occasions they came under fire and he watched men die. It was still the rainy season and he was wet for a week. He came back to Saigon early one evening tired and dirty, his clothes rumpled from sleeping rough and stubble on his chin. He caught a taxi from the airbase to his apartment and humped his kit up the stairs, nodding his 'bon soirs' through the open doors of his neighbours as he passed. He let himself into his own apartment and there was Phuong sitting at the table reading a magazine.

She looked up and smiled her grave smile. 'Welcome home.'

He did not ask her how she had got in. He did not want to question his good fortune. It was enough that she was there.

Later that night as Phuong lay in his arms and he lightly stroked her bare back he said, 'You are the most mysterious woman I have ever met, Phuong. I want to know everything about you.'

'Don't try to know me too well. It is better that a bit of the mystery remains.'

Bing laughed. 'No I want to know everything, who you are, what you think, what your hopes and fears are. Everything about you. Why did you wait for me tonight?'

Phuong rolled on top of him. Her hair cascaded forward over her breasts. She gently laid a finger across his lips. 'Hush my darling, don't talk.' She lifted clear for a moment to allow him to enter and began to move. Bing forgot all about conversation.

Even after Phuong moved in with him there was a reserve about their liaison. Despite their intimacy Bing felt he did not really understand her. She made love with grace and tenderness and when she reached her panting climax Bing saw a glimpse of the passion hidden within, but at all other times she remained slightly removed. It was as if there was another, deeper Phuong, he had yet to know. Later he would wonder if even these displays of passion were real, or were they too part of the elaborate deception she wove. Other questions would haunt

49

him. Why, for instance, did her father accept without a murmur a Westerner living with his daughter? Was any part of their love real or was it all a careful conspiracy?

He met her father once, when Phuong asked him to drop by his home in Tanh Banh, a residential district where middle-class Vietnamese lived. While she went off to fetch something in an inner room Bing made stilted conversation with a serious, intense man who gave no indication what he thought of his daughter's liaison. He knew her mother was alive, but on that day there was no sign of her. Phuong's brother, Nguyen, behaved exactly as before. His work was without fault. He was polite, diligent and formal as always.

They lived quietly. He forsook his bachelor round of bars and restaurants and tried to get home as often as he could in the evenings. She went to work each day at the embassy and most nights she came home and cooked Vietnamese food for him.

One or two evenings a week Phuong left Bing alone, saying she had family matters to attend to at home. What these matters were she did not say and something about her careful manner prevented him from asking. It was only much later that he realised the deadly nature of her absences, but by then it was too late.

One evening before dinner they were sitting at a cafe on Tu Do Street. Bing was drinking pernod and Phuong as usual was sipping lemonade. The rain had just ceased and the air smelled fresh and cool. Bing began telling her about a pet project he had been working on for many months.

'I want to go behind the lines with the Viet Cong.'

Phuong showed no surprise. 'It's a good idea. People never hear what life is like on the other side.'

'So you think I should do it?'

'Oh yes.'

Bing took a sip of pernod. 'Do you know what's unusual about you Phuong? You never ever try to stop me from doing things that might be dangerous.'

'Of course not. It is your job.'

'Do you worry when I'm in the field?'

'Yes I worry.'

'You're strong. You never show it.'

'Well, you know I am not a demonstrative person.' She toyed with her glass and, as always when they strayed onto intimate ground, deftly changed the subject. 'Have you been in touch with the VC?'

'I've spoken to half a dozen contacts, but I've had to be very circumspect. If the South Vietnamese found out what I was up to they'd never let me out of their sight. A month or so ago I finally found a direct channel to a local VC company commander. It'd be a great scoop if I could pull it off but they're cautious, it's taking forever.'

Phuong sipped her lemonade and watched a boy about eight years old with a portable shoeshine stand touting for business. 'Who have you been talking to?'

'The name wouldn't mean anything to you.'

'Perhaps not. Why don't you tell me anyway.'

Bing named the chief of a village twenty miles to the west of the capital. Phuong nodded absently and began telling him about her sister's plans to marry a friend of the family.

One week later when he had a quiet day, Bing took the office Peugeot out along the highway towards the village. It was a slow journey. The road was blocked every mile or so with a concrete maze guarded by soldiers. Long queues of vehicles banked up at each checkpoint. Approaching each one he handed the soldier in charge his passport with a five dollar note folded inside and was waved through without having to undergo a search. He drove into the village, pulled up outside the chief's house and picked up his gifts from the back seat.

The old man was sitting in a hammock strung between two trees. He had a wizened face and a wispy Ho Chi Minh beard. He wore a pair of voluminous khaki shorts and plastic sandals but no shirt. His ribs showed through his dirty skin. A few chickens pecked in the dust and nearby three naked children played with some broken toy cars. In the distance there was the faint boom of explosives. Bing offered his gifts: some rice, a carton of American cigarettes and a box of chocolates. 'I thought these might be useful. I know you rarely get to the market.'

The old man nodded and called to one of the children to take them inside.

'How is the harvest looking this year?' Bing enquired.

'If we survive long enough it will be a good harvest.' He cleared his throat noisily and spat in the dust.

Bing nodded in the direction of the fighting. 'The war is close today.'

'That's right. I think it will soon be over. And you? Do you agree?'

'Yes I agree. That is why I want to speak to you again about your friends. I am afraid if I don't receive permission soon it will be too late. I wonder if you have heard any word yet.'

The old man lifted his feet from the ground and lay back in the hammock. 'Poussez, s'il vous plaît.'

Bing leaned forward and gave the hammock a push. The old man rocked back and forth in silence. The children commenced firing imaginary weapons at each other. One of them clasped his chest theatrically and fell to the ground.

The old man contemplated them for a moment and then spoke. 'There has been a decision. Come here in two days' time. Tell no one where you are going, bring nothing but the clothes you are wearing. Be prepared to be away for four days.'

Bing could hardly conceal his excitement. He knew it would not be seemly to ask too many questions but he could not restrain his curiosity. 'Thank you. I have only one question. What has changed? What made them say yes?'

The old man folded his arms comfortably behind his head and gazed up at the sky. 'Poussez, encore. Poussez.'

Bing did as he was told and after a time the old man continued. 'You have a reputation as an objective reporter with an understanding of our country, but until now my friends have never been completely sure about you. They received word that you were to be trusted.'

Driving back towards the city Bing puzzled over what the old man had said. He had continued his cautious dealings with several different contacts but could think of nothing they had said which indicated there was going to be a change of heart. Still, the ways of Asia were often impenetrable. Forgetting his questions, he began to plan what he would say to excuse his absence.

As he had been instructed, two days later Bing presented himself at the village. Late that night he was led on foot away through the rice paddies and into the jungle, where a force of Viet Cong soldiers were camped. The record of the four days he spent with them, his documentation of their daily lives, their meagre rations of rice levied from local villages, their effectiveness in battle with weapons inferior to those of the Americans, their high morale and of course the graphic description of their engagement with an American patrol, are now part of newspaper legend. These were the facts. What made the story more controversial was the tone of Bing's writing. In objectively reporting what he saw, it was inevitable that he would be accused of sympathy for the enemy. If he had cared more about perceptions and less about his craft Bing may have modified the writing to suit, but he could no more do that than knowingly publish an untruth. He knew when his account of life with a VC fighting unit was splashed across the front page it would cause a sensation in America and plenty of trouble for him in Saigon.

Two days after his paper ran the story he was sitting in his office when the door opened and a South Vietnamese army private walked in and handed him a handwritten note. Bing opened it and read the contents without surprise. It was a summons for him to attend a meeting with the Colonel in charge of counterintelligence in the South Vietnamese Army. Bing went with the private out into the gathering heat of the morning and drove across town to military headquarters.

Unusually for a Vietnamese, Colonel Nguyen Dac Mao was tall and well muscled. He and Bing knew each other and had chatted occasionally at social events at which they treated each other with polite mistrust. He ushered Bing into his office with icy formality. An old-fashioned ceiling fan rumbled round and round on worn bearings, on the walls there were maps with flags stuck on them, an empty water cooler squatted uselessly in a corner. Bing sat down in front of a desk with half a dozen telephones on it, stacked with reports. Among them he noticed a photocopy of his story. The Colonel lifted the sheet of paper a foot into the air and let it float back down to the desk. He said with an air of regret, 'Mr Connick, I am very unhappy about this.'

'I'm not surprised.'

'Do you want to see this country fall to the communists?'

'We both know it's going to fall, what I want has nothing to do with it.'

'Do you have any idea what sort of damage it causes when reporters like you write your anti-American stories? It undermines morale. That is not enough for you. Now we have an approving account written by you of a VC military operation in which allied soldiers were killed.'

'It was a factual account of what happened.'

The Colonel regarded Bing with dislike. 'You must have some very high-level contacts to pull off a stunt like this.'

'I have good contacts, yes.'

'I want you to tell me how you came to be in the field with a VC unit.'

'You know I can't do that.'

'Nonsense. All you have to do is give me a name. No one will know where it came from.'

'If I gave you the name no source would ever trust

me again. You know this, Colonel. I don't know why you bother.'

The Colonel tapped the photocopy thoughtfully. He picked it up and crushed it into a ball and dropped it into a wastepaper basket beside him. 'You will appreciate that you are operating here with accreditation supplied by the South Vietnamese Government. That accreditation can be withdrawn.'

Bing laughed aloud. 'Come on, you know that's not going to happen. Not even this government could be so stupid.'

The Colonel shook his head. 'You are liaising with some dangerous people Mr Connick, I hope you realise that. We shall have to do something about it.'

Bing stood up. 'Are we finished? I have some work to get on with.'

The Colonel remained seated. 'We are finished.' Bing began to leave when the Colonel held up his hand. 'Correction. We are finished for the moment.'

Bing's story was a cause célèbre for a few days, then life returned to normal, although normality now was tainted by a desperate edge of panic. At night the dull boom of artillery fire, like a distant thunderstorm, could be heard on the outskirts of the city as the North Vietnamese forces drew inexorably closer. Banks and airline offices were filled with panic-stricken people trying to flee the country. Some correspondents began to leave, convinced that when Saigon fell the victors would kill anyone with round eyes.

Phuong and Bing had just finished eating a bowl of pho ga, a beef soup made with rice noodles, and Phuong was preparing to visit her parents. The fear in the city had become tangible in the last few days. There was an air of desperation and despair at the inevitable defeat that was soon to come. Phuong emerged from their bedroom with her handbag and as she walked over to say goodbye Bing almost gasped at her beauty. He was gripped by a sudden unreasonable fear of what his life would be like if he lost her. He caught her by the hand and said, 'Do you have to go tonight?'

She held his hand for a moment and then slipped her fingers free. 'Yes, it's all arranged. Why, what's the matter?'

'I don't know. The city feels dangerous. I don't think it's safe for you to be out alone at night.'

Phuong slid onto his lap and put her arms around his neck. 'You've never worried before. You know I can look after myself. I'll be back about midnight.'

She kissed him, got up and walked to the door. Bing followed. She turned and he held her as she kissed him lightly again. He had an impulse to hug her close and implore her to stay with him, but he fought it. It was foolish for him to feel apprehensive. Besides, he had a story to write. He patted her lightly on the rump and said, 'Be safe, I'll wait for you.' She smiled her trace of a smile, turned and walked down the stairs to the street.

It was past midnight and Bing had written his story and was nodding off over a book when the telephone rang. It was a contact in the police department. He was speaking urgently, as though afraid that he might be interrupted at any moment. There had been a raid on a suburban house and police had arrested a high-ranking Viet Cong officer. Shots had been fired. The informant gave the address, a street in Tan Banh. It was the same street where Phuong's father lived.

Bing felt his bowels loosen with fear. Carefully he asked if he knew the exact address. His contact had no further information. Police were at the scene now.

Bing slammed down the telephone and thundered down the stairs to where the Peugeot was parked. Cursing the slow-moving traffic he headed towards Tan Banh. Logic told him that the shooting could have taken place at any one of a hundred houses, nevertheless he was gripped by an unshakeable pessimism. Despite his impatient rush, one hand on the horn as he barged the cyclos and bicycles and motorbikes and tiny farting Renault taxis aside, he dreaded the moment when he would know the truth. It took him twenty minutes before he was free of the traffic and he turned with squealing tyres into the street. Ahead he could see the flashing police lights and an army staff limousine parked halfway down on the eastern side. With mounting panic he slammed the door and ran for the front entrance of the professor's house. Just as he was about to pound on the door it opened and Colonel Dac Mao stood before him. He gave him a wintry smile. 'Ah, I'm glad you turned up, Mr Connick. So convenient. Otherwise we would have had to come and fetch you.'

Connick stared at him, too shocked to speak. 'You will please accompany us,' the Colonel continued. 'We would like you to assist us with a matter of identification.'

'What are you talking about?'

The Colonel smiled coldly again. 'You reporters like to get close to your stories. This time you will be able to write the personal angle.'

Bing was seized by a terrible fear. 'You bastards,' he whispered. 'You've killed her, haven't you? You've killed her.'

'A suspected Viet Cong agent was killed trying to escape, yes. We believe she was known to you.'

Bing stumbled to the police car and allowed himself to be driven through the teeming streets to the city morgue. The Colonel, a police detective and two other soldiers showed him in through the door, past the stainless-steel tables and into a cold concrete room with a row of refrigerator doors down one side. He stood dumbly as they slid out the tray and lifted the plastic sheet. The Colonel stood by with a slight smile raising the corners of his mouth, waiting patiently. Bing steeled himself and looked down. Her eyes were open and her lips were drawn back in agony. He stepped forward, touched her hair and stroked it. A wave of intense grief swept over him. His body shook with a great sob. With tears running down his cheeks he bent and put his lips to her cold skin.

As if from a long way away he heard the police officer

say, 'Can you identify this as Phuong Ngo, daughter of Professor Nguyen Kao Ngo?'

He opened his mouth and uttered a cry of sheer animal pain. Thrusting past them he ran out into the night to scream his agony to the world.

Bing had spent his life reporting the human tragedy all around him, but nothing could have prepared him for the loss of Phuong. She had been his refuge; a gentle, mysterious companion who had brought some meaning into his life. Until he met her he had not believed himself capable of deep emotion. It was only when she was gone he realised that what he had been experiencing was, after all, love.

He threw himself with savage zeal into his work, reporting the daily horrors dispassionately, without emotion. The war possessed him. He had nothing else. His obsession left other correspondents wondering about his state of mind. He had never shirked danger before, but since the death of Phuong he appeared to seek it out with a relentless disregard for his safety. On a couple of occasions Dave Lindley refused to go with him into obviously suicidal situations.

It was two weeks before the fall of Saigon. The Vietnamese army was fighting a last-ditch battle at Xuan Luoc, the provincial capital just to the north. For days the beleaguered soldiers had managed to hold the city against repeated assaults by North Vietnamese regulars. The South Vietnamese were desperate for good news and when there was a lull in the fighting they hastily organised a press tour to show correspondents the victory. Bing, Dave Lindley and a few television crews and newspapermen piled into a Chinook helicopter and took off from Bien Hoa Airbase.

Below they could see the roads jammed with refugees heading for Saigon. In the distance faint smudges of smoke indicated where fighting was taking place.

The chopper flew high and fast to avoid stray ground fire. Away from the city they passed over areas of rice paddy with peasants working up to their thighs in water. He could see the blur of their faces as they paused and looked up at the Chinook passing overhead. After about half an hour the buildings of Xuan Luoc came into view. As they drew closer they began to see the extent of the damage. Buildings were shattered by heavy shell fire and in places rows of houses were reduced to rubble.

They touched down on an airfield still smoking from the battle and at the urging of the army public relations man ducked and ran under turning rotor blades to the airport building. A row of two dozen sullen prisoners had been lined up for them. They were all suffering wounds of one sort or another and three of them had cuts and yellow bruises from beatings. Dave said, 'They're going to have to come up with something better than a prisoner parade if we're going to get a run.'

The correspondents asked a few perfunctory questions about the prisoners and were then led to a briefing room where a dapper little Colonel was waiting to lecture them on the battle which had just taken place. The Colonel was wearing an immaculate uniform with a cravat at his throat and perfectly polished shoes, gleaming in spite of the dust. Springing up and down on his heels he motioned to the newsmen to gather around a map of the area pinned to the wall.

'Take a look at this joker,' said Dave. 'Now he's going to tell us how they're winning the war.'

Bing put up his hand and said, 'How are you going to hold Xuan Luoc, Colonel?'

The Colonel squared his shoulders. 'They will keep coming but we will knock them down.' He looked around to see if the correspondents were writing down his words and repeated for emphasis, 'We will knock them down.'

Bing had been to too many press conferences and heard too many phony battle assessments to be impressed. He said, 'Colonel, is the city secure at the moment?'

'Perfectly secure. The enemy are in retreat.'

'Can we have a tour and see things for ourselves?'

'That is not possible, I'm afraid. No spare transport you see.'

'But I'll bet you've got a body count all ready for us,' Bing said.

'Ah yes.' As the Colonel reached for his briefing papers the first incoming mortars shook the building, bringing down a shower of plaster onto the assembled correspondents.

Bing hit the floor alongside Dave. 'Some victory,' he said. 'We'll be lucky if these bastards don't get us killed.'

'Dammit,' said Dave. 'I had a dinner appointment tonight.'

Bing could hear the communications officer radioing for the helicopters. Nearby, artillery pieces began returning fire. The exchange continued for about five minutes, then there was a lull. In the distance came the clatter of the twin-engined Chinooks homing in on the airfield. The PR officer told them to get ready to run for it.

On a signal from the officer Bing bent double and ran across the airfield. The Chinook was hovering four feet above the runway, with the boarding ramp down, unwilling to touch down. Bing sensed rather than saw others running beside him. Not only newsmen, but soldiers and civilians as well. He had no idea where Dave was.

As he got closer he ran into a stinging cloud of dust and debris. The wash from the rotors knocked him off his feet and he smelled his eyebrows singeing in the heat from the jet exhaust. He struggled to his feet and was knocked down again by frantically running soldiers. A woman with two small children in tow was on the ground and one of the children cried out with fear and pain as she was trampled.

Bing reached the boarding ramp just as the chopper took off. Around him Vietnamese soldiers and civilians were screaming for it to wait. As it gained height another chopper came down through the dust to hover just clear of the ground. The ramp thumped down and the crowd made a frantic rush for it.

The mob was out of control, driven by blind fear

towards the ramp. As the first ones tried to climb up they slithered on spilled hydraulic oil. Some managed to get a purchase and made it into the belly of the chopper, while the weaker ones were dragged aside by others more desperate. Bing was badly positioned and before he could get anywhere near, the roar of the engines increased and the chopper lifted clear. He knew it was only a matter of time before the shelling started again. He couldn't understand why they had not begun already.

The next chopper was closer, although there was still a sea of people in front of him. He felt the pressure of the crowd behind him as the first ones scrambled up into the yawning belly. Punching and clawing, Bing fought his way to the ramp and arrived at the same time as a Vietnamese woman clutching a little girl about three years old. They touched the ramp together and their eyes met. Above them the loadmaster was urging them to hurry. There was room for just one more adult. Infected by the fear all around him, Bing acted instinctively. He shoved the woman roughly aside and scrambled up the ramp. Seconds later the helicopter took off. For a moment the woman held tight but when she was two feet from the ground she let go and fell back. The last thing he saw as the earth slipped away was her stricken face looking skywards, arms raised beseechingly. The image remained imprinted on his memory forever.

That was the last chopper out of Xuan Luoc. Minutes later the North Vietnamese renewed their attack, pulverising the airstrip and everyone on it. Dave Lindley was among those killed. A short time later the city fell.

'Another drink sir?' The voice filtered through Bing's reverie. The barman was looking curiously at him. How many times had he asked, Bing wondered. How long had he been staring fixedly ahead as the memories flooded his mind?

'No thanks,' he mumbled. He put the empty glass back on the counter and signed the bill. Making his way outside he took the lift to his room, undressed slowly and climbed under the covers. For a long time he lay there willing himself not to close his eyes for he knew what would happen when he did.

At last he could fight fatigue no longer. In his sleep the dream came back. As ever it was a confusion of many images: the Vietnamese mother, eyes wide with fear and hate as he pushed her aside, her face and that of her child diminishing in size as he pulled away from the earth. Other unrelated scenes, somehow connected to the first. The morgue in Saigon, smooth polished tables, a row of doors, the blank-faced attendant sliding out the tray and the police detective flipping back the sheet. Phuong staring sightlessly up at him. As if he was a detached observer he saw himself bend down in an agony of grief to embrace her and as always he woke screaming as he touched her cold flesh.

The bedclothes were in disarray. He disentangled himself, got up and poured himself a shot of whisky from the mini bar with trembling hands. He tossed it down with one gulp and sat down on the bed feeling the alcohol steady his nerves. It was a long time since he had had the dream. Lately he had almost allowed himself to believe he had got rid of it.

Six

Laura and Bing were seated in the Oriental's breakfast room finishing their coffee when a bellboy threaded his way amongst the tables carrying a varnished wooden rod with a sign on the end of it. 'Telephone for Mr Connick,' he cried. 'Telephone for Mr Connick.'

Bing signalled the boy and asked him to bring a phone to the table. It was McCormack. 'How are you this morning, Bing? I trust the Oriental's looking after you? Do they still replace the damned fruit in your room every time you turn your back?'

Bing grunted a reply.

'You're not much fun in the morning are you?' sighed McCormack. 'Well I might as well get straight to it. Buggins has had an accident. His wife found him dead at home this morning.'

'His wife?' said Bing.

'Not exactly a wife. She was away last night staying with a sister who was ill. Came home this morning to a nasty surprise.' McCormack gave a snort of laughter.

Bing and Laura took one of the Oriental's Mercedes hire cars to the address McCormack had given them. It was in a rutted back street, running between down-at-heel buildings. The sleek grey car looked out of place as they cruised along slowly, looking for the number, dodging bicycles, three-wheeled taxis and people pushing hand-carts. Ahead they saw a police car pulled up on the side of the street and McCormack stepped out from the shade of an awning to wave to them. While he had been waiting he had been composing in his head the obituary he would write for Buggins' hometown paper. It was a rare misfortune which did not have something in it for McCormack.

'Bad business, eh?' he said insincerely, as they got out of the Mercedes.

'How did it happen?' asked Laura.

'The police say he must have surprised a burglar. The place looks as though it's been robbed, although I wouldn't have thought Buggins had much worth stealing. As far as I could tell he just scraped a living on his military pension. He certainly showed no outward signs of wealth.'

'We'd better go up and take a look,' said Bing.

The three climbed the staircase past apartments noisy with conversation, children crying, radios playing. The smell of spices and shrimp paste permeated the old building and curious faces looked out from open doors as they passed. On the fourth floor they came to the apartment. A uniformed policeman made an attempt to stop them but McCormack spoke to him in Thai and he stood aside. Inside was a two-room apartment, which once must have been neatly furnished. There were several black and white photographs of a younger Buggins on the walls. Buggins posed beside a jet fighter, Buggins in uniform with half a dozen other servicemen mugging for the camera, Buggins with a Thai woman sitting at a restaurant table laden with food.

'His wife?' asked Bing.

'Yes.'

The pictures were still geometrically straight, but the rest of the room had been ransacked. Drawers were pulled out and papers were scattered over the floor. The cushions of the cane furniture had been slashed and their insides flung aside. Laura looked around apprehensively, half expecting to see Buggins' body lying on the floor. There were a few rust-coloured stains on the rush matting which looked like blood. A man in plain clothes recognised McCormack and greeted him in Thai. They spoke together for a few moments, then McCormack turned to the others.

'He says it's a simple case of robbery. Some of the other residents heard him come home last night, shortly after he left us it would seem. No one saw anything or heard any signs of a struggle. Or if they did they're not saying so. It sometimes makes life easier to be deaf and blind.'

Bing bent down and picked up some of the papers which had been scattered on the floor. One was a letter. 'Dear Congressman,' it began. 'I am writing to you with vital information concerning the fate of American servicemen still missing in action in . . .' Riffling through other papers he came across a stack of sworn affidavits concerning missing airmen. He picked up a letter which seemed to be addressed to the family of an MIA. 'Dear Mrs Jankowski, in regard to your letter about your son John, from my research it seems that it is more than probable that he was still alive when . . .' Rummaging some more he found a pile of painstakingly drawn maps of Vietnam and Laos showing the positions of enemy anti-aircraft batteries and US surveillance positions. Other maps showed what appeared to be the sites where American planes had crashed. Each site was marked with an identification symbol which would probably point to a reference sheet. Bing was looking at the record of Buggins' obsession. He could imagine him labouring in this cheap room, chain smoking as he desperately wrote letters to anyone he thought might listen; the years of correspondence with families as tortured as he was over their missing loved ones. He leafed systematically through the piles of scattered papers but could find no sign of the reference sheet, nor of any list containing the names of the airmen whom Buggins had designated MB. Bing recalled Dean's words the night before that the list was 'in a safe place'. He addressed McCormack. 'Can you ask the officer where we can find his wife?'

McCormack spoke in Thai with the police officer. 'She's with her sister. He's given me the address, I'll take you.'

The morning sun was now high in the sky. Outside the heat settled over them like a warm wet blanket. The traffic had built up until it could only move at a slow crawl. The air was acrid with exhaust smoke. 'It's only a couple of blocks away,' said McCormack. 'We might as well walk.'

By the time they reached the address, an apartment block similar to the one they had just left, they were damp with sweat. The apartment this time was on the fifth floor. They were all panting heavily from the climb when they knocked on the door. After a time they heard a shuffling within. The door opened and an attractive Thai woman, aged about thirty-five, stood before them. Recognising McCormack she put her hands together and made the traditional Thai gesture of greeting. 'Please come in.'

A woman who looked slightly older was sitting at a table on which she had been grinding spices with a mortar and pestle. 'This is my sister Nitia and I am Somi.' The sister stopped work for a moment and gave them a nod, then continued with her task as though they were not there.

McCormack introduced Laura and Bing. Somi put her hands together and made a Wai to each and then waited. 'We're sorry to hear about Dean,' Bing said. 'We hardly knew him. We only just met him last night, but he seemed like a good man.'

There was no sign of grief. The woman before them seemed perfectly composed. 'Thank you,' she said.

'Had you been together long?' Bing asked.

'Five years. We were together five years.'

'How did you meet?'

'I worked in a jewellery shop. Dean came in one day

to buy a gift for his daughter in America. It was her birthday. We began talking and he asked me out.' She paused as though trying to find the words to sum up their life together. 'He was good to me.'

Watching this exchange Laura realised that Bing was genuinely compassionate.

Somi's sister paused in her work and spoke for the first time. 'I tell Somi she should marry, but she no marry. Now what she do?' Tears began silently to roll down her face. She was grieving not for the death of Dean Buggins, but for the stolen promise of a secure future.

Somi remained dry-eyed. She put an arm around her sister and said, 'My sister is worried about what will happen to me. Life is very hard in Thailand, but I can work. Perhaps I can work in the jewellery store again.'

Bing said, 'Somi, you know about Dean's interest in the MIAs?'

'Oh yes. I could never understand why they were so important, but the MIAs, they were his life.'

'Dean was going to give us something which is very important to us,' said Bing. 'A list of Americans who were shot down in Vietnam. There were a lot of papers in the apartment this morning but the list wasn't among them. Do you have any idea where it might be?'

The sister said something in Thai which sounded like a warning and a short conversation followed.

'He asked me to keep some papers in a safe place, but I am not sure that I should give them to you.'

'Could we at least have a look at them?'

Somi glanced at her sister. 'I don't know.'

'Dean is dead, Somi,' Bing said gently. 'I think he would want you to show them to us.'

Somi hesitated for a moment longer, then got to her feet and walked into the next room. She returned carrying an aluminium briefcase with a combination lock. She spun the wheels, clicked the lid open and turned the briefcase round on her knee so that Bing could look inside. With a graceful Asian gesture, a slight upward sweep of the palms, she invited him to examine the contents. Bing picked up a sheaf of computer printout and scanned it rapidly. From the size of it, it appeared to be a complete list of Americans missing in action in Indochina. He knew there would be nothing especially secretive about that. The list would be available from any of the veterans' groups in the United States. He put the list aside. Next he lifted out a blue manilla folder and opened it. Inside was a typewritten list of about fifty names in alphabetical order. He scanned rapidly down until he came to P. There, together with his rank and serial number and the date he had been shot down, was the name Daniel Parkinson. Without a word he handed it to Laura. Her face distorted. She put her head down on her knees and quietly wept.

Later that day Laura, Bing and McCormack were back at the Oriental Hotel sitting at an outdoor table beside the pool. McCormack had suggested they go to the Glitter Bar, but Laura insisted they meet on her territory. They were seated in the shade of a large umbrella, cooled by a gentle breeze wafting off the river. The afternoon storm was building up, dark clouds rolling in from the horizon, accompanied by the growl of distant thunder. McCormack looked around with distaste at the immaculate pool attendants and well-to-do Europeans relaxing on chaiseslongues. The waiter put down their drinks, three iced beers. McCormack disregarded his glass and took a deep swallow straight from the bottle, raising an eyebrow with surprise as Laura followed suit. While they were driving back Laura had recovered her composure and now she took the initiative.

'It's obvious where the trail leads. We'll have to go to Russia.'

'And do what?' said McCormack. 'Put an ad in the paper? Would anyone knowing the whereabouts of Dan Parkinson, formerly of the United States of America, please call this number?'

'I don't know. But if Americans were taken to Russia,

there must be a record of it somewhere. The Cold War's over now, couldn't we simply ask the Russians, or enlist the help of the US Embassy?'

Bing had been silent during the car ride back. Now he said, 'Russia's been a closed society for seventy years. It just wouldn't be in their nature to come out now and be open about what they did in the war. They certainly aren't going to admit anything without a lot of careful thought about the consequences.

'Let's just think it through further. It's unlikely the Americans would want to stir the pot either. The MIA question is nicely dead and buried. Like Buggins said, no one's interested any more. Just when the Cold War's over no one wants embarrassing inquiries about abandoning our boys to the Russians.'

McCormack joined in. 'Exactly. And how do you even know that it's true? What have you got? A list compiled by an obsessed ex intelligence agent who worked it out from intercepted conversations in code twenty years ago?'

Laura listened to the cynical logic of their arguments. She was beyond logic. How could either of them understand the nature of her quest? They avoided involvement, McCormack because he was probably incapable of it and Bing because for some reason he was afraid of it. Only Buggins had been involved and now Buggins was dead.

'Back in Sydney you gave us no chance of finding so much as a clue,' Laura said. 'Now at least we have a lead. Your contacts have got us this far. Surely if you put your mind to it you could think of a starting point in Russia.'

Bing was silent. He was thinking about Buggins' death. Perhaps he had been the victim of a burglar, or perhaps there was something more sinister behind it. He gazed into the middle distance, weighing up his options. Return to Australia now and slip back into the old life, or press on to who knew what? He told himself that Laura, with her boots-and-all approach, had no idea what she would be letting herself in for if she began blundering about in Russia. She thought she could handle anything, but she needed to be protected from herself. But he was too much of a realist to kid himself about his reasons. In spite of himself, he was becoming caught up in the search. He said to McCormack, 'Remember David Bellamy? I heard he was Bureau Chief in Moscow now.'

'I believe so.'

'He was a good hand in Saigon.'

'Not bad.'

Bing turned his attention to Laura. 'Well, I guess it's your party.'

McCormack shook his head in amusement and gave a small snort of laughter at this confirmation, yet again, of human folly. He thought to himself, Bloody Bing Connick, never did know when to back off.

Seven

Sergei Bulak stood beside the bench with his foreman and a technician, contemplating a TV set which was ready for testing. He knew with depressing certainty that it was faulty. The whole batch of fifteen hundred colour tubes just off the assembly line was faulty. Still, he wanted to see the disaster with his own eyes. Out of politeness he addressed the technician in Lithuanian, eliciting a slight grimace of censure from his foreman. The foreman could never understand why the manager took so much trouble with the workers. He always spoke to them in Russian.

The technician plugged a lead from a pattern generator into the back of the set. At a nod from Sergei, he switched the machine on. A cross-hatched pattern of vertical and horizontal lines appeared on the screen. The lines were black and white and towards the edges of the screen they were red, blue and green. The technician made some adjustments with a screwdriver. The pattern remained the same, confirming what Sergei already knew. The deflection yokes on all fifteen hundred tubes would have to be junked. A week's production had been wasted.

'How could fifteen hundred deflection yokes be faulty?' he said to the foreman.

The man shrugged his shoulders. These things happened. There was no point in getting excited about it.

The man's lack of interest was a familiar irritant to Sergei. It wasn't just him. The entire workforce was the same. He should have been used to it by now, but still he felt a hot flush of anger redden his ears.

'Didn't you test before you started the run?' he said.

'I'm afraid not.' The foreman gave him a blank look. He could not understand why these things upset his superior. It made no difference to anyone if they had to remake the deflection yokes. They still got paid. Life went on.

Sergei could not let it go. Three weeks ago it was the diodes wired arse-about, before that it was the wrong capacitors. 'Doesn't anyone care that we're not going to meet the quota?' he said angrily.

The foreman was sick of hearing about quotas. Figures dreamed up by some bureaucrat in Moscow meant nothing to him. Sergei Bulak was the only man he knew who took quotas seriously, but then there had always been something strange about him.

'No one ever meets the quotas, Comrade, you know that.'

'Well they're going to have to start,' said Sergei.

'Ah yes,' said the foreman derisively. 'I was forgetting perestroika. We all have to work like Americans now don't we? Produce, produce, produce.'

'This country would be a damn sight better off if people did work like Americans,' retorted Sergei. 'Even when we manage to make a TV set that works it falls to pieces in a couple of years.'

'A shame, Comrade, that you weren't born an American if you admire them so much.'

Sergei was about to respond, but he checked himself. He knew there was no use descending into pointless bickering with his foreman. Better to try and maintain good relations and cajole him into getting the work done. He couldn't really expect him to understand a concept like pride of workmanship when it had never mattered how well or badly he did his job.

'Never mind,' he said. 'Let's get the new run under way. And do some tests this time eh? There's a good chap.'

Sergei looked at his watch. It was a thick Russian-made timepiece with a manual winder. The cheap imitation leather band was about to break again. He would have to ask his wife, Palmyra, to try and find a new one, but like everything else in Vilnius, a new watchband could be hard to obtain. Sometimes weeks would pass by without being able to find one and then suddenly watchbands would be everywhere. It was irritating, but the erratic supply of watchbands was as much a part of life as food coupons and power cuts. Perhaps he would be better off being like the foreman and just accepting that this was the way things were. He tried, but he couldn't help chafing at the inefficiencies.

It was time for lunch. He took his watch off and put it in his pocket for safety, then walked down a long assembly line containing dozens of half-made sets. The shoddy plastic casings were all red. For the next few months anyone lucky enough to buy a TV would have no choice. Red or nothing. He chuckled quietly to himself, not at the system, although he found much to amuse him there, but at the foreman's last retort. If only they knew, he thought, but they could never know. No one could ever know.

Sergei made his way to the canteen and joined a long queue of assembly workers waiting to be served their daily hot meal. He could have gone to the head of the line, but he liked to mingle with the workers and see what they were thinking. They would never officially approach him with suggestions for improvement but, chatting to them informally, he sometimes discovered problems before they became disasters.

'Are you going to the cathedral tomorrow Sergei?' Sergei turned to see who was addressing him. It was one of the maintenance men, a Lithuanian of about thirty who had spent all his working life in the plant. Tomorrow was 16 February, the anniversary of Lithuania's Declaration of Independence, in 1918, from the Russian Tsars. Normally a Lithuanian would never ask such a question of a Russian, but the workers knew that the manager was a bit eccentric. It would be just like him to turn up with his family in the main square for tomorrow's celebrations.

Sergei shook his questioner's hand. 'How are you, Algis?' he asked warmly. 'Yes of course I'm going. I want to hear the speeches.'

'Better to go in person I think,' said Algis. 'You may not read about it in the newspaper. I hear the presses broke down again.'

Everyone knew that when the presses broke down it usually meant they had been sabotaged. It was one way for Moscow's agents to check the growing stridency of the independence movement, Sajudis. The Russian President, Boris Ivashov, had recently visited Lithuania and taken the unusual step of going into the streets to talk to the crowds. Ivashov had been harangued by ordinary men and women demanding to know when they would be given their freedom. He had left for Moscow making it clear that no such move was contemplated in the near future.

They approached the counter and Sergei held out his plate for a watery stew and potatoes. 'How are your kids?' Sergei asked Algis. The maintenance man began to tell him all about his five-year-old's prowess on the toboggan. The two men walked together to a table where they joined a dozen other workers. For half an hour the manager chatted away with them. Across the room, the foreman dined alone. He watched the scene unhappily. Managers should dine alone in the office. It wasn't right for Bulak to mix with the assembly-line workers like that. He said to himself, not for the first time, that there was definitely something strange about him. Even his hair was strange. Who had ever seen a red-headed Russian?

At the end of the day Sergei caught a trolleybus to his apartment building in the suburbs of Vilnius. As usual the elevator was not working, so he climbed the stairs to the third floor and let himself in. He hung up his coat and left his shoes in the tiny vestibule. Palmyra was in the kitchen cooking. She turned around to greet him with a smile.

'I got lucky today,' she said. 'I was in the market and there was a woman selling rabbit.' She dipped her ladle into the pot and held it out to Sergei to taste.

Sergei sipped appreciatively and pronounced the stew delicious. Palmyra continued gaily, 'And some Azerbaijanis had some fruit. I got two oranges.'

'You're amazing,' he said. 'A rabbit and oranges. A triumph.' He gave her an affectionate slap on the rump, left the kitchen and went into the sitting room. The apartment was of a higher standard than average; a reward for his cooperation. There were two bedrooms, almost unheard of, even for a factory manager. The furniture was the usual shoddily built Russian issue, but he had several luxury items. There was a TV set and a record turntable with a collection of long playing classical discs. On a sideboard table was a short-wave radio on which he could listen to the BBC Overseas Service or Voice of America. One wall contained shelves full of books in Russian and English. On another were two restored icons and a Van Gogh print of a bridge over a river in Holland.

Sergei looked in on one bedroom and saw his son bent over his desk, doing his homework. Alvidas looked up and smiled at his father's greeting. Sergei went over, tousled his red hair and for few minutes they discussed his day at school. When he was born fifteen years ago, Sergei and Palmyra had been in a dilemma over what to name him. Palmyra was Lithuanian. It had come down to a choice between a Russian name, Mickhael, or the Lithuanian one. In the end they had decided on Alvidas. It had been a bold thing to do at the time. Sergei had only been in Lithuania for two years and he was still being closely monitored to see if he was behaving appropriately. They were not at all sure how this gesture might be interpreted. He had never heard anything about it. Now, seventeen years after first arriving, he rarely had contact with his case officer but he assumed that he was still watched and his activities reported on.

Palmyra walked in to the lounge room and joined him on the couch. 'I've been thinking about tomorrow,' she said. 'Do you think it might be better if we didn't go?'

Sergei touched her shoulder with his palm in a gesture of affection. As a young man he had never been a touchy person, but now he seemed to need tactile contact with his loved ones, as if to reassure himself of their existence. 'Why not? Are you worried?'

Palmyra put her hand on his. She looked at him with a serious expression. 'We have a good life don't we?'

'Good for the Soviet Union, yes.' He could never quite bring himself to embrace wholeheartedly the fiction that he was content.

'I'm just afraid there will be trouble. You know the speeches are going to call for independence don't you?'

'Yes my dove.' He used the Russian term of endearment, although he spoke Lithuanian. 'I know. But so what? They told Ivashov the same thing to his face the other day.'

'I just think you should stay out of it, that's all. You shouldn't get involved.'

'I believe in Sajudis, you know that.'

'I know. You think after all these years you're free to believe what you want, but you're not. You never will be.'

'Look, they may call me a Russian, but they'll never make me think like one. Independence is coming. They can't stop it.'

'They stopped it in Prague and Budapest. What makes you think they won't bring in the tanks here?'

'Because the world's changed. Ivashov wouldn't dare.'

Palmyra shook her head. 'You're always so certain about everything aren't you? You know what they did to people in Hungary and Czechoslovakia. They'll do the same thing to people here who speak out. You'll be no different. Worse. They'd be more harsh with you than a normal dissident.'

Sergei knew Palmyra's fears for him were well-founded. He had been allowed to build a life, but its stability depended on him keeping a low profile and playing the faithful party member. He had been given a good apartment and a job where his knowledge of electronics could be put to use. He hated the job but he tried to do it well. He loved his wife and son and would never do anything to put them in danger. Still, he was stirred by the talk all around him of freedom and democracy. He knew better than any Lithuanian the practical beauty of those words. He squeezed Palmyra's hand. 'Look we'll only be a couple among thousands. We'll just go and listen to the speeches that's all. OK?'

Palmyra gave him a worried smile. 'All right we'll go. But please don't get involved.'

All next day crowds slowly built up in the old town and around the main square of Vilnius. By nightfall thousands of Lithuanians were strolling about dressed in their best clothes. The town and the people in it had remained perversely European despite being occupied twice by the Russians. The Tsars had ruled them for over a century. They had broken away after the First World War, they were occupied by Germany during the Second World War and after a secret deal between Russia and Germany Stalin took over again. Now the Lithuanians and their neighbours, the Estonians and Latvians, were clamouring for their freedom.

Palmyra and Sergei strolled past a group of hunger strikers protesting against drafting their children into the Red Army. A bearded man stood beside a display board of black and white photographs showing dead Russian soldiers in Afghanistan. They were artless, as news pictures usually are: a body sprawled with its arms akimbo and the mouth open in a death grimace, another shot of three dead soldiers piled together like discarded dolls, the blood showing as black blotches against the white snow, a burnt tank with two more dead Russians beside it. A small crowd had gathered around the parent to hear him rail against Moscow. Sergei wanted to stop and listen for a while, but Palmyra hurried him along.

Further on they came to the cathedral which stood in the middle of the main square. It was built of white stone and a stark belltower, made of the same material with a red roof like a cap, stood separate to it. The cathedral was the symbol of Lithuania's subjugation. It had been used by the Nazis as a headquarters during their occupation. When Stalin took over, after the signing of the Molotov–Ribbentrop pact, he had torn down the decorative saints, banned the practice of religion and turned it into a communist art gallery. A year ago, in a gesture of reconciliation, the Party had allowed the cathedral to reopen. The faithful were preparing for evening mass.

'There's a feeling in the air,' murmured Sergei to Palmyra, 'which reminds me of the anti-Vietnam movement.'

Palmyra shushed him and glanced about her nervously. Not even Alvidas knew of his father's earlier life. It was something he and Palmyra spoke about only when they were alone and sure of absolute security. Although Sergei had described it to her, she could only dimly imagine what it would be like to live in America, but she knew how much her husband ached for the freedoms of his upbringing. She could understand how all this talk of independence stirred him, as it frightened her. She had lived under the communist system too long to believe that glasnost was anything more than an illusion which would be shattered the moment Moscow found that it was no longer expedient.

The sun had gone down and a black, crisp night crept upon them. Now, one by one, the people lit candles until there were thousands of flickering yellow lights dancing like fireflies. Carrying the candles before them in the still air, they began walking slowly and silently down the streets of the old town towards the main square, solemn faces lit by the glow. Searchlights bathed the cathedral in red, yellow and green, the colours of the Lithuanian flag. When they reached the cathedral the walkers stopped and waited for the bell to signal the beginning of the service. Palmyra and Sergei drifted with the crowd. They looked around for signs of a military presence, but there was none. A few police cars were parked on the outskirts of the square. The officers were sitting inside looking bored. Still Palmyra, with instinctive caution, contrived to insinuate them deep into the crush where they would merge.

The bell tolled and inside the cathedral a choir began to sing, their voices ringing with electric passion across the square. Tentatively at first and then with abandon, the crowd in their thousands joined in. The singing was one of the things Sergei loved about Lithuania. It was a nation of choirs. Every large factory and communal farm had one. Some nations protested with guns and bombs, but the Lithuanians' was a singing revolution. As the voices harmonised and held, he felt something like longing, although for what he did not know. The singing came to an end and the crowd listened in silence as the priest read the mass and then gave communion.

A platform had been erected to one side of the cathedral. When the mass was over there was a crackling of loudspeakers and the first of the speeches began in Lithuanian. The candle-lit audience listened reverently as speaker after speaker called for an end to communist rule. After some time a tall man wearing a black overcoat walked forward to the microphone and began to speak in English with an American accent. He was a practised orator and although few of the audience could understand him they stood transfixed by the power of his delivery. He spoke for several minutes, building up to a passionate climax.

'We stand here today as one nation,' he declaimed, 'which has returned from the Gulags in Siberia, from exile, from eternal oblivion and we ask all peoples of goodwill in the West to help us in our quest to return to the map of history.'

Sergei was the first to put his hands together and in a few seconds the crowd were applauding in a roar of approval. Sergei looked at Palmyra beside him and saw that her eyes were shining. When the sound died down the choir began to sing 'Lietuva Brangi Mano Tevyne'. Stalin had banned the national anthem, but this song, 'Lithuania My Dear Country,' by the beloved poet Maironis, had become the rallying song for the nation:

Lithuania my dear fatherland
A land where our warriers sleep in tombs
Beautiful is the blue of your sky
Because you have suffered so much misery and pain
You are dear to us.

After the first stanza the crowd joined in. The sound of thousands of harmonising voices filled the town square like hope. Swept up in the wave of emotion, Sergei sang lustily, with tears coursing down his cheeks. Singing for freedom, for Lithuania, for himself.

At home that night he and Palmyra chattered like teenagers. They went to bed and made love slowly, exploring familiar pleasures. Soon afterwards Palmyra went to sleep but Sergei lay awake, thinking. He had been caught up in the patriotic fervour in the square, but now he felt a wave of depression settling over him. As sometimes happened in the night's blackest hours, he was confronted by the reality of his situation. He was a man without a country. A traitor. In his dark bed he faced the bleak truth that he was ultimately alone.

Eight

Rod Landauer entered the State Department building at the corner of C Street NW and 23rd in Washington, DC. He showed his pass to the marine guard and caught the elevator to the seventh floor housing the Executive Secretary. Walking through deserted corridors he came to a locked door. He punched in his key code and entered the Operations Centre. It was eleven o'clock at night and for the next eight hours he would monitor cables. Landauer was a Foreign Service Officer. The centre was manned twenty-four hours a day and as long as he did it Landauer could never get used to working the graveyard shift.

Yawning, he went to the coffee machine and filled a polystyrene cup, sprinkled creamer on top and stirred in two satchels of sugar. He nodded and said hello to the other half dozen officers and prepared for work. Rows of printers spewed forth rolls of paper, a relentless, never-ending avalanche of information from US embassies all over the world, most of it, Landauer knew, entirely useless. There were summaries of what the local media were saying about the United States, economic reports, gossip picked up at embassy cocktail parties, tips from low-level informants and intelligence reports.

Landauer's job was to summarise these reports and distribute them to the heads of various government departments. Sensitive cables were marked NODIS, meaning no distribution. These were circulated only to specific high officials. At the top of each report a series of acronyms indicated their destination—SOS for Secretary of State, SOD for Secretary of Defence, NSA for National Security Adviser, POTUS for President of the United States.

Landauer put down his coffee, loosened his tie and picked up his first cable. It was a NODIS from the Bangkok Embassy referring to an informant named McCormack. He remembered a cable sourced to the same man yesterday where McCormack had advised his controller about a meeting between a former NSA analyst and a journalist. Pretty routine stuff except later the same day the analyst had met with a fatal accident. Cursing the bureaucrat who had decreed such small print, Landauer scanned the text. The journalist, one Bing Connick, had left Bangkok and was on his way to Moscow. He glanced at the top. It was flagged attention NSA.

Landauer threw it into the tray and moved on to the next cable.

Despite the temperature, which was hovering near freezing point, Laura waved aside the shabbily dressed men with their filthy Lada taxis waiting outside her hotel and set off on a walking tour of Moscow. She planned to sightsee while Bing went to look up his old colleague from the Vietnam days. Going through the pedestrian tunnel which leads under the street to Red Square, she was shocked to see beggars squatting on their haunches against the tiled walls. Most were old women with lined faces and toothless mouths. One younger woman had a child of about five, swaddled in layers of clothing, who held out a tiny mittened hand for coins. The mother and son were doing a lot better than the babushkas. Laura was struck by the obvious poverty all about her. The Muscovites, trudging unsmilingly through the tunnel, were grey-faced, with lank hair and shabby clothing.

Emerging at street level she entered Red Square. As she headed across the cobblestones towards Lenin's tomb a young man in army uniform came up to her and, in halting English, attempted to sell her the belt from his greatcoat. Shaking her head politely she walked across to stand in admiration before the extravagant spires and minarets of St Basil's.

Laura walked back across Red Square and pushed through the swinging glass doors of GUM. She had always heard it described as a department store, but it was like no department store she had ever seen. It consisted of scores of separate shops gathered together in a vast arcade. Stairways led from ground level to catwalks running alongside more shops above. Many of the stores were closed while those that had a few old-fashioned-looking goods for sale mostly had long queues outside. She saw nothing that she wanted to buy.

She headed back towards the hotel. There was a crowd gathered up ahead. As she approached closer she could see that the footpath was packed from the buildings to the gutter with men and women standing stoically in the cold. Each person held a small item for sale, a tube of toothpaste, a toy tricycle, a fur hat. As Laura threaded her way through the narrow path that had been left clear for pedestrians there was no attempt to importune her. If it was a street market in America the vendors would have been shouting their spiel, but the Russians had not yet learned this particular trick of capitalism. They simply stood there waiting patiently for a sale.

A little further on Laura was approached by half a dozen gipsy children. One girl, perhaps ten years old, with swarthy skin and dark flashing eyes and wearing a long cotton dress, its hem filthy from dragging in the snow, walked backwards ahead of her with her hand out in a begging gesture. Two other children held onto her legs so that she was forced to a halt and two more each held onto an arm. They were all murmuring for alms. Laura was effectively trapped. With a shock she realised that yet another gipsy child was fiddling with her handbag. She tried to wrench herself free but the little hands clasping her legs and arms were impossible to prise away.

Laura was capable of punching a man or throwing a steer, but she was at a loss how to combat a gang of children clinging like limpets to every limb. She looked around for help. The street was crowded with people, but no one seemed interested in the tribulations of the well-dressed foreigner. She was about to take violent action when a tall, dark-skinned man stepped forward and began berating the gipsies. He cuffed one on the ear and in a moment they let her go, running jeering into the crowd.

Flustered, Laura stammered out her thanks in phrase book Russian. 'Please don't mention it,' the man replied in English. 'But you must be careful walking alone in Moscow these days, especially of gipsies. Never stop for them, just walk on.'

He was about thirty years old with faintly Oriental features and straight, jet-black hair. He looked strikingly different to most people she had seen walking about the streets.

'Easier said than done,' she replied with a smile.

He smiled back. 'My name is Askar.'

'Laura Bailey. I'm visiting here from the United States.'

'And you are staying at the Metropole?' he said, indicating the imposing Stalinist building towards which Laura had been heading.

'Yes.'

'I know Moscow well. If you need any help, a guide, assistance with shopping, I am available.'

'Oh well, I'm not sure yet just how long I'll be here, but yes, that's nice of you. Thank you.'

Askar dug into his pocket and produced a business card. 'Please, if I can be of any help, you can call me on this number. Now goodbye and, as I said, take care.'

David Bellamy was what Bing might have been if he had remained in the profession of journalism. As head of a wire-service bureau in Moscow he had long passed the stage of merely reporting events. He was more like a diplomat, cultivating high-level contacts, keeping his finger on the pulse, strategically directing his staff as they tried to keep pace with the bewildering changes besetting the Soviet empire.

Bellamy's office was located on the second floor of a building occupied mainly by joint-venture companies. Bing walked down a corridor past a door with 'Russo Finnish Enterprises' written in fresh paint and entered a shabby room filled with utilitarian office furniture. Although it was a decade since Bing had visited a wire-service bureau he felt instantly familiar with the scene. A word processor took up most of Bellamy's desk and what space was left was littered with newspapers and magazines. In the corner a television set showed CNN with the sound turned down. Bellamy shook Bing's hand and gave him a friendly examination.

'Look at that suntan. Living in the Antipodes obviously agrees with you.'

'How are you, David? How's Moscow.'

'If you really want to know it's a bastard of a place, but it's the best damn story in the world. It's the place to be right now and probably for the next four or five years. So what about you? I thought you'd given all this nonsense away. A bit of freelancing?'

'You could say that, David.'

'Well welcome to Moscow. Anything I can do just ask.'

'As a matter of fact, there might be. I've landed here absolutely cold and I need a couple of contacts for a specific project.'

'Tell me about it and I'll see if I can help.'

'I'm interested in Russian involvment in the Vietnam War.'

Bellamy laughed. 'Is that all? Why don't you try something difficult? You know the Russians were never officially involved.'

'I know. And you know and I know that's bullshit.'

Bing looked around him. Through the grimy window of Bellamy's office he could see reporters telephoning and typing up stories. He didn't want to tell Bellamy everything but he would have to go some of the way if he was to get help. 'I have information that Russians may have interrogated American POWs in Vietnam. I'm after confirmation.'

'I've heard those rumours,' Bellamy said. 'That's KGB business.'

'I know.'

'Hmm. Let me tell you about the KGB these days. We're told that they're no longer the old repressive organisation they used to be. That's true to a point, but not entirely. There are two factions. One wants to open the place up to the world and reveal all the dirty secrets, a sort of public cleansing of the spirit. Your best chance of finding out anything about involvement with Americans would be to gain the confidence of someone in this camp. There is, however, another faction which is determined not to see their old powers eroded and they're still a powerful force within the organisation.'

'So I need to make contact with the liberals.'

'That's right.' Bellamy paused. 'You don't need me to tell you that you're treading on pretty tricky ground here. These guys can still play pretty rough when they want to.'

'I'm aware of that, David.'

'It must be a pretty good story.' Bing said nothing. 'What are you doing this weekend?' Bellamy continued.

'Nothing in particular.'

'I'm going out of town to a dacha owned by someone who might be helpful. If not directly at least they might be a start. Want to come?'

'I'm not alone. I'm travelling with a woman. A colleague.'

'All the better. Bring her along too.'

Bing stood up. 'Thanks David.'

'That's all right. I owe you a few from the old days.

I'll pick you up at the Metropole at nine Saturday morning.'

Laura thanked Askar again and walked the remaining few hundred yards to the hotel. As she approached the main entrance two hard-faced men looked at her carefully. It was obvious she was a guest. No one could have mistaken her clothes for those of a Russian. They swung the doors open and she stepped inside to another world. Well-dressed men and women sat on plush, red covered sofas discussing business in French, German and English. Porters and bellboys hurried about, while the front-desk staff handled the comings and goings of guests with professional efficiency. She crossed the spacious reception area with black and white marble flooring and turned left to the bistro where she had arranged to meet Bing. He was sitting at a table with a coffee in front of him. She sat down with relief and said, 'I just nearly got robbed out there. A bunch of gipsy children were all over me begging and one almost had my handbag open.'

'Are you all right?' It was the first time Bing had ever asked her a personal question.

She smiled her appreciation of his concern. 'Yes. I'm a little shook up, that's all. How did your meeting with Bellamy go?'

'Quite good. I didn't tell him the whole story, just enough for him to get the drift of what we need.'

Bing related some of Bellamy's background briefing. A waiter came and placed fresh coffees in front of them, making an elaborate show of pouring them out and fussing with the sugar bowl. He had already learned one of the basics of a market economy, that service translates into tips. Bing waited until he left before continuing his conversation.

'Tomorow we've been invited to a dacha outside Moscow to spend the weekend. Bellamy says there may be some useful contacts among the guests.'

'Wonderful. A country weekend in Russia, it sounds fantastic.'

Bing was irritated by her enthusiasm. It was unprofessional. He would rather be doing this by himself. He blurted out, 'Look it's not too late to back away from this now.'

Laura gave him a surprised look. 'Back away, why?'

'This may sound melodramatic, but there's a good chance we're stirring up something which people don't want stirred up.'

'What are you trying to say Bing?'

What was he trying to say? Was he really annoyed at her, or was he was just annoyed at himself for being here? 'You saw for yourself today how dangerous this place can be,' he said. 'Just be careful, that's all.'

David Bellamy called for Laura and Bing in a black Zil limousine driven by a young Russian. In half an hour they were clear of the city, speeding along a three-lane roadway. The opposing lines of traffic occupied the lanes on either side while the centre lane was used by both for passing. The Zil spent most of its time in the centre and the two Americans found it a little unnerving watching vehicles approaching head-on only to swerve aside at the last minute back to their side of the road. The country through which they passed was covered in snow. Now and again they spied groups of drab dwellings with wisps of smoke spiralling from their chimneys. Paling fences were half-buried under drifts of white.

As they travelled Bellamy told them about the people they were going to meet. 'Pavel Rezchikova is an entrepreneur. He comes from an influential Russian family and is involved in setting up joint ventures with foreign companies. He's an ardent supporter of the new free-market economy and likes the West. I think you should approach him circumspectly. He's very well connected with the new regime and if he decides to help you he could be useful.'

'And what about the dacha?' Laura asked. 'Whose is it?'

'It's owned by a friend of mine. I think you'll find Giorgiou fascinating.'

'What does he do?'

'His profession is, well, unusual.' Bellamy smiled enigmatically.

Laura was intrigued. 'Come on David,' she said. 'Why the mystery?'

'Please allow me to keep you in suspense for a little longer. You'll find out soon enough when we arrive.'

After about an hour the limousine left the highway and began travelling slowly along a narrow road with snow banks piled high on each side. They came to a village of large, well-kept wooden houses, bright paint showing out gaily against the white. A man and a woman made their way along the side of the road on cross-country skis. A little further on a man, markedly better dressed than most Russians Laura had seen, was walking a German shepherd. 'These are all dachas owned by the elite,' Bellamy said. 'You have to be someone pretty special to earn one of these. As you will see our host falls into that category.'

The driver turned in through a pair of eight-foot-high gates which had been left open, drove up a sweeping driveway and came to a halt outside a two-storey, green-painted dacha. A door opened and a small man with a neatly trimmed beard came out and greeted them warmly.

'David, I see you've survived the traffic unscathed yet again. Good to see you.' As the others stepped out of the Zil he continued effusively, 'You must be Laura Bailey and of course Bing Connick. Welcome, welcome, come on in.'

The English was perfect, without the slightest trace of an accent. He could have been a country squire in England welcoming guests for a weekend of shooting.

Their host led the way into a large lounge room with dark panelling and Persian rugs on the floors. Another man, who had been relaxing on a sofa, rose to his feet and was introduced as Pavel Rezchikova. Their host took their coats and asked them to make themselves comfortable. He headed towards a large samovar which was bubbling on a table. He had a way of bounding about as though full of energy waiting to burst out. As he poured tea Bing said, 'Thank you for inviting us here, Giorgiou.'

The man Bellamy had called Giorgiou gave a delighted laugh. 'Ah David, you do like your little surprises don't you. In Russian you would call me Giorgiou, but I'm still more comfortable with George. George Blackwell.' He paused to gauge the effect this announcement had on his guests. Laura smiled politely. Bing said, '*The* George Blackwell?'

The little man beamed delightedly. 'I doubt if there are any other George Blackwells between here and Vladivostok. Oh yes I am *the* George Blackwell.' He held out a steaming cup. 'Tea?'

Bing accepted the black tea wordlessly. Blackwell was one of the most celebrated British spies ever to defect to the Soviet Union. As a highly placed member of MI5 he had for years passed valuable secrets to the KGB. Bing remembered the details of the story clearly. He had been discovered, arrested and sentenced to forty-five years imprisonment. After two years he had escaped from his British prison in a dramatic breakout and was smuggled to the Soviet Union, where he was welcomed as a hero and given a high-ranking position in the KGB. He remembered reading somewhere that Blackwell had been responsible for unmasking dozens of British spies in the Eastern bloc, many of whom had probably been executed. It was difficult to reconcile his Machiavellian reputation with the cheerful little man who now sat before him.

Taking note of Laura's incomprehension Blackwell said to her, 'I can see my place in history has escaped your notice Mrs Bailey. I am what Fleet Street and no doubt the American press was pleased to call a spy. Back in the fifties there were many of us at Oxford and Cambridge who saw in communism a great ideal. We were drawn to the idea that all men and women could be equal, working together for the good of all, where the physician and the professor were no more esteemed than

90

the factory worker. Think of it, free education, free housing, work for all. A modern utopia. What a seductive idea.'

Blackwell gave one of his effusive chuckles, as if he was relating some lark that the undergraduates had got up to. 'After university and the war I ended up working for British Intelligence, running agents behind the Iron Curtain, as they called it then. I was able to tell the Soviets who they were and what they had access to. As a result they were able to seed them with a great deal of misinformation and eventually to eliminate them.'

'What do you mean by eliminate them?'

The hint of a mood change passed for a moment over Blackwell's face. The new student was not getting into the spirit of the caper. But in a moment his effusiveness returned. 'Oh, no harm came to them. They were simply caught that's all.'

'And when you came to Russia, did you bring your family?'

'I left my wife and daughter behind. They could have followed me here, but they preferred London to Moscow.'

'So you dedicated your life to communism,' Laura said disbelievingly.

'Yes. Without hesitation.'

'It was a high price to pay wasn't it?'

'I was idealistic. At the time it seemed like the right thing to do.'

Bing said, 'Communism's not looking too good now is it?'

'Oh I knew it had failed a long time ago. You only had to live here for a while to realise that the grand vision didn't work in practice. Marx forgot about one thing, the human factor. People aren't created equal and you can't make them so.'

Pavel Rezchikova spoke for the first time. 'Still, George, you shouldn't complain, the system has been good to those who served it, as you did.'

'Yes, I don't deny that for a moment. I have an

apartment in Moscow, I own a car and the dacha here. I have interesting work to do. Good friends. But I wonder what will happen to an old spy now that everything is changing.'

'We have to change with it,' said Pavel. He was a big, fleshy man with hard eyes. 'Change means opportunities, whether you are a businessman or a KGB officer. The trick is to be on the right side of the changes. It is the same game as it has always been, only there are a few new rules.'

Blackwell nodded seriously, then was the charming host again. 'Come come Pavel, we're boring our guests. They don't want to talk about politics. Let's enjoy our weekend.'

After finishing their tea, the four men and Laura rugged up and went for a walk through the snow-covered streets of the village. Blackwell, talking away with nervous energy, filled them in on his life as an exiled British spy. His persona was that of a sprightly leprechaun, enjoying life immensely, but Bing detected beneath his prattle a mind as sharp as a razor and probably as dangerous. A hint of steel showed through when they called in at the village shop for bread. Half a dozen people waited patiently at the counter while the shop assistant sat reading a newspaper. Blackwell chatted away, apparently unperturbed by the delay. Suddenly he broke off, turned towards the shop assistant and barked angrily in Russian. It was as though another person was speaking. When she attempted to argue he unleashed a torrent of abuse. Catching the authority in his voice, she shrugged submissively and served him his loaf of bread.

When they continued on their walk he was the affable guide once more. They passed by large, fenced-off dachas, most of which were closed for the winter. Blackwell kept up a steady who's-who commentary about his neighbours. The businessman, Pavel, was polite but reserved. To Bing it felt as if they were applying for a position and had not yet proven themselves suitable. He did not know how much Bellamy had told them, but he had the feeling that underneath the hospitable veneer he and Laura were being sized up.

Back at the dacha they lunched on hot borscht, hard brown bread with cheese and sausage and more tea. After lunch Pavel suggested a game of chess. Bing demurred, saying that he was a poor player. Bellamy accepted the challenge and Laura said she would watch. Blackwell also excused himself, saying that he would take a sauna and invited Bing to join him.

The sauna was in a small, timber-lined room at the back of the house. Wearing towels around their waists, they sat down on the slatted wooden seat. Blackwell ladled water onto the superheated rocks and a cloud of steam rose with a hiss to envelop them. For some minutes they sat without speaking. Blackwell broke the silence. 'Bellamy has told me a little about the reason for your visit,' he said. 'If you would care to elaborate I may be able to help you.' The leprechaun had been replaced by the serious professional.

Bing replied carefully. 'Forgive me for being cautious, but why would you want to help?'

'For a very un-Marxist reason, self-interest. For thirty years I've been unable to leave the Eastern bloc for fear of being arrested and extradited to Britain. I've seen my daughter only twice in all that time. She has visited me here, but I'd like to be able to move freely in and out of Britain. The world's changing. The Cold War is over. My sins were committed a long time ago. It may be that if I could assist in a good outcome for you it would be useful to me in the long run.'

Bing dabbed the sweat out of his eyes with his towel. The movement was designed to give him time to think. Was this devious little man trying to set him up? He was a KGB officer, after all. If he told him everything about his search would he find himself bundled onto the next plane out of Moscow? Blackwell had been a traitor once, responsible for who knows how many deaths. Why should Bing trust him now? But if he was to make any headway he had to trust someone. Bellamy had introduced him and Bellamy was a good hand.

He decided to lay his cards on the table. He told Blackwell about Laura Bailey, about the clues gathered by Dean Buggins and lastly the identity of Laura's fiancé. Blackwell heard him out in silence. When he had finished Blackwell nodded his head. 'It's possible. Yes it's possible. It would make sense for the KGB to interrogate American air defence experts. But why bring them to Russia? Why not just question them and hand them back to the Vietnamese?'

'I don't know.'

'Perhaps they wanted him to help them further.'

'Do you think so?' Bing looked sceptical.

'Who knows? If he was an expert he could have been seconded to the weapons industry. The most likely thing of course is that he was questioned and then executed.'

'Yes I think that's more likely. Or else returned to the Vietnamese. God knows what would have happened to him then.'

Blackwell frowned. 'Interesting. Maybe the Vietnamese would have kept him as a bargaining chip for future negotiations with the Americans. You know they did that with the French.'

Bing nodded.

'Intriguing. Tell me when Parkinson was shot down, and where.'

Bing told him. The two men had been in the sauna for over half an hour. Bing was feeling enervated. Suddenly Blackwell was the energetic host again. He slapped his knee. 'Come on. What we need now is a snow bath.'

Opening a door in the side of the house Blackwell led Bing outside. He showed him how to squat down and scoop up handfuls of snow and rub them all over his body. After a couple of minutes they were both gasping with the cold. They went back inside for a warm shower, dressed and went to join Laura observing the chess game. Rezchikova was within one move of checkmating Bellamy.

'I am afraid we are about to witness a victory of East over West,' Bellamy quipped.

Rezchikova slid his piece into place and smiled. 'Checkmate.'

'That'll teach me to play chess with a Russian,' said Bellamy ruefully.

'It was a good fight, I enjoyed it.' said Rezchikova.

'Come on, Pavel, you're too modest. You've been toying with me. I have the feeling you could have beaten me ten moves ago if you'd wanted. I lack your devious mind.'

Rezchikova spread his arms apart and shrugged elaborately, the modest victor. 'Devious? Nonsense, I'm just a simple businessman. Next time we play you'll whip me.'

That night they dined simply but well on stew and after a couple of glasses of chilled Stolichnaya vodka in front of the open fire, went to bed. Next day they went for another long walk in the snow during which Blackwell and Rezchikova kept them entertained with stories about the changes taking place in Russia.

'It's wide open for entrepreneurs,' said Rezchikova.

'Yes,' said Bing. 'But how many entrepreneurs could there be in a country where you get paid whether you work or not?'

'There are plenty. Let me give you an example. Recently an army general was caught selling military hardware abroad. He was part owner of a cooperative which was set up to sell surplus military materials. Apparently he bought a trainload of tanks, complete with instructions in English. He said he was going to convert them to tractors. Instead he was about to ship them off for sale on the arms black market.'

Rezchikova laughed heartily. While he was affable enough, Bing felt instinctively wary of him. There was something indefinable which did not quite ring true. Although he had several opportunities he made no mention of MIAs.

As the group were loading their luggage into the Zil

to return to Moscow and saying their goodbyes, Rezchikova shook Bing's hand and kissed Laura boisterously on both cheeks. They got into the car and wound down the windows. Rezchikova handed a card to each of them and said, 'If I can be of any assistance at all while you're here, please let me know.'

Blackwell, standing beside him, raised his hand in farewell. 'I know where you're staying. I'll be in touch.'

Nine

Bellamy dropped them off at the hotel and the big limousine glided off through a slush of melted snow. As they entered, uniformed attendants hurried forward to help them out of their coats. The sound of a string quartet drifted from one of the reception rooms. The lobby was busy with the comings and goings of guests. According to the brochure placed in each room, the hotel used to be a Tsarist palace and had fallen into disrepair during the communist rule. It had been restored recently by a consortium of Russian and Western European owners, to cater to the rich international clientele streaming in and out of the Soviet Union seeking business opportunities. Unlike most things in Moscow, the hotel worked. It was possible to make international telephone calls, the Russian staff were uncharacteristically efficient and courteous and made certain that guests received their messages. When Laura and Bing approached the reception desk for their keys they were welcomed by name. The front-desk clerk, a buxom Russian woman with a blonde, beehive hairdo, handed Bing a slip. 'There was a telephone call for you an hour ago, Mr Connick.'

Bing glanced at the slip. The handwritten message asked him to please call Mr Eugene Hammond at the

American Embassy. There was a telephone number included.

Bing had never been one of those correspondents who mixed with the embassy crowd. He disliked their habit of pumping him for information which they would then include in their situation reports. He knew that many journalists were happy to pass on tidbits and to receive a few scraps in return, but he had always preferred his information from less tainted sources. Once, in Vietnam, he had been approached none-too-subtly by an embassy second secretary attempting to recruit him as a CIA informant. He had told him rudely where to shove the offer. His instinct now was to screw up the message and throw it away, but he was intrigued. How did the Americans know he was in Moscow and why would they want to talk to him? He was no longer a celebrated war correspondent and was an unlikely guest for a cocktail party.

He showed Laura the message.

'What do you think it could be about?' she asked

'Probably just some get-together for visiting Americans.'

'Do you really believe that?' Laura said.

'No, not really. But unless I call back we'll never know.'

They entered the elevator and rode up to their rooms in silence. He dialled the number on the message slip. The telephone gave a weak sounding beep which in most parts of the world would be a busy signal. On the second beep a resonant American voice boomed down the line. 'Hammond.'

'Bing Connick, Mr Hammond. I had a message to call you.'

'Bing, nice to hear from you,' said the voice with clubby familiarity.

He's only said half a dozen words and I dislike this man already, thought Bing. He said to the phone, 'Have we met?'

'No, but everyone knows the famous Bing Connick. I

used to read your stuff all the time. I'm the Press Attache here, I thought we might get together for a chat.'

'I no longer work in newspapers,' Bing said, trying to put some frost into his voice to counter the jollity on the other end of the line.

'A free agent eh?' boomed the voice. Hammond laughed as though he had uttered a witticism. 'And what brings you to Moscow, Bing?'

Bing bridled inwardly again at the overly-familiar use of his first name. 'A private visit.'

Hammond laughed again as if they were at a convention swapping jokes. Now it was his turn again. 'Look here, I know you newshounds, always want to know what's going on. Why don't you come on over for a briefing. I can fill you in on the situation.'

'What situation?'

The voice boomed on, as irrepressible as a salesman. 'This is an extraordinary time in history. Fascinating. I know you'll want all the lowdown. You'll find it interesting I assure you.'

'What do you have in mind?'

'Oh I thought something private. Just you and me here at the embassy. Shall we say about five? The hotel driver will know where to go.'

Reluctantly Bing replied. 'OK, at five.'

'I'll be expecting you.'

Bing called Laura and told her about his appointment. She suggested they might spend the next few hours sightseeing, but Bing had never liked being a tourist. Instead, he went down to the newsstand in the lobby and purchased an armful of English-language news magazines and papers. For the next few hours he immersed himself in world events. Several of the papers carried feature stories about American plans for an aid package to Russia. There was sharp division in Congress, some senators arguing that it was vital to help the new Russian President, Boris Ivashov, through the difficult winter, while the hard-liners pushed the view that the former communists should be left to founder. At four-thirty he closed his metal Halliburton suitcase, spun the combination dial to a certain sequence, went into the bathroom and dabbed soap on his fingertip. He then smeared on two faint films and plucked a hair from his head which he stuck across the lid opening. He felt slightly foolish taking these precautions, but on previous assignments to the Soviet Union during the Brezhnev era, the 'time of stagnation' as the Russians now liked to call it, he had been followed, his room had been searched and no doubt bugged as well. There was supposed to be a new freedom in Russia, but the old habit of paranoia was hard to break. Satisfied with his preparations, he went down to the lobby where he had ordered a hotel car to be waiting.

Outside, a light snow was falling. The afternoon traffic turned the flakes into grey mush as soon as they hit the road. It was getting close to rush hour. Queues of people, swathed in shapeless coats and wearing scarves or fur hats on their heads, waited in the cold for trolleybuses which would take them to the high-rise apartment blocks surrounding the city. Private car owners cruised by on the lookout for paying passengers. Hordes of people descended into the metro stations. The hotel Mercedes drove up Gorky Street past the newly built McDonald's restaurant. There was a 200-yard-long queue waiting in the falling snow for the opportunity to pay half a day's wage for a Big Mac and a bag of fries. High up on a building Bing saw the current temperature picked out in lights. It was minus 2 degrees.

The American Embassy was a low building near the Russian parliament. Across the street from the entrance Bing noticed a derelict Orthodox church and remembered being told once that the Russians used the belltower to observe comings and goings at the embassy. The car was stopped at the electric gates by a Marine guard. When Bing gave his name he told him he was expected and directed him up a sweeping drive to the main building. They drove past some row houses on the left where embassy staff lived. On the right was an eight-storey building which had been abandoned only half built. Bing smiled as he recalled the story. The Americans had discovered that the Russian workmen were installing surveillance equipment during construction. The only way to be certain that the new building was secure was to abandon it and start again, this time with US workers. The Mercedes came to a halt and he walked down a dozen steps below ground into the embassy complex.

An athletic looking man with a crew cut, wearing a well-cut grey suit, white shirt and a plain dark tie came forward to meet him. He seized Bing's hand in an iron grip and squeezed it harder than necessary. 'Bing Connick, I'm Gene Hammond. Nice of you to come over.'

Bing retrieved his crushed hand and muttered hello. Hammond went on with the same florid cheerfulness which had irritated him on the telephone. 'Welcome to a little bit of the USA. We've got everything we need here to feel at home. Gymnasium, basketball court, indoor pool, cafeteria, a commissary with American groceries and up in my office I think I might be able to rustle us up some real American bourbon whiskey.' Hammond gave the braying salesman's laugh which seemed to accompany most of his utterances. Bing noticed that the laughter did not extend to his eyes.

Hammond's office looked out on the massive building known as the White House which housed the Russian parliament. It was a peculiarly impersonal room, just a desk with a blotter and telephone and two chairs in front of it. There was none of the usual clutter that one would expect to find; no family photo, no papers waiting to be signed. Along one wall there was an informal setting of chairs and a lounge with a coffee table in front of it. A picture of President Blanchard hung on the wall above, but there was nothing to indicate what sort of taste the occupant might possess. It was as if Hammond had hired the room for the afternoon. He indicated the lounge and sat down.

'Whiskey?'

'Yes fine, thanks.'

Hammond strode over to the opposite wall and opened

a cupboard door to reveal a small sink and refrigerator. He pulled down a bottle of Jim Beam and poured out two glasses with ice. His movements were fluid and athletic. Bing had the impression of a man who spent a lot of time working out in the gym. The sort of man who would play sports hard, to win. Handing over the glass Hammond said in his resonant voice, 'God bless America.'

Was this another joke? Bing thought. But Hammond for once did not laugh.

'Cheers,' said Bing. He took a sip of the Jim Beam and waited to hear what Hammond would say. Hammond remained standing. After sipping his own drink, he indicated the White House through the window.

'Know what that is?'

'Yes it's the White House.'

'What happens in that building and in the Kremlin in the next couple of years is of crucial importance to the United States.' He paused, as a coach giving a pep talk might, to allow the message to sink in. 'Ivashov is up against it. There are still powerful forces in Russia who want him to fail. Your friends at the *Washington Post* and the *New York Times* keep saying communism's dead. It's not, it's just taken a setback. It could still come right back again.'

Bing was tempted to reiterate that he was no longer a journalist but decided there would be no point. Hammond had obviously formed a certain impression of him which would be pointless to try to dispel. Hammond began to stride up and down. 'This is going to be a hard winter for the Ivans. Food shortages, inflation gone mad. They've been told they have to make the market economy work but none of them have ever had to compete for anything in their lives and they're finding it hard to cope. This winter is going to be a real test.' He put his glass down on the desk. With his hands now free Hammond slapped his fist into the opposite palm, emphasising his words. 'We want Ivashov to succeed, Bing. The American President wants Ivashov to succeed. The American people want him to succeed. What we don't want is anything that's going to make that task more difficult.'

'I'm sure you're right,' Bing said. He was puzzled. He was trying to see the real Hammond beneath the veneer, for he was certain this buffoon mouthing patriotic cliches was not real.

'You've been here before, haven't you?'

'Once or twice.'

'In the old days it was dangerous to go around asking too many questions, wasn't it?'

'Well it was dangerous for the people answering them. If you were a dissident and you were seen talking to an American, it could be very unpleasant, but not necessarily dangerous for us, no.'

'OK, but what I'm saying, Russia has always been the sort of place where you have to tread carefully, am I right?'

'Yes. But you're talking about the past. Russians are allowed to talk to whoever they like now.'

'Don't be so sure.'

'What do you mean.'

'There's no such thing as absolute freedom. Even in America there are certain things, let's say things bearing on national security for instance, which are sensitive. Things which it would be dangerous to inquire into too deeply.' Hammond stopped his pacing, reversed a chair and sat on it opposite Bing, his forearms resting on the back. Bing was aware again of suppressed physical energy. It was tangible.

'Yes, you could be right,' he said.

'It's the same thing here. There are still some areas where questions, too many questions, could be dangerous for the one asking them.'

'I'm not here to steal Russia's defence secrets, Mr Hammond.'

'No of course you're not. We're talking hypothetically here. What I'm saying is that the country is in turmoil. Who knows what's safe and what isn't? Questions which might seem quite innocent to some people may be acutely sensitive to the Russians. If people were to get into trouble, even American citizens, the embassy might not be in a position to help. Diplomacy, as I'm sure you know, can be a tricky thing. A question sometimes of priorities.'

'I've seen enough of diplomats to understand all too well what they call priorities.'

'Well you'd also understand that I'm speaking to you as a friend, as a fellow American.'

'It's kind of you but it's always worried me when a diplomat professes friendship. I think I told you this is a private visit. I'm no longer a correspondent.'

'Ah yes. You don't ask questions for a living any more do you?' Hammond grinned at him conspiratorially before continuing with exaggerated cheerfulness. 'So. This conversation has probably been unnecessary. I hope so.'

Hammond jumped to his feet and returned to where he had left his glass on the desk. He took a sip and chuckled loudly to himself as if he had been forgetting his manners. The pep talk was over, now it was time to show that he was one of the team again. 'Look at the time. I'm afraid I've got another appointment waiting. Nice of you to drop by, Bing.' Again the christian name, as if they were a couple of old friends who had been having an informal chat. 'Let me show you down.'

Night had fallen while he had been inside the embassy. The snow was coming down more thickly and the Mercedes made its way back to the hotel at a careful crawl. Sitting in the back, Bing went over what had just taken place. Underneath Hammond's inane bluster there was a warning. That was clear, but the motive behind it eluded him. Back at the hotel, Bing sat down at the small desk in his room. There was no telephone book, such things did not exist in Russia, but the hotel had provided a list of convenient numbers, among which was the general switchboard of the American Embassy.

He dialled the number and an American voice

answered. 'I want to send a fax to the Press Attache, can you tell me his name please.'

There was a pause while the operator consulted her computer. 'Yes sir, the Press Attache is Mr Battle. Would you like his fax number?'

'No thank you, I have it already. By the way, do you have a Mr Hammond on the staff, Eugene Hammond?'

Again there was a brief pause while the operator punched the keys. 'No sir,' she said brightly. 'There's no Mr Hammond listed on the embassy staff.'

Bing thanked her and carefully replaced the receiver.

Ten

When Laura had found that she had nothing to do for the rest of the day she was determined to make the most of it. Remembering the man who had rescued her from the gipsies, she rummaged in her handbag until she found his card. There it was, the name Askar and an unpronounceable surname followed by a telephone number. She had been intrigued by his exotic appearance and the charm which had shown through even in their brief encounter. She knew the sensible thing to do would be to use one of the guides provided by the hotel, but Laura had gone beyond doing the sensible thing. She dialled and the number answered on the second ring. Laura reminded him who she was and asked if he was available to guide her in Moscow that day. Askar said he was free and they arranged to meet in an hour in the hotel lobby. He asked her to inform security, otherwise he would not be allowed in.

When she entered the lobby she saw Askar standing waiting before he saw her. While he was unaware of her scrutiny she was able to study him for a few moments unobserved. Where the people she saw in the street were pasty-faced and overweight, Askar was lean and hard. His features seemed to her to be Mongolian. With his olive skin, he looked as though he would be more at home on a horse, riding across a frozen steppe, than in the drabness of Moscow. Laura guessed his age at about thirty-five. Askar turned and, seeing her approaching, stepped forward to greet her courteously in good but overprecise English.

'Mrs Bailey, how are you? I hope you have had no more adventures since we met?'

'Fortunately no. Thanks again for rescuing me. I don't know what would have happened if you hadn't stepped in when you did.'

'What would you like to do? There are many sights I can show you. Moscow has some wonderful museums, Lenin's tomb, GUM, Saint Basil's, but I suspect you were coming from there when we last met.'

'Yes, I saw all the sights around Red Square. I'm not much for museums.'

'If you would like to go shopping I can take you to places where I can ensure you won't be overcharged.'

'What I'd like to do is just see Moscow, how ordinary people live. I'd like to get a feel for the place.'

'Are you sure?'

'Yes I'm sure. Show me the Moscow you know.'

Outside, Askar had one of the ubiquitous Ladas waiting for them. It was in better condition than the dilapidated vehicles plying for hire as taxis and once they had made themselves comfortable in the back seat Laura noted with relief that the heater worked well. Askar spoke to the driver who set off through the downtown streets. As they cruised along Askar indicated points of interest. They passed a queue outside a nondescript doorway. There was no sign to indicate what might be going on inside.

'It's a cheese shop,' Askar said. 'The trouble is inflation has made cheese so expensive no one can afford it. It's the same for meat. Now that the centralised pricing system has been abolished no one can afford meat any more either.'

A little further on he pointed out another queue. 'A vodka shop. The government has rationed vodka because people get so drunk they cannot work. Before, it didn't matter if people worked or not but now they are supposed to produce.' His manner, Laura noted, was that of a sardonic observer, almost contemptuous of the poverty he saw all around, as though it really had nothing to do with him.

'It sounds as if communism might not have been all that bad,' said Laura. 'I mean at least everyone had food to eat didn't they?'

'You can say that because you've never lived in a communist society. I hate communism. This was, what was it your President said, an evil empire? He was correct. Things are bad now, but in the long run, they will get better.'

'That's what President Ivashov says.'

'I believe him. They have to. Nothing could be as bad as before.'

The car pulled to a halt and Askar motioned to Laura to get out. With their breath turning to mist in the freezing air they set off down a long street of pink cobblestones which had been blocked off to motor vehicles. In contrast to the grey drabness they had passed through, the buildings in this area were painted brightly. Some even had shop windows displaying hand-crafted goods for sale.

'This area is known as the Arbart,' explained Askar. 'It's a place for artists.' He searched for the right word in English. 'Bohemian.'

They came up to a square where small crowds were gathered around speakers reciting poetry, playing musical instruments, or declaiming passionately, about what, Laura could only guess. The scene reminded her of Speakers' Corner at Hyde Park in London. She had gone there once on a holiday with her husband. They stopped on the edge of a group surrounding a wild-looking man with long black hair and a great bush of a beard. He was speaking passionately in Russian.

'What is he saying?' asked Laura.

'It's a poem. An anti-communist poem. If he had stood

108

here a year ago saying these things he would have been arrested. See how the people listen to him? It is hard to get used to the fact that you can say these things now.'

They listened as the poet's rendition came to a dramatic climax and the crowd broke up, some surging forward to speak to him. Laura and Askar started walking again side by side. 'What would it be like for an American to have to live in the communist system?' Laura asked.

Askar looked at her with surprise. It was an odd question. The tourists he dealt with were usually interested in monuments. 'I don't know if I could explain it to you.'

'Please try, I'm interested.'

They were approaching a doorway with a sign in Cyrillic over the lintel. Askar looked at his watch. 'If you are hungry may I suggest we stop for lunch and I will tell you a story about life in the Soviet Union.'

They went inside to a long narrow room with a polished wooden floor and wooden trestle tables. They sat down at one which was already laden with bottles of mineral water, wine, fruit cordial and vodka. The bottles were all warm.

'The food here is Georgian,' said Askar. 'It is very good. I would advise against the wine, however. It is also from Georgia, and Russians think it's wonderful, but I think you would find yourself unable to drink it.' He smiled. His English at times had a stilted quality as though he was translating from another language as he went along.

Laura left the ordering to Askar and within minutes a waiter came out and placed a large plate of fresh legumes on the table. Then followed a dish of dumplings stuffed with meat and rice. The dumplings were shaped like a little parcel with the edges gathered together on top. Taking her lead from Askar, Laura seized one in her fingers and bit into it. It was highly spiced and delicious.

'I'm surprised to find food like this in Moscow,' said Laura.

'There's good food here if you're rich. The customers are mostly black marketeers and foreigners. When we leave you will have to pay in hard currency.'

After they had finished the dumplings the waiter placed a plate of kebabs on the table. They were flavoured with some exotic marinade. As they ate they confined their conversation to the food and Russian customs. Laura said little, happy to absorb the information that Askar was offering. After they had finished eating, the waiter brought thick, sweet coffee with a cardamom seed floating on the surface of each cup. Askar took a noisy sip and leaned back in his chair.

'You were going to tell me a story,' Laura said.

'Yes. It is of my own family. It is by no means unusual but it may help you to understand what life used to be like here. Taking another sip of coffee, he began to tell his story.

Zenimenka was a small village in Kazakhstan made of rough-hewn stone buildings and pressed-tin roofs huddled on the dusty plain a hundred miles from Semipalatinsk. Askar lived there with his parents, three brothers and two sisters, in a house like all the others. His father, Kenes, was a great bear of a man, with dark eyes, fierce moustaches and a lust for life which made everyone in the village his friend. Whenever there was a celebration Kenes would be in the middle of it, dancing, laughing, drinking and flirting with noisy good humour. Every day he went off to work on a collective farm, along with most other men in the village. However, unlike the others, he was never content to unquestioningly obey their Russian supervisors. He was always the first to argue with orders he thought were stupid; always ready to speak out against injustice.

Kenes had the intelligence and strength of character to become a leader in whatever field he chose. If he had wanted to join the Communist Party and work within the system, he could have gone far in life. His failing was that he hated his Russian masters and he could never keep his feelings to himself. He regarded the Russians as occupiers of his country. In communist Kazakhstan the majority of people agreed with him but few put their feelings into words. Kenes had a reputation amongst the local party functionaries as a disruptive individual who needed to be kept firmly in his place. Despite his intelligence and vitality he would never be allowed to become anything but a field worker.

Kenes' lust for life included a thirst for knowledge. Somehow or other he had obtained a short-wave radio. At night, when the family were in bed, he would sit up and listen to illicit broadcasts from Voice of America or the BBC Overseas Service. Askar was his eldest son and he worshipped his father. Sometimes, when the day's work in the fields was over, the big man would seize his son's hand in his great fist and walk with him away from the village. Father and son would find a hummock to sit on where they could see to the horizon, and talk for hours. When Askar was small his father would tell him fairytales and stories about the great armies of Genghis Khan marching in from the east conquering all before them. Askar listened wide-eyed as he wove magic tales of the glorious Kazakh past when they were a nation of nomads following the seasons with their herds, free and beholden to no one.

From about the time Askar turned ten, Kenes began to lead these conversations along forbidden paths. He told him how the Russians had come to Kazakhstan and forced the sheep and goat herders to give up their traditional ways and work on the giant collectives or in factories. In his deep, resonant voice he said, 'The Russians are invaders in our country, son, and don't you ever forget it. One day we Kazakhs will own our own land again. In the meantime we will never be wealthy, but there are riches which are more valuable than money.'

Askar was entranced. He had already learned the value of money as only a child born into poverty can. 'What could be more valuable than money, Papa?'

Kenes motioned to the little boy beside him to come

closer, as though the secret he had to impart was too important to be overheard by even the goats grazing nearby. Askar leaned in to his father until he felt the whiskers of his great moustache tickle his ear. 'Knowledge, my son, is the greatest gift of all. Not just the knowledge they teach you in school, although that is important, but knowledge from the outside world.'

'You mean the knowledge you hear on your radio?'

'Yes. The radio tells me about a world outside Russia where people are free to say and do what they like. And one day if people are prepared to speak out, Kazakhstan will be the same.'

To little Askar knowledge sounded interesting, but it was difficult to see how it could be more important than money, especially during a hard Kazakh winter when they did not have enough roubles to buy meat and flour.

Askar remembered vividly the first time he became aware of the atomic tests on the range near his village. He and his family were in the little garden beside their home tending their vegetable patch when suddenly the earth shook with a rumble like a thousand earthquakes. In the distance there was a blinding flash. They dropped their tools and stood at the front fence with their mouths open as a great cloud shaped like a mushroom slowly rose into the air, blotting out the sun and casting a shadow across the land. No one made any attempt to protect themselves. They were too absorbed by the incredible display of energy they saw before them. Even when the dust from the cloud began to rain down on the village they were too much in awe to move.

The Polygon, or test centre, was just fifteen miles from Zenimenka. The blasts were a regular event in the life of the village. For years the tests had been conducted above ground. In the sixties they began detonating the bombs in underground tunnels. They were so poorly constructed that the very earth itself blew apart and the tests ended up being at ground level anyway.

One day the peace of the village was disturbed by the rumble of heavy transports. A column of army trucks carrying uniformed soldiers ground down the main street, raising clouds of dust and sending dogs and chickens scurrying to get out of their way.

The villagers stood and stared at the soldiers seated on benches, some of them only teenagers. The soldiers in turn gazed back at them without expression. The convoy did not stop but instead headed out of town towards the Polygon. Two days later the the ground shook to another great explosion.

Kenes had not been able to contain his curiosity about the soldiers. He asked questions of his friends who worked at the Polygon and learned that they had been sent by their commanders to walk through the cloud from the bomb so that doctors might see what effect it had on them.

No one in Zenimenka cared about the fate of a few Russian soldiers, but soon the effects of the tests began to be felt among the villagers themselves. Askar's mother, Ainur, was the village midwife. When a child was born with a cleft palate or a harelip, or with some other deformity of body or mind, it was regarded as simply another burden sent by fate to add to the many others the villagers had to bear. Such things were part of life. However, she began to notice that more and more children were being born with something wrong with them.

Young Zhamal Nurgozhin, three houses away, gave birth to a child with no hands or feet. Then a year later she bore a boy without eyes. There were merely two lumps where they should be. People in the village who were still in the prime of life began dying of cancer.

The villagers began to remark on the unusual incidence of misfortune which had come to plague them, but even then life might still have gone on as usual in Askar's household if two things had not happened. One night his father was listening to his radio when he heard a broadcast about the effects of radiation sickness caused by atomic bombs. The report mainly concerned the victims of Hiroshima and Nagasaki, but as he listened with mounting horror it became clear to Kenes that what they were describing in far-away Japan was exactly the same thing that was happening to his own people.

Despite his anger, he said nothing. He was determined to think carefully before he acted. Next morning he went off to work as usual. When he came home that night he could sense from the moment he walked in that something was wrong. Ainur, normally as cheerful and vibrant as he was, was long-faced and sad. The children were strangely quiet. He strode across the room to Ainur. 'What is it, what is wrong?'

'A terrible thing happened today. You know young Bakhyt who was having her first child? This morning after you left she went into labour. As you know she is a young healthy woman and everything went normally. After about five hours the child was born.'

Ainur paused for a moment while she relived the awful scene she had witnessed. Kenes waited impatiently. Then gathering courage she continued. 'It was a monster. It had one eye in the middle of its forehead. Oh God what is happening to us, Kenes? What is causing these disasters?'

Kenes clasped his wife to him for a moment, then let her go and roared with anger. 'These accursed Russians are killing us. They've got to be stopped.'

The family listened wide-eyed as Kenes explained to them what he had learned; that the tests which had been going on as long as they could remember were responsible for the horrors now besetting the village. 'I shall speak out,' he said. 'Someone has to try to stop it.'

Askar by now was a teenager. He knew what it meant to speak out against the system. Yet no member of the family argued against the rightness of what had to be done. Next day was a day of rest. Kenes went from house to house urging each family to come to a meeting in the village square in the early afternoon. At first many refused. They knew how dangerous it would be to stage a public meeting without permission. Some, more bold than the rest, left their homes at the appointed time and walked down to the square. Emboldened by this, the timid followed and by the time the meeting was due to begin five hundred men and women were gathered to hear what Kenes had to say.

Standing on a wooden table he called for silence. Gradually the murmur of the crowd died away. He began to address them in solemn, measured tones. 'Men and Women of Zenimenka, I have called you together because there is a tragedy in our midst and the time has come to do something about it.'

The crowd were silent and attentive. Kenes' booming voice held them spellbound. 'You all know that people are dying of cancer. There is barely one family which has not suffered some bereavement. Our children are being born crippled and with damaged minds. You all know that yesterday Bakhyt gave birth to her first child and most of you will have heard by now that it was not normal. The child was born dead and that at least is a blessing.'

There were a few murmurs of sympathy. Kenes reached down and took a bundle wrapped in a rug from his wife who stood waiting at his feet. With every person's gaze upon him he gently pulled back the rug and held up the dead cyclops over his head for all to see. There was a gasp from the crowd. Some women began to wail in fear, then Kenes' voice boomed out again. 'Why was this child born a monster? I will tell you. It is because of the Russians and their nuclear tests. The clouds which rain dust on Zenimenka are full of poison and it is this poison which is killing us. We have to protest about it. We must march to the Polygon and voice our feelings. The tests have to stop.'

There was not one man or woman in the village who would have argued against Kenes that day. In commandeered buses and trucks they travelled the fifteen miles to the test site and staged the first demonstration anyone could remember since the Stalinist days when Kazakhs had died while protesting against the rape of their country.

The military guards regarded the demonstrators massed outside the facility with passive silence as they called for an end to the tests, but they had orders to do nothing. Eventually the protesters went home. Everyone knew that they had not heard the last of it.

Two days later, just before dawn, Askar was woken by a heavy thumping at the door. One of the younger children, afraid at the unfamiliar sound, began to wail. Askar threw back his blankets and fearfully peeped around the door of the room he shared with his brothers in time to see his father open the front door himself.

The KGB squad was led by the local party chief. Kenes looked him in the eye and spat at his feet with contempt, then he stood aside and ushered in the men who had come to arrest him. He motioned to them to wait while his family, still dressed in their nightclothes and wrapped in blankets and coats, came nervously into the room. Solemnly he went to each one in turn and embraced them. His wife Ainur was last. Turning away from her he addressed Askar. 'You are the eldest son, Askar. It is up to you to look after the family until I return.'

Without another word he turned on his heel and walked out of his house followed by four KGB officers and the party chief. He was charged with fomenting unrest and encouraging dissident elements within the village and sentenced to fifteen years in a labour camp.

Laura listened to Askar's story, spellbound. He had spoken quietly but with obvious emotion. Now it seemed he had said all he wanted to say. There was one question which Laura had to ask. 'What happened to your father?'

'Sometimes people went into those camps and simply disappeared. Many of them died of overwork or went mad in solitary confinement or died of cold. He survived, but he came out a broken man.'

'I don't know what to say. I can't imagine what it must have been like growing up like that.'

'Because of my father I was never allowed to go to

university, but I never forgot his advice about knowledge. I learned English from books and by listening illegally to his radio.' Askar smiled. 'Oh yes, he knew he was going to be arrested and he hid it well. But he told me where it was. I lived in Zenimenka nearly all my life. Then when things relaxed a little I decided to come to Moscow.'

'Why Moscow?'

'This is where the opportunities are. With all the people coming here from the West I can scrape a living. I do a bit of business now and then, some translating or guiding tourists. I send what I can back to the family.'

Laura asked, 'What sort of business?'

'Oh I deal in this and that,' Askar said vaguely. He looked at his empty coffee cup and said, 'There are not many tourists here at this time of year. Are you here on business, Mrs Bailey?'

For a moment, Laura was tempted to tell him the real reason for her visit, but instead she said ambiguously, 'I've always wanted to visit the Soviet Union.'

'It will not be the Soviet Union much longer. We Kazakhs want our independence and so do the Azerbaijanis, the Georgians, Ukraine, the Baltic States. It's only a matter of time before we get our freedom.'

Laura could have listened to him all afternoon. As if he realised that he had stepped far outside his role, Askar suggested that they pay the bill and continue with their tour.

It was mid-afternoon by the time they walked back to the car. The weather was colder than before, a flinty coldness which foretold of the snow to fall that evening. Askar spoke to the driver and they set off again. He turned to her and said, 'You asked me to show you the real Moscow.' He gestured out the window. 'This is it.' They were passing through a suburban area where acre upon acre of identical high-rise buildings towered above a dreary, snow-covered wasteland. The Lada topped a rise and then began descending a hill. Askar pointed. 'Over to the left. This also is the real Moscow.'

Laura looked out on a frozen lake, a bare white expanse, at the head of which was a fairytale structure of white towers topped by golden onion domes. After the dreariness they had just passed through, the sight was breathtaking.

'It used to be a monastery,' said Askar. 'In summer it's beautiful but I like it best in winter when everything is white.'

'It's gorgeous,' murmured Laura.

They sat in the car and absorbed the serenity of the scene. A group of children were playing on snowshoes in the middle of the frozen lake. Laura heard faint squeals of laughter coming across the expanse. She felt comfortable in Askar's company, and intrigued. He was exotic, gallant and mysterious. She was sorry that their tour was coming to an end. After some minutes Askar tapped the driver on the shoulder and they headed back towards the hotel. When they arrived Askar escorted Laura back inside and presented her with an invoice for his services. She paid him in American dollars. As he was about to leave Askar said, 'Forgive me, Mrs Bailey, but you will remember the circumstances of our first meeting?'

'They're hard to forget. It's not everyday someone tries to hold me up.'

'You can see that it's not safe to walk alone in Moscow these days. I don't wish to alarm you, but when we left the hotel there was a fellow sitting outside in a car. I noticed him because he was wearing a black leather coat which is unusual. I saw him again at the Arbart. And again when we arrived back here.'

Despite the warmth of the lobby, Laura felt a chill raise the hairs on the back of her neck. 'Perhaps it's just coincidence,' Askar continued, 'but it may be something more. He could be a criminal. You should be careful.'

'Thank you, I will.'

Askar looked at Laura, his Mongol eyes slitted thoughtfully. 'I don't know what your business is in Moscow, but if you need help, any kind of help, you know where to find me.'

With that he turned and walked out. The promised snow had just begun to fall.

When Bing put down the telephone to the American Embassy, he remained motionless for some time, staring blankly at the mirror the hotel had thoughtfully provided on the wall facing the desk. If he had bothered to study his own face, he would have seen a man in his late forties, still sunburned from his life on the river, deep crow's feet around the eyes, short, slightly unkempt hair flecked with grey, a close-cropped grey beard, a face with experience written on it. Bing, however, was unaware of his own image staring back at him, he was thinking about Hammond.

He had initially assumed that Hammond was CIA. He knew that there was always at least one CIA representative at every embassy, certainly several here in Moscow. But if Hammond was CIA, with cover as an embassy employee, why was there no record of him on the staff? Perhaps he was from some other arm of government, but if so it must be very important for the embassy to allow the use of its premises for the kind of meeting which had just taken place. Offhand he couldn't think of any agency which would have that kind of pull, although he had to confess that he was no expert on American covert activities. The bottom line was that he had been given a warning to back off. Now he had to decide what to do about it. If he quit now he would have to tell Laura Bailey why. Equally, if he decided to press on he could not do so without telling her what had just taken place. He called Laura's room and they arranged to meet in the coffee bar downstairs.

Their waiter greeted them and showed them to a table, fussing about them as if they were old and valued customers. He probably thinks we're a married couple, thought Laura wryly. She couldn't imagine being married to Bing Connick, in fact she couldn't imagine anyone being married to him. They'd never get through his

119

defences. Laura ordered a gin and tonic. Bing asked for a martini, dry with a twist of lemon.

'Up?' inquired the waiter. Someone had trained him well in the ways of Americans. Bing nodded assent. While they were waiting for the drinks to arrive he glanced around the room. The clientele were the usual business types, with a smattering of casually attired tourists. No one was close enough to overhear their conversation. The drinks arrived and Bing said, 'We have a problem.'

'We do?' Laura replied. 'Why?'

'The embassy visit was curious. A man called Hammond as good as warned me to back off what I was doing.'

Laura was incredulous. 'What do they mean back off? Back off or what?'

'Well, that was left unclear, but there was no doubt there was a threat there. He was trying to convey the idea that I, we, are messing about with something they would prefer left alone.'

'Who's Hammond?'

'I don't know. The most obvious answer is CIA, but maybe that's too obvious.'

'Whoever he is, how would he have known we're here, or why we're here? Do you think Bellamy might have said something?'

'No I'm sure Bellamy wouldn't have told him anything.' Bing thought for a moment. 'But what about Blackwell? He's spent his whole life double-dealing. Maybe he's got a little business going on the side selling information to the Americans.'

Laura said nothing. Bing took a sip of his martini before continuing. 'Damn, another thought just occurred to me. McCormack. He knew we were coming to Russia and he knew what we were coming for. It wouldn't surprise me in the least if he was a part-time spook. It's just the sort of thing he'd be involved in. Damn his bloody corrupt soul.'

'McCormack or Blackwell, what does it matter?'

120

Laura said indignantly. 'We're American citizens, aren't we? The CIA can hardly stop us making inquiries if we want to.'

Bing regarded Laura. Anger made her features come alive. Her cheeks were slightly flushed and her mouth had a firm set to it. She was, he realised, attractive. He said, 'Don't be so sure. The CIA are capable of practically anything if they put their minds to it.'

'Why would they be against us anyway? Surely they'd want to know the truth just as much as we do.'

'The MIAs are political,' said Bing. 'Politics and truth don't necessarily go hand in hand.'

While they had been talking, Laura had forgotten all about her afternoon with Askar. Now she briefly related how she had spent the day.

'Askar said something strange just before he left. He said he thought someone had been following us. He saw a man in a black leather coat when we left the hotel and again along the way and he said he was there when we got back.'

Bing looked thoughtful. 'It could be some crim sizing you up.'

'That's what Askar thought.'

'Or it could be directly related to what we're doing here.'

'Do you think so?'

'To tell you the truth I don't know what to think. It could be nothing. Or it could be Askar playing some game of his own, trying to make himself look big for some reason.'

'I don't think so,' Laura said.

'Why not? Who is this Askar?'

'I told you, I met him when I had that trouble with the gipsies.'

'But what do you know about him?'

'Well, he's from Kazakhstan and he's a sort of freelance businessman. He does some guide work. I don't know. What else do I need to know? He's nice. I liked him.'

'Did you see the man in the leather jacket yourself?'

'No, Askar told me about it just as he was about to leave.'

Bing shook his head. 'I don't like it. There's too much mystery about this whole exercise. We're fishing in the dark here and all the signs are telling me to reel in my line and go home.'

'Go home?' Laura looked shocked. 'We're just getting started. We haven't even heard back from Blackwell yet.'

'Who may be relaying everything we say and do to the KGB and possibly the CIA as well.'

Laura continued as if she had not heard this last remark. 'He's the only lead we've got. We've come this far. At least we could wait until we hear from him. You never know, he might come up with something.'

'Look, let's talk about this realistically,' said Bing. 'What do you really expect? Do you really think we're going to find a live American?'

'No, I guess not. But I think if there's just a chance of finding out what happened to Dan, even if I can establish once and for all that he *didn't* come to Russia, that Buggins was wrong, then that's something. I can't just walk away now.'

'My instinct is that's exactly what we should do. Let it rest. It's ancient history. Get on with your life.'

Laura leaned forward impulsively and grasped Bing's hand resting on the table. 'I know you find it hard to understand what's driving me, but I can't let it rest and I can't go on without you.' She looked at him earnestly. 'Please Bing, don't quit on me now.'

At the bar, where he was waiting patiently for another order, their waiter smiled to himself. It was good to see a couple their age who could still hold hands, he thought.

Bing withdrew his hand to take another drink. He had never been able to counter the weapon of vulnerability. Against his will he said, 'I won't quit on you Laura. At least not just yet. We'll give it another couple of days and see what turns up.'

122

Eleven

The flak had ripped through the front of the cockpit, destroying the controls and blowing off the canopy. A piece of flying shrapnel tore off the pilot's head. A great gout of scarlet arterial blood swept back in the slipstream and splattered Dan's face and chest. He had time to radio briefly that they were hit without knowing if the message was received and then ejected into space. As he floated down he saw the F101 explode in a ball of flame. The patchwork rice paddies grew larger as he descended and he noted with detachment small details: some peasants shepherding a pair of oxen along a track, a huddle of people crouching in a ditch, wisps of smoke still coming from a village. He splashed down gently into a rice paddy. Some peasants watched him warily from a distance as he floundered through the paddy to a dry bank. They were unarmed and he thought that if a chopper got to him quickly he might just get out alive. For half an hour he sat while the peasants stared at him across the water. Then he heard a truck in the distance. A military vehicle stopped a few hundred yards away and half a dozen soldiers came up to him with their weapons at the ready. He held his hands up and the commanding officer approached him, motioned him to lower his arms and clubbed him to the ground.

As they walked him to the truck, the peasants beat him with their farm implements. His hands were tied behind his back, his feet were bound and he was thrown onto the tray. Trussed like that, it was impossible to get comfortable as the harshly sprung vehicle bumped its way over unmade roads for an hour before arriving at a military camp. He was cuffed and kicked out onto the ground and they untied his feet so he could walk to a cage which had been set up in the open. They kept him there for forty-eight hours without food or water, his tongue swelling from thirst and his fair skin blistering in the sun. Then they took him inside to a small room where the questioning began.

At first he had genuinely believed he would not break. When he refused to answer with anything other than his name, rank and serial number, they beat him savagely with clubs. They forced him to double up into a ball, with his head on his knees and his ankles hard against his buttocks and tied him so that he was immobile. Then they lifted him onto a table and resumed the interrogation. When he refused to answer again they pushed him off onto the concrete floor. They repeated this torture for four hours until he passed out with the pain. He remained trussed like a chicken for a day and a night and another day. Thirty-six hours of agony. When they untied him he could not straighten up or walk. Then came more questioning and more beatings. After a week he was ready to tell them anything.

All the time he was being interrogated he never saw another prisoner. After a time, a routine established itself. He would be taken from his cell soon after dawn across the compound to a small room furnished with a table and a few chairs. They wanted to know about his squadron, how many aircraft, what type, what armaments, the names of his fellow airmen and his commanding officer. Questions, questions, questions. The sessions would last about four hours, after which his interrogators would break for lunch. He would be taken back to the cell and fed rice, laced usually with a few scraps of offal. In the afternoon they would do it all over again.

The cell was about eight feet long by five feet wide. There was a wire bed but no mattress, just a grimy blanket. There was a bucket which he used for a toilet. He noticed when he pissed that there was blood in it. The door was solid timber and there was a small window high up which let in the mosquitoes in swarms, but very little light and air.

After ten days the interrogations suddenly stopped. He was left alone in the cell. During this time he thought often of Laura. He remembered mundane happenings: a shared hamburger sitting in the Chevvy on a knoll over-looking the airbase, watching the B52s and F101s take off and land; her excitement when he bought her a silver and turquoise ring for her birthday; her belief in him. He wondered how he could explain to her that he had broken under torture and spilled his guts. Would she understand? She thought he was so strong, but when it came down to it he had not had the strength to stand up to the pain.

Every couple of days a guard would open the door and make him carry the reeking bucket to a latrine dug into the earth, where he would empty it. Apart from that he never left his cell. He had been in solitary confinement for two weeks when, one morning, shortly after eating a plate of dried fish and rice, the door opened and two guards stood there with rifles at the ready. They motioned with the weapons for him to follow them and set off across the compound. He was still bent double like an old man and barely able to hobble. There was something about their demeanour that made him certain they were about to execute him. Then he saw they were heading for the interrogation room again and he began whimper-ing with fear at the thought of more torture. He was led inside and one guard remained, watching him impassively. Five minutes later the door opened. Instead of the Vietnamese, a grossly fat man dressed in rumpled trousers and a too-tight shirt straining at the buttons, walked in. His Slavic features were covered in a sheen of perspiration and he wheezed with the effort of breathing. He lowered his great body carefully into a bamboo chair, pulled out a handkerchief and mopped his face. When he had finished he looked at Dan and said, 'How do you do, Mr Parkinson, I am Timashov,' then added as if in afterthought, 'Major.'

Dan stared at him. 'You're Russian,' he said stupidly.

'As you see,' said Timashov. 'Yes I am Russian. I have come to ask you some questions.'

'I've already told everything I know,' said Dan.

Timashov patted his shirt pocket and pulled out a cigarette pack. Taking his time, he shook one out and placed it in his mouth. He lit up and blew the smoke out noisily. Absurdly, Dan was reminded of a horse snorting on a chilly morning on a boyhood farm holiday in Ohio. Delicately for such a large man, he picked a flake of tobacco from his tongue and flicked it aside. Dan noticed that his hands, in contrast to his massive body, were quite small, almost a child's hands. Timashov coughed, an unhealthy wet sound. He tossed the packet onto the table and indicated it with a wave. 'Cigarette? They're Vietnamese I'm afraid, not American.'

'I don't smoke,' replied Dan.

Timashov gave a lugubrious sigh. 'Very wise. Keep your health. For me it is too late. The doctors tell me to stop but I am too old and too fat to be healthy. What difference will a few cigarettes make?' He inhaled again and shuddered as he fought back the urge to cough with lips pursed shut. His cheeks bulged and his eyes watered from the effort and he dabbed them with the handkerchief. When he had regained his composure he gave Dan a compassionate look. 'How have you been treated?' he said solicitously, as if enquiring after the quality of food in a hospital visit.

'How do you think?' said Dan bitterly. 'These people are animals,' he gestured towards the guard who stared back at him with uncomprehending dislike.

'They use harsh methods. Harsher than we would.' Timashov shook his head reflectively and his multiple chins wobbled. 'Knowing them as I do I cannot blame you for breaking, but I wonder if a military court would be as sympathetic.'

'What do you mean?' said Dan.

Timashov shook his head again, and continued as if he had not heard the question. 'At least you're still alive,' he said ruminatively. 'War. It brings out the worst in men. Imagine seeing your village napalmed, children mutilated, loved ones lost. Who can blame them for being harsh? Two weeks ago we had five American fliers here. They were interrogated and then, when they had given all the information that was useful, our friends cut their throats.' Timashov drew a dainty finger across his throat to demonstrate. 'All five, dead.'

'Is that what you're going to do to me, cut my throat?'

Timashov tapped the ash from his cigarette. Disregarding Dan's question, he went on. 'The Vietnamese have suffered so much . . .' he let the sentence trail off with a wave of his hand. He inhaled again, this time without an accompanying spasm. 'Of course if I had known it was going to happen I could have tried to talk them out of it, but I only heard about it after it was too late. A pity.' He regarded Dan sorrowfully out of a pair of small eyes buried in flesh. 'I only hope the same thing doesn't happen to you.'

Timashov paused to allow the last remark to register. 'Would you like something to drink?' he asked.

'Yes please.'

Timashov spoke to the guard, who gave Dan a hard stare before leaving. In a few moments he returned with a glass of cool water with some limes floating in it. Dan drank appreciatively. It was the first cool drink he had had since being captured. Timashov watched him in silence. 'What do you want?' Dan said.

'You have had a difficult time,' replied Timashov. He gestured towards the empty glass. 'I can make things easier for you.'

'Yeah, and why would you want to do that?'

'Why are you here?' said Timashov.

'You know the answer to that. I was shot down.'

'No, I mean why are you here at all? In Vietnam, flying a military aircraft, engaged in hostile acts?'

Dan bridled. It was the same sort of jargon his interrogators had been using. 'I'm an officer in the US Air Force, I follow orders.'

'Exactly,' said Timashov. He smiled, as if pleased at an adept pupil. 'The American government says to fight and you fight. Drop bombs here, strafe that target there and you do it. You do as you are ordered. I also do as I am ordered. We are both soldiers, isn't that right?'

'Well I know what I am,' said Dan. ' But you haven't told me yet what you are.'

'Do you know what happened during the First World War at Christmas time?' Timashov said irrelevantly. 'English and German troops in the trenches stopped firing and walked into no-man's-land where they spoke peacefully before resuming hostilities. A few moments of peace in the middle of the carnage. It says something about war does it not?'

'I've heard the story, but it always sounded like bullshit to me.'

'To me the story illustrates a truth. The soldier is just a small part of a larger plan. The Vietnamese are fighting over two different political systems, but,' Timashov leaned forward and lowered his voice, 'does it really matter so much whether they are communist or capitalist? My superiors would not like to hear me say these things, but you're an intelligent man. You and I know political ideology is not worth so much pain and suffering.'

Dan was tired of following the fat man's meandering thought patterns. He said, 'I asked you before, what do you want?'

Timashov settled back into his chair which gave a tortured creak. He pulled his handkerchief from his sleeve and flapped the air in front of his face. Sweat dripped onto his shirt which clung to his fleshy form in wet patches. He began an answer, but to a different question; his conversation seemed to be following a

128

divergent path to Dan's. 'You ask me what I do, I will tell you. I work for the KGB, First Directorate. I am here to advise our Vietnamese friends. They tell me that you have told them everything you can and they see no reason to keep you alive any longer. I have asked them not to be hasty. I would like you to remain alive, but in return you will have to do something for me, a small thing,' he waved the handkerchief to indicate the insignificance of what he was about to propose. 'You operated the missile-jamming system. We need to know how it works, everything about it. All you have to do is help us and you will stay alive. If not,' he shrugged, 'who can say what our friends might do?'

'I won't do that.'

'May I suggest you think about it? What has this war got to do with you? It is a politicians' war, we are merely soldiers,' said Timashov. 'Like the English and the Germans,' he added. He had apparently forgotten Dan's disbelief in that story. He plodded ponderously on, 'You can tell me what you know and I will see to it that you remain alive. Who knows, we might even become friends.'

Dan looked at the fat man in astonishment. What sort of friendship could he possibly have in mind? It would be easier to be friendly with a Martian. 'You're asking me to be a traitor,' he said.

'You are already a traitor,' said Timashov. 'Now it is only a question of degree.'

'And what happens afterwards?'

'As soon as you agree to cooperate you will be taken from here to more comfortable quarters.' Timashov paused, like a bad actor delivering a key line. 'In Russia.'

'What?'

'Yes, in Russia. After you have helped us you will have a new life. No one need ever know that you talked.'

'You're offering me a life in Russia? I'd rather be dead.'

'Yes I know, better dead than red. That's how it goes isn't it? How easy it is for the politicians to mouth slogans. But they're not the ones who have to fight, or endure pain are they? It's the soldiers like you and I who have to die for their slogans.'

'Look, spare me the damned philosophy,' said Dan. 'The answer's no. Not now, not ever. No.'

Timashov hauled himself to his feet and spoke to the guard. The Vietnamese walked over to Dan and cuffed him savagely across the side of the head with a round-house slap. Timashov regarded him glumly. 'A pity. I would like to save you from further brutality, but,' he paused to mop his face again, 'perhaps you will think about it.'

That night Dan was lying awake on his filthy blanket when the guards came and dragged him to his feet and methodically beat him with clubs. Afterwards they left him lying there, aching all over. Towards morning, despite his pain he fell asleep to dream fevered dreams in which he was surrounded by a ring of air force officers who kicked him and jeered at him. Laura was among them.

He was asleep when the guard prodded him with his rifle. The first thing Dan saw when he opened his eyes was Timashov peering down at him with concern. Dan's face was bloodied and his body and limbs had ugly purple bruises on them. Timashov shook his head and tut-tutted with sympathy.

'My dear friend,' he said, as if they had known each other a lifetime. And indeed it seemed to Dan in his beaten state that he had never known anything else but this cell and the pain wracking his body. 'My dear friend, you can make it so easy for yourself. All you have to do is agree to help us and I can take you away from all this.'

Dan opened his mouth and spoke in a whisper. 'God-damn you, you're not my friend.' He tried to rise from the bunk.

Timashov laid a moist hand on his shoulder. 'I will be. You will see. I will be.'

Two days later, when Timashov came waddling in again, full of solicitude, Dan agreed.

In his prediction of friendship, as with many matters to come, Timashov was right. The air defence research facility at Priazorsk was a tight little world of cliques and jealousies. Dan was an interloper, a traitor who spoke no Russian and to whom the scientists were often forced to defer. His days were spent working in the laboratory assisting the men who were attempting to unravel the secrets of the Wild Weasel by assembling captured fragments. Timashov was with him constantly, acting as his translator and adviser. He came to depend on the fat Russian as the hostage depends on his captor.

When he finished work each day, Dan would go to the one-room flat which he had been assigned in the accommodation block. There he would undergo an hour of instruction in the Russian language, administered by a mousy man with a schoolmasterly manner. His meals were taken in the staff canteen. Afterwards in the evenings there was little to do. Timashov taught him to play chess, a diversion he had never learned in his American childhood, and they formed the habit after a time of retiring to Dan's apartment or Timashov's for a few games to while away the time.

Timashov's room was identical to Dan's, but where Dan's was militarily neat the Russian's matched its owner's apearance. The bed remained unmade for weeks on end, clothes were tossed carelessly on to furniture or in a corner awaiting cleaning. There was a table upon which stood some books and a record turntable. Underneath, the only neat thing to be seen was an orderly pile of long-playing records. As they sat at the chessboard Timashov would play classical music softly in the background. One evening, after Dan had just checkmated him, Timashov went to his cupboard where he rummaged for a few moments before returning with a bottle of vodka. He poured two shots and placed them on the table beside the board. He then waddled to the record player and turned up the volume slightly. The lyrical tones of a Mozart piano concerto filled the tiny flat. Finally he sat down again, lifted his glass and sipped with appreciation.

'Mozart,' breathed Timashov. 'The greatest composer who ever lived.'

'What, greater than the Russians? What about Prokofiev? What about Rachmaninov?' Dan had learned just enough about composers from Timashov to needle him gently. 'Does the KGB know that you feel this way?'

Timashov's chins wobbled as he chuckled. 'Of course this is a private preference on my part. Publicly I prefer the Russians.'

Dan sipped his vodka. He had begun to like Timashov. The fat man had a humanity about him which was in contrast to the barely concealed hostility he had to deal with every day in the laboratory.

'Can I ask you something?' he said.

Timashov was conducting the orchestra with his free hand, the glass in the other. 'Anything.'

'What puzzles me is why people put up with this system. In America no one gives a damn what sort of music you prefer, or what books you read or who you talk to. Here you're told how to think.'

Timashov wagged a dainty finger at Dan. 'Careful, my young friend. You can say these things to me, but please don't repeat them elsewhere. Do you know you can be sent to a psychiatric ward for saying what you just said. If you are going to survive in Russia you will have to work within the system. You may have your opinions, but keep them to yourself or else only discuss them with people you know you can trust. Believe me, this is important.'

'I'm not sure I can do it,' said Dan.

'You must do it. You're not an American now, you're a Russian.' Timashov tossed back his vodka and shuddered with pleasure. 'You will find that life is not so bad. You will miss luxuries but there will still be music, friends, work to do. It is hard now but you will see. It won't be so bad.'

In the weeks and months to come, Dan had much to thank Timashov for. Timashov taught him how to play the party game, to mouth the phrases which would look right in the reports and keep the hard men in Moscow off his back. And Timashov was right. After a time, a long time, it wasn't so bad.

He came to love music as Timashov did and in Vilnius, five years after being shot down, Sergei Bulak, factory manager and good Party member, met his future wife while shopping for a record. Classical records were one of the few luxuries the average Russian could afford and Sergei had become a collector, although unlike his mentor, he preferred the power of the Russians to the prettier melodies of Mozart. Palmyra was a music teacher at the Vilnius Polytechnic. She neither looked like Laura nor did she have her American self-confidence. Small, dark haired and womanly, she fell hopelessly in love with the red-haired man from a mysterious background who spoke Russian with such a strange accent.

When Sergei told Timashov he wanted to get married, Timashov cautioned him to wait while he consulted with Moscow. He must have put up a convincing case because word came back that the marriage could go ahead, although he was cautioned never to mention his true background to his wife.

On their first anniversary they caught a bus to Lake Galve, thirty kilometres outside Vilnius. They walked into the hills to admire the castle which rises from the middle of the lake. It was a mild spring day and the sun for once shone down from a clear sky. Clouds of hatching mayflies sprinkled the air. Sergei spread a blanket on the grass and they sat listening to the cattle lowing nearby. Palmyra was lying on her back and Sergei was beside her, propped on one elbow.

'There's something I haven't told you. Something about my past,' he said.

Palmyra's eyes were shut. 'Is it good or bad? If it's bad please don't tell me.'

'It's bad.'

She opened her eyes. 'What is it?'

'You told me not to tell you,' said Sergei, smiling.

'Of course I did, but I didn't mean it.'

'If I tell you, it's going to be a burden to you, but I can't share my life with you and not share this as well.'

Palmyra reached up and pulled his face down to hers. 'I don't care what it is, I want to know. Tell me.'

He kissed her lightly and drew back. 'My accent. Do you wonder how I got it?'

'You told me. Your father was a diplomat and you moved around a lot when you were young.'

'Yes I know. That's what I was told to say. It's English.'

'From the International School in Moscow.'

'No not from there. From America.'

'You lived in America? I didn't know that.'

'I didn't just live there. I am American.'

Palmyra sat up and stared at him. 'I don't understand.'

'I'm American. I was born and raised in the USA. My parents were American, I went to American schools, an American college, I joined the American Air Force. I'm American as . . . as apple pie.'

Palmyra searched his face, looking for a trace of a smile. 'What are you talking about, apple pie? You're not making sense.' Fearfully she shook him. 'Tell me what are you talking about.'

Sergei took both her hands in his. 'Listen to me my dove. I was an airman in the US Air Force fighting in Vietnam. I was shot down and captured. I had knowledge of a weapons system that the Soviet Union wanted. They told me if I helped them they would make a new life for me in Russia.'

Palmyra was looking at him wide-eyed with astonishment. She could think of nothing to say. 'I . . . I don't understand.'

Dan took a tuft of his hair in his fingers and pulled it lightly. 'Have you ever seen a Russian with hair like this?'

Palmyra realised he was serious. This was not some

134

elaborate joke. Sergei was telling her the truth. 'Oh Sergei,' she said, 'they must have tortured you. I know you would never have given in otherwise.'

'I tried to fight them but I couldn't. I just couldn't stand the pain. I'm a traitor, Palmyra. I've been living a lie and I'll have to live a lie for the rest of my life, but I can't lie to you any longer.'

Palmyra took his face between her hands and kissed him. 'You're not a traitor to me, you're my husband and I love you.'

Sergei lifted her hands and kissed them. 'Thank you. I'll never let you down. I promise. You're the best thing that's ever happened to me.'

'I want to know everything,' said Palmyra. 'About your childhood, your parents, friends, lovers, your job, everything.'

Sergei began to speak. He told her about his boyhood in America, his engagement to Laura, being shot down and tortured, his betrayal and the time at Priazorsk. Palmyra listened to these revelations in a state close to shock. When she was able to speak the questions came pouring out in a torrent. She wanted to know every detail about this new man whom she had never known existed.

'What was the name of the girl you were going to marry?'

'Laura.'

'Tell me about her.'

'It was so long ago I can hardly remember. She was strong, earthy. She would never avoid an argument just because it was the easy way out. She could be wearing sometimes.'

'What did she look like?'

'Typically American I suppose. Blonde hair, blue eyes, long legs.'

'She sounds beautiful.'

'Well yes, I suppose she was.'

Palmyra gave Sergei a serious look. 'Do you ever think of her?'

'No, not for a long time. She's part of the past which

I can never revisit. She's probably married and fat with a couple of kids and would have forgotten all about me. There's no point thinking about her. I have you.'

'If she loved you like I do, she will never forget you.'

'Maybe, but we'll never know will we?'

'I suppose you're right.'

Palmyra's questions were spent. She was lying on her back looking up at Sergei who was propped beside her on one elbow. She reached up to him. 'Make love to me.'

Palmyra pulled him down towards her. They hugged each other tightly and loved shamelessly on the open hillside as if the act would seal the secret that they both now shared.

To Palmyra this new knowledge explained many of the mysteries which had troubled her about Sergei, the sadness which she detected in him and his inability to accept the system. The shared knowledge brought them closer together. She understood now the reason for the six-monthly visits from Timashov. She could never trust him completely as Sergei did and she was glad when, after their son was born, the visits became rarer. Someone in Moscow had obviously decided that he was safely in place and would cause no trouble. They had not seen or heard from his fat friend now for two years.

Twelve

Laura met Dan when she was at college. She had been invited to a party by a man she was half-heartedly dating. The Beatles were full blast, the air smelled of marijuana and spilled liquor. The rooms were packed with young men and women dancing, arguing and shouting at each other to be heard. By midnight the party was potent with barely suppressed violence and sexuality. On couches and on the dance floor, couples were necking and in a few instances openly petting, too stoned or drunk to care who saw them. There was a feeling that things were at the outer edge of control.

Laura, who had been raised on a ranch near a small town in Nebraska, still did not feel at home with student debauchery. She had not seen her date for an hour or more and stood alone in a corner watching the couples throwing themselves around with abandon to the music. A young man whirling by alone, with a glass of liquor held high, bumped against her and the drink splashed down the front of her dress. She pulled back and was about to say something but the dancer had already reeled away.

She wondered if her date had perhaps had too much to drink and passed out. Anyway, drunk or sober she was going to find him and tell him she was leaving. Dodging her way carefully through the crowd she searched the lower floor of the house. There were one or two inert bodies draped in chairs or lying in corners but he was not one of them. She climbed the stairs and came to a landing with a hall leading down past a row of doors. She went into the first bedroom she came to. By the time she realised what she had walked into it was too late to pretend that she had not seen what was happening. Her escort was lying on the bed on his back with his trousers down around his ankles and his feet on the floor. A young woman was on her knees in front of him with her head down. They both looked up startled as she entered. She paused for an instant and within a second of taking in the scene, turned and ran out. Behind her she heard the sound of giggling.

Laura went back downstairs, determined to leave. As she reached the bottom of the stairs she walked right into a group of men and women arguing loudly about America's involvement in the Vietnam War. It was the time of moratorium marches and draft-card burnings. Voices were raised and faces were distorted as they hurled invective across the room. It all seemed to be directed at one man, a tall redhead with hair cut short in contrast to the fashionably unkempt mops of the others. He was the only one in the group putting the case for involvement.

She began to follow the argument. One of the redhead's opponents was built like a footballer, over six feet tall with a thick neck and massive shoulders. He was clutching a paper cup full of liquor which spilled as he gesticulated.

'You're a fuckin' coward. You fly over in your fuckin' plane and drop your bombs on innocent women and children.'

'That's not right,' the redhead replied evenly. 'We only attack military targets.'

'Military targets, bullshit. Watch the news, man. There's civilians getting slaughtered out there.'

'Civilians get killed in every war. But Americans are

dying too. At least they're prepared to lay their lives on the line for what they believe in.'

The big man raised his fists, slopping the last of his drink over the man's clothes. 'Oh so you're a hero are you? Let's see how heroic you are in a *fair* fight.'

The redhead's arms remained by his side. 'I don't think so.'

Until this stage Laura had been silent. Now she could contain herself no longer. She planted herself squarely in front of the big footballer, eyes blazing. 'Look at you. I thought you people were all about love not war. Pretty hypocritical don't you think?'

The big man focused drunkenly on her. He was at a loss for words. Laura could hear some of the onlookers tittering at this new turn in the argument, but her eyes remained locked on the man before her. For a few moments more he stared back. For a second Laura thought he might hit her. She bunched her fists and then his eyes dropped. He turned to his friends and said with an attempt at a grin, 'Feisty little thing isn't she.'

'You'd better believe it,' said Laura.

The heat had gone out of the moment. Some of the big man's friends stepped in and pulled him away into the crowd. As the onlookers broke up she became aware of the red-headed man beside her. 'Is that right,' she said, 'you actually fly bombers?'

'Fighters. I'm not a pilot. I sit in the back and play with a lot of electronic gadgetry.'

'And have you been to Vietnam?'

'Not yet. But it's only a matter of time.'

'For what it's worth I think you were right just then.'

'Well thanks. Not many people do these days. I felt like I was down behind enemy lines waiting for rescue.' He smiled. 'Then you came along.'

Laura smiled back. 'Here comes the cavalry.'

'Just in time.'

And so it began. Laura forgot about going home and instead she and Dan spent hours talking. After he drove her home and dropped her off she had trouble going to sleep. She kept thinking about the man she had just met. With surprise she realised she was attracted to Dan Parkinson. She wanted to see him again.

Right from the beginning she understood he was different to the other young men she had dated. Where other 24-year-olds didn't know who they were or where they were going and seemed only intent on drinking and drugging as much as their bodies could stand, he was steady, mature, level-headed and uncomplicated; a highly trained military careerist with a real war to fight.

She had never been tempted by the clumsy gropings of her suitors. When Dan kissed her she felt an unfamiliar stirring. At home in bed she imagined him making love to her and found herself on the edge of sleep thrusting her hips involuntarily, caressing herself. For the first time in her life she began to have disturbing, erotic dreams.

One weekend, about two months after they met, they drove home from a movie in Dan's rattletrap Chevvy. It was about midnight. Laura's room-mate was away. Dan pulled her close in the car and kissed her and asked quietly if he should see her inside. They both knew what he meant. Laura had already decided some time ago what the answer would be.

He led her in the dark to her bedroom, held her close and kissed her under her ear. His lips moved to her throat. The light from a half moon spilled through the window, throwing the two of them into silhouette. Stepping back he ran his hands from her shoulders down to her breasts and his thumbs lightly stroked her nipples. Laura felt a tingling as she hardened. Slowly he undid her blouse and slipped it off. He went onto his knees and slipped her skirt over her hips. It fell in a pool of cloth around her ankles and Laura stepped out of it. Dan guided her to the bed and pushed her gently down.

Standing back he undressed quickly. Kneeling beside her on the bed he gently pulled her panties down. She lifted her hips slightly to help. Tenderly, he began to kiss her, first her mouth then her throat and her breasts, slowly oh so slowly. By the time he touched her with his hands she was ready.

Afterwards Laura began to sob quietly. Dan regarded her with concern. 'Why are you crying?'

She laughed through her tears. 'I'm crying because I'm so happy.'

They could not meet every day. Dan was often tied up at the airbase in the evenings and Laura took her college course seriously enough to spend a lot of her nights studying. But they called each other when they could not be together. They had known each other six months when, one morning just as she was about to leave for college, the phone rang in her apartment.

'Hi. I haven't got long, I'm taking off on a training exercise in ten minutes, but how about we get together tonight?'

'I'd love to, but I've got a really full day of lectures and I have to finish an assignment. How about tomorrow?'

'Honey, it's really important.'

'What is it? Tell me now.'

'It's not something I want to tell you over the telephone. I need to be face to face.'

Laura was intrigued. She was already running late. Whatever it was she would hear about it tonight. 'All right, see you at Kenny's Castle at six o'clock. Gotta run.'

Kenny's Castle was their favourite meeting place. The drinks were reasonably priced and the decor shabby but homely and, importantly, it was a place where servicemen knew they would not be harassed by the anti-war protestors. Laura arrived five minutes late to find Dan already sitting by himself in a booth towards the back of the bar. He was sipping a beer. He ordered Laura a beer as well and when the waitress had gone, leaned forward over the table and took her hand.

'I got orders yesterday. I'm going to Vietnam.'

Laura stared at him, speechless.

'I'm sorry to be so stark, honey. I've been trying to

figure out how to tell you, but the only way I know is to say it straight out.'

'When?'

'A week from today.'

Ever since she had known Dan she had known that sooner or later he would be called up for active duty. It had always been hypothetical, so far in the future as to be not worth worrying about. Now that it was here, she was struck by the realisation that what Dan did for a living was dangerous. Servicemen were dying every day in Vietnam, you read about it in the papers and saw it every time you turned on the television. They were just names and faces she did not know, but now it involved the man she loved.

Laura took his hand. 'Are you scared?'

'No I'm not scared. I'm excited. This is what I've been training for all this time.'

'*I'm* scared. I'm afraid you won't come back.'

'Hey sweetheart, I'm not going to let some VC come between you and me. I'll be gone six months and then I'll be back. It'll pass in no time.'

She became aware that she was gripping his hand tightly. She released him and gave him what she hoped was a nonchalant grin. 'You're right. I'll hardly notice you're gone. I need to catch up on some study anyway and I can't seem to get it done with you around.'

'Speaking of distractions, could I talk you out of that assignment tonight?'

'Why? Do you have a better offer?'

'How about a steak at Mario's and afterwards we go out to the lake?'

The lake Dan referred to was fifteen miles out of town. They had spent a magical weekend there once in a hired cabin, swimming, canoeing, sunbathing and making love. It held special memories for them both. Dan reached into his pocket and pulled out a key with a wooden tag attached to it which he dangled in front of her. 'Look familiar?'

'You're an awful man. You planned this didn't you?

Soften me up and get me all misty-eyed and then bribe me with a steak.'

'That's right.'

'What can I say?'

Later that night, well fed on prime rib and Idaho potatoes with sour cream and chives and half tipsy from an unfamiliar bottle of Californian red wine they tumbled laughing into bed. They could hear the sound of the water lapping the shore only a few yards away from their window. Off in the reeds somewhere a frog croaked and an owl gave a solemn, honking call. Their laughter died and they began to caress each other. In seconds they were tearing at each other's clothing and Dan was on top of her thrusting savagely. There was something desperate about their lovemaking. Laura had never allowed herself to become completely abandoned like this. She did not know if any of the nearby cabins were occupied and she did not care who might hear her cries of pleasure or the frantic bumping of the four-poster bed against the wall. When Dan collapsed panting on top of her he buried his face in her shoulder. After a few moments he lifted his head and looked into her eyes. 'That was scary,' he whispered. 'I never knew I could feel like that. God how I love you.'

Laura put her hands on his buttocks and gently began to move her hips, pulling him against her. Dan felt himself grow hard again inside her and began to move more urgently. Next morning, sated, and closer than they had ever been, they went back to town. A week later Dan left for Vietnam.

She never saw him again.

Alone in her room in Moscow, Laura decided to write some postcards. She scribbled some hasty homilies about the freezing weather and how much she missed everyone, and addressed them. That done, she paced the room for a while, unaccountably restless. She rang room service and ordered tea, then sat down at the desk, opened her purse and pulled out the photograph of Dan.

143

The last time she had looked at it was in Sydney. Then it had brought back vivid images from the past. She stared at his image and willed the memories to return. She was filled with longing; aching with the need to feel flesh and blood instead of this grainy picture of a young man in military uniform, as impersonal as a stranger in a magazine. She tried to imagine what he would look like now if he were alive. Would his hair be thinning? His face lined? What would it really have been like if they had married and spent their life together? Would the determined, confident young man she had adored have grown into a strong and loving partner or would he have turned into one of those overly masculine military career-ists whose women took second place in their lives? Would they have remained in love? Questions. Questions with no answers.

Laura settled further into her chair and closed her eyes, trying to recreate in her mind the living Dan she had loved. It had all been so long ago and the images stubbornly refused to come. Her optimism deserted her. The very idea that he had survived at all, let alone come to live in Russia, seemed preposterous. She was slumped in her chair with the photograph held tightly against her breast when there was a knock on the door. It was the room service waiter, with the tea.

Laura placed the photograph back inside its envelope and went to answer the door.

Thirteen

Next day was one of frustration and boredom for Bing. He did not want to stray far from the telephone in case a call came through, so he spent most of the time in his room, reading, watching CNN and in-house movies on television. It was late. Rambo was defeating half the Vietnamese army while rescuing some Americans who had been held captive. Bing was annoyed with himself watching this nonsense but had reached that stage of stupefaction where he was incapable of summoning the will to turn it off. When the sound of the telephone overrode that of the automatic weapons, flame-throwers and grenades, he jerked back to alertness. He fumbled at the volume control but the sounds of war became even louder.

Worried that the telephone might stop he picked up the receiver. 'Connick here,' he said. 'Hang on a moment and I'll fix this damn television.'

Putting down the receiver he found the correct button and Rambo continued wreaking mayhem in silence.

'Sorry, I was watching Rambo and couldn't figure out how the volume worked.'

George Blackwell sounded puzzled. 'Rambo? I'm sorry I don't understand.'

Blackwell had been a Russian citizen for the last thirty

years. It was unlikely he had the taste for Hollywood blockbusters even if he had access. 'I'm sorry,' Bing said. 'It's hard to explain. It's a movie about a GI who's sent into Vietnam to bring back a group of MIAs. Along the way he single-handedly destroys about ten battalions of enemy soldiers.'

'And he is called Rambo?'

'That's it.'

Blackwell chuckled. 'It sounds as though Hollywood is even sillier than I remember. What a pity you didn't bring Rambo with you. It might have made the whole thing much simpler. Then real life is never like the movies, is it?'

'Have you managed to come up with something?' Bing asked.

'I've had to be very discreet, as you will understand, but I do have something which might be helpful.'

Rambo, his chest bare and glistening with sweat, was running through an enemy village firing an automatic weapon. Communist soldiers fell in droves. Some of them fired back but they were all bad shots. Rambo brought his flame-thrower to bear and the grass huts began burning, sending silent sheets of flame into the sky. Bing said, 'When can we meet?'

'I think now would be best.'

'OK. Where?'

'There is a nightclub not far from you, the Baku. Any taxi driver will take you there. It'll cost you a packet of Marlboros if you have them, otherwise a couple of American dollars. Don't try to give them roubles. No one wants Russian money these days.'

'The Baku. I'll leave now.'

It was midnight but there were half a dozen Ladas waiting outside the hotel. After travelling for five minutes the driver stopped outside a nondescript doorway. Bing paid him and went inside. Two hard-looking men with Middle Eastern features silently stared at him as he shrugged out of his overcoat and handed it to an old man behind a counter, who gave him a numbered marble in return. He stepped through the swing doors into the nightclub to be greeted by a wail of Eastern music. On stage a woman was performing a contortionist act. Her head seemed somehow to have ended up underneath her well-shaped legs, which were in a sort of knot around her neck. Bing peered through a fug of cigarette smoke and saw Blackwell sitting in a corner as far away as possible from the musicians. He went over and sat down.

'Delightful place.'

'It's owned by the Mafia. In Moscow we have various factions, chiefly Georgian, Russian and Azerbaijani. This place belongs to the Azerbaijani Mafia. It's good food and a good place to meet. Also a good place to find drugs, women, boys, weapons, black-market goods, whatever you want. But don't be alarmed, they pay the police a lot of money to leave them alone. We won't be disturbed.'

Blackwell poured out a shot from a vodka bottle and passed the glass to Bing. 'Confusion to our enemies,' he said and chuckled. He was playing his cheerful undergraduate role, out for a night on the town.

Bing did not smile. He held up his own glass. 'Cheers.' A waiter approached and Blackwell waved him away. He seemed to sense that Bing wanted to come straight to the point. Leaning forward he said, 'I have a friend, an Army major, who writes articles in military newspapers. One of the papers he writes for is *Red Star*. He is on the editorial board. I'm sure you've heard of it.'

'Yes. I've heard of *Red Star.*'

He writes for another paper which is published by the Urals Amalgamation of Air Defence. As its name suggests, it specialises in air defence matters. It circulates all over the Soviet Union, from the Volga to Tumin in Western Siberia and from the Arctic Ocean down to Kazakhstan in the south, a very large area.'

'And what is this newspaper called?'

'Na Stradze. It means "On Guard". Now this friend of mine was doing some research into air defence during the Vietnam War and he came across some information

which seems to support the theories of your man in Bangkok, Buggins was it?'

'That's his name, Dean Buggins.' Bing had not mentioned Buggins' death to Blackwell and he saw no reason to bring it up now.

'While he was interviewing people for his articles, my friend spoke to a man who used to be a major with the Soviet air defence advisers. He's in his sixties now and retired from active service, but he still remembers clearly what went on in Vietnam.

'He told my friend that in about 1967 there was a specific directive from Kosygin prohibiting Soviet Air Force pilots from engaging or intercepting American aircraft. That was one part of the directive. The other part you will find interesting. It ordered air defence to specifically try and capture American pilots.'

'Did he see these directives?'

'No he did not see them. They would probably have been sent to the Soviet Ambassador in Hanoi who would have passed them on to the Head of Air Defence Advisers. He would then have issued orders to the major.'

'I've never heard of them.'

'Maybe not, but they're not secret. They're quite common knowledge amongst certain military officers.'

Blackwell paused and glanced at the stage. The contortionist had unravelled her limbs and was now standing upright, performing a fire-eating routine. He returned to his narrative. 'Now this major actually took part in downing an American plane and capturing the crew. He was in charge of a missile battery which brought them down. In fact he was awarded a medal for it.'

Bing was incredulous. 'Come on George, the Soviet Union has never admitted to active participation in Vietnam. How could he be awarded a medal?'

'It's the Order of the Red Star. The citation says the standard thing, "awarded for the performance of international duty", except that they say it was for Afghanistan.' He gave a cynical laugh. 'Never mind that the major had probably retired by the time the Afghan war was on, that's how it was done.'

'So he helped capture an American. Does he remember his name?'

'Don't forget that this information was given to my source as part of a general interview. He didn't go into details.'

Bing thought for a moment, grasping for a way to pin down the information more precisely. 'Could he contact the old man now and ask him?'

'No, I don't think so. If he suddenly starts asking specific questions there's a good chance he'll get scared and just clam up. My friend could also find himself in trouble. I doubt if the idea of glasnost has been whole-heartedly embraced by the military just yet.'

Bing was silent. The major's story strengthened Buggins' theory but it took them no further towards finding out what happened to them afterwards. He said, 'Did the old man mention Americans being taken to the Soviet Union?'

'No he didn't.' Blackwell paused. 'My friend has more information bearing on that question.'

Blackwell was clearly enjoying himself, revelling in the intrigue of the scene. The late-night meeting at the shady nightclub, the information doled out piece by piece, the criminals hovering in the shadows. Earlier he had sneered at Hollywood but his own life was like an espionage movie in which he was a leading player. Bing sensed he was waiting for a question.

'What information?'

'Again it's second-hand stuff that came up in the context of his Vietnam researches. At the time he did not think too deeply about it, but he remembers the details.'

'And?'

'During the war, when Russia and China were still on good terms there were special windows created on their border which were used to transport classified hardware through to the North Vietnamese. My friend spoke to a former KGB officer who is now retired, who was in charge of a window near Alma Ata, in Kazakhstan.

'Why would the KGB be in charge of a border crossing?'

'Actually the border troops and the KGB used to be the same until only very recently. They were different directorates of the same agency. In Autumn of 1967, somewhere in September or October, four KGB officers came across the border from China with an American. He was taken to Alma Ata and then to Saryshagan.'

'He saw this American?'

'He saw him.'

'How old was he?'

'He said he was aged between twenty-four and thirty.'

'How did he know he was an American?'

'It is impossible to mistake an American for a Russian.'

'And how were they travelling?'

'By car.'

Bing felt an excitement he recognised but had not experienced for a long time. It was the feeling every journalist gets with the first scent of a story. He deliberately looked for holes. 'Why would a KGB officer, even if he's retired, tell your friend this story?'

'I wondered the same thing. The service is not noted for treating informers kindly,' said Blackwell dryly. 'It seems this officer was indebted to my friend. You know that in 1979 there was a war between Vietnam and China?'

'Yes. It was a secret war. It was hardly reported.'

'Exactly. Well by '79 Russia and China were at loggerheads. This officer served with the Vietnamese during that war. When he retired, that year of overseas service was not included in his pension. Because it was a secret war it was never acknowledged. As a rule your years of combat service are multiplied by three when they calculate the pension. My friend put him in touch with a veterans' union and they lobbied the Ministry of Defence and had his pension increased. That extra three years made a big difference to him. He now gets 347 roubles, two and a half kilos of meat, a month. So you see he is grateful to my friend for his intervention.'

'OK. An American was taken across the border at Alma Ata, then to Saryshagan. What happened then?'

'My friend doesn't know. But we can speculate a little. Saryshagan is near Lake Balkhash. Near the lake but not on it. Nearby there is a smaller town which is not on the map, called Priazorsk. It means in Russian, "on the lake". Now Priazorsk is an air defence installation. It's a military base and nearby there is a missile test-firing range. If this American was an airman with knowledge of the Wild Weasel jamming system, it is logical to assume he was taken to Priazorsk.'

'Is it possible to travel to Saryshagan?' said Bing.

'Yes, you can go there and walk around just like any tourist. On a clear day you can see Priazorsk about twelve kilometres away.'

'And can you go to Priazorsk?'

'There is a regular military flight, a TU-154 which carries officers and their families in and out. Of course it's not available to civilians.'

'And that's it?'

Blackwell raised his shoulders and spread his hands. The fire-eater blew her last flaming breath to a frenzy of music and drums. There was a smattering of lukewarm applause as she exited from the stage. The musicians put down their instruments and began smoking. A couple of them wandered off the stage and over to the bar. Bing needed time to think. He poured himself another shot of vodka and one for Blackwell.

'It's pretty tantalising,' he said. 'But it's second-hand information, third-hand now. How likely is it to be true?'

'I don't think that there were droves of Americans being brought to Russia,' Blackwell said thoughtfully. 'But one or two perhaps? I can believe that. It's the way the KGB might work. He would have to agree to coop-erate. Then he would be brought to the air defence base, perhaps with some hardware from a downed F101, and he would help them learn how the Wild Weasel worked.'

'So you think part of it is credible?'

'I think so, yes.'

'And afterwards? After he had spilled his secrets, what then?'

'Well presumably a deal was made. Tell what he knew and he would be given a new identity and allowed to live. Refuse and he would be executed. I could see another scenario which would be attractive to the KGB. He is an American. Give him a new identity, slip him back into the United States. He is already skilled in electronics, he gets a job in one of the firms in the military industrial complex. Maybe it doesn't happen for a long while, maybe it takes ten or fifteen years, but eventually he reaches a position where he has access to sensitive material which he then passes on.'

'Why wouldn't he just reveal his true identity?'

'Do you remember what happened to Bobby Garfield when he escaped from North Vietnam?' said Blackwell.

'He was charged with being a traitor.'

'The same thing would happen to this man. He would have to confess to giving away secrets. He'd end up in prison.' Blackwell chuckled. The scenario appealed to him. 'It does have a certain beauty doesn't it?'

'If he's still here, how could we find him?' Bing asked. 'The trail ends in Saryshagan. And it's more than twenty years old.'

'I can't tell you. And it would be better if you don't tell me what you intend to do. I can only suggest one thing. Be very very careful. I've enjoyed the game so far, but be in no doubt that the KGB can get very rough if it finds out what you're up to.'

If they don't know already, Bing thought. They drank some more and Blackwell made small talk, as if reluctant for their meeting to end. Bing listened to his chatter warily and as soon as he politely could, rose to go. He thanked Blackwell and left him sitting alone at the table.

At the door he retrieved his coat and stepped outside into the street.

It was about 2 a.m. There was not a taxi to be seen. He thought of going back inside and asking them to telephone for one, then realised how fruitless that would be in Moscow. The snow had stopped falling and the streets gleamed slickly under the occasional light that was working. The footpath was covered in a light dusting of powdered snow. He knew roughly where he was. It would only be a fifteen minute walk back to the hotel. Wrapping his scarf around his chin and hunching his shoulders, he set off at a brisk pace.

He had been walking for about five minutes, his breath coming in puffs of white, when he became aware of the car travelling slowly behind him, just keeping pace. Shit, he thought, I'm about to be mugged. He continued walking, looking about him for some avenue of escape. He heard the car approaching. It ranged up alongside and the window wound down to reveal a pudgy face under a fur hat. A cigarette was jammed in the corner of the driver's mouth and one eye was screwed up against the smoke. Looking across him he could see the vague shape of another man in the passenger's seat.

The driver spoke with a heavy Russian accent, 'Where you go? You want taxi?'

'Nyet.'

'Ten dollar. Taxi to hotel.'

Bing disregarded the man and kept on walking. The car accelerated fifty yards up the road and stopped. The passenger got out and began to walk back towards him holding an unlit cigarette in his hand. He held up the cigarette. 'You have a light?'

The man was standing squarely in front of him so that Bing would have to step around him to pass. If I punch him now, thought Bing, I might get a chance to run before the other guy gets out of the car. The man was thickset and capable-looking, wearing a heavy coat with a wide leather belt. If he was going to hit him it would have to be in the face.

Out of the corner of his eye Bing saw the car door begin to open. He brought his right fist up from about belt level and connected with the man's chin. He felt the solid crunch of bone on bone and saw him stagger against a lamppost. The driver of the car shouted and began to swing his leg out onto the pavement. Bing ran and slammed the door hard on his ankle and he screamed with pain and anger. Catching a glimpse of the first man reeling, but still on his feet, Bing took off at a run, trying hard not to slip on the icy pavement.

In front of him was a side street, filled with garbage bins, the road badly potholed. He turned and ran down the street, looking desperately for some place to hide. Behind him he heard the car accelerate, and glancing back, saw light lick the walls. The suspension banged in protest as it slammed through the potholes.

To the side there was an archway which led into a courtyard. Think! Continue on and be run down? Or hope to find escape in the yard? He ran through the archway, his shoes scrabbling for purchase on icy cobblestones, and saw that he'd made the wrong choice. The yard was surrounded by the doors of private dwellings, grimy windows shut tight, each with a row of stalactites suspended from the sill.

Headlights appeared at the entrance to the courtyard, the car doors slammed and he heard footsteps clattering. The ice snapped off cleanly in Bing's hand.

The thickset man was advancing swinging a short club by a strap. The driver of the car was hanging back. I hope he's not armed, thought Bing. If he's armed I've had it. Bing advanced towards the man, holding the stalactite low. For a second they faced each other. The club swung high and Bing stepped in close plunging the shaft of ice upwards into the underside of his jaw.

The weight of the Russian dragged Bing onto the ground and for a few panicked moments he was trapped underneath him before dragging himself free. He whirled to face the second man but he needn't have bothered. He was leaning against the car, grimacing with pain every time he tried to put weight on his ankle.

Bing approached him warily and their eyes locked. The driver gave him a look of pure hatred and said something in Russian. Bing carefully kicked his injured ankle and he went down screaming. He leaned in through the open door, removed the ignition key and threw it as far as he could. As he walked away he thought, I'm too damned old for this.

When Bing reached the hotel he was breathing hard. The doorman gave him a curious stare as he stepped inside to the deserted lobby where everything was strangely normal. A woman was guiding a vacuum cleaner across the marble floor, two reception staff were yawning away the graveyard shift, a porter was dozing on a chair. He asked for his key and when he held out his hand it was shaking with delayed shock. Letting himself into his room, he poured himself a drink from the mini bar and tried to calm down. Bing had made a career out of reporting violence, but he himself was not a violent man. Gradually, his hands steadied. Too exhausted to wash, he dragged his clothes off and climbed under the bed covers, his mind swimming with the events which had just taken place. His thoughts were a jumble. As he hovered on the edge of unconsciousness he was thinking that there was something about the driver of the car that he should remember, but before he could think what it was he slipped into grateful oblivion.

Fourteen

Bing woke late, got out of bed and padded across the carpet to the window. Pulling aside the curtains he looked out onto another bleak Moscow day. The sky, the buildings and the ground were a uniform grey. He had always needed an environment of light and water but had not seen the sun since he got here. His shoulder was aching where he had hit the ground last night and there were grazes on his hands, knees and elbows. He walked to the bathroom and ran the shower as hot as he could stand it. Twenty minutes later, after cleaning his teeth and shaving, he felt almost normal again. He knew that he and Laura would have to have a council of war. For a moment he toyed with the idea that they might go outdoors and walk in open space, but he knew it would be too cold for that. Instead he called her and suggested they meet in the hotel's breakfast room.

He guessed the room must have been a ballroom when the place was a Tsarist palace. It was vast, and beautifully appointed. Graceful columns drew the eye skywards to a curved stained-glass ceiling. It was not hard to imagine the noble families gathered here in their splendour, the men with moustaches and pointed beards and wearing uniforms jangling with medals, the women in gorgeous gowns, dancing the night away while the peasants starved outside. Even now nothing had really changed. Along one side of the room tables were laden with food which no Muscovite could aspire to. There were fresh fruits, hams, cereals, smoked fish, four different sorts of eggs, pancakes; the smorgasbord would have been remarkable even in a Western five-star hotel. Here, amid the poverty of Moscow it was almost obscene.

At one end of the room was a stage upon which sat a young woman in a formal black dress playing a harp. Bing saw Laura sitting at a banquette beside one of the columns and waved. As he sat down she looked at him with concern. 'Are you all right? You look as though you haven't slept all night.'

'I went to a nightclub.'

'Oh really? Well I have no sympathy for you.' Laura smiled to show she was kidding.

'With Blackwell.'

'Ahah. And how's the espionage business?'

'We've got to decide where we're going with this thing, Laura.'

'You look serious. Something happened.'

For the next twenty minutes Bing related everything which had occurred the night before, beginning with Blackwell's midnight call. He told her about the Kosygin directive, the American allegedly taken through the border window and about the air defence installation in Kazakhstan. Laura listened without interrupting. As he described the two Russians bailing him up Laura reached over and placed her hand on his arm. 'You must have been terrified. How did you get away?'

'I outran them.'

'I'd heard about muggings in Moscow, I guess they're real.'

'Well mugging's one explanation, but I can think of another.'

'Someone trying to stop us from investigating?'

'It's a possibility. Remember Hammond's warning? This could have been to reinforce the point.'

'Do you think so?' said Laura doubtfully. 'It doesn't sound very professional.'

'Maybe good help is hard to find in Moscow.'

'It could also have been the KGB, couldn't it?'

'The KGB would know we're here,' said Bing. 'But how would they know *why* we're here?' He took a sip of his coffee. 'I don't know. Maybe it was just a clumsy mugging attempt. I just don't know.'

The thought that he had been trying to focus on as he went to sleep suddenly came to him. 'I just remembered, the driver of the car that attacked me was wearing a black leather coat. Maybe your friend Askar wasn't grandstanding after all.'

A waiter approached with a coffee pot. Bing waited while he refilled his cup. Laura watched him speculatively. 'What do you think of Blackwell's story?'

'Well we have a third-hand report of an American who was supposed to have been taken across the border. *An* American, not necessarily *your* American. If Buggins is correct and there were fifty MBs, that makes it pretty long odds that it was Dan.'

'The American was supposed to have been brought across in Autumn 1967 wasn't he?'

'That's what Blackwell said.'

'Dan was shot down in July.'

Bing counted off the months. 'July, August, September. The informant said he crossed the border in August or September. He would have been interrogated by the Vietnamese first. It would have taken a while for them to hand him over.'

'So the time frame fits.'

'We can look at Buggins' list and see how many others fit. Scrub all those who were shot down after late September '67. That will give us more of an idea.'

'I think we're onto something,' said Laura. 'Don't you?'

'Quite possibly, but last night worries me. This is the Soviet Union, remember.'

'Well I'm game,' Laura said. 'What about you?'

Bing had begun by being being uninvolved, but he knew he had changed. The newsman's instinct was something he could not kill. He was enough of a realist to admit to himself that he wanted the adrenalin rush of a big story again. He looked at the woman opposite, waiting for his reply. She had intelligence and determination and he realised he was in danger of becoming involved in more than just the story.

'The next step in the trail is Kazakhstan,' he said. 'I know nothing about it except that it's an Asian republic on the edge of China. We couldn't just turn up without some sort of cover story.'

'I wonder if Blackwell could help.'

'He made it pretty clear last night that he'd done all he was prepared to.'

Laura hesitated for a moment, then said, 'What about Askar? He's from Kazakhstan.'

'What do we know about him, though?' He smiled at her, 'Apart from the fact that you think he's charming.'

Laura grinned back. 'Not much, but I do know one thing, he hates Russians and communism.'

'That would help. Does he hate them enough to risk helping a couple of Americans who want to go sniffing around a secret military establishment?'

'A fee paid in American dollars might go some way towards persuading him.'

Bing was silent. He looked around him at the ornate room with the harpist playing incongruously up on the stage. It was easy to sit here and fantasise. Outside there was a real world, a powerful empire in the throes of disintegration, with another great power, America, on the sidelines playing a role which neither of them fully understood. He knew with bleak self-knowledge that he could not step back. 'Why don't you call Askar,' he said to Laura. 'We can at least talk to him.'

When Laura told Askar on the telephone that they needed to talk somewhere where they could not be overheard, he immediately sensed the seriousness in her voice. He suggested they meet in a metro station and take a train ride. They followed his directions and walked to a subway entrance near the hotel. About five minutes later Askar arrived, walking fast, unwinding a scarf from around his neck as he came. Laura introduced him to Bing who shook his hand briefly before leading them down through a dank concrete tunnel onto the platform. As they arrived they felt the cold rush of air being pushed ahead of an oncoming train and a few moments later the leading carriage glided past. A car stopped directly in front of them and Askar gestured them aboard. For a couple of kopeks they could ride all day if they liked, and talk undisturbed.

The doors closed with a soft thud and the train pulled away, its rubber-shod wheels making a mild hum on the rails. Askar ushered Laura and Bing to a pair of bench seats facing each other. The train was clean, warm and comfortable. It was early afternoon. Despite the fact that the Metro moved three million people every day, the carriage was deserted.

They had already agreed that there would be no point in half-telling the story. If Askar was to help them, he would need to be fully informed. Nevertheless, Bing was loath directly to broach the subject of their meeting.

'What do you do in Moscow, Askar?' he said.

'I do what everyone does these days. I try to survive.'

'By working as a tourist guide?'

'By doing whatever is necessary.'

'Laura mentioned a business of some sort.'

'I buy and sell things.'

'What sort of things?'

'Oh this and that.'

'But what sort of this and that?'

'I am interested in any sort of business. The commodity does not matter. I buy cheaply and I sell for a profit.' Askar grinned. 'This is capitalism is it not? I am a capitalist.'

Bing sensed that Askar was attempting to disarm him. He guessed he was some kind of black marketeer or perhaps a drug dealer, though he wondered if they had drug dealers in Moscow yet. He decided he liked him. If he was operating on the fringes of the law he could have precisely the sort of skills they were looking for. He began to steer the conversation a little closer to their interests.

'Laura told me how you feel about communism.'

'What I said to Laura is what I feel.'

Bing sensed that Askar wanted him to get to the point. He glanced at Laura, who nodded. 'What do you know about Russia's involvement in the Vietnam War?'

Askar thought for a moment. 'I know Russia was in Vietnam. We were always told that we were helping them fight American imperialism. I was only young then, but I remember there was often news film on television of Russian advisers instructing North Vietnamese soldiers.'

'They did a lot more than that. Russian intelligence interrogated prisoners of war who had military information.'

Askar shrugged. 'Really?'

'You don't seem surprised.'

'No I'm not surprised. It seems a logical thing for them to do.'

'Even if they weren't supposed to have an active role?'

Askar shrugged again as if the answer was too obvious to put into words.

'They also helped to capture Americans.'

For the first time Askar showed mild incredulity. 'I never heard that. But then they lied to us about so much. What is one more lie?'

The train pulled into a station and the doors slid open. Bing paused, looking up to see if anyone entered their carriage. A man on the platform seemed about to step inside but apparently changed his mind and disappeared into the carriage behind theirs. The doors shut again and Bing continued. 'We believe that some Americans were brought to the Soviet Union for interrogation.'

'Oh really? This is not so easy to believe,' Askar said.

'Why would they go to that trouble? Why not interrogate them in Vietnam?'

'These prisoners had information about a weapons system which was destroying the North Vietnamese air defences. The Russians needed them to help develop their own countermeasures.'

'I understand,' Askar said.

'So they brought them to the Soviet Union where they had the scientific facilities.'

'We think at least one American went to Saryshagan,' Laura added. 'To an air defence establishment near there.'

'Ah, Priazorsk.'

'You know it?'

'Everyone knows it. But no one knows what goes on inside there.'

'We are not particularly interested in what happens at Priazorsk,' said Bing. 'What we want to know is what happened to the American.'

'I understand your problem. You cannot just ask.'

'Exactly.'

'We want your advice, Askar. How can we find out what happened?'

Askar looked slowly from one to the other. 'Who do you represent?' he said. 'Are you CIA?'

'No, we have no connection with the American government,' replied Laura. 'I want to know about the American for personal reasons.'

'And Mr Connick? Where does he fit in?'

'Bing is helping me. As I hope you might.'

Askar contemplated them both thoughtfully. 'When do you think the American was taken to Priazorsk?'

'In Autumn of 1967.'

'A long time ago.'

'That's right,' said Laura. 'A long time ago. But even after so long there may be someone there who knows what happened.'

The train was pulling into another station. As the doors opened the conversation stopped again. A middle-aged

162

Russian woman stepped into their carriage, carrying about twenty toilet rolls on a string. They were one of the rarest commodities in Moscow and she had obviously decided to capitalise on her good fortune at finding some. She sat at the far end of the carriage and began rummaging in her handbag, muttering to herself.

'We want to go to Saryshagan,' Laura continued. 'And we'd like you to help us when we get there.'

She was not quite sure how she expected him to react. With derision perhaps, or amusement, but Askar merely nodded thoughtfully. 'This American must have been important to you?'

'Yes, very.'

'You know, just a year or so ago it would have been practically impossible for you to travel to Kazakhstan. You needed a visa to go further than forty-five kilometres outside Moscow, but things are easier now. You are tourists, Americans who want to see something out of the ordinary. You are fascinated by the Asian republics. I am a guide who has been hired to take you. This part would not be difficult. I could arrange it. The problems would begin when you get there. Perhaps, though, there would be ways to overcome them.'

'Do you have any suggestions?' Laura said.

'I have an uncle there, my father's brother. We could stay with him. Perhaps he could help us.'

'You said you were a businessman,' Bing said. 'What would you expect to get out of this?'

'I would charge you my normal daily fee.'

'That's not enough,' said Laura. 'You don't need me to tell you that you could be at risk.'

Askar chuckled. 'If we do find out about this man it could embarrass the Russians couldn't it?'

'I think you can assume that,' Bing said.

'Well that will be my bonus,' said Askar, grinning broadly.

Fifteen

President Blanchard was speaking on the telephone when Brandon Paine entered the Oval Office. The President was discussing with the Secretary of State the overnight situation report from Moscow. There had been a demonstration in the streets by old-guard communists and the reactionaries within the parliament were becoming more strident by the day. The Russian President's grip on the country was tenuous at best and could slip any day.

Looking up, the President waved a greeting and motioned to Paine to take a seat. As Paine waited for him to finish his conversation, he looked at him with a mixture of respect and wariness. He had known Tom Blanchard for thirty years, since Blanchard had been Director of the CIA and Paine an Army general. During their long political careers, they had been friends and confidants, at least as friendly as two ambitious Washington movers can be. Theirs was a political as much as a personal friendship. They had thrust their way upwards in parallel. Paine had served as Assistant Secretary of State in a previous Republican administration while Blanchard had been Vice-President. When Blanchard became President he had appointed Paine Head of National Security.

He knew that the President had a lot riding on Russia.

He would be up for re-election in two years and had already earned himself political points by presiding over the end of the Cold War. He now had to do everything possible to help the Russian leader maintain stability. The better the Russians did, the better he would look. The State Department experts were saying the Soviet Empire would soon begin to disintegrate. The Baltic states, even now, were on the verge of declaring independence. Once they seceded there would be a queue of others wanting to follow. On the streets of Moscow, events were reaching a critical stage as the crippled economy staggered on through a bitter winter. It was a worrisome situation for the President and Paine knew that what he had to say now would add to his burden.

President Blanchard put down the telephone and turned to Paine. 'It's going to get worse before it gets better,' he said. 'That Ivashov's a tenacious son of a bitch.'

'And a smart one. He could teach some of the operators on the hill a thing or two.'

'I hope you're right. He'll have to be damn smart to manoeuvre his way through the next few months. And he'll need all the help we can give him.' Blanchard looked out the window. Snowflakes were drifting down past the panes, turning the Rose Garden white. To his left he could see a glimpse of the south lawn. It was a scene of beauty, which another man might have savoured for a moment or two, but the President had never acquired the habit of introspection. The ambition which had driven him all his life had left no room for it, and now that he had attained the presidency he had to be even more tough-minded. He turned back and said, 'What do you have for me, Brandon?'

'It's about Buggins.'

'The nutter from the NSA? That was taken care of wasn't it?'

'We thought so, but things got out of hand. The operative got a little overzealous.'

'Jesus, Brandon, what happened?'

165

'You don't want to know, Mr President. The bottom line is that the journalist Connick turned up in Moscow a few days ago with the woman, Laura Bailey.'

'Why didn't you tell me?'

'Well we didn't think there would be any need to. Hammond made two attempts to put him off, one verbal, the other more persuasive, but they didn't work out. And now it seems he's come up with something.'

'How the hell could he? The Russians wouldn't help them.'

'I don't know. Remember he was a hotshot once. Maybe he still is.'

'I know he was a damn hotshot. And now he's suddenly in Moscow with this woman looking like he's about to embarrass the hell out of me.'

'He's got a long way to go yet before he puts it all together,' Paine said.

'Well he's made pretty good progress so far.' Blanchard slammed his fist onto the desk. 'Jesus, Brandon, you know what sort of damage this can cause.'

Brandon Paine was only too aware. The intercepts which Buggins had painstakingly analysed, his speculations about Americans being taken to Moscow, had been known to the President when he headed the CIA at the time of the Vietnam War. Buggins had been quite correct when he told Bing that Blanchard must have known. What Buggins did not know is why nothing was done about it. Paine did not know either, but of one thing he was certain, if it came out that Blanchard had sat on the reports, the repercussions both for the President and for America would be disastrous.

'Mr President,' Paine said. 'You never told me why you did nothing about Buggins' reports.'

'Are you sure you want to know?'

'At this stage I think I should.' Blanchard understood the unspoken subtext. Paine was prepared to help his political patron up to a point, but before plunging in further he wanted to know how far the ripples spread. He had his own career to worry about.

166

'At first they were just theories,' the President said. 'By the time the war was coming to an end we were desperate to get out of it. If we had brought up the fact that these MIAs might still be alive the peace talks would have broken down. We slipped it under the carpet, Brandon. It was the right thing to do at the time.'

Paine recalled the national rejoicing when American POWs were released. Perhaps it had been the right thing at the time, he mused. Certainly it made political sense to end America's involvement in an unpopular conflict as tidily as possible. Now it looked as though the decision might come back to haunt them.

Blanchard interrupted his thoughts. 'Connick has to be stopped, Brandon. Don't tell me how you do it, I don't want to know. There's too much at stake here to allow some retired journalist to torpedo us.'

'He will be stopped.'

President Blanchard rose and walked around from behind his desk. At the door he shook Paine's hand and clapped him lightly on the shoulder. 'You know, Brandon, you've been a loyal friend over the years, I won't forget this.'

Paine, knowing that he had just placed the President further in his debt, smiled silkily. 'Leave it to me, Mr President.'

Sixteen

It took two days for Askar to get in touch with his uncle and arrange the visit to Saryshagan. One morning, Laura, Askar and Bing caught a taxi to Moscow's domestic airport, a huge, chaotic building with long lines of people at the counters waiting patiently to be processed. The thermometer had plunged to minus 20 degrees Centigrade and Laura could see airport service vehicles ploughing through a blur of falling snow. Dozens of aircraft with the blue Aeroflot stripe and drooping dihedral wings sat on the tarmac, drifts of snow piled against their wheels and building up on wings and fuselages. It was hard to believe that the airport could be operating, but now and again groups of travellers would drive out in buses to board their planes and the sound of roaring jet engines indicated flights taking off and landing.

After a wait of about two hours there was an announcement in Russian and passengers in the waiting room began straggling to their feet. The doors opened and a blast of freezing air entered. Moving at a slow shuffle, they advanced outside and boarded a bus which set off across a white wasteland.

Laura glanced at her ticket. There was no seat number. The bus came to a halt and the passengers stepped out into the weather and headed in a mob for the stairs. Askar was beside her. 'How do we know where to sit?' she asked.

'It's every man for himself. Keep close to me and I will find us seats wherever I can,' he replied.

At the top of the stairs there was a jam as passengers tried to get through the door. One by one they disappeared inside the plane. They were beginning to turn numb by the time their turn came. As they stepped into the main cabin Laura was amazed at the number of people who seemed to be squeezed in. They were crammed four deep on either side of the aisle in narrow, thinly padded seats. The three made their way slowly towards the back of the plane where they found an empty row.

Once she was seated Laura looked out the window where she could see ground crew de-icing the wings with powerful water jets. Glancing along the length of the plane she noted that the seats were now all occupied, but still passengers kept arriving. There was a babble of voices, much gesticulating and shouting as some passengers squeezed up to allow children to share a seat. A few men with the wind-burned faces of peasants elected to stand. The stewardesses, in badly fitting light blue uniforms, watched the passengers sorting themselves out with looks of contempt on their faces but made no attempt to impose order on the chaos.

Eventually, after much pushing and shoving and a few minor arguments, the doors were closed and the engines started. Bing was sitting next to Laura. He leaned over and said, 'You know all those television pictures we see of Russians in space stations? I don't believe it. They were all taken in a TV studio at some secret location, with sets made out of cardboard. They could never have got organised enough to send anyone into space.'

Laura smiled, grateful for the levity. She was finding her first Aeroflot flight terrifying and the plane hadn't even taken off. Askar meantime stared ahead impassively.

Outside, the ground vehicles rolled back and the aircraft began to taxi. Laura and Bing fastened their seat belts, but few of the other passengers bothered. In the row across from her a family of Kazakhs pulled down their tray tables and began to cut up bread and sausage. Others lit up cigarettes. The stewardesses had disappeared. A safety demonstration was evidently not deemed necessary. Laura remembered reading somewhere that Aeroflot planes crashed frequently but the accidents were never reported. The sound of the engines grew to a scream and the big airliner gathered speed down the runway, the G force pushing her back in her seat. Laura closed her eyes. She felt the plane lift into the air and when she eventually looked out the window all she could see was dense, snow-laden cloud.

The airliner climbed steeply for several minutes and then levelled off, the sound of the engines dropping to a low whine. Two stewardesses appeared and began distributing plastic glasses which they unsmilingly filled with warm, salty mineral water. Laura said, 'I'm not usually nervous about flying, but this is terrifying.'

Bing grinned back at her.

'I'd hate to think what would happen if there was an emergency.'

'Statistically you're more likely to crash on take-off or landing,' Bing said. 'It's a five-hour flight so we can probably count on staying alive at least that much longer.'

Laura tasted her mineral water, grimaced and put it aside. 'You must have flown on some pretty outlandish airlines in your time.'

'I sure did, but this comes close to the worst. Still, I had a friend who was a helicopter pilot in Vietnam and he used to say any flight you walk away from is a good one.'

'Maybe we should adopt your friend's attitude,' Laura replied. She noted that Bing's mood seemed almost jaunty and she had a sudden insight into the sort of correspondent he must have been, poking around in outlandish corners of the world, enjoying the danger. 'How long were you in Vietnam?' she asked.

'All up, five years.'

'A long time. Did you get to know many Vietnamese personally?'

'Some. We had Vietnamese working for us, of course. Photographers, interpreters and so on.'

'But apart from work.'

'I lived with a Vietnamese woman in Saigon.'

Laura was surprised. For some reason she had not imagined Bing being involved with a woman. It gave him a new dimension.

'What was her name?' she asked.

'Phuong'

'What a beautiful name. What was she like?'

He thought for a moment and echoed Laura's question. 'What was she like?' The words of Buggins' mistress sprang to mind. 'She was good to me.'

'And what happened?'

'She was killed,' said Bing, then added bitterly, 'she was another casualty of the war.'

'I'm sorry,' Laura said.

'Thanks. Who knows how it would have worked out? I don't think she would have liked it away from Vietnam.'

'I feel the same thing sometimes. I wonder how it would have worked out with Dan. Realistically I've got to consider that if he had come back we might not have made it as a couple anyway. What is it? One in three marriages fail, don't they?'

'What happened with yours?'

'It was one of the failures.'

'You never did tell me much about home.'

'There's not much to tell. Small town girl goes away to college, graduates and finds that everything she really wants is right there on the ranch.'

'And somewhere along the way small town girl found a husband.'

She said nothing. Bing wondered if he had touched a nerve. 'You don't have to tell me about him if you don't want to.'

'No it's all right. It's been over a long time and I never really loved him anyway.'

Bing's face must have reflected his surprise.

'Oh I thought I did. I had known him since we were both kids. He was the boy next door.'

'What was he like?'

'Too good-looking, too much money. Too confident. The first time I was ever alone with him he made a pass at me. I'd been to a dance in town and my car wouldn't start. Griffith offered me a lift home.'

'That was his name, Griffith?'

'Yes. Griffith Harvey.'

'Having trouble, Laura? Griffith Harvey was twenty years old, tall and well built, with chiselled good looks which fell just short of perfection because of an over sensuous mouth. He was too certain of his effect on women for Laura's taste, but most of the girls she knew did not agree with her. In the few short years since he had reached puberty, Griffith Harvey had notched up a long list of conquests around town.

'Oh, hi Griffith. The battery's dead. I guess I'll have to call my dad.'

'Don't bother about that. I'm heading home, I'll give you a ride.'

Laura locked her car and got in beside him. He put the car in gear and they began to move. It was a new coupe of some sort and the interior still smelled of leather. Harvey's parents were well off and they didn't hesitate to indulge their only son. They left the lights of town behind and after a few minutes hit the dirt road which wound into the hills where the Bailey and Harvey places were situated.

'That's a fine horse your daddy bought you, Laura.'

'He's beautiful isn't he?'

'Palomino. Just like you.'

Laura wasn't sure she liked being referred to in the same breath as a horse, but that was Griffith, not much finesse but plenty of confidence. The road led them

172

through open pasture country as it gently climbed into the hills. They passed through a heavily wooded area. Griffith was wearing a short-sleeved shirt with the sleeves rolled up almost to his shoulders to reveal the muscles of his biceps. A slight sheen of perspiration glistened on his forearms in the glow from the dashboard as he swung the wheel through the curves. Laura could feel the warmth emanating from him beside her. He slowed and pulled off into a side road.

'What are you doing, Griffith?' said Laura.

'I want to talk to you about something.'

The car came to a halt and he turned to Laura. 'You know when I saw you the other day riding that horse I thought I should be more neighbourly and ask you out sometime.'

'Well I don't go out much with boys.'

'I know. And I've been saying to myself, I wonder why that is? It must be that you just haven't found a boy that excites you yet.'

Harvey moved his arm onto the back of the seat and touched her on the shoulder. She was wearing a thin summer dress with narrow shoulder straps. He began to stroke lightly, his fingers straying under the strap. Laura was confused. One part of her told her she hated his smoothness, but there was an undeniable animal magnetism about him which she found at the same time repellent and attractive. She said nothing.

Harvey shifted closer to her. 'You need someone to light your fire, Laura.'

It was a hot night and she could smell a heady mixture of perspiration and aftershave coming from him. It was not unpleasant. She could feel perspiration prickling her own skin. He slowly pulled her towards him and put his mouth on hers. Laura had kissed boys before. Usually they tried to put their tongue in her mouth, which she found revolting. Kissing Griffith was different. It was nice. Her breath began to quicken. Griffith's free hand was stroking her leg under her skirt. For a moment she yielded then she put her own hand on top of his and held it tight. 'No Griffith, please don't do that. I'd like to go home now.'

Griffith Harvey knew that when girls said no they often really meant yes. All that was needed was a little persuasion. Little Laura Bailey with her tomboy pigtails and her gorgeous body was no different to the rest. He forced his hand higher up the inside of her thigh. Laura took her hand away and he smiled inwardly. All it took was a bit of persistence. He was about to touch her panties when her right fist caught him squarely in the right eye. He shook his head with surprise and she hit him again in the other one.

'Jesus Christ, what are you doing!'

'Take me home Griffith Harvey or I'll bust your goddamn nose.'

Bing laughed at the story. 'So you were a tough guy even then.'

'With Griffith you had to be. Anyway I went away to college and I didn't see him for a few years. I was working in a law firm as a researcher when the news came that my daddy had died in an air crash. Mother had died when I was very young and, well, Dad had brought me up himself. We were very close.

'I came home for the funeral and that's when I met Griffith again.'

The little town church was unable to accommodate all the mourners. They were packed shoulder to shoulder in every pew, cattlemen and their wives most of them, sweating in their Sunday best. Those who could not squeeze into the church crowded around the open doors to listen to the eulogies. Jim Bailey had been a popular and respected member of the farming community. His spread had been one of the best run and most profitable cattle ranches in all of Nebraska and his sudden death had come as a terrible shock to everyone.

Laura managed to fight off the tears all through the service and during the short trip to the churchyard. But when the first sod of earth fell with a dull thud onto the wooden lid she could hold back no longer.

As the crowd began to move away from the graveside they murmured messages of sympathy to the beautiful young woman dressed in black. Many of them remembered Laura from before she went away to college. She was Jim Bailey's only child, but if he was disappointed that she was a girl he had never showed it. He had done a fine job raising her. Why, from practically the moment she could walk she was in the saddle and by the time she was a teenager she could ride and rope and work a herd as well as any cowboy in the country.

How could anyone help but feel sorry for her? There had been that tragedy when the boy she was going to marry, a fine young airman by all accounts, had gone missing in the war, that damn war out in Indo-China that had taken so many young men. And now here she was, a lovely young woman suddenly finding herself the owner of a huge cattle ranch.

Griffith Harvey stood before her, turning his hat in his hands. 'Hello Laura, I'm awful sorry about your daddy, he was a good man and a fine rancher.'

Laura hardly registered what he was saying. Her thoughts were still full of images of the earth being shovelled in on top of the coffin. 'Thank you Griffith.'

'If there's anything I can do, any advice you need about running the ranch I'd be only too happy to oblige.'

'Thanks. That's neighbourly of you. I'm going to have to sit down and figure out what I'm going to do, but I'm kind of numb at the moment.'

'Of course. I understand. My own folks passed away some years back. Maybe I'll drop by in a day or two to see how you're getting on.'

Laura looked unseeingly at him and nodded.

At eleven o'clock in the morning five days later Griffith Harvey drove up in his Jeep station wagon and knocked on the door of the house. Laura let him in and led him through to the wood-panelled study where her father used to do his paperwork. It was a comfortable, homely room, with an old-fashioned roll-top desk with a thickly padded green leather swivel chair. On the walls were crowded together pictures of prize bulls, favourite horses and family portraits showing Laura in various stages of growing up. The carpet was worn and there was a couch where Jim Bailey sometimes used to take a nap in the afternoons. There were a couple of comfortable leather chairs and a low coffee table. Laura motioned Griffith to one of the chairs and sat down in the other. She had been drinking a cup of coffee and there was still some left in the pot. She poured one for her neighbour and another one for herself.

'Thank you kindly Laura, I believe I'll take one of those little bitty lumps of sugar you've got there. Thank you.'

Laura stirred her coffee absently. Griffith said, 'How are you getting on? I'm worried about you being here all by yourself with no one to talk to.'

'Oh I'm OK. I've got the place to run. Roy Aldridge is a good manager. He was with my dad since before I was born and he knows how to keep things going day to day.'

Laura took a sip of her coffee. She was putting on a brave face, but the truth was she was in a state of acute depression. The years of fruitless waiting for some news of Dan, the bland rebuffs by officialdom every time she attempted to find out if there was anything new, and now the sudden death of her father had left her in a vulnerable state. The coffee cup jiggled in the saucer and spilt. Wordlessly Laura placed it on the table and two tears began to roll down her face. Griffith put down his own cup, walked over and sat on the arm of the chair and put his arm around her. Laura buried her face in his shoulder and wept. 'There there, Laura,' he said. 'You just let it all come out. Old Griffith will be here when you need him.'

As he spoke his eyes roved over the pictures on the wall. There was some mighty nice breeding stock there. Mighty nice.

Laura gave up her job with the law firm in Los Angeles and moved back to the ranch for good. Griffith Harvey was an ever-helpful neighbour and an attentive friend. He advised her on matters relating to the running of the ranch and courted her with country manners. She saw no hint of the spoiled youth who had once attempted to molest her in his car. During all this time she remained faithful to the memory of Dan, persuading herself that when the war ended he would be released from whatever prison he had been held in for so many years and would come home.

When the Paris peace meetings began she followed every development avidly through newspapers and television. Then the accords were signed and it was announced that 591 prisoners were to be released. By then she knew that Dan would not be among them, yet still, with a last desperate hope, she watched the live television coverage of the POWs' arrival. Dressed in immaculate uniforms they filed down the aircraft steps and ran forward to embrace their loved ones. Laura scanned each face anxiously as if even now, by some miracle Dan's might be among them. The jubilant crowd waved American flags and a brass band played. The President, swept up in the emotion of the moment, spoke from a rostrum high above the assembled well-wishers. When he said the words, 'All of our brave men are back home again,' she knew she could wait for Dan no longer.

Griffith Harvey and Laura Bailey were married in the same church where the service for her father had been held. All the people of the district agreed it was a perfect match. The union brought together under one name two families and two of the richest cattle ranches in Nebraska.

Bing said, 'What went wrong?'

It was a question Laura had asked herself many times. The fact that she did not love her husband did not come as a blinding revelation. At some time, perhaps in the fourth or fifth year of marriage, she simply accepted that there was no passion in their partnership. Making love with Griffith was never a tender experience. He was quick and rough and afterwards she felt used and unfulfilled. She could have lived with this, but she came to realise very early on that he was not the upright, courtly countryman he portrayed. Rather he was a deal-maker and a politician, dabbling in businesses all over the state and thick with the inner circle of cronies who ran the town.

Why did she continue with a loveless marriage to a man she was beginning to despise? Later she came to the conclusion that she simply didn't care enough to do anything about it. She was busy with the ranch and when they attended social events together they managed a veneer of cordiality which fooled everyone. After the emotional turmoil of the past years it needed a catalyst to spur her into action.

It was one of the rare evenings when Griffith was home. After they'd eaten together he asked her to sit with him for a moment on the verandah. She was sipping coffee, enjoying the faint chill of early fall. In the distance there was a rumble of thunder and the horizon was lit now and then by lightning. The air smelled moist with coming rain. He swirled brandy in a balloon glass, held it to his nose, sniffed it appreciatively, tilted his head back and swallowed.

'I've been planning a few changes next door, Laura, and I want to discuss them with you. I've been talking to some people in town, rural industries are on the decline, the future lies in tourism. We've formed a consortium to develop the ranch into a hotel and holiday resort.'

Laura was stunned. 'Why? The ranch is doing well. We've had one of the best years ever.'

'The money you can make out of ranching is nothing compared to resorts. I'm not talking about some tin-pot little development, I'm talking about a major enterprise: golf courses, tennis courts, swimming pools, horse riding; it'll put this place on the map and it'll make me a very rich man.'

'Aren't you rich enough already?' said Laura.

He grinned and shook his head. 'That's something you've never understood about me, Laura. You've never approved of my business interests. Well, honey, despite your disapproval I'm just getting started.'

'I don't see how you can do it anyway, Griffith. The whole area's zoned rural. You'll have to get it rezoned. The town will never allow it.'

He tapped the side of his nose. 'Don't you worry about the rezoning, that'll all be attended to.'

Until now Laura had been merely curious. Now the implications of the scheme began to sink in. 'And what do you think it'll be like having a monstrous resort right next door to here? Have you thought of how that kind of development might affect this place, not to mention the environment generally?'

'It's progress, Laura. Can't you see that? If you'd like to put some money in you can get in on the ground floor.'

'You can't seriously think I'd help finance the destruction of everything I hold dear. My father would turn in his grave if he thought I was a party to a scheme like that.'

Griffith leaned forward and patted her knee. She instinctively recoiled from his touch. 'Look,' he said smoothly, 'it's a lot to take in. I've got all the plans and income projections, everything you need to see how it'll work. When you're ready I'll explain it all to you in detail. Just think about it.'

Laura got to her feet and looked down on him with contempt. 'I'll fight you on this Griffith, I'll fight you with everything I have. *You* think about *that.*'

She stalked away from the verandah and went into her father's study. It was exactly as it had been when he died. She'd kept it unchanged in memory of him. She sat down at the roll-top desk and began to pore over the accounts. After a time she realised she'd been staring at the same set of figures for several minutes. Still angry, she went into the bedroom and got under the covers but she could not sleep, she was seething at the thought of him planning his betrayal for goodness knows how long without telling her.

Next morning she could not put the development out of her mind. Griffith had already left. She thought if she could just sit down and talk some sense into him, explain to him that what he had in mind could ruin not only the ranch but the character of the community they had both been raised in, he might still see some reason. She had a hurried snack and headed off.

She knew where he'd be. As his business interests had burgeoned he had turned his old home next door into an office. He had been in the habit lately of going there on Saturday mornings to work alone. He said he could get much more done that way, without interruptions. Laura drove up the sweeping drive which led to the house and parked under a grove of pine trees next to Griffith's Lincoln and a little red sports car. It looked as if he had been unable to avoid interruptions after all.

She walked up the front steps to the open front door in her sneakers. Griffith's office was down the hall and to the left where the dining room used to be. As she started down the hall she heard him laugh and then the murmur of a woman's voice. The door to the office was shut. She opened it onto a scene similar to the one she had stumbled upon on the night she met Dan. This time the man was not lying on a bed in a darkened bedroom but sitting in her husband's padded office chair. There was one other similarity which struck her. The woman who raised her head in alarm from Griffith's lap was about the same age as the teenage girl she'd surprised all those years ago.

It was mid-afternoon the same day when Griffith Harvey arrived back home with a squeal of brakes. It was a windless day and the dust hung like a shroud through which her husband strode, heading towards the yard where Laura was watching some rousebouts castrating young steers. She stood with her hands on her hips and watched him coming. Roy Aldridge tipped his hat. 'Afternoon Griffith.'

Griffith ignored him. 'Could I have a word with you, Laura?'

'I'm busy, Griffith.' Laura took the knife that one of the men had been using and motioned to his assistant to throw the steer.

She bent down to the squirming animal and with a few deft movements sliced its testicles off. Clasping them firmly in her hand she walked over to where Harvey stood. 'You've got half an hour to get all your possessions out of here. If you ever come back I'll cut your balls off.' She threw the bleeding gonads in his face. 'Now get off my land.'

Bing had been listening to her narrative with rapt attention. 'What happened to his development plans?'

'I made it clear to him that if he went ahead I'd see that the Internal Revenue Service had a good close look at some of his deals. I knew they wouldn't stand up to close scrutiny. He shelved the idea and a little while later we were quietly divorced.'

'And you decided to find out once and for all about Dan.'

'If I'd been happily married I probably never would have felt the need.'

'I wonder.' He paused, absorbing the story he had just heard.

Sensing that further questions would not be welcome, he merely sat there in silence. Laura was getting used to these silences. When he had nothing to say Bing did not rush to fill the gap but would unembarrassedly slip into repose. She did not feel the need to talk further. They sat together companionably, each lost in their thoughts, as the airliner thrust its way blindly through the clouds.

Seventeen

In Washington the day had begun badly for President Blanchard. The *New York Times* and the *Washington Post* had both carried prominent stories about the likely defeat of his tax reform bill in the Congress and he had had a silly argument with his wife over the guest list for next week's state dinner with the Japanese Prime Minister. Brandon Paine called and asked for a meeting and he could tell by the tone of his voice that he had unpleasant news. When Paine walked in the door of the Oval Office, Blanchard was behind his desk. He did not get up to greet him as he normally would.

'What have you got Brandon?' he said.

'I got a NODIS from Hammond in Moscow overnight. Connick and Bailey have already left for Saryshagan.'

'Shit,' said the President. 'Saryshagan. Where the hell is this place?'

'It's about fifteen hundred miles south-east of Moscow, over there on top of Afghanistan and near China.' Paine thought for a moment, choosing his words carefully. 'The location presents a problem. It's a small Kazakh town and we can't operate there the same way as in Moscow.' He paused again for a moment. He wanted to get the timing right. 'But the Russians could.'

The President looked at Paine in appreciation. He had

come bearing bad news but it was typical of him that he had already thought of a solution to the problem. Automatically, he began to think through the ramifications of the suggestion. Both of them understood well enough if it became public knowledge that Americans were taken to Russia in secret it would give added strength to those hawks on the hill who wanted to cast the Soviet Union adrift and watch it disintegrate. The question was, would the Russians see this? It took him only a few moments to decide that President Ivashov would grasp the implications instinctively. He would be just as anxious to prevent exposure as Blanchard.

The President turned to Paine and said, 'It's a good idea, Brandon, but I can't just ask Ivashov for help with a thing like this.'

'It doesn't have to be a direct request, Mr President. You can put it in oblique language. Outline the problem, explain the repercussions. Ask politely for any suggestions he might have which will help us to attain our mutual goals of stability and world peace. One statesman to another.'

Blanchard nodded. 'How would we communicate with him?'

Paine knew what he meant. It was practically impossible for anyone at the higher levels of the administration to have a completely private conversation with his opposite number. At the State Department, for instance, all telephone calls were routed through the Operations Room, where even internal conversations were randomly recorded as a routine security measure. The State Department had secure lines to the US Embassy in Moscow, designed so that conversations could not be picked up by satellites. But this was too sensitive to go through the embassy where extra people would be involved.

Even the President found it difficult to communicate with his opposite number in complete privacy. There was the so-called hot line, which was commonly thought to be a red telephone sitting on the President's desk but in fact was in the Situation Room in the bowels of the White

House. It looked like an ordinary, black, telephone-fax machine. Conversations on the hot line were automatically recorded and, as with calls through the embassy, they would have to be interpreted at one end or the other.

'We could call in Popov,' suggested Paine, referring to the Russian Ambassador to the United States.

'Hmm. Even if he came late at night there's always the chance some journalist might spot him,' said Blanchard. 'And you know the staff here leak like sieves. I think it would be too risky.'

'Yes you're right,' said Paine. 'I was going to suggest he came to my private address, but the same thing applies. The last thing we need is for some damn newsman to start sniffing around.'

The two men discussed other ways of using the Russian Ambassador and finally rejected them all. They knew the Ambassador had his own channels of communication back to Moscow, but even if they got a message to him in secret they would have no control over how many people would become privy to it.

Some US Presidents, notably Ronald Reagan, wrote letters in longhand to their opposite number, which would then be delivered through a third party. In order to ensure that the exact nuances of language were correctly conveyed, the translation was always done at the American end. As they pondered the problem further, Blanchard and Paine came to the conclusion that a combination of methods might work best. The President could call on the hot line and tell the Russian leader to expect a hand-delivered message. A courier could be despatched to London via Concorde and would then fly on the regular London-to-Moscow service. It would be slow but reasonably secure. The only flaw was that someone would first have to translate the message at the American end. There was no shortage of fluent Russian speakers in both the State Department and on Paine's staff. The problem was finding one whom they could trust. After mulling it over for a while Paine said to the President, 'I'll give it some thought.'

'Find the right man, Brandon,' said the President. 'For both our sakes.'

Paine left the President to compose his message and returned to his office, where he called for the personal files of all fluent Russian speakers available to the National Security Agency. When he began going through them he realised that he had a problem. The Agency was full of extremely bright, ambitious, highly motivated people. They all had the sort of flair which would carry them to the heights of the bureaucracy, but which would make them a dangerous choice for the task he had in mind. It wasn't until he had reached the seventh file that he found what he was looking for. Leaning over to his intercom he punched his secretary's button and said, 'I'm expecting a sealed envelope from the President. As soon as it arrives, I want you to bring it in and have Ross Sellars come to the office.'

'Ross Sellars, sir?'

'He's a translator.'

Sellars was a career foreign service officer attached to the NSA. Paine knew from his personal file that he was not a self-starter. He was steady, reliable, loyal and showed little sign of initiative. He was perfect.

After a few minutes the secretary ushered in a short man with dark curly hair and horn-rimmed glasses and handed Paine a sealed envelope with the Presidential seal on it. Paine greeted Sellars, walked him over to an informal lounge setting and asked him if he would like coffee. Surprised, he accepted and waited nervously for his boss to come out with whatever was on his mind.

'I've been looking at your file,' Paine said. 'You've been doing good work, Sellars. You've got talent and it hasn't gone unnoticed.'

Sellars muttered his thanks for this unsolicited panegyric, but it did not dispel his wariness. He had been around government long enough to know that this was leading somewhere and he was waiting for the 'but'. Paine put the President's envelope down on the coffee table. 'This is a personal letter from the President to

Ivashov. I want you to translate it and return the translation and the original to me.'

Sellars knew that a letter of this sort would normally be handled by the President's office or someone at State. However, he did not express his surprise to the National Security Adviser. Instead he nodded and said, 'No problem sir, I can get onto it right away.'

'You'll see when you read it that the contents of the letter are sensitive. They are of the utmost importance to the security of this nation. I'm sure I don't have to tell you that absolute secrecy is essential.'

'Of course not, sir, that goes without saying.'

'Just so. Now, how will you write the translation?'

'On a computer sir. I have a program with the Cyrillic alphabet.'

'Is your PC connected to the mainframe?'

'It can be.'

'I want you to isolate it completely. And when you've printed it I want you to trash the document. No copies. No trace of it. Do you understand?'

Sellars was even more intrigued. 'Yes sir, you've got it.'

Paine rose to signify that the meeting was over. Sellars gulped down the last of his coffee and put the letter in his coat pocket. As they walked to the door Paine clapped him on the back. 'Well done, Ross. I've got my eye on you. You're going far. Depend on it.'

Back in his office, Sellars closed the door, sat down at his desk and opened the President's letter. Skimming quickly through the formal salutations at the beginning, he reached the main text. He read with amazement about the President's knowledge of the MBs and his analysis of the damage it could cause if the details ever got out. When he reached the part describing the activities of Bing Connick and Laura Bailey, he whistled quietly behind his teeth. The request for Russian intervention was couched in diplomatic language, but to Sellars, as it would be to the Russian leader, it was obvious what he was asking.

Sellars shook his head in wonder, locked his office door and began work. It took an hour to translate the document onto his computer screen. After he had finished he read through both the English and Russian texts carefully again, making sure that every nuance was correct. Then he printed out two copies. Sellars took the original letter in the President's handwriting and photocopied it. He then placed the original plus one copy of the translation in a sealed envelope. The copy of the original and the other copy of the translation he put in another envelope and placed under some papers in the bottom drawer of his desk. He would find a safe place for it later. This done, Sellars lifted the telephone and called Brandon Paine. He tried to make his voice noncommittal. 'All done sir. I can bring it over right away.'

'Well done, Ross, and you understand now what I meant about the importance of secrecy.'

'Oh yes sir, absolutely. No copies.'

'That's right, Ross. No copies.'

The airliner carrying Laura, Bing and Askar descended in a series of sickening lurches. Passengers who had been circulating as if at a social gathering swayed along the aisles like drunken sailors, heading back to their seats for landing. The peasants remained standing in the aisle, chatting animatedly, grasping the overhead parcel shelves like straphangers on a bus. The stewardesses had disappeared again. Laura and Bing checked their seat belts nervously and tried to appear calm.

Outside, the air was still opaque. As Laura peered through the window the cloud began to thin and she caught glimpses of flat, barren-looking country with patches of vegetation showing through the snow. The ground was coming up fast, too fast it seemed. The lights marking the end of the tarmac flashed past but still the airliner seemed to hover as if reluctant to touch down. It dropped heavily the last few feet and the engines screamed.

'Looks like we made it,' said Bing.

'I wasn't worried for a moment,' grinned Laura.

Balkhash airport was a neglected-looking grey concrete building full of people waiting to welcome friends and relatives from the Moscow flight. There was no baggage carousel. Some attendants wheeled two steel trolleys into the main concourse and left the passengers to rummage through the pile of cheap cardboard suitcases and packages tied with string. They collected their bags and walked through into the main hall. A man wearing thick baggy trousers and an old suit coat buttoned across a couple of shapeless pullovers stepped forward. He had a white beard and was wearing a black skull cap decorated with a silver coloured motif. He stepped up to Askar and embraced him, kissing him on both cheeks and murmuring something in Kazakh. When he disengaged himself Askar turned to Bing and Laura and introduced them.

'This is my Uncle Nurlan,' he said.

Nurlan, who looked to be in his sixties, seized their hands one by one and shook them. His palms were hard and callused. Askar had explained to them that his uncle had worked all his life on a collective farm. Under perestroika agriculture was being privatised. Nurlan had obtained a small parcel of land on which he raised cattle and sheep and grew fruit and vegetables.

Outside the airport the temperature was near freezing point but nowhere near as extreme as it had been in Moscow. There were few cars and the passengers were dispersing into buses and trucks. Nurlan spoke briefly to Askar before disappearing into the crowd. Askar said, 'My uncle has managed to borrow a vehicle. He'll be back in a minute.'

A short time later Nurlan pulled up in a battered-looking van. Askar got into the front seat and the others climbed in the back where a couple of packing cases had been placed for them to sit on. With a grinding of gears the decrepit vehicle moved forward and away from the airport environs. Askar leaned over the back of the seat and said, 'It's 140 kilometres to Saryshagan. It should take us about three hours.'

The road took them through flat, impoverished-looking country. Here and there they came across small settlements of drab, cement-rendered houses, mostly unpainted. Herds of scrawny cattle and sheep stood stoically in the cold. As they travelled Askar engaged in animated conversation with his uncle. The old man swivelled round in his seat to give them a broad smile.

'I was telling him about Dan Parkinson,' said Askar. 'I told him if we find out what happened to him it could be very embarrassing for Russia. My uncle likes that. He hates Russians. There are more of them here than us. They have always had the best jobs and we are second-class citizens. He is very pleased to be able to help you.'

Bing nodded and clapped the old man lightly on the back.

'My uncle knows everyone,' Askar continued. 'Including people working at Priazorsk.'

After about three hours the van turned off the main road and began bumping along a dirt track, the springs and body rattling and groaning. Askar explained that the settlement where his uncle lived was off the road just before the town of Saryshagan. Ten minutes later they came to another cluster of dwellings like the ones they had passed along the way. They squealed to a halt beside a house painted pastel green. Three children aged from about eight to twelve ran out to greet them. They threw their arms around Nurlan and then Askar, chattering excitedly. When Askar introduced them to Laura and Bing they fell into shy silence.

'These are my uncle's grandchildren,' said Askar, tousling the eldest boy's hair affectionately.

'Where are their father and mother?' asked Laura, smiling at the children.

'Their father is out with the animals,' replied Askar. 'And their mother is inside. Come.' He motioned for them to follow him.

They followed Askar into a big room with wooden

189

floors covered with exotic looking rugs. More rugs hung on the walls. The room was furnished with a mixture of cheap, mass-produced and heavy, hand-made furniture. A long wooden trestle table stood in the centre. A woman of about thirty, wearing a voluminous dress which covered her from throat to ankles and a headscarf, stepped forward and welcomed them. 'This is Gulnar,' said Askar. 'My uncle's daughter-in-law.'

Gulnar smiled a welcome and said something in Kazakh. It was apparent that no one, apart from Askar, spoke a word of English.

Laura and Bing were each shown to a room which they presumed must be the childrens' bedrooms. They were simply furnished with narrow beds piled high with rugs and blankets, a chair and little else. By the time they returned to the main room of the house, the sky outside was turning dark and cooking smells were permeating the atmosphere. The children had begun setting the big trestle table for dinner when there was a stamping of boots outside the front door. The door banged open and a man of about thirty years of age entered the house. It was Nurlan's son, Kanat.

Askar stepped forward and embraced him before introducing him to the others. 'How do you do,' said Kanat, stiltedly. 'Welcome to our home.'

'Thank you for having us,' said Laura, but from his blank smile it was evident that Kanat had reached the limits of his English.

They sat down at table. The three travellers had not eaten all day and the smell of cooking food was intoxicating.

'What do you normally eat in Kazakhstan?' Laura asked Askar, while the children busied themselves in the kitchen.

'A lot of meat,' he replied. 'At the start of winter two or three families kill a horse or a cow and then we salt or dry the meat so it will last.'

'And how do you cook it?' said Laura.

'We boil it mostly.'

Gulnar was watching this exchange with interest. 'Can I see?' said Laura, smiling at her.

Askar spoke to her and she giggled with appreciation. Gulnar stood up and, taking Laura by the hand, led her to the kitchen at the back of the house. There she pointed out a crude fuel stove with a neatly stacked pile of dried cow dung beside it. On top of the stove a huge, round-bottomed pot was simmering. Beside the stove were plate-sized sheets of pasta waiting to be served. She pointed to the pot and the pasta in turn and said, 'Beshbarmack.'

Laura turned to Askar. 'What is it?'

'Salted cow.'

With Askar translating, Gulnar explained how they cooked the pasta in broth from the meat. Gulnar pointed at a smaller pot of simmering broth with lumps of meat submerged in it.

'And this?'

'Kazy.'

'A kind of sausage made from the rib of a horse,' Askar explained. 'We put it bone and all into a skin of intestine and cook it.'

Gulnar dipped a ladle into the pot and offered it to Laura to taste. This she did, with much smacking lips and noises of approval.

They all returned to the main room and at a word of command from their father the children brought the great pot out to the centre of the table. Each person's plate was covered with a slab of pasta onto which were ladled chopped pieces of meat.

Nurlan had been noting their curiosity with approval. Now he took the ladle from his son and dipped it in the pot until he found the delicacy he was looking for. With a flourish he offered it to Bing, who held out his plate upon which Kanat deposited an eye. He leaned back and looked at Bing expectantly. There was a hush as the others all waited for his reaction.

Without hesitation Bing speared the glistening orb with his fork and popped it into his mouth. He chewed appreciatively and put his thumb and forefinger together in a universal gesture of approval. The silence broke. The rest of the family began eating and soon the table was loud with conversation.

'The eye is always given to the guest of honour,' Askar said. 'I was wondering how you would react. Nurlan and Kanat are already impressed by you both.'

Laura said, 'Have you explained to Kanat why we're here?'

Askar nodded and began speaking in Kazakh to his cousin. As he spoke, Laura had a chance to observe the powerfully built herdsman. He had the same ruddy-cheeked Mongol features as the rest of his family, and there was a certain gravitas about his demeanour. Kanat was listening attentively, without interruption. In contrast to Askar's street-smart intelligence, there was an air of quiet capability about him. If he was surprised or alarmed at what Askar was telling him he did not show it. When Askar had finished talking, Kanat looked at them both and nodded.

'Is it possible to go to Priazorsk?' asked Bing.

Askar repeated the question to Kanat and translated his reply. 'He says that there is a regular bus from Saryshagan to Priazorsk and back each day for people who work on the base. But you have to have a special pass. There are also checks along the road and sometimes helicopter patrols as well. There is no way an unauthorised civilian can go there.'

Kanat spoke again at length and Askar again translated. 'Our family has been here for many many years. They know many people, including some who work on the base. It may be that some discreet inquiries could be made. Also, you have one thing which is in very short supply in Kazakhstan and which may be very helpful.'

'And what is that?' said Bing.

'Dollars.'

Bing laughed. 'What's the penalty for bribing someone on a military base?' he said.

Askar translated for the benefit of the rest of the

family. Kanat grinned mischievously and replied with a word they could all understand.

'Gulag,' he said. His face split into laughter. Chuckling merrily, he rolled his eyes hideously and put an imaginary gun to Bing's head.

'Boom,' he said and, slapping his knee at the joke, laughed even harder. Bing could not help himself. The laughter was infectious. Before long he too was rolling in his seat with helpless merriment.

Laura was smiling uncomfortably. 'They have an odd sense of humour,' she said.

Clutching his sides, Bing found it difficult to speak. Finally he gasped out a few words. 'I think I'm going to like these people.'

The next day the household woke early and Kanat left before dawn to milk and feed his cattle. The travellers could hear movement in the house but they remained where they were, luxuriating in the warmth of the rugs piled high on their beds. When they arose, there was a pale sun shining and the house was warm from the stove. Gulnar gave them each breakfast of kozhe, semolina boiled with yoghurt, nan, a flat crusty bread and tea. They had just finished this meal when there was a knock on the door. Gulnar opened it and ushered in a big man with an overfed, jowly look about him. He removed his overcoat to reveal a shiny double-breasted suit, a white shirt with a grimy collar and a thin tie. He was Abdullah Omarov, Askar explained, the local Communist Party chief. Even before he was introduced, Bing could tell that he was a petty bureaucrat of some sort. There was no mistaking the air of pomposity with which he conducted himself. Omarov launched into a flowery speech.

'Comrade Omarov says he welcomes you to Kazakhstan and he trusts that your stay will be a pleasant and fruitful one,' said Askar.

'Please thank him for his kindness. We are looking forward to making many friends here.'

'He asks if there is anything he can do to assist you?'

'Thank you, we have everything we need.'

'He says he hopes your visit will give you a greater knowledge of the Kazakh people and further understanding between our two countries,' said Askar, winking at Bing.

The overblown exchange went on with Bing smiling at the official as he made his replies. Omarov smiled back.

Gulnar came in with tea and they all sat around the big table. For half an hour they exchanged platitudes. At last, with much bowing and hand-shaking, Omarov got up and left. When the door had closed Askar said, 'I told him you are a couple of crazy American tourists, here to sample Kazakh village life.'

'Do you think he believed you?' Bing said.

'Probably not. He will report back to party headquarters in Saryshagan. By this afternoon there will be a message to Moscow saying that you are here.'

'We need to start work,' said Bing.

'Nurlan will go into Saryshagan and see his friends tonight.'

'Ask him not to mention the name of the American. Just the approximate date we think he would have been there.'

Askar tapped the side of his nose and winked. 'Not a problem,' he said.

Later that day they were sitting at the big table drinking tea. Bing asked, 'How hard will it be to find people to help us, do you think?'

'It will be easy,' replied Askar. 'And I will tell you why. The people around here used to be nomadic. In the 1930s Stalin decided to industrialise Kazakhstan. He set up mines and factories and heavy industries and then imported Russians and Germans to run them. The herdsmen were forced to give up their way of life and were sent to work on collective farms. If they resisted they were massacred.'

He paused to angrily slurp his tea. 'Near my home in Sempalatinsk they used to test their nuclear weapons and

194

they didn't care where the fallout went. In my village 50 per cent of the people are affected by radiation. There are children born without eyes, or with deformed limbs. There was one child born dead who had only one eye in the middle of his forehead. Very few people live to an old age, they all die of cancer.

'In the Aral Sea to the west of here they dumped so much fertiliser and wastes from the factories that almost half the people in that region suffer from sickness. The pollution is in the air and in the water. You can't escape it. Because of all the water they have drawn from the streams feeding the sea it has shrunk so much that the fishing industry has died. You can see the fishing fleets sitting on the mud, just rusting away. Whole fishing towns which used to be on the shores have had to be abandoned.'

Askar waved his arm in a savage gesture and continued. 'Over there in the east the Caspian Sea is the same. They diverted the rivers for agriculture and industry and the lake has shrunk by five thousand square miles. The sturgeon industry is on the verge of collapse. Those bastard Russians have turned this country into a toxic wasteland. You can see why it will not be difficult to find Kazakhs willing to help you.'

'I hope Nurlan can turn someone up soon,' said Bing. 'The longer we're here, the more uncomfortable I feel.'

'There are people who work at the base whom he can trust. Maybe soon we will hear something.'

Eighteen

Igor Bakutin, the Director of the KGB, had been only recently appointed to the post, but President Ivashov had had his eye on him for a long time. One of the things he liked about Bakutin was that his career had been outside the intelligence community. He had proven himself an able administrator in a number of difficult posts, had been ambitious and tough enough to prosper during the years of hard-line communism, and had been politically aware enough to roll with the changes which had swept many less flexible bureaucrats into obscurity. The President was sure he would understand what needed to be done when he showed him his American counterpart's letter.

The letter had been hand-delivered at nine-thirty in the morning. Within an hour Bakutin's black Zil limousine had made the short trip from KGB Headquarters to the Kremlin building in Red Square. He was ushered into the President's office, wondering what was so important that he had suddenly been asked to drop everything.

After welcoming him, the President pushed across the letter. Bakutin read it in silence. When he had finished he handed it back. 'Interesting.'

'Do you know anything about Americans being brought here?' asked Ivashov.

'Nothing. But I would not rule out the possibility. The KGB has always been a law unto itself, as you know.'

It was a criticism with which he knew the President agreed. 'I don't doubt it either,' said Ivashov. 'The question is what do we do about it?'

Bakutin noted the 'we' with satisfaction. He had the ear of the President and there was no telling how far he could go if he acquitted himself well in his new job. His first reaction was that they should agree to help the Americans but he wanted to hear what the President had to say first.

'Blanchard is correct when he writes that the political repercussions could be a hindrance for us,' Bakutin said.

'And for him, Igor,' said Ivashov. 'Don't forget that. And for him.'

'He is asking us for a pretty big favour.'

'Yes. And as much as I hate to help him out, the fact is we need him firmly in control. We can't just let these two pursue their inquiries unhindered.'

Now that Bakutin could see where his President was heading, he decided it was safe to offer his own suggestion. 'They'll have to be stopped.'

'I agree. They seem to have remarkably good sources of information to have got as far as they have,' said the President. 'KGB sources perhaps,' he added pointedly.

'You know what I inherited. The organisation is a mess. Who knows what leaks there are.'

'Indeed,' said the President drily.

Bakutin was silent. 'I have made a decision about this,' the President continued. 'You will take steps to stop the Americans. It will have to be handled quietly. No fuss.'

Bakutin nodded. 'We'll look after it. Saryshagan is a wild place. Far enough from Moscow for news to be confused. I'll have someone see to it.'

'And by the way. Find out what happened to this prisoner, Parkinson. He may be another loose end that will have to be tidied up.'

Fifteen minutes after arriving, Bakutin was in his limousine heading back to the office. When he arrived he made two telephone calls. The first was to the Head of Counterintelligence whom he summoned to his office at once.

It was a new experience for Bakutin to order an assassination. He was not exactly aware of how it was done, only that such things were handled by Counterintelligence. The head of the department, Pasha Ponomaryov, was a product of the Cold War years; clever, a careerist and an implacable enemy of the United States. Bakutin did not particularly like him and he was sure his Counterintelligence chief returned the distrust, so he decided not to tell him everything about the background. It would be better if he painted the Americans in simple terms as spying against Russian interests.

'Comrade Ponomaryov,' Bakutin began, deliberately formalising his language. 'We have a problem at the air defence establishment at Saryshagan.'

'Kazakhstan.'

'Yes. I congratulate you on your knowledge of geography.' Bakutin could not help his sarcasm. He knew Ponomaryov regarded him as an amateur. Well, he would learn soon enough who was running this show.

'There are two Americans there, a man and a woman. They are travelling on the pretext of tourism, but their true purpose is to make inquiries about Priazorsk.'

The Head of Counterintelligence wondered how Bakutin had come by this information, but he held his peace. He listened impassively while the KGB director explained what was known about Laura and Bing's movements. He longed for the old days when the organisation was run by hard-nosed professionals like himself. However, the political climate had changed and for the time being at least he would have to accommodate this blow-in whom the President had seen fit to put in charge.

'They will have to be stopped,' said Bakutin.

'You mean eliminated. Might as well speak plainly, Comrade Director. Don't you agree?'

Bakutin allowed the implied slight to pass by unremarked. 'How will you do it?' he asked.

Ponomaryov stared at his boss without expression. 'We have people who are very good at this sort of thing. Professionals.'

Bakutin gazed back at his Counterintelligence chief with distaste. 'I'm sure you have,' he said drily. 'Please let me know when it is done.'

The second telephone call was to the Chief Archivist. Bakutin told him to investigate the files and see if there was any record of an American prisoner of war named Parkinson being brought to the Soviet Union for interrogation and to find out what happened to him. The search was to be given priority over anything else the archivist was working on and he was to report in person back to the Director.

The KGB archives occupy a labyrinth of underground rooms beneath the headquarters building. The files are kept in folders stored on rows of shelves behind wire-mesh doors. Dusty and yellowing, they contain stories of terror and death dating back to the beginnings of the KGB under Beria. They record the terrible purges of Lenin and Stalin as they administered a political system which relied upon fear for its survival. The Chief Archivist decided to look after this search personally.

Walking down two flights of stairs from his office to the file room, he instructed a clerk to find him the appropriate references. He returned with a red-bound book which looked like a bank ledger. The Chief Archivist sat down at a wobbly table with a reading lamp over it and proceeded to pore over the handwritten entries. After twenty-three years the ink had faded, but still he could distinguish the writing well enough to find what he was looking for.

After a few minutes he nodded and motioned to the clerk to take him into the archive room. Taking a key with a large wooden tag attached by a twist of rusty wire, the clerk led him down a dusty corridor past several wire-mesh doors. Arriving at the correct one he inserted the key and slid the door back on squeaking rollers. He clicked on a light and led the way down to the end of a row of shelves. Leaving his boss, he went off and after a few minutes returned with a stepladder.

Dismissing him, the Chief Archivist mounted the rungs and on a top shelf found the pile of folders he was looking for. Using his handkerchief to flap off the dust, he selected a grey folder, climbed back down to floor level and left the archive room, making his way back to the desk.

He opened the folder and began to read. The first interrogations of the prisoner Parkinson had taken place at Son Tay prison camp in North Vietnam. They had been carried out by Vietnamese with KGB personnel sitting out of sight behind screens, occasionally passing through written suggestions for questions. The prisoner had proved obstinate at first but, as is usually the case, when he broke he told everything. The file did not go into detail about the information except that it was to do with anti-missile warfare.

The prisoner had proved so useful that he had been taken to the Soviet Union, travelling with a KGB team through a special border post into Kazakhstan. As he read on about the subsequent history of Parkinson the Chief Archivist pursed his lips and uttered a soft whistle. That was what he liked about this job. People thought it was boring spending your days with indexes and files, but they were full of history and every now and then you came across something really amazing. He looked forward to delivering the file personally to the Director and could not wait to see the look on his face when he told him what it contained.

Nineteen

The children cleared away the plates from breakfast and Laura and Bing stepped out of the hut into a pale, faintly sunny day. The landscape was drawn in shades of grey: grey steppe stretching away to infinity, merging into grey sky. Kanat was in the yard beside the house staring at a cow, a worried expression on his face. As they watched, the animal bellowed in pain and its stomach convulsed rapidly. Its tail was sticking out horizontal to the ground. It bellowed again, bent its knees and delicately collapsed onto the ground.

Laura walked over and stroked the cow, then stepped around behind. About six inches of a calf's leg was sticking out. 'How long ago did the water burst?' she said.

Askar repeated the question. Kanat gave her a quizzical look and murmured a reply. 'About four hours ago.'

'It's a breech birth.'

'How can you tell?' Bing said.

'Look at that foot, the bottom of the hoof is turned upwards. Not only that, the other leg is caught in the uterus. Someone's going to have to do something soon or the cow and the calf will die.'

Askar and Kanat launched into a conversation in Kazakh, then Askar turned to Laura and said, 'He would try to pull it out but is afraid the leg will damage the mother.'

'He's right, it will. They've got pretty sharp little hooves, even when they're first born. Would he like me to help?'

Askar shook his head in amazement, but he repeated the question. Kanat shrugged and gestured with an upraised palm to the cow. Laura took off her coat, rolled up the right sleeve of her blouse and plunged her hand into the cow's vagina. Her arm disappeared past the elbow and she began feeling around inside. 'It's a bit tricky. You've got to feel for the hoof and manoeuvre it around into position. I can feel it now.' The others watched curiously as Laura concentrated on her task. The cow lay patiently without struggling. After several minutes she let out a grunt of satisfaction. 'There, that's got it.'

She withdrew her arm and the second leg emerged. Laura turned to Kanat. 'Come on, we'll pull it out together.'

Laura sat on the ground with one foot against the cow's rump and two hands firmly grasping one of the calf's hooves. Kanat sat down beside her with the other. 'OK. One, two, heave.' The two of them pulled together and the leg emerged a few inches. Laura counted again. 'One, two, heave.' A few more inches of leg came out.

Working together to Laura's instructions, the two of them gradually pulled more and more of the calf clear until the shoulders and head were all that remained inside.

'This is the hard part,' said Laura. Nodding to Kanat she grasped the calf's leg again. 'One, two, heave.' Together they pulled. The cow bellowed in pain. Laura counted down again and they leaned back like a pair of scullers straining at the oars. For a few seconds nothing happened, then the calf began to move. The shoulders appeared and the glistening wet newborn slithered out onto the ground. The cow bellowed once more, heaved itself to its feet and began to lick its baby.

Laura and Kanat grinned at each other. They got to their feet and Kanat said something, motioning towards the open steppe.

'He asks if you would like to accompany him while he watches the herd today,' Askar translated.

'Yes,' said Laura, 'we'd love to.' Kanat opened the gate and shooed the cattle out and away from the village. Walking slowly behind them he allowed them to spread out across the landscape like insubstantial ghosts. Snow lightly dusted the ground. A chill wind rippled the grass like water. Flanking the herd, the three people strolled along without talking. Nothing needed to be said.

They were sitting on a mound, watching the herd grazing when Kanat broke into song. It was a mournful atonal chant, the progressions and rhythms sounding alien to a Western ear. Laura had the feeling that she was in a place where time had ceased to have any meaning. She could imagine a herdsman no different to Kanat sitting here a hundred, a thousand years ago, singing his wild discordant song and watching the herd with exactly the same sense of endless patience.

When they returned at the end of the day and herded the animals inside the yard the newborn calf was on its feet suckling happily. Kanat turned to them with a grin and said again the only words in English that he knew, 'Welcome to our home.'

There was nothing that Bing or Laura could do except wait. With her background on the land, Laura adapted easily to the life of the family. Bing took to going out every day with Kanat. Even if he had been able to converse with him it is unlikely they would have spoken much. Bing had become taciturn living alone on his Australian river, and Kanat too was used to spending his days in solitude. Occasionally one would tap the other for attention and point out some sight, such as an eagle soaring or a marmoset sitting on its hind legs looking around with comical intensity before it broke and ran for its burrow. Bing enjoyed the elemental nature of the work and he proved good with his hands and adept at handling the animals.

The cattle were free to roam, but they needed to be constantly watched to protect them from hungry packs of wolves which shadowed the herds in winter. Occasionally, they heard them howling in the distance, but they rarely came close enough to see. Kanat carried an ancient, single-shot rifle of Russian make, slung over his shoulder.

One bitterly cold day, stray flakes of snow were whirling about, filling the air like confetti. They had heard the wolves howling all day, a primeval, dangerous sound which made Bing feel on edge. As they drove the beasts along a small gully towards the village, Kanat and Bing at the rear gave the stragglers an occasional flick with a stick to hurry them along. Kanat stopped and touched Bing on the arm. He pointed to a slight rise about six hundred yards away. A wolf, grey like the gathering dusk, was silhouetted against the sky, watching them. Kanat slipped the rifle from his shoulder and gently drew back the bolt. Holding it to his shoulder, he sighted on the tiny target. The crack of the bullet startled the herd into a loping run. The wolf fell instantly. Bing knew enough about guns to know that he had just witnessed a remarkable feat of marksmanship. In the language of gesture which they used he offered congratulations by patting Kanat on the shoulder. He acknowledged the compliment by a slight upward thrust of his chin.

As evening approached Kanat and Bing would herd the animals in close to the house before retiring indoors to eat with the family. Laura and Bing ceased to mention the search. Like the Kazakhs, they were becoming immersed in a routine in which time ceased to have meaning.

In a small fenced paddock beside the house were two wiry little horses, a chestnut and a bay. Leaning over the fence one morning after helping feed the herd, Bing said to Laura, 'I'd love to go for a ride.'

'Where did you learn to ride?'

'I used to spend holidys on a farm in Ohio when I was a kid.'

'Why don't we ask Kanat if it's all right?'

Kanat helped them saddle up and watched them trot away from the settlement. They turned and waved before disappearing from view. Bing was familiar with the country by now and led the way out onto the flat plain. It was a clean, crisp day, with a hint of pale sun out of focus behind thin cloud. A light breeze was blowing, frosting their cheeks.

'Want to step up the pace a little?' said Bing.

Laura kicked her heels in reply and the bay broke into a canter, then a gallop. Bing nudged his horse forward and the two of them pounded along abreast, the horses' hooves raising powdered snow in clouds, their breath whorling like smoke.

Bing let out a whoop and Laura answered with an Indian yell. It was a race. For a minute or two they were at full gallop, both riders stretched low over their horses' necks. Then the terrain changed to a series of hummocks, forcing them to slow the pace as they weaved around them. Laura's horse was moving at a trot when it tripped, sending her flying out of the saddle and into a snowbank. Bing reigned in his mount and rode back. Laura was lying on her back, covered with snow, laughing breathlessly. The horse stood nearby, waiting.

Bing dismounted and ran to her. 'Are you OK?'

'I'm fine,' she laughed. 'I've got so much clothing on I can't feel a thing.'

Bing held out his hand. She took it and he helped her up. As she rose to her feet they were momentarily close, face to face. Their eyes met and a charge crackled between them for a second, then the moment passed.

'We'd better take it a little slower on the way back,' said Bing. 'You're lucky you didn't bust something.'

They mounted and headed soberly towards home and for the rest of the journey neither of them spoke.

That night after they had finished their meal, Nurlan told them he was going into town and would return with someone who had information. He put on his overcoat, went outside to the van and bumped off into the darkness. After half an hour they heard the van pull up and moments later there was a stamping of boots outside. The door opened and Nurlan entered, followed by a small man with thinning sandy hair. He sat down at the table and glanced at Laura and Bing nervously. Gulnar brought tea and disappeared discreetly into the kitchen while Askar introduced them.

'Our friend wants to be known only as Josef,' he said. 'He has worked at Priazorsk for ten years as a file clerk.'

Laura and Bing each shook Josef's hand. His grip was damp and limp. He withdrew his hand quickly, as if from danger.

Askar continued. 'Nurlan has told Josef about your interest in Priazorsk. He thinks he can help us.'

Laura said, 'Go ahead, we're listening.'

'He heard that in the late sixties there was an American who was helping scientists with the SAM anti-aircraft missile program.'

Laura said, 'How did he hear this?'

'He can't say exactly, it's just a rumour that he has heard from time to time.'

Bing said, 'Tell him rumours are interesting but we'd like to know if anyone has seen the American personally.'

'He says he doesn't know anyone. There are not many people at Priazorsk who were there that long ago and if there are they would not necessarily talk to him about it.'

The Russian was silent while Askar translated. His head moved from side to side as he watched the exchange of English like a spectator at a tennis match.

'What else can he tell us?' said Bing.

The little man looked around nervously and spoke in Russian to Askar. 'He says he has access to the files and can tell us more but he wants to be paid. It's very risky for him.'

'How much does he want?' asked Bing.

The Russian spoke again briefly. 'Five hundred American dollars.'

'Tell him before we can give him anything we need proof that he's not just making up a story for money.'

'What sort of proof?' said Askar.

'The name of the American.'

Askar translated and Josef said something in reply. To the two Americans he seemed to be equivocating. Askar replied sharply. The Russian shrugged.

'Parkinson,' he said.

'Jesus!' said Bing.

'How does he know?' asked Laura.

Josef had been watching their reactions carefully. He seemed pleased at the response. Now he appeared to preen himself as he replied. 'He has already looked in the file,' translated Askar.

Laura's face had drained of colour. 'Can he tell us what happened to Dan?'

'He says he knows what happened to him.'

'Well for God's sake what?'

'He says he wants to be paid before he will give that information.'

Laura turned to Bing beside her. 'What do you think?'

So far they might just get away with the fiction that they were tourists. Once they paid money to Josef they would be technically guilty of espionage. He had no doubt that Laura was prepared to take that risk. She was asking him if he was.

Bing studied the Russian who was shifting uneasily in his chair, eyes darting everywhere. Josef might be a KGB plant sent to entrap them, but he didn't think it was likely. He was too nervous. And he didn't think Nurlan would be fooled easily. He looked around the table at Askar, Kanat and Nurlan. They had made their commitment already. There was no turning back for them.

'Let's find out what he has to say.'

Laura left the table and went to her room. She opened her suitcase and counted out five hundred dollars. She returned and laid the money on the table. Josef picked it up and counted slowly. He put the wad in his pocket and began to speak while Askar translated.

'Daniel Parkinson arrived at Priazorsk on 27 September 1967. He was brought in by a special KGB squad of four men under the command of a Major Timashov. Timashov remained at Priazorsk to liaise between him and the scientists.'

Laura was watching Josef intently, as if she could interpret what he was saying by sheer force of will. As Askar translated she listened impatiently. She was bursting with questions but she forced herself to keep quiet while the story unfolded. 'At first he was kept under very close security,' Askar continued, 'but he was so cooperative that, after a year, he was allowed a more-or-less free run of the base. He was of course not allowed anywhere else and the base security was so tight it would have been impossible for him to escape. Even if he did, where would he go?'

Laura could contain herself no longer. 'What happened to him?' she asked.

The Russian went on, taking his time. 'By 1970 his knowledge was becoming outdated and his usefulness to the air defence program was not so great. In November 1970 the files show an order from Moscow for him to be moved.'

'Moved? Moved where?'

'He was taken to Lithuania, to the capital, Vilnius.'

'For what reason?'

'He doesn't know.'

Laura was incredulous. 'What does he mean he doesn't know? It just can't end like that, there must be more.'

'The file tells only what happened at Priazorsk. After he left there . . .' Askar shrugged.

Laura stood up, seized Josef by the lapels and shook him. 'There must be some other file you can look up, something which gives us a clue.'

Josef shrank back from her intensity. His eyes darted to Askar and he spoke defensively in Russian.

'That's all there is,' said Askar. 'The KGB keeps everything in compartments. The full story will be somewhere in a central file in Moscow, but there is no chance of getting to it.' He looked pityingly at Laura. 'I'm afraid the trail ends in Vilnius.'

Laura let go of the Russian and slumped back in her seat. Bing spoke. 'Tell him we want to know whatever else he has. Any detail, no matter how small, might be helpful.'

'He says that's all he can tell us,' said Askar.

An animal shifted outside. Josef glanced apprehensively at the door and spoke urgently to Askar. 'He wants to get back to Saryshagan,' said Askar. 'He is very nervous about being here. Is there anything else?'

Laura looked at Bing imploringly. He shook his head. 'I guess that's it.' The Russian got up and offered another limp handshake before scurrying out the door with Nurlan.

When they had gone, Gulnar came into the room and hugged Laura. Bing went to his room and returned with a bottle of vodka. Gulnar fetched some glasses and he poured a generous shot into each. Bing raised his glass but could think of nothing to propose as a toast. They clicked glasses and solemnly drank.

'Look at it this way Laura,' Bing said eventually. 'At least you know he was alive when he left Priazorsk.'

Laura gave him a wan look, 'Nineteen-seventy. Twenty years ago. Anything could have happened since then. How will we ever know?'

'Look what they do with Russian defectors in the States. After they debrief them they give them a new identity and then they live happily ever after as American citizens. Why not the same thing here?'

'Why would they risk that?' Laura said. 'Isn't it more likely he was imprisoned or executed?'

Bing tried to find words of reassurance, but he knew what she said was the most likely outcome. He had never learned to lie easily, even out of kindness. He poured more vodkas and they sat around, talking desultorily, waiting for Nurlan to return. By the time they heard his boots stamping on the doorstep they were all morosely drunk. There was a feeling of anticlimax. They had reached a milestone but they seemed as far as ever away from their goal.

'The next flight to Moscow is the day after tomorrow,' Askar said. 'I should book seats. Maybe tomorrow we'll think of something.'

That night Laura dreamt she was walking down a long road. Dan was in the distance coming towards her. He was wearing his Air Force uniform and his red hair was cut short, as in her photograph. As she got closer she began to run towards him, but he continued walking doggedly ahead without acknowledging her. As he got closer she saw that it was not Dan at all, but a man with no face wearing a fur hat. She cried out to him and held her arms wide but he walked right by as though she wasn't there.

Another pale day stole across the steppe, bathing the household with pastel light. For once Bing did not go out with Kanat at dawn to help with the animals. He and Laura got up late and ate a desultory breakfast. Laura looked puffy eyed, as though she had not had much sleep. Bing wished her good morning as usual. If she was hoping for some sign of sympathy it was not forthcoming. Whatever he felt about their failure, he kept it to himself. His barriers, as usual, were firmly in place.

As he had done on their first day there, the party boss, Abdullah Omarov, came calling soon after they had finished eating. He stepped inside and took off his overcoat, handing it to Gulnar without thanking her. He was wearing the same shiny suit and soiled shirt and tie as on his last visit. Omarov sat down, acepted an offer of tea and began oozing the same unctuous pleasantries. Eventually he got to the point of his visit. Speaking through Askar he said that he would like the two Americans to come with him to Saryshagan. It was necessary for them to fill out some registration forms.

After Askar had translated, Bing said, 'If we had to register as foreigners, why not when we first arrived? Why now?'

'Maybe we can stall him until we leave,' Askar said. 'I'll say that it's not convenient today and that you'll come in tomorrow.'

Bing agreed. Askar spoke in Russian. Omarov's reply was accompanied by doleful looks of apology in their direction and exaggerated hand-wringing. It was obvious before the translation was through that he was not to be put off.

'He insists that you go now,' said Askar.

Omarov spoke again. 'He wants you to go without me,' said Askar. 'He says there is someone at party headquarters who can translate. I don't like it at all, but I'm afraid you will have to go.'

Smiling and bowing, Omarov shepherded them into his mud-covered Lada. Omarov ground the gears and the car lurched forward. They drove for ten minutes through the mud and potholes to the highway and turned right.

'What do you think this is all about?' said Laura. 'Do you think they know about . . .' Bing silenced her with a squeeze of her arm. She glanced at him and he shook his head. Perhaps the odious Omarov was not as ignorant of English as he made out. They rode the rest of the way in silence.

Saryshagan was a showcase for everything bad about communist architecture. The predominant building material was concrete; for the most part unpainted, rust-streaked and diseased. The grey was unrelieved by advertising signs. Occasionally they passed some heroic statuary depicting workers toiling together for the common good, or soldiers uniting in battle for the glorious motherland. The impression was one of depressing drabness. The Lada drove around a central square dominated by a statue of Lenin, turned into a side street beside a five-storey building and came to a halt opposite a side entrance. Omarov, all smiles, ushered the two inside. The interior had been freshly painted in a bilious green. Paint had spattered on the floor and where it had been applied to the windowsills it had been carelessly brushed onto the glass panes as well.

Omarov led them down an unheated passageway, their shoes ringing on the concrete floor. He came to a wooden door and knocked once before entering. Laura and Bing stepped into a room painted the same green colour. It must have been a standard government issue. There were some grey steel filing cabinets, and a steam heater gurgled quietly on one wall. Directly in front of them was a wooden desk with some hard-backed chairs in front of it. Behind the desk sat a short, thickset, bull-headed Russian wearing a suit similar to Omarov's. He did not get up. When he opened his mouth to speak he revealed a row of tombstone teeth, two of which were made of steel.

'Please sit,' he said. It was an order, not a request.

They sat down and with a wave he dismissed Omarov, who shot them a last apologetic glance before he left.

The man behind the desk did not introduce himself. Instead he looked at them speculatively for a few moments and said, 'Why have you not registered with the police? It is necessary for all foreigners to register.'

Bing had been detained many times during his career as a journalist and knew that there was nothing to be gained by bluster at this stage. He decided to adopt a conciliatory approach. 'We didn't realise we had to register. We apologise.'

'What are you doing here?' The tone was rude. Unnecessarily rude, Bing thought.

'We're tourists.'

'And what does a tourist find to do in a village in the middle of Kazakhstan?'

'We're interested in the Kazakh people, the way of life.' Bing knew as he said it that it sounded lame.

The Russian snorted as if to register his contempt at the lie. 'Ah, I see. The way of life. Very nice. And are you also interested in the way of life at Priazorsk?'

Bing willed his features to remain impassive. He

hoped Laura was doing the same but he dared not look at her. 'Priazorsk?' he said. 'I don't know what you mean. Where is Priazorsk?'

'You know very well where it is, Mr Connick. And you know also that it is a restricted military area. It is against Soviet law to spy on military establishments.'

'Undoubtedly,' Bing agreed. 'But we're not spies. We're what we say we are, tourists.'

'Tourists do not hide from the authorities like criminals, Mr Connick.' The bull-headed man seemed to be giving only half his attention to the conversation. Bing had the uneasy thought that the end to the wretched scene they were playing had already been written and the Russian was merely arguing to pass the time.

'Are you a police officer?' asked Laura.

'The police do not deal with matters of national security.'

Laura was afraid, but she was also becoming angry, as much at the insolence of their interrogator as at their situation. 'Are we under arrest, then?' she demanded.

'Not yet.'

'If we're not under arrest, I'd like you to tell us what the problem is, allow us to sort it out and let us go. We're American citizens and we've done nothing wrong.'

'This is not the United States, Mrs Bailey. You are in the Soviet Union and subject to the laws of this country. There are no Miranda rights here.'

The Russian looked at his watch. As if he had suddenly tired of the exchange he picked up the telephone and spoke into it briefly. He then sat back and regarded them with a steel-toothed smile. There was a knock on the door and two men in suits entered.

'You will go with these gentlemen,' he said.

'I'm not going anywhere,' said Laura. 'I demand to be allowed to speak to the American embassy.'

The Russian laughed. 'You demand do you? Very nice. She demands. Incredible.' He turned and spoke in Russian to the two men, who laughed dutifully. 'Please do not give me any more trouble. Go with these men.'

Bing spoke up. 'We're American citizens, here on a legitimate visit. Our papers are in order. If you don't want to be seriously embarrassed, I advise you to think carefully about what you're doing. Allow us to get in touch with our embassy and I'm sure this can all be cleared up.'

The Russian looked at them both with contempt. 'Go,' he said. The two men moved in beside them and led them out of the room. They marched down the corridor and descended a flight of stairs. At the bottom they entered a small room without a window. They were ushered inside without a word and the two men left, closing and locking the heavy door behind them. Bing listened for footsteps receding back up the stairs, but heard none. Then a low murmuring and the shuffling of feet told him that they were stationed outside the door, keeping guard.

Laura looked around the bare room. It was like an interrogation room from a B-grade movie: a bare bulb hung from the ceiling, the sole furnishings were two straight-backed chairs and a table, scarred with cigarette burns, in between. The walls were painted the same green as the rest of the building she had seen. She sat down and looked at Bing. A corny line from a dozen Nazi jokes leapt into her mind. She had a hysterical impulse to lighten the moment by leaning forward and uttering conspiratorially, Ve haff vays of makingk you talk. But bravado failed her. Instead she said, 'We're in trouble aren't we?'

'We are that. These guys are KGB.'

Laura said uneasily, 'Why have they just left us here? No charges, no interrogation. Nothing. What do you think it means?'

The casual way they were being treated worried Bing too. If they were being accused of espionage, why had they not been formally charged? He had an uneasy feeling that he was not aware of all the facts. He said, 'They're probably just waiting for instructions from Moscow.' He looked around the room. It was in all likelihood bugged. 'Anyway, we've done nothing wrong. Don't worry, we'll be out of here in an hour or two.'

Laura looked at him curiously. As usual, she could not read what was really going on in his mind.

'This must be a familiar situation for you I suppose,' she said.

'Not lately and never in Russia,' Bing replied. He was trying to understand how the KGB could have learned about their interest in Priazorsk. The Americans knew, that was obvious by his encounter with Hammond, but how could the Russians have found out? Could Nurlan have been indiscreet with his inquiries? He had the feeling that the old man, steeped in the communist system, would be too canny to have been caught. Could Blackwell have informed? It made no sense for him to send them off on the trail, only to betray them. Could Josef have spilled their secret to the KGB? Having compromised himself by accepting the bribe, it was unlikely. No matter how he worried at the questions the answers made no sense.

At one o'clock there was a shuffling outside the door and one of the guards brought in some bread and a watery soup. Laura asked to use the toilet and was led to a filthy cubicle with two footrests and a hole in the floor. The guard waited outside and led her straight back to their room when she was finished. Bing and Laura picked at the food. At two o'clock the guards came back and took the plates away. Bing was taken down the corridor to the toilet. When he tried to engage the guards in conversation they wagged their fingers and shook their heads.

Back in the room, the long day dragged on. Because there were no windows they could not see the light change, but their watches told them that outside it was dusk. At six o'clock the door opened again and the bull-headed Russian, flanked by the two guards, stood before them. They still did not know his name.

'Turn around,' he said to Bing.

Bing turned and as he did so he was seized. His arms were forced behind his back and his wrists were handcuffed. Laura had scarcely begun to protest when she too was handcuffed. He had to admire their professionalism, it was over in ten seconds. Upon another order from the KGB man, the guards blindfolded them and they were marched awkwardly out of the room and up the stairs. With a guard guiding them each by the elbow, Laura and Bing were led down the concrete corridor. They heard a door open and a freezing blast of wind told them they were outside. Slipping and sliding on the icy pavement they were led to a car. Their heads were forced down and they were shoved inside. Not a word was spoken. They heard the doors slam. The starter groaned half-heartedly in the cold and for a moment Bing thought the engine would not start, but after two or three attempts it caught and revved and the car began to move.

'What's going on?' demanded Bing. 'Where are you taking us?' He hoped the fear he felt was not apparent in his voice.

No one spoke. There was no way of knowing how many people were in the car. Laura huddled against him. They had not been able to put on their coats and he could feel her trembling through her sweater, but whether through cold or fear he couldn't tell.

They felt the car stop and start a few times as it negotiated the sparse traffic of the town, then the tyres began to hum steadily as they presumably got onto the highway. They were obviously heading out of town.

Bing had a flash of memory about an incident in Nicaragua. The Sandinistas had put up a roadblock near a village which had been savagely brutalised by soldiers. The press were not allowed in. Bing had argued with the soldiers, but when he saw the futility of it he had given up. A freelance photographer with whom he was travelling kept arguing. He was new to Nicaragua and also, because he was a freelance, he was hungry. When the soldiers began to lose patience Bing tried to jolly the photographer away, but he could not sense the atmosphere. He kept on and on insisting that 'La Prensa' should be given access to the village, as if the press had rights.

A soldier walked up to him and, reversing his rifle, clubbed him to the ground. Bleeding and dazed, he was dragged to his feet and led away. Bing could do nothing. His photographer friend was never heard from again. The Soviet Union was changing but he had no illusions that the KGB had undergone an overnight transformation. Their deaths would be easy to stage. Two American adventurers travel to a wild corner of the Soviet Union where they meet with . . . what? A traffic accident? A violent robbery which goes wrong? A wrong turn while hiking on the steppes in sub-zero weather? The possibilities were endless, and far away in Moscow no one would even bother to ask questions.

These things happened in his profession. You took the risk and if you miscalculated you paid the price. And knowing this helped not at all. Bing did not feel philosophical about it. What he felt was scared.

He said, 'The embassy in Moscow knows we're here. If anything happens to us they'll be asking questions.'

There was no reply from the front seat. Bing went on, 'I suggest you tell us where we're going. We're American citizens. You don't want to start an international incident.'

Laura did not know what to do. What was happening to her was outside her experience. She felt like hitting out at her abductor but the handcuffs held her immobile. Maybe they're just taking us to some other place for more questions, she thought. The blindfolds and the sinister lack of communication told her that was a vain hope. It was a pity they had not even found what they were looking for. She tried to think of Dan, but like the faceless man in the dream, he eluded her. Trying to find him had been an unreal exercise, she now realised. What was real was this car, the man with steel teeth, the blindfolds, the handcuffs pressing painfully against the small of her back and Bing sitting helpless beside her.

The car was slowing down. It turned off the road and bumped over rough ground for a few moments before coming to a halt. The engine was switched off and there was silence, the absolute silence of the steppe. The exhaust pipe ticked as the metal contracted in the cold. The front door opened and the KGB man told them to get out.

Bing knew with sudden clarity that the man was alone. Then he realised just as quickly that it made no difference. He could not even tell where he was standing. He felt the prod of a gun barrel in his ribs and then heard the crunch of boots as the man quickly stepped back. He was careful and professional.

'Walk, both of you.'

They began to walk. 'Turn slightly left. That's it, now straight ahead.'

Laura could not speak. She felt warmth running down her legs and realised she had wet herself. It did not matter.

Bing's mind was racing. Should they try to run? He knew it was a ridiculous thought. He could feel Laura beside him. 'I'm sorry,' he said. 'I should have been more careful. I should have known when to stop.'

'It's all right, Bing. Don't worry. It's all right.'

They had gone about ten paces when they heard the gun cock loudly in the still air. They continued walking like automatons, waiting for the hot steel to rip into them. Oblivion.

The expected shot rang out, but they remained standing. Behind them there was a sound like someone gargling and then a thump as a body fell to the ground. They heard running feet coming towards them and rough hands ripped the blindfolds from their eyes. It was Kanat, his rifle was slung over his shoulder.

Kanat saw the handcuffs and walked over to the body of the KGB man. He rummaged in his pockets and in a few moments returned with the key. He freed Laura first and then Bing. Laura was shaking uncontrollably. She hugged Kanat tightly and then motioned Bing to her. With her free hand she hugged him. The three of them stood for a few moments, a tableau in the vast landscape, before disengaging.

'Thanks Kanat,' said Bing. 'Nice shot.'

Kanat grinned. He walked over and looked down at the body lying in the snow. 'KGB,' he said and spat on the dead face. He walked to the dead man's car, switched off the headlights and motioned for them to follow him. Several hundred yards down the road was the van in which he had trailed them. Laura and Bing climbed into the front seat alongside Kanat. As they drove back to the village, Bing put his arm around her and held her tightly against him until her trembling had ceased.

When the van pulled up outside the house, Askar and the others ran out to greet them. They went inside and Bing fetched a bottle of vodka from his suitcase. He had never tasted anything so good as the spirit slid down his throat and the warmth spread through his body. Gulnar was fussing over Laura like a mother over a hurt child.

As Kanat related what had happened, Askar translated. 'We were worried when you didn't return by the afternoon. Kanat went into town and watched the building until you were brought out. He followed you out onto the highway without using his lights and when he saw the car stop he stopped too. He was a long way back. He couldn't get too close because the KGB man would have heard his footsteps in the snow. He shot him from about three hundred yards.'

'Tell him thank you for saving our lives,' said Laura.

'He knows,' said Askar.

Bing said, 'There's a KGB hit man gone missing and a body out there. We're going to have to do something about that.'

'We'll go back tonight and get rid of the car and the body. They won't be found until summer. Maybe not even then.'

'You'll be questioned when it is found.'

'Yes, but they won't find any connection.'

'You'll have to get rid of the rifle. They can match the bullet.'

'We will. Today I booked you on Aeroflot back to Moscow. The flight leaves at nine tomorrow morning. By the time they start to worry about the missing man you will be on your way. But I think you should leave Russia quickly. It'll only be a matter of time before they come looking for you.'

'Askar,' said Bing. 'I don't know how to thank you.'

'Thank me when your plane takes off from Moscow. It may not be over yet.'

Twenty

Laura and Gulnar were weeping as they said goodbye. Bing shook Kanat's hand and embraced him. Kanat said, 'Welcome to our home,' and the two of them burst into laughter.

'Goodbye,' said Bing. 'Maybe we'll meet again.' They knew this was the last time they would ever see the family. Nurlan hurried them into the van with exaggerated gruffness. He said little as he drove them back down the highway to the airport. He unloaded their bags and embraced them. When he stood back his eyes were glistening. They turned and waved before entering the aeroplane, and by the time they had found a seat and looked out the window for him he was gone.

The terrors of Aeroflot seemed trivial after what they had just gone through. When Laura, Bing and Askar picked up their baggage in Moscow they thought it would still be too early for the alarm to have been raised, but they could not be certain. As they walked out onto the concourse they were half expecting to be stopped. Askar scanned the crowd suspiciously. 'You should not go to a hotel,' he warned. 'I think it is best if you come back to my apartment.'

'Are you sure it's all right?' asked Bing. 'You've risked enough already.'

'You will be noticed, certainly, nothing is private here. But it should only be a short time, with luck only a few hours.'

Askar lived in a run-down building close to the Arbart. The stairwell was strewn with rubbish and smelled of cats. His room was pathetically poor, containing a gas ring, a sink, a couch which converted to a bed, and little else. There was, however, a red plastic telephone with an old-fashioned rotary dial. While Laura and Bing sat apprehensively, Askar called the airlines. There was a British Airways flight to London that evening. They had six hours to wait.

It was mid-afternoon when the call came through from the Communist Party Chief in Saryshagan to the Head of Counterintelligence at KGB Headquarters in Moscow. Abdullah Omarov had difficulty getting through on the telephone. Twice he made a connection only to have the line drop out suddenly. It was always the way. When he finally got through to the switchboard it took some time for him to find someone who would accept his call. Eventually, after being transferred several times, he reached a duty officer, who realised at once the importance of his information. Not wishing to be the bearer of bad news, the duty officer routed the call directly to his boss. It was a very poor line and Ponomaryov of Counterintelligence was irritated by the obsequious manner of the man at the other end. He was hard to understand over the hisses and crackles and he took forever to come to the point. He was further irritated to hear that one of his best and most experienced operatives, along with the two Americans, had gone missing.

'How often do you have flights to Moscow?' he shouted.

The line crackled and fizzed. The reply was faint, but he could just understand it. 'Three times a week.'

'When is the next one?'

'There was a flight this morning and there is another one in two days' time.'

222

The Head of Counterintelligence swore angrily. 'Who is in charge of police there?' he asked.

Omarov told him. 'Well have him call me immediately. We'll have to get a proper search underway.'

'Yes, Comrade,' said Omarov and rang off.

Ponomaryov hung up. First they would have to determine if the Americans had been on today's flight. Better check the hotels as well. Also an alert at Sheremetyvo Airport. If they were here they would be found; they would have to be. The KGB did not take failure lightly. It wouldn't take much for that bastard Bakutin to roll him and replace him with another damned amateur. He picked up his telephone and began to issue orders.

The BA flight was due to depart Moscow at 8.20 p.m. Laura and Bing planned to leave a bit after six, allowing an hour to get to the airport and another hour to clear passport control. The hours ticked by with leaden slowness. While the fugitives fretted at the inactivity a dozen KGB officers began calling hotels in Moscow. The coordinator of the operation, Oleg Tsarvulanov, was one of the KGB's bright young men, smart, ambitious and resourceful and something of a protégé of Ponomaryov. Tsarvulanov did not know why the Americans were being sought, but he knew it was important. It wasn't every day that the Head of Counterintelligence took charge of an operation personally. While his subordinates plied the phones he rang airport security personally.

There were several international flights departing that evening. JAL and Virgin Airlines both had flights to Tokyo. The Polish airline LOT had a direct flight to Warsaw; Swissair, Finnair and Czechoslovakian Airlines had movements. There were several Aeroflot departures and there was also a British Airways flight to London. Tsarvulanov requested that passport controllers be alerted to watch out for two Americans carrying travel documents in the names of Laura Bailey and Bing Connick. He gave them their passport numbers and requested that they be entered into the computer with a signal to detain them when found. At the same time he asked for the passenger lists of all outgoing flights to be scrutinised. So far the hotel enquiries had yielded nothing. Tsarvulanov called his boss. 'There are quite a few flights leaving Moscow this evening,' he informed him. 'I think we should take some men and get out to the airport.'

Ponomaryov agreed and called down for a car and driver. Tsarvulanov would ride with him to the airport and a minibus would follow with a team of back-up agents.

Because they were travelling first class, there was no waiting at the British Airways departure desk and Laura and Bing were processed in a few moments. They thanked Askar. Bing shook his hand warmly and Laura gave him a kiss on the cheek. With a final wave they wished him goodbye and walked through to passport control. The passport officers were in glass-fronted booths with a small shelf and a slot through which passengers slid their travel documents. Laura stepped forward first and stood in front of the window. The officer was an unsmiling young man with pimples. His uniform was badly fitting, but he made up for his callow appearance by scowling at the foreigners and deliberately taking his time. He looked carefully at Laura, down at her passport photograph and back again at her. He was in no hurry. Laura tried to look nonchalant, but she was shaking under the youth's impassive gaze. His hands, hidden below the shelf, poised to type her details into the computer. He grimaced as his mind wrestled with the Roman numerals. These American names all looked the same to him. Suddenly the screen blinked at him and went blank. Damn. The computer was down. It was always doing that. Reluctantly, he handed Laura her passport and waved her through.

Bing was next. He stood in front of the booth for several minutes while the young man gave him the same painstaking examination. He would go far in the bureaucracy, Bing thought. At length Bing too was allowed to pass.

The computer glitch was reported to the airport security office. It took some time to type and copy the passport details of the two Americans, Mrs Laura Bailey and Mr Bing Connick. By the time it had been done and an officer dispatched to go down the row of passport control booths distributing the information, they had walked past the duty free store selling perfume, babushka dolls, badly made fur coats, caviar and vodka and mingled with hundreds of other passengers waiting for flights. Another officer was dispatched to go around to the airline offices and collect the passenger lists. No one told him what it was for and he saw no reason to hurry. By the time the men from KGB Headquarters had arrived at the airport, he had not returned. Ponomaryov paced the floor in a fury of impatience while another officer was dispatched to find the first one and bring back what he had already collected.

Laura's nerves were jumping as she settled back into the seat of the Boeing 737. Her hand shook as she accepted a glass of orange juice served by a professionally friendly stewardess. Bing did not show the tenseness he felt. He was sure that by now the hue and cry must have begun. It was still not too late for them to be arrested.

The passengers seemed to move with maddening slowness as they filed on board. Bing glanced at his watch, but the hands seemed not to have moved since last time he looked. He peered at the second hand to check that it was working, then told himself to sit tight and wait. There was nothing he could do to make the plane depart any earlier.

With the delays back in the terminal it was eight twenty-five by the time the KGB men began rapidly scanning the first passenger lists. It took only a matter of minutes to eliminate JAL and Virgin. It was unlikely the fugitives would be flying to an Eastern bloc country and they put aside Aeroflot until later. The British Airways manifest was the third one they looked at.

It was Oleg Tsarvulanov who found their names. He gave a quiet shout of triumph to his boss and glanced at the top of the list to see the departure time. It was eight-twenty. As his boss grabbed for the telephone, he raced out of the office to the British Airways desk. With luck the flight might be running late. The desk had closed for the night. Outside there was the roar of jet engines. A Boeing 737 with blue and grey livery was just beginning to taxi away from the terminal.

Tsarvulanov raced back to the office with the news. Ponomaryov looked up from the telephone. 'I'm onto the control tower now. They're just about to take off.'

'We could order it to return,' said the young agent. 'It's still in Soviet territory.'

The Head of Counterintelligence regarded his eager protégé with appreciation. He spoke a curt order into the telephone, nodded and put it back on the receiver. 'I've told them to hold the plane on the tarmac,' he said. In the old days he would have just dragged them off the flight, but it was not like the old days any more. 'I'll call Bakutin,' he added savagely. 'He's the politician, let him make the decision.'

'Why do you think it's taking so long?' Laura asked. They had been sitting on the tarmac with the engines idling for ten minutes. It seemed like an hour. The longer they waited, the more anxious she was becoming. She had a terrible feeling that it was all about to go horribly wrong, just when they thought they were safe.

'Probably just heavy traffic,' said Bing. He hoped he sounded convincing.

'What are we going to do if they call the plane back?'

'Go back with it I guess. We can hardly jump off.'

'You know what?'

'What?'

'I'm scared, I'm not used to this sort of tension.'

'There's nothing to be scared about. It's just a normal air traffic delay, that's all.'

Laura turned sideways in her seat to look at Bing. 'Do you believe that?'

'Absolutely. Nothing to worry about.'

Ponomaryov was talking urgently into the telephone. 'The plane's sitting out on the tarmac now. We've told air traffic control to delay it until we give permission to take off. What do you want to do?'

Bakutin leaned back in his office chair and thought for a moment. The operation was meant to have been clandestine. If they took two Americans off an international flight, the political repercussions would be impossible to contain. He cursed silently. 'Tell the control tower the flight can proceed,' he said. 'And I want to see you in my office first thing in the morning. I hope you'll have a good explanation for this disaster.'

The whine of the Boeing's engines increased in pitch. The aircraft began to move slowly forward. Laura tensed, fearing the worst, then relaxed. The speed was increasing. They were not taxiing back to the terminal. They were taking off. The nose lifted and she looked out the window, watching the ground fall away. She turned to Bing and said, 'Phew. You must have nerves of steel.'

He grinned at her. 'I wasn't worried for a moment.'

Twenty-one

There are few people in the world who can pick up a telephone, dial the White House and be put through directly to the President of the United States. The Soviet Ambassador to Washington is one of them. Three days after Laura and Bing left Moscow for London, a courier arrived in Washington bearing a letter from President Ivashov to be relayed to President Blanchard. He delivered it in a sealed envelope to Ambassador Popov, along with written instructions to pass it on unopened. Popov called the President and told him that the letter was there and within minutes a White House courier had arrived to pick it up. The President, sitting at his desk in the Oval Office, slit the seal with a gold opener which had been a gift from an African dictator whose name he could not recall and unfolded the letter within. It was written in Russian. The President buzzed his secretary and asked her to get Brandon Paine on the line.

'Brandon, I've got a hand-delivered letter here from Ivashov. The damned thing's written in Russian, but we can guess what it's about.'

'Good news I hope, Mr President.'

'I'll send it over to you. And get that translator, what's his name, the one who did the original letter?'

'Sellars.'

The President wasn't really listening. 'Whatever. Get him to translate and we'll take a look at it.'

'OK. The moment it gets here.'

'Thanks Brandon.' The President rang off.

Ross Sellars was eating lunch alone in his office as usual. When other people who worked on his floor got together in the canteen or went out to one of the cheap little restaurants within walking distance of the NSA offices, Sellars was never invited. The easy male bonhomie, the jokes about rival baseball teams, the office gossip did not come easily to him and people sensed it. It had been the same since he was a schoolboy. He had been brilliant academically, excelling especially at languages, but in the playground and later in the workplace, there was something about him which put people off. He was not overly aggressive, or overly sycophantic; he was not overly anything. He was invisible, a friend to no one.

He lived alone in an apartment not far from his place of work, where in his spare time he indulged his hobbies of reading Russian literature and painstakingly putting together model ships, accurate in every detail. No friend ever dropped in unexpectedly to chat or to invite him impulsively to a movie. There was no woman in his life. He had tried computer dating, but after two or three failed encounters he had given it up. Once a month he would furtively visit a whorehouse where in a few expensive moments his sexual needs would be allayed. His work and his hobbies were his life.

Sellars had realised at an early age that he was a misfit, but he had never become reconciled to it. The easy friendships which he saw springing up among his colleagues galled him, as did the advancement of others whom he knew had no greater ability than he.

When he saved the President's letter to Ivashov against the express orders of Brandon Paine, he realised that it was too dangerous to leave it in his desk so he had spirited it out of the office and taken it home with him where it lay rolled up and hidden with some model boat plans in a cupboard. He had no clear idea why he had kept it, but he felt good just having it there, hidden away. Somehow it made him feel that he was not quite as insignificant as people thought. Having the President's letter gave him a sense of power.

Despite Brandon Paine's promise that he would go far, he had heard nothing from him since he had translated the letter, when was it? Well over a week ago it must have been. His heart gave a slight jump when the telephone on his desk rang and the secretary asked him to hold for the National Security Adviser. Maybe this was the call he had been waiting for.

'Sellars,' said Brandon Paine, 'I want you drop whatever you're doing and come to my office immediately.'

He smiled to himself. At last. However, when he arrived at Paine's office after hurriedly combing his hair and straightening his tie, he was in and out in less than a minute. Paine handed him an envelope addressed to the President and instructed him to translate it as soon as he was able.

Returning to his office he closed the door, although the likelihood of anyone coming to interrupt him was slim. With slightly shaking fingers, like a man who has been waiting for the next instalment of a serial, he opened the envelope and began reading the words of the Russian President.

He had been wondering what had happened to Laura Bailey and Bing Connick and he suspected that the letter would say that they had been—what was the word Blanchard had used?—'Neutralised'. In context, the nuances of the word had proved difficult to translate into the Russian. He was surprised to read that far from being neutralised, the two Americans had managed to visit Kazakhstan and had subsequently left the Soviet Union for London. There was no mention of the murder of the KGB operative in Saryshagan and President Ivashov had not gone into the details of their flight from Russia, but the inescapable message was that there had been a balls-up. The Russian President had no advice to offer. The ball was back in the Americans' court.

Using his special word-processing program, Sellars set to work translating. Within an hour he was done. As before, he carefully photocopied the Russian letter and printed an extra copy of the translation which he slipped into his desk drawer. Then he called Brandon Paine to tell him it was ready. Paine asked him to bring the translation around to his office personally, for the sake of security.

'Goddamn it to hell, Brandon, they fucked up.'

President Blanchard threw the translation onto his desk and rose to his feet. He was too angry to sit still. Paine picked up the letter and skimmed it quickly. 'I don't believe it,' he said. 'I just don't believe it.'

The President was pacing in front of the window, oblivious to the view. 'Is this the superpower we've been worried about all these years? They can't even round up a couple of amateurs.'

'Question is what do we do about it?' Paine said. He looked down at the translation. 'Ivashov says they did get to Saryshagan, but he doesn't say if they found anything.'

He doesn't say because he damn well doesn't know,' retorted the President.

'OK, so we've got two scenarios. One they went to Kazakhstan, they sniffed around, found nothing and now they've given up the search and we all live happily ever after.'

'I like that one,' said the President. 'What I don't like is the second. What are the chances they were successful do you think?'

Paine reflected for a moment. 'I'd say too good to rule out. Connick's followed the trail to Saryshagan and he's managed somehow to elude Ivashov's people. That's a pretty good act so far. I think we'd be unwise to assume that he's come up empty-handed.'

'Jesus, he could be writing his story now. And wouldn't those bastards on the *Post* just love to get their teeth into another President.' It was times like this that

Blanchard momentarily wondered if the struggle to attain the presidency had really been worth it. No one could fully understand the nature of the job unless they'd done it. He did not consider himself an evil man. It was just that sometimes to achieve an honourable result, dishonourable acts were necessary. The liberal news media would no doubt love to wring their hands over his shelving of the intelligence reports back in the Vietnam days. What they would fail to appreciate was that the alternative would have been for the peace negotiations to have stalled even further. It took leadership to act for the greater good and make the hard decisions. Unfortunately the press would never see it that way.

Paine said, 'Let's just think this through. Say he's confirmed that an American, or Americans, were taken to Russia. He writes it up with the inference that you knew about it. Is it deniable?'

The President shook his head. 'You know how it is with these things, Brandon. Once they get a sniff the papers won't let it go. Who knows how it would end up?'

'There's only one loose end that I can think of,' said Paine.

'And what's that?'

'Hammond used the embassy in Moscow to communicate.'

'That communication would make no sense to anyone who didn't know what it referred to.'

'That's true.'

'Who the hell is Hammond anyway?' said the President.

'Well you won't see his name in any government employee list, Mr President. He's someone we use from time to time for delicate operations, but there's nothing anywhere that says he exists.'

'How do you pay him?'

'He comes under Discretionary Funding. The Senate Budget Committee's always bitching that we won't itemise it. The reason is that it covers people like Hammond.'

'He hasn't exactly covered himself with glory so far,' snapped the President.

'He was never meant to get as involved as he did. We thought a warning, ostensibly from the embassy, would put Connick off. When it didn't work he took it upon himself to take stronger action. I think he underestimated the difficulty of the problem and the resourcefulness of Mr Connick.' Paine had neatly put the blame on Hammond rather than himself.

'And what about that fellow in Bangkok? Was he an underestimation too?'

'Buggins? An overzealous operative. These things happen.'

'Don't forget it was a minor balls-up which led to Nixon's downfall.'

The President seemed to have a fixation on Watergate, thought Paine. He reviewed the chances of his own role in the attempted cover-up being discovered and rapidly reached the conclusion that he was safe. He returned to the problem confronting his President. 'I think we're going to have to get someone more removed to handle it,' he said.

'It has to be untraceable,' said the President. 'I know the CIA does that sort of stuff.'

'It widens the knowledge.'

'Hmm, you're right. Does the NSA have that capability?'

'We do.'

Blanchard stopped pacing and sat down again. He was due to meet the Prime Minister of Australia in five minutes and had been looking forward to a few pleasant platitudes about trade and mutual understanding. The Aussies could always be relied upon not to be too assertive. This news had put a sour complexion on the day. Still, he had not got where he was by being pessimistic. He pulled his shoulders back and slapped the desk with an air of decision.

'OK, Brandon, let's do it. And for Christ's sake let's do it right.'

On the flight from Moscow, Laura and Bing hardly spoke at all. It was not a conscious thing. They were still in a state close to shock. Laura tried to forget the blindfolded walk, the click of the pistol being cocked, the KGB man's body lying sprawled on the ground, the patch of red staining the snow, but the images were impossible to shake off. She was grateful that Bing was impassively silent. It was not something she could talk about. Not yet.

It was after midnight by the time they cleared customs at Heathrow Airport and climbed into a taxi to take them into London. The Cockney driver slid back the window separating him from the passenger compartment and enquired where they were going. They had not booked anything from Moscow for fear of being traced, but Laura remembered she had once stayed at the Athenaeum on a trip with Griffith and asked him to take them there.

As they left the airport and headed out to the M4 the driver threw them a glance over his shoulder and asked where they had come from. For the rest of the journey he gave them the benefit of his opinions on the state of Eastern Europe and was moving on to the shortcomings of the British government when they mercifully arrived. The Athenaeum had two rooms available and without further delay they went straight upstairs and collapsed into exhausted sleep.

Next morning promised one of those clear days which can unexpectedly brighten a London winter as it teeters on the edge of spring. Well rugged-up, they walked out of their hotel situated at the top of Piccadilly and crossed over to Green Park. Some joggers strode along the pathways, one or two nannies pushed prams with the hoods up, their baby passengers swathed under fluffy rugs. A few tourists and idlers strolled about enjoying the unseasonal day. Laura had always thought of London as a shabby place and the English as a poor people. Compared to Moscow, with its beggars squatting in the snow, its pathetic crowds of black marketeers and its crumbling roads and buildings, it now seemed extravagantly wealthy. She felt secure. Nothing, she thought, could happen to them now. Here they would be safe.

The shared danger had changed their relationship in some indefinable manner. Laura took Bing's arm, something she would never have contemplated before, and in this way they strolled along, remarking now and then on the sights and talking about anything other than Russia or MIAs.

At lunch time they found themselves in a pub in Chelsea. The clientele were office workers and a smattering of bright young Sloane Rangers. They watched a darts match in progress and marvelled at the normality of the scene. In the afternoon they went to a movie. It was a comedy, but an hour after they had left the cinema neither could recall what it had been about. They returned to the hotel and rested for a while, meeting in the bar at eight for a drink. It was a small, wood-panelled room, holding no more than thirty people. The barkeep was a Frenchman, five feet tall in his uplifts and flamboyantly homosexual. Through some mysterious trick of hotel management he already knew their names when they walked in. He made a fuss of them and thereafter treated them, as he did everyone, with saucy familiarity. They chatted with an American couple who were visiting London to do the theatres. After an hour Bing and Laura excused themselves and went into the dining room, where they were seated at an elegantly laid table. They ordered food and wine. It did not seem believable that just two days ago they had stood in the snow waiting to die.

The plates had been cleared and they were drinking coffee. 'Well, what do you think?' Laura asked. 'Do you have a story?'

Bing pondered the question. He could write about Buggins and his radio intercepts, the trip to Kazakhstan, the Russian clerk Josef's revelations, the KGB murder attempt, but who would believe it? Where was the evidence? It was unsaleable. He felt no disappointment. He had never believed they would find out what happened to Dan. His original idea had been to write up Laura's obsession, but now, after having been part of it, to do so would seem a violation. 'No, Laura. I don't have a story,' he said. 'What about you? Can you let it rest now?'

'I don't want to, but I can't think of where to go from here.'

The waiter came over to ask if they wanted more coffee, but they waved him away. Laura toyed with her spoon. She looked up and found Bing gazing at her steadily. 'You were very brave out there,' he said.

'I was terrified. I wet myself.'

'Maybe, but you didn't break down. You didn't plead with him. You just walked away. It was,' he searched for a word, 'admirable.'

Laura held his gaze. 'Are you trying to be nice to me, Bing Connick?'

'I guess so.'

'Well you're doing just fine. Don't stop now.'

'It's not something I'm used to, being nice. It's been a long time since I seriously tried it.'

'I think you were pretty admirable yourself,' said Laura.

'I misjudged badly. I shouldn't have let you go to Kazakhstan in the first place. It was a mistake.'

'Why did you keep going, when it would have been so easy to quit?'

'I thought of it plenty of times.'

'So why didn't you?'

'The lure of a good story I suppose.'

'I suspect you never really believed in the story.'

'Not at first, but I guess I got caught up in it. In things.'

'Things?'

'Yes.'

They were both silent. There was no one left in the dining room. The waiters had all disappeared save for one who was fussing unnecessarily in a corner, too polite to hover over them. Bing glanced at him. 'I think we ought to let this poor fellow get to bed.'

'Me too,' said Laura.

236

'I'll walk you home.'

They left the dining room and caught the elevator to the fourth floor. As they got out and turned down the corridor, Laura took Bing's arm, as she had in the park that morning. They proceeded in silence. When they reached the door Laura gave Bing her key and he put it in the lock. The door swung open. He handed her the key and stepped aside to let her in. Now was the moment for him to say goodnight and walk away, but he hesitated. Laura made no attempt to leave either. They stood there looking at each other for a long moment.

'Nightcap?' said Laura.

'Yes, thanks, I could handle a brandy. Help me sleep.'

They walked into the room. It was at the front of the hotel and looked out over Piccadilly to Green Park. The maid had closed the curtains. Laura walked over and drew them aside, revealing the lights of London below. A light rain was falling and the cars' headlights caught the raindrops as they slanted down. The blacktop glistened under the streetlights. The tops of umbrellas hurried along, borne by invisible pedestrians. Bing opened the mini bar and poured two cognacs. He went over and joined Laura at the window. They stood gazing out at the scene in silence. They raised their glasses and sipped. There was no denying the tension between them. 'I'm not a very casual person, Bing,' Laura said at last.

'And I'm not a very committed one.' They spoke without looking at each other. Both were staring out the window as if discussing the view.

'You live on a river in Australia. I live in Nebraska.'

Bing said, 'You've got a ranch to run. I've got no family and no responsibilities.'

'Not exactly a perfect match, would you say?'

'You're right.'

She put her glass down on the windowsill. Bing did the same. Laura turned to him and stepped into his arms. He held her tightly, enfolding the length of her against his body. She closed her eyes and squeezed him hard, feeling his strength. She murmured, as though it was relevant, 'I have to go home soon.'

Still holding her Bing said, 'I worked in London for a while. I used to go out of town to a little pub down at the seaside in the Solent. We could go there. A holiday before you leave.'

Laura released him and stood back. 'I must be insane,' she said and added 'Yes, I think I'd like that.'

She had no idea what to do next. She had known two men in her life, Dan and her husband. She felt as gauche as a schoolgirl. Bing kissed her. She smelt a faint odour of cognac. His body, pressed against her, felt hard. She felt her blood pounding in her ears, an unfamiliar stirring, moistness. He was walking towards the door. As he opened it he said, 'Tomorrow then,' turned and was gone.

Twenty-two

Ross Sellars was discontented. After the work he had done for Brandon Paine and the President he had expected his situation to change. Hadn't Paine promised as much? It was ages since he had got involved in the presidential dialogues, yet he had not heard from Paine since he handed in the last translation. There had been no hint of the promised promotion. He continued to be given the routine work at the office, while his intellectual inferiors got the plum assignments.

Sellars was tempted to send a memo to the NSA Director reminding him of his promise of advancement, but he dithered. Perhaps if he waited just a little longer word would come through that things were going to change. After all, Brandon Paine had plenty of other important matters on his mind. He was probably just waiting for the right job to come along for him. It wouldn't do to appear over-anxious.

In the last few days Sellars had felt a familiar stirring. He had been waking up in the mornings with an erection. It was three weeks, no nearly four, since he had last visited the Daily Planet. It was that time of the month again. He would go this evening after work. Maybe that young Vietnamese girl would be there. He'd give himself a treat and have oral as well as the usual. It cost more but maybe it would cheer him up.

At 6 p.m. he closed down his computer and put his translations into the internal mail system. A few other employees were leaving as well, with their usual noisy goodbyes. Some of them were going to a bar for a drink after work, but as usual no one invited him. He looked at them with contempt and thought of the correspondence between the Presidents of Russia and the United States which he had hidden away. Screw them. They didn't know what he knew.

He pulled on his coat and scarf and left the office. The Daily Planet was only a short cab ride away and within ten minutes he was entering a plain doorway which looked like the entrance to an office building. The door opened into a small anteroom with a reception desk, behind which sat a rather worn-looking blonde woman with heavily made-up eyes. She was reading a magazine and smoking a long cigarette with a white filter. As Sellars approached she looked up and recognised him. She took the cigarette out of her mouth and he noticed with distaste her red lipstick adhering to the filter. 'Hello dear, we haven't seen you for a while. How have you been?'

'Fine thank you.' Sellars hated this part of it. He glanced nervously at the street door. It would be disastrous if someone he knew came in. The receptionist caught his mood. She was used to nervous men. 'Anything special you have in mind today?' she asked.

'Well I was wondering if the Vietnamese girl was here, I forget her name.'

'Rosie,' offered the receptionist. 'No Rosie's not here, she's having a night off, but we've got a new girl who I think you'd love. Dark hair just like Rosie, very petite and very friendly.' She paused expectantly, wishing the little creep would hurry up.

Sellars glanced nervously at the door again. He wasn't sure. Well yes, he heard himself say, certainly, if you recommend her, that sounds fine. The receptionist picked up her telephone, pressed a buzzer and spoke to someone on the other end. 'Gentleman coming in to see Belinda,' she said. She turned to Sellars and said, 'That'll be a hunnert twenty. You can pay for any extras afterwards. Cash or credit card?'

'Cash,' said Sellars. She took the money, pressed a button and a plush, padded door clicked open. Sellars walked through into the lounge. The decor was in muted good taste. The furnishings were expensive, modern and comfortable. The carpet was a pale grey, the walls grey also, decorated with modern abstracts. There were low lounges and glass tables scattered about and a bar at one end. A few attractive young women were sitting around waiting for the evening to liven up. As Sellars walked in one of them stepped forward to welcome him. She was, as promised, petite and dark, perhaps twenty-four years old. She gave him a practiced smile and asked his name. 'John,' said Sellars.

'Hello John. I'm Belinda. Would you like to have a drink and relax a little?'

'No thanks,' said Sellars. 'I'm in kind of a hurry.'

Mentally the woman placed him. She remembered Rosie talking about him. A real nerd apparently. Never time for a chat or a laugh, just slam bam and thank you ma'am. The smile revealed none of her thoughts. She said archly, 'If you don't feel like a drink, what would you like, John?'

'Oral,' said Sellars. 'Then the normal.'

'Boy you're straight to the point aren't you?'

'Right,' said Sellars. 'I'm a busy man.'

Oh man, what a lulu this one was. Belinda turned and said, 'OK John, follow me.'

Sellars followed her swaying bottom down a passage and into a room with a spa and a king-size bed. It was decorated in the same discreet taste as the lounge. There was a TV set in the corner showing a pornographic movie with the sound turned down. Belinda, professional despite her instinctive dislike of Sellars, moved close to him. 'Would you like me to help you get undressed, John?' she said.

'No thanks, I'll handle it.' Sellars slid off his jacket, shirt and tie and laid them carefully over the back of a chair. Then he sat on the bed and took off his shoes and socks. Finally he dropped his pants and waited seated on the bed in his undershorts.

'I'll just have to take a look at you John,' said Belinda. She walked over to him and pushed him back on the bed. She slid his shorts down and gave his flaccid penis a quick examination for signs of venereal disease. 'My, you're a big boy aren't you? I'll bet you drive the girls crazy.'

Sellars decided he didn't like this Belinda. She'd talk about him later, laughing with the other girls, and he regretted allowing himself to break from his normal pattern. He should have come back when Rosie was here. He liked her because she didn't come on with this smart-ass hooker's patter. These encounters were a delicate thing which in the past had led to embarrassment and he hoped this wasn't going to be one of those times.

'Would you like a spa first, John?' said Belinda.

Normally he would have accepted the offer, but it meant he would have to engage in more unwelcome conversation. 'No I don't think so, thanks.'

'You just lie back there, John, while I get comfortable and join you,' said Belinda. She crossed her arms in front of her, bent down and grasped the hem of her short skirt with both hands. In one swift movement she pulled it over her head revealing her naked body. She turned towards him and he noticed that she had shaved her pubic hair. Oh no, he hated that. This was getting worse. The woman approached the bed and knelt over him. His penis remained flaccid. She stroked it and murmured her pat phrases. He noticed that she had a mole on one breast and that her teeth were slightly crooked.

'Look, I think the moment might not be quite right,' he said.

'Come on baby, let me turn you on,' she whispered.

She bent down and took him in her mouth. Sellars, lying on his back, looked down glumly at her dark thatch of hair. It was no use. He just couldn't make it with this one.

'I'm sorry,' he said, 'it's no good. I'm just not in the mood.'

Belinda lifted her head and looked up at him. For a moment the professional mask slipped and the contempt showed in her eyes. 'I can keep trying if you like, but whether you make it or not there's no freebies.'

'No of course. Thank you. My fault entirely. I'm happy to pay.'

She got up from the bed and slipped her dress back on. Now she was all business. 'I'll see you outside,' she said and walked out, leaving him to put his clothes back on again. When he walked back out into the lounge he saw Belinda with two other girls. They were giggling about something. Probably about him. He walked towards the door and Belinda broke away from them to wish him goodbye. It was one of the house rules. As she came up to him he opened the door himself. 'Don't bother me,' he hissed. He turned and went out into the street, feeling humiliated. The evening had been a complete disaster. He knew from past experience it would be weeks before he would be able to summon up the courage to return.

Ross Sellars picked up a takeaway pizza on his way home. He unlocked the door to his apartment, walked through to the kitchen and ate it straight out of the box, standing up at the kitchen bench. When he had finished he went into his bedroom and got out the translations from the wardrobe. He took them to the lounge where he sat down with a sense of excitement. He opened the first letter and began reading. As he did, the humiliation of the evening slipped from his mind. That dumb hooker, if only she knew what he had here she'd look at him with more respect. He put down President Blanchard's letter and picked up the reply from the Russian President. As he read he felt a familiar stirring in his loins. He was becoming erect.

Twenty-three

Igor Bakutin had mixed feelings about the events in Kazakhstan. On the one hand, failure to stop the Americans had been an embarrassment. When informed of the news President Ivashov had sworn and cursed for some minutes and smashed a rather fine glass paperweight by throwing it against the wall. However, Bakutin thought he had been able to lessen the damage. He had reminded the President that even if the story of the American prisoner got out, he had been taken to Russia long before Ivashov's time and he could hardly be blamed personally for it. Through some careful talking, without ever directly saying so, he had managed to suggest that the fault had nothing to do with him but was directly due to the incompetence of his Head of Counterintelligence, to whom he had entrusted the operation. Their meeting lasted for half an hour. At no time did either of them express concern over the disappearance and presumed death of the agent entrusted with the job. They were both more concerned with lessening the political damage. By the time Bakutin left, the President was at least somewhat mollified. Bakutin suspected that the real reason for Ivashov's anger was his mortification at having to explain his failure to the American President.

In his own political sphere, the exercise had not been

without its positive side. He had handed out a scathing dressing down to Ponomaryov and had enjoyed doing so immensely. Ponomaryov fully expected to be relieved of his post, but Bakutin preferred to let him remain, with the knowledge that he had to make just one false move and his career would be finished. He would have no more trouble from that quarter for quite some time. He allowed himself a moment to savour that pleasure and then recalled something President Ivashov had mentioned during their first meeting. 'No loose ends,' he had said. He reached over for the file which the Chief Archivist had brought him. Opening the fading folder he read through the details of the prisoner Parkinson's arrival in Saryshagan, his work at the air defence research facility and his ultimate transfer to Vilnius where he had apparently been settled for many years in obscurity. Bakutin noted that the case officer for Parkinson was one Major Timashov of the First Directorate. Tapping the file thoughtfully, he leaned back in his great leather chair and contemplated a bank of black switches set into a white plastic console on his desk. They had been installed by one of his predecessors and allowed the Director of the KGB to communicate directly with offices throughout the Soviet Union simply by picking up the telephone. He allowed the chair to swing forward into its normal position. It was a pity not to use the technology, but the call he had to make was a simple one. He buzzed his private secretary in the office next door and asked him to get in touch with the First Directorate. If Major Timashov was in Moscow he would like to see him. If he was elsewhere, he was to get here as fast as possible.

Timashov was indeed in Moscow and only a few hundred yards away through the corridors which snake through the Dzerzhinski Square building and underneath the roadway to surrounding buildings. Vladimir Timashov had changed little in the twenty-three years since he first met Dan Parkinson. He was still as fat as ever, but the cares of his job had not etched themselves on his face as they might have on a leaner man. His bulging cheeks were smooth and baby-like. There was perhaps another chin or two, but added to the multitude already there they made little difference.

He had never before been summoned to the Director's office. He heaved himself out of his chair and slowly lumbered off down the corridor, pacing himself so as not to arrive out of breath. After five minutes of walking and two elevator rides, he arrived at the Private Secretary's office next door to the Director. Tall, bald and impeccably dressed, the Private Secretary sat bolt upright at his desk, as though comfort were a sign of weakness. He looked with distaste at the rumpled figure which presented itself before him and buzzed the Director. After listening to his reply he unsmilingly pointed to the door.

The Director was signing some papers when Timashov walked in. Without looking up he asked him to sit down and went on with his work for some minutes. Finally he pushed the papers into a tray and contemplated the man before him.

'Timashov, thank you for coming. Sergei Bulak is one of your cases I believe.'

'That's right, Comrade Director. At one time I had quite a lot to do with him, but no doubt you've read the file, so you would know about that. I see him rarely now. Just a routine visit now and then to check that there are no problems.'

'And are there any problems?'

'Not that I know of,' said Timashov cautiously.

'How often is now and then?'

'Well, to be absolutely accurate I have not seen him personally for two years, but there are six-monthly reports from informants in the factory where he works and from certain neighbours.'

'Do you have any doubts about him?'

Timashov recalled their conversations about freedom and the poverty of the communist system. He phrased his reply carefully. 'He is happily married, he has a child and as far as I can tell he is a model citizen. Why, is something wrong?'

246

'No. Nothing is wrong. At least that we know of.'

Timashov did not relax. If nothing was wrong why was he here? The KGB Director went on, 'I am personally interested in the case of Bulak. You are on good terms with him I presume?'

'Quite good. Yes.' He did not add that they were friends. He was too wily for that.

Bakutin regarded him skeptically and for a second Timashov's heart fluttered beneath the fat. After a long moment he said, 'I would like you to go to Vilnius and see him. Spend some time there. I want to know if anything has changed in his life. If anything unusual has happened. If he is content.'

'If he is content,' repeated Timashov. 'Of course.'

'And report back to me, say, in a week.'

'Yes Comrade Director.'

As Timashov waddled off he was thinking hard. He did not believe for a moment that the new Director had suddenly taken an interest in a twenty-year-old case of defection out of curiosity, yet he could not think of any reason why it should be revived now. The reports on Sergei arrived with routine regularity every six months or so. In fact one was due any day now. Over the years there had been no hint of any change in his attitude. Timashov had simply read them and filed them away. Practically speaking, the case of Dan Parkinson aka Sergei Bulak had been as good as closed for years.

On his return he settled into his chair with a grunt of relief, paused a few moments to recover his breath and reached for the papers in his in-tray. Just before lunch he came upon a folder marked 'Bulak'. He opened it and began to read the latest report from the foreman at the factory where Sergei was manager. It noted, with a malicious attention to detail, that Manager Bulak had told certain employees, known to be sympathetic to the Sajudis freedom movement, that he planned to attend a rally on the occasion of the anniversary of Lithuania's declaration of independence from Russia.

It had come to the foreman's attention, he wrote, that

the subject, Bulak, had subsequently attended the rally with his wife and had joined in an anti-Russian demonstration by dissident Lithuanian elements.

When Timashov read the report he shook his head in dismay. He could understand that Sergei would be attracted to the Sajudis movement. But he was surprised that, despite his careful tutoring, he had been so foolish as to make such a public show of interest. Shaking his head and tut-tutting to himself, he carefully filed the folder and filled out a requisition for travel and expenses for a trip to Vilnius.

Two days later, when Sergei returned from attending a minor crisis on the factory floor, he found Timashov in his office waiting for him. He was surprised and delighted. After they had shaken hands Timashov lowered himself onto the hard visitor's chair, his buttocks sagging over either side like sacks. Sergei said, 'It's been two years since I saw you last, Vladimir, what brings you here?'

Timashov gave him one of his mournful looks. 'Just routine, Sergei. You know I'm still your case officer. I just have to check to see how you are getting on.'

'I'm fine. The same as always.'

'And Palmyra and Alvidas?'

'Fine too. Alvidas is doing well at school and he is a good boy at home. Palmyra is wonderful. I suppose you would say I am a lucky man.'

'Nothing has changed? You are content?'

'Well, Vladimir, contentment is relative isn't it? I am undoubtedly more content than, say, someone in a Siberian labour camp. I have a family and a good position. But am I as content as a factory manager in England, or France or West Germany, or America? I think they would have a quite different standard of contentment, don't you?' Sergei smiled to show he was not serious, but he did not fool Timashov. He knew him too well not to sense the underlying bitterness.

Timashov shook his head from side to side. His mannerisms had not changed since he first confronted Sergei in Vietnam two decades ago. He still affected the same lugubrious air of patience in the face of impetuosity. 'I know very little about those countries,' he said. 'They are not really relevant to me.' He paused and added, 'Or to you.'

'Unfortunately, Vladimir, you are right.' Sergei smiled again to lighten the moment. 'But yes, to answer your question, I am content.'

'Do you hear much talk of independence?' asked Timashov.

'You can't live in Vilnius and not hear it.'

'And do you take part in this talk yourself?'

'Are you asking me as a friend or as my case officer?'

'As a friend.'

'Well I don't mind telling you, as a friend, that I am excited by it. I went to the rally the other day. It was very moving. There's a feeling that things are really going to change soon.'

'I know you went to the rally the other day, Sergei.'

Sergei looked surprised. 'Oh?'

'I am not the only one who writes reports on you, you must know that.'

'I simply went to listen to the speeches. Thousands of others did the same.'

'Thousands of others may do what they like, but you are not like thousands of others. If you remember you have a unique past.'

Sergei bridled. 'Come on, Vladimir. Are you telling me that after twenty years I can't even go and listen to a few speeches? You've heard of glasnost. Things have changed since I first came here, you know that.'

'Maybe things have not changed as much as you think.'

'What do you mean? Are you trying to tell me something?'

'I am telling you to be careful. Keep your nose clean. Do your work. Look after your family. Stay out of politics.'

'Is this an official warning?'

'No, Sergei, not official. The official Timashov would not be allowed to issue a warning. The official Timashov merely writes his report on what he sees.'

'Well write in your damn report that I'm tired of playing the game. Tired of pretending that this system is anything but corrupt and useless. Write that Sergei Bulak thinks it would be a good thing if the communists were defeated and we had a democratically elected government.'

Timashov tut-tutted with disapproval. 'Please be calm, Sergei, and listen. Something has changed in Moscow. You have been invisible for years and all of a sudden people are interested in you again.'

'What people?'

'Very important people. *Very* important people. More than that I cannot say.'

'Why?'

'I don't know.' Timashov looked at Sergei with concern. 'If you insist on being flamboyant you will place me in a delicate position. At the end of the day I am an officer in the KGB. If you get into difficulty I cannot help you.'

'I'm not going to get into difficulty.'

'I hope not.' Timashov patted his shirt pocket for cigarettes, then changed his mind. Today he was, for some reason, aware of mortality. 'You remember in Vietnam the little lizards called, I think in English, gekkos? They used to live in the huts.'

'Sure, gekkos, I remember.'

'They adopted the same colour as the surroundings. That is how they survived.'

Sergei knew that Timashov was about to make one of his ponderous analogies and tried to lighten the moment. 'Yeah, and if you chased them they shook off their tails as a decoy. I know what you're going to say, Vladimir.'

But Timashov was not to be stopped. 'Be like the gekko, Sergei. Blend in with the background.'

Sergei laughed. 'Like the gekko. OK you've got it. Now how about a glass of vodka.'

Timashov stayed in Vilnius for three days, interviewing various informants who had been reporting on Sergei's activities. It was obvious to him that the foreman had developed an unreasonable dislike of his manager and put the worst possible slant on even the most innocuous acts. Face to face, his vindictiveness was obvious, but in print his observations had a ring of authority which was damaging.

When he returned to Moscow Timashov composed a careful report saying that he had found Bulak unchanged. There was no denying that he had attended a dissident rally and had been seen talking with Lithuanians known to be Sajudis supporters, but he put this down to the fact that he was after all living in a Lithuanian community. He had found no reason to suppose that Bulak represented any danger to the state. No signs of restlessness. He signed his report and sent it off to Bakutin's office. He hoped that he would hear no more about it, but he knew his profession too well to believe that was likely.

Twenty-four

After Brandon Paine left the President's office he put in a call to Hammond, who had returned to Washington from Moscow. He told him that the matter of the two Americans was still causing anxiety and it must be seen to a successful conclusion. Whoever Hammond used must be far removed from the US administration. The NSA chief knew that such people existed and he knew that Hammond would know where to find them.

That same day Hammond boarded a flight to Beirut where he entered as Mr James Scofield, businessman. Installing himself in the Commodore Hotel, one of the few still operating in that shattered city, he put through a telephone call to a small import-export company and asked for Hamid. After a brief conversation they arranged to meet for dinner at an Italian restaurant that evening.

Things had improved since Hammond had last visited Beirut. There was no longer a curfew and it was possible to travel through the city without having to stop constantly at roadblocks operated by the various militia groups. The vogue for kidnapping Westerners had passed but that was not to say that the city was entirely safe. Firefights were still an everyday occurrence and snipers were still likely to pick off pedestrians at random. One had to be careful.

The restaurant was called Mama Maria's and was run by a buxom Italian woman who had doggedly remained open for business throughout the worst of the fighting. When Hammond arrived Maria showed him to a table already occupied by a very dark Lebanese man with an eroded face, over-long hair and stubble like a dirty smudge. Hamid rose and gave Hammond a limp hand to clasp. Hammond remembered in time that Arabs do not place the same importance on a firm handshake as Americans and restrained himself from his usual hearty grip, but he could not restrain his Dale Carnegie manner.

'How are you, Hamid? Long time no see. When was it last? Must have been '85 was it? The time the Maronites had that big car bomb.'

'Eighty-four. Yes, a hundred and twenty killed. One of the more memorable days in our history,' said Hamid drily.

The restaurant looked out over the rooftops to the surrounding hills. There was a series of flashes in the distance and, a few moments later, the thud of heavy ordnance reached their ears.

'Looks like someone's having a little fun out there tonight,' said Hammond.

'Yes. It will make a nice show for us while we have dinner,' replied Hamid. He indicated the menu. 'What will you have? Madame tells me the osso buco is very good tonight.'

'Sounds fine,' said Hammond. More flashes lit up the hills and the chattering of small arms punctuated the night. 'Shall we have a bottle of wine?' He knew the Moslem religion did not allow alcohol, but in Beirut he had found that the faithful tended often to forget the Prophet's teachings in this matter. Especially if it was a good French red.

'By all means. I presume your company is paying.'

'Entertainment expenses.' Hammond gave his braying laugh and a few diners looked in disapproval at the crass American who was obviously some sort of salesman, dining with his Lebanese client.

The wine came and Hammond tasted it, pronouncing it drinkable. Hamid sniffed his glass and took a taste, rolling it around in his mouth before swallowing. Hammond noted that he had developed a connoisseur's airs since they had last met. Business must be good. He had no idea what business Hamid pursued except that it had little to do with import or export.

The waiter was hovering. 'Two osso buco,' said Hammond. 'And a green salad.'

The waiter nodded and headed towards the kitchen. 'What brings you to Beirut?' said Hamid, carefully avoiding the use of his name. Hammond noted that he had developed a Westerner's directness too. Five years ago they would have had to engage in small talk until the end of the meal before getting to the real point of their meeting.

'I have an assignment which I think will interest your Pakistani associate.'

Hamid regarded him with interest, a client listening to a presentation about a new product. 'Go on.'

'Two people, US citizens, presently in London. It's important that it's clean. No bombs, no shooting. It mustn't look even vaguely political.'

'US citizens. Interesting. It's a little different.'

'They're a man and a woman, mid-forties, travelling together, but not lovers. At least I don't think so. We don't know how long they intend to stay in Britain. The male is resident in Australia, the woman lives in Nebraska. It needs to be done quickly. Once they leave London they may split up, we don't know. It would be much simpler if it was done in London.'

'I don't know how busy my associate is at the moment,' said Hamid. 'Also, he doesn't like haste. He has a reputation for thoroughness which he would not like to jeopardise.'

Hammond recognised this sally for what it was. It seemed Hamid had not lost all of his Arab qualities. He said, 'We appreciate his thoroughness and would be prepared to pay a premium for speedy action.'

254

On the hillside an orange glow showed where a building was burning. The gunfire had ceased. Perhaps the shooters had fulfilled their objective. Maria arrived and placed two plates of osso buco on the table along with a fresh green salad.

'I don't know how she does it,' said Hammond, 'keeping a restaurant running during all this.' He gestured out the window towards the hills.

'Oh, she was brought up here,' said Hamid. 'Maria's more Lebanese than Italian. She's like everyone else, she copes. Life goes on.'

'I wonder why she stays?'

'Where else would she go?'

Hammond tasted his food. 'She'd make a goddamn fortune in Washington with this cooking, I tell you.'

'Not everyone regards Washington as preferable to Beirut.'

'Yeah? Well I know which one I prefer.' Hammond glanced about him to make sure Maria was safely out of earshot. 'We were talking about money.'

'Yes. I shall have to confer with my associate. He may have to hire additional people. Costs have risen considerably lately.'

'Don't worry about the cost, we want it done well, that's the important thing.'

'And you have photographs, personality profiles, the usual?' asked Hamid.

'Yes. We can supply all that.'

'Well then I'll see him tomorrow if I can catch a flight out. Where will you be?'

Hammond gave Hamid an address in London. They discussed methods of communication and identification procedures and, their business at an end, they made polite conversation until the coffee arrived. As they sipped the sweet, thick liquid from tiny cups, they were careful not to talk politics, which in truth held little interest for either of them. It was the deadly games which surrounded politics that they enjoyed, for their own sake.

Next day Hammond, using a passport in the name of

Donoghue, flew to Frankfurt. There, using the name Brewer, he continued on to London, where he booked into a hotel under yet another name. Upon checking in, he paid in advance and went up to his room. After an hour, he left, carrying his small suitcase with him. He walked two blocks and then took a taxi to a street in Islington. When he had paid off the driver and the taxi had disappeared around the corner, he walked two blocks to a nondescript Victorian detatched house and let himself in with his key. The Islington house was Hammond's permanent London operations centre. Once installed, he set about immediately to find the whereabouts of his quarry.

In America investigators were already taking steps to track down friends who Laura or Bing might stay with in London, Laura's telephone had been tapped and her mail was being intercepted. The same facilities were not available in Australia, but in London Hammond began methodically to check hotels. Recalling their accommodation in Moscow, he surmised that he should begin at the top end of the market. He started with the As in the telephone book, skipping those establishments which were obviously too cheap. The Athenaeum was only the third telephone call he made. It was a small but exclusive hotel which prided itself on the personal touch. When he asked for Mr Connick or Mrs Bailey, the telephonist told him that they had booked out that morning. His heart missed a beat until she added, seconds later, that they were expected back in three days. By any chance did she know where they had gone? Unfortunately no, but perhaps he would like to leave a message for their return? Hammond declined, thanked her for her trouble and rang off.

He left the house and walked three blocks to the tube station where he caught a train to Euston, emerged into the crowds and quickly hailed a taxi. Getting out at Piccadilly Circus he walked west along the Green Park side of Piccadilly until he was opposite the Athenaeum. The iron railings which fenced off the park were hung with cheap paintings for sale. On the pretence of inspecting them he was able to watch the comings and goings from the hotel. He lingered by the paintings for several minutes until a hopeful artist approached him. Politely waving him away, Hammond crossed the road and wandered up the side lane which runs from Piccadilly into the labyrinth of twisting streets behind. What he saw left him satisfied. The Athenaeum was in many ways a better location for their purposes than some of the bigger hotels. There was one main entrance opening onto Piccadilly and a service door on the side lane. Both could be observed by a single watcher from a vantage point across the road. The disadvantage was that it would be almost impossible to enter and roam around inside unnoticed.

He returned to the house in Islington by a roundabout route and settled down to wait. There was not much else he could do until the Pakistani arrived. The break, while they had their dirty weekend or whatever it was, would be useful, thought Hammond. The Pakistani should arrive in London tomorrow. All he had to do was brief him and then his job would be over.

Tirath Gavaskar was born in Pakistan, but it had been many years since he resided there. His home base was Tangier, just across the Straits of Gibraltar from Spain. He liked Morocco because it was handy to the Middle East, Europe and Africa where the majority of his clients came from. The authorities did not bother him and, an important point, it was a Moslem country. Tirath Gavaskar was a devout Moslem and to live in the Christian world would have been unthinkable. He had his principles.

His professional skills were known to only a few people who operated at a high political level. They included arms dealers, the leaders of certain countries sympathetic to terrorist causes, Latin American drug barons, and operatives in various intelligence agencies around the world. Those who wished to use his services did not just pick up the telephone and call. There were two or three trusted intermediaries through whom the approach could be made. He liked to keep his distance and so did his clients.

Hammond was sitting in the lounge room watching a soap opera on television. The theme song was a sentimental ditty about neighbourliness. The show featured a cast of healthy looking young people with nauseating Australian accents who spent their lives having affairs with each other. Each scene seemed to end with the actor giving a long soulful look into the camera before the commercials came on. Hammond found it difficult to believe that people actually watched this sort of rubbish in enormous numbers, but apparently the British loved it.

There was a knock at the front door. Hammond turned off the TV and peered through the spyhole. On the other side, distorted by the fish-eye lens, was a slight man with Pakistani features, dressed in a cheap-looking overcoat and carrying a briefcase. He looked like a typical, underpaid, door-to-door salesman. Hammond opened the door.

'Good afternoon Tirath.' He did not offer to shake hands.

'Mr Hammond. A moment before we go inside.' He offered an illustrated brochure for encyclopedias to Hammond, who perused it for a few moments before nodding and ushering him in.

'Thank you for coming at short notice,' said Hammond, closing the door.

'Not at all. It was the least I could do for a valued client.'

'Can I offer you something?'

'Nothing thank you. I understand that time is important. Perhaps we should discuss our business straight away.'

The Pakistani took off his coat and sat down. Hammond had no idea how many assassinations he had performed but guessed it must be over a dozen. And no one had ever come close to linking his name with any of them. Hammond stole a glance at him. Death came in a neat package. Under the shabby overcoat the Pakistani was tidily dressed. His clothes were conservative, made of top quality material and expensively tailored. On his wrist was a wafer-thin gold watch. These trappings contrasted oddly with the unshaven face. 'Do you have some photographs and documentation for me?' he said.

Hammond opened a sideboard drawer and produced a Manila envelope. He withdrew a photograph and handed it to the Pakistani. 'Bing Connick. Journalist. Fifty years old. Single. American citizen resident in Australia. He's worked all over the world, a lot of the time in war zones. Can look after himself and understands politics. His career's on the skids now but he's smarter than you'd think. Street-smart.'

The Pakistani contemplated the photograph in silence as if trying to see something which would give him a clue to Bing's personality. 'Street-smart, you say?'

'That's right. He's already given us trouble. There was an attempt to dissuade him from a certain course of action just recently which was not successful. He's a lot more resourceful than we gave him credit for.'

If the Pakistani had any criticism to make of American methods he did not reveal them by so much as a flicker of an eye. 'I see,' he said. 'So he will be wary. That always makes things more difficult.'

Hammond said nothing. He handed the Pakistani another photograph. 'Laura Bailey. American. Divorced. Travelling with Connick. She runs a cattle ranch in Nebraska.'

The Pakistani again contemplated the photograph for some moments in silence. 'A cattle ranch. Fascinating.'

'She has certain information which we prefer to be kept out of the public domain.'

'About cattle?'

'No, not about cattle. It's political.'

'Ah. And she was with Mr Connick during this previous attempt?'

'Yes. They were together.'

'Do we know where they are staying?'

'They're out of town at the moment but they're returning tomorrow to the Athenaeum.'

'I see. They travel in style.'

'Mrs Bailey is well off. She's paying the bills.'

'And how long are they planning to stay at the Athenaeum?'

'We don't know.'

The Pakistani held up both photographs and looked at them again before placing them carefully on the coffee table in front of him. His movements were fastidious, almost reverential, like a jeweller handling a precious stone. 'Two Americans staying in Central London. Do you know how hard it is to be alone in London? There are always crowds. This calls for something imaginative. An interesting case. Quite challenging really.'

'It has to be done discreetly. No fuss. No mess.'

The Pakistani gave Hammond a pained expression. 'Of course. Hamid has already mentioned that.' He added, 'We haven't spoken of a fee.'

'Hamid said you would discuss that personally.'

'Three hundred thousand. A hundred now, the rest to be paid upon successful completion.'

'That's fine. The money will be transferred today.'

The Pakistani reached into his pocket and pulled out a folded piece of paper. 'That is the name of the bank and the account number. I'll begin work right away. When I have confirmed that the down payment has arrived I will complete the assignment.' The Pakistani stood up. 'Thank you, Mr Hammond. You won't see me again. Happy to be of service.'

The Pakistani did not shake hands. He shrugged into his cheap overcoat, opened the door and emerged into the street, a salesman with shoulders slumped after another rejection. Without another word he was gone.

Twenty-five

The morning after their encounter in her room, Laura left
London with Bing in a hired car and headed south. She
felt a sense of unreality. The headiness of the night before
had passed and in the sober light of day she was not at
all sure she was doing the right thing. It was as though
the decision to leave town with Bing had been ordained
and now nothing could stop it. Bing was silent as he
threaded his way through the city traffic. Within an hour
they had cleared the red-brick uniformity of London
suburbia. Bing avoided the motorway and meandered
along on minor roads which took them through farming
country. The fields were an impossible green and the
villages through which they passed had the neatness of
architect's models. Every now and then they saw white-
washed cottages and the odd thatched roof. Picture-post-
card England.

The town was situated at the mouth of an estuary, a
collection of neat shops standing back from the seawall
looking out through small windows to the sea. The tide
was coming in, sending rivulets of water stealing among
the mudflats. Fishing boats and pleasure craft sat half-
afloat. Seabirds wheeled and screamed and a few fishermen wearing boots and rollneck sweaters under their
smocks were mending nets. Bing and Laura booked into

their hotel as Mr and Mrs Connick. The receptionist gave them a key and directed them up a flight of creaking stairs to a double room which looked out over the sea.

Bing deposited their suitcases, went to the window and drew the curtains aside. Laura was standing in the centre of the room, looking indecisive. 'What about a walk?' said Bing.

'Good idea,' said Laura gratefully.

Bing walked into the bathroom and dabbed some soap on his finger. He returned and placed two light smears on his suitcase. Then he walked over to Laura and reached up to her hair.

'May I?' he said and plucked a hair out.

'What on earth are you doing?'

'Being paranoid.' He put the hair in place and gestured towards the door. 'Shall we?'

Shaking her head with amusement Laura said, 'You go on ahead. I want to freshen up. I'll see you outside.'

Bing left and Laura began to unpack her suitcase, placing some wrinkled clothes in the cupboard in the hope that the creases would hang out. She wanted time alone to think. Although she dealt with men every day running her ranch, she knew very little about man–woman relationships. There had been a few suitors after her divorce, but none of them had interested her. She had never felt the need to sleep with a man merely for the sake of sex. With Griffith, sex had been a marital duty, like cooking meals or going to social events together. She had not felt the same passion as she had with Dan. Last night, there had been a reawakening of long-forgotten urges. She was physically attracted to Bing, yet she was still not wholeheartedly ready to take the next logical step.

Fifteen minutes later Laura walked downstairs and left the hotel. The tide had advanced further and the mudflats had disappeared under water. A slight sea breeze had sprung up carrying ashore the iodine smell of seaweed and salt air. A few fishing boats showed signs of activity on board as their crews prepared to put to sea. She looked along the seawall and saw Bing with some of the men who had been mending nets. He was helping them load equipment into a big rowing boat to ferry it out to the moorings. They were talking to each other as if they were old friends.

As she came up to them the men were climbing into the boat. Bing gave them a push off. 'Thanks Bing,' one of them said gruffly. 'We'll have that pint when we get back.'

'Good fishing,' said Bing and gave them a wave.

'It doesn't take you long to make friends,' said Laura.

'I understand fishermen.'

They strolled along the seawall and down some steps to the beach. The sand was hard-packed and easy to walk on. Laura took Bing's arm and they set out along the shore. 'There's something about the sea that clears the mind,' said Bing. 'It's therapeutic.'

'I know what you mean. With me it's the range. If ever I need to unwind I get on a horse and ride. After Dan disappeared I went back to stay with my father and used to go out every day by myself and let the country heal me.'

'Was it your father who taught you to be so determined?'

'I suppose that comes from him. He taught me that you can get whatever you want if only you try hard enough.'

'Do you still believe that, after Russia?'

'I must say when I was walking blindfolded in the snow and I heard that gun being cocked, I was having my doubts.'

'Me too.'

Laura said, 'You're a bit like my father.'

'Oh? How?'

'You don't say much and you came on like a tough guy, all hard-bitten and cynical. But underneath you're a lot softer than you make out.'

'Well if I am it's because you've brought it out in me.'

'Maybe so. Maybe we have complementary personalities. You know, Yin and Yang.'

'I guess we'll find that out,' said Bing.

'Maybe. I still don't know if it's a good idea or not.'

Their feet crackled on dried seaweed which had been stranded above the tideline. 'Are you looking forward to going home?' said Bing.

'I'm still disappointed we haven't been able to find out what happened. I'm a little mixed up about a lot of things.'

'You don't have to go home,' said Bing.

'Oh yes I do.'

'You could come to Australia. Cool out on the river for a while. Take a holiday.'

'Are you inviting me?'

'I believe so.'

She thought for a moment. 'Well, let's see.'

The beach stretched away for a mile to a large headland. They walked towards it for an hour or so until the sun began to set, then they turned around and headed back towards the village. When they entered the pub the bar was full of people. They were a mixture of fishermen and yachtsmen and the talk was of weather and sails, of storm-tossed races and record catches. They ordered drinks and within minutes they were drawn into the crowd. Bing fitted in immediately and they listened attentively as he spoke of his own life with sailors and fishermen on a river in Australia. It was not until near midnight that the talk turned to current events. A bearded fisherman was bemoaning the intrusion of European fleets onto British fishing grounds. As far as he could see it was only going to get worse. The whole map of Europe was changing. Why, just this evening on the news he had heard that one of the Baltic states had broken away from the Soviet Union. Before long they'd have bloody commies wanting to join the Common Market. Where would it all end?

Laura was talking to a yachtsman about his cruise to

France last summer and only half-heard the comment. She turned to the fisherman. 'What did you say?'

'I said where will it all end,' he repeated.

'No about the communists.'

'Haven't you heard the news?'

'No. What news?'

'They've declared independence. They broke away today. It's all over the telly.'

'Who has?' Laura asked impatiently.

'Lithoowania.'

Bing turned to the fisherman. 'Did you say Lithuania?'

'That's right, Lithoowania.'

'We have CNN in the room,' Bing said to Laura. 'Maybe we should go and have a look.'

They said their goodbyes and climbed the staircase to their room. Stepping inside, Bing shut the door. Out of habit he checked that his suitcase had not been disturbed, then turned on the TV. The picture came up on a shaky shot of the parliament building in Vilnius. A crowd of people were celebrating in the street outside. With much shouting of slogans they lowered the hammer and sickle flag and raised the Lithuanian one in its place. The reporter's voice-over outlined the details of the declaration and described a mood of jubilation coupled with apprehension sweeping the country. He warned that it was unlikely the Soviet President would simply let Lithuania go without a fight. There were fears that he might call in military forces to suppress the rebel regime.

The scene shifted to Washington, where a spokeswoman for the State Department was giving a press conference. Laura turned the volume down and turned to Bing. They had both been standing immobile in front of the TV set. 'Well. That changes things,' she said.

'It does? How?'

'If Lithuania's no longer part of the Soviet Union, we could go there.'

Bing sat down on the couch and Laura made herself comfortable beside him. 'And do what?' said Bing.

'What do you think? Find out what happened to Dan.'

'It's a long jump from declaring independence to it becoming a fact. You heard what that reporter said. This is only the beginning. No one knows how Ivashov will react.'

Suddenly Laura was sick of her helplessness. It seemed that everyone always found some reason why nothing could be done. At first it had been the Washington officials and their bland stonewalling, then when she thought she was finally on the verge of a breakthrough in Kazakhstan, more dangerous forces had conspired to defeat her. Now even Bing wanted to put up obstacles. 'Dammit, Bing,' she snapped. 'I'm tired of caution. Let's just go there and do something.'

Bing shook his head at her impetuosity. 'We can't just go there. For all we know we're wanted criminals.'

'You're too cautious!' Laura yelled at him.

'And do you know what?' Bing shouted back. 'You're too pig-headed. You want everything to happen straight away. You can't see the subtleties in a situation. We nearly got killed a few days ago because I stopped being cautious. Don't be so damned stubborn. Back off, Laura, for your own sake.'

Laura raised her fists beside her face and shook them in anger. She gave a kind of howl. 'I just feel so impotent, not being able to do anything.'

Bing seized her wrists and held them firmly. He looked into her eyes. 'I know you do, and so do I. Look, give it time. Maybe the situation there will change.'

Laura lowered her arms and leaned against him. Her anger had subsided as quickly as it flared. 'I'm sorry, I can't let it go, Bing. I just can't. As long as there's a chance I have to keep looking.'

'But can't you see how impossible the task is? The trail's cold and there's no Blackwell in Lithuania to help us.'

Laura was silent. He put his arm around her. 'I'll tell you what, we'll go back to London tomorrow and try to think of some plan. OK?' He knew as he said it that it was a hollow promise. He had no plan and no likelihood of one.

'All right,' said Laura.

'I want to help, you know that.'

'I know. I'm impossible. It's just that I'm used to getting things done. This frustrates me beyond reason.'

They sat together for a time, staring at the State Department spokeswoman goldfishing silently on television. 'It's late,' Bing said.

'I know. You first. I'll be there in a minute.'

They kissed, but Laura's lips were unyielding. As she rose and went into the bathroom, Bing cursed the news which had soured the evening. He undressed and got into bed. This wasn't how he had imagined it would be. He wished he knew how to recapture the chemistry they had shared last night, but he had never been adept at the rituals leading to love. He knew she had awoken feelings within him which he thought were dead. Despite their spat just now he realised it was Laura's directness which attracted him to her. It balanced his own reticence. And she had courage. But was this love that he was experiencing? Perhaps. When he was young he had loved women with far less reason.

The light was out and he heard Laura approach the bed. The mattress sagged with her weight and he felt her slip under the covers beside him. She was wearing a nightgown. She turned and she felt her hair brush his face as she moved half on top of him. He reached up with both hands and ran his fingers through the long locks, gently pulling them back behind her neck. He felt rather than saw her face descend to him and their lips met. Her lips were hard. Together they rolled over so that their positions were reversed. Bing stroked her breast lightly through the thin nightgown. She was stiff, unyielding beneath him.

'I'm sorry,' she said. 'It was all right until tonight. It's the news. It's broken the spell.'

Bing lay on his side. He was throbbing with desire.

267

'It's all right. We've got time.' It wasn't all right. He wanted her now.

Laura turned away from him and reached behind her to pull him close. They lay with their bodies nestled together spoon-like. Bing caressed her gently but Laura did not respond. She was there, but far away, staring at the wall. Her mind was racing with the scenes she had just seen on TV of the events in Lithuania. Was Dan there, alive, celebrating tonight? Gradually her thoughts calmed. On the edge of sleep other images swam into her consciousness, images which had haunted her before: Dan's fighter spiralling to earth; the faceless man walking towards her; reaching out to find he had slipped away, as insubstantial as a ghost. Beset by these dreams she finally slipped into fitful sleep. She did not feel Bing roll away from her, nor was she aware of him later shuddering with his own erotic dreams, waking and going to the bathroom for a towel. In the morning when she awoke he was up and dressed. He went over to the bed, placed his hand on her shoulder and looked at her silently for a few moments, with what? Love or regret, she could not tell. He told her he would see her downstairs for breakfast. After she had showered and dressed she joined him. They said little. After breakfast they packed, loaded the car and headed back to London.

Twenty-six

When he left Hammond, Tirath Gavaskar travelled by underground back into London, changing trains twice, watching his back carefully out of habit. In London he liked to stay at the Savoy. As he approached the hotel he slipped out of his shabby overcoat and draped it over his arm. The well dressed man who approached reception for his key looked as if he belonged in the plush lobby.

The Pakistani prided himself on his professionalism. When an operation required more than one person he would not use common criminals. Although such people often had the skills required, they could never be trusted to remain silent afterwards, and he valued his reputation for discretion too much to risk it lightly. He had two or three trusted colleagues who had proven themselves on a number of occasions and who could be relied upon not to brag about their exploits afterwards. They were scattered about various parts of the world and if called upon he knew they would be available at short notice. They too liked working with the best.

It was a pity, he thought, that the Americans had not come to him in the first place. They had no subtlety. Although he had not asked Hammond about his bungled operation he could guess easily enough how it would have been. Probably a crude attempt to attack the targets in the street, using hired help of an inferior standard. He would devise something subtle. Already the outlines of a plan were forming in his mind. The first thing he needed to know was the floor on which Connick and Bailey were staying. He knew that hotels would not give out guests' room numbers, but it would not be difficult to find. When he entered his suite he picked up the telephone and dialled a number. His conversation was short and to the point. He named a time one hour hence and a location, a bench in Green Park, the same park where Laura and Bing had strolled on their first day in London. Disconnecting the call, he left the hotel and strolled through the streets window-shopping. After travelling three blocks he stopped at a public telephone box and dialled a number in Damascus. There was an answer after the third ring. The Pakistani spoke three sentences into the mouthpiece and hung up. He then placed another call, this time to Berlin. Again the conversation was only a sentence or two. Next he looked up the number of the Athenaeum. When the receptionist answered he identified himself as a travel agent and requested the name of the hotel's manager.

Satisfied so far, he began to walk in leisurely fashion towards Green Park, timing his progress to arrive at precisely the time he had specified for his appointment. A man was already sitting on the wooden slatted seat. The Pakistani sat down beside him and remarked upon the beautiful spring weather. A casual observer would have taken them for two men who had chanced to meet by accident. The Pakistani uttered a few sentences, gesturing at the surroundings, obviously commenting on the scene before him. After a few moments he nodded a polite goodbye and continued with his stroll, a well-to-do foreign visitor killing time between business appointments.

Shortly after the Pakistani departed, the other man left the park and took a taxi into the city where he bought a packet of good-quality A4 envelopes. He then went to a newsagent and bought a copy of *Time Out*, which was devoted to entertainment in London. Putting the magazine in the envelope but leaving the flap unsealed, he wrote on the front, 'Ms L. Bailey, arriving guest.' Leaving the newsagent he caught another taxi to Piccadilly Circus, paid it off and set out to walk along Piccadilly. On the way he dumped the rest of the envelopes in a trash can.

When he arrived at the Athenaeum he went straight to the reception desk and asked to leave a message for Ms Bailey. The receptionist keyed the name into her computer to see which room had been pre-assigned, picked up her pen and wrote the number on the envelope. Just as she went to put it away the man said, 'I'm sorry, I just thought of something else I should add. May I borrow your pen and some stationery please?'

She handed them over. He wrote, 'Welcome to London, Ms Bailey. If I can be of any assistance please don't hesitate to contact me.' He signed it, 'Nigel Warrington, Manager,' sealed the note in the envelope and handed it back making a mental note of the number on the front. Thanking the receptionist politely, he left the hotel and walked northwards into the maze of side streets behind the hotel. There he stopped at a cafe and ordered a cappuccino. While it was being made he took out a cellular telephone and dialled the Savoy, asking for the Pakistani's room number. When he heard Gavaskar answer he said three words, 'four one five' and disconnected the call.

Tirath Gavaskar dialled the Athenaeum and asked for reservations. Introducing himself as Suresh Prasad, he requested a double room, single occupancy, for a week starting from tomorrow. He would particularly like the fourth floor if possible, room 413. Mr Prasad explained with a laugh that he had had his honeymoon there some years ago and he would like to stay in the same room for sentimental reasons. It would be fun to call his wife back in India and tell her where he was. The receptionist, forever accommodating to the guests' whims, said she would try. Even if it meant a little bit of juggling they would do their best. Next day Mr Gavaskar left the Savoy and a short time later Mr Prasad took up residence at the Athenaeum in the room he had requested.

Laura and Bing checked back into the Athenaeum and spent the following day separately. It seemed to both of them that they had come to the end of something. They were as distant as lovers who have argued passionately, except that they had never experienced passion, only its promise. They each listened to news bulletins and read the newspapers, but nothing they saw or heard gave them hope. Lithuania was in turmoil and independence was far from an established fact. Bing was preparing to go home. Laura knew she should start making arrangements to return but she could not bring herself to begin the process. As long as she remained in London she could cling to the hope that her search was not over.

Bing looked up a couple of old friends in Fleet Street and spent the evening getting mildly drunk in a journalists' pub. Laura went alone to a West End play, returned early and went to bed.

When she woke early the next morning and pulled the blinds back she looked out on a depressing sight. The weather had broken. The radio report spoke of sleet and freezing wind coming down from the Arctic Circle to lash the metropolis. The news from Lithuania was about conscripts deserting the Soviet army at the suggestion of the new government. Soviet troop movements within the country were leading to fears that President Ivashov might be about to move to crush the fledgling independence.

Laura decided that today she would book her flight to America. She showered and had just completed dressing when there was a knock on the door. 'Who is it?' she said.

A male voice. 'Hotel maintenance.' She opened the door and saw two men in overalls carrying tool boxes. 'Sorry to disturb you ma'am, but we have a report of a leak in the room below and we think it might be coming from your bathroom. Would you mind if we came in and had a look?'

'No, come in,' she said. 'I was just going out.'

The two men walked into the room, the second one shutting the door as he entered. As the first man started towards the bathroom, Laura began following him, turning her back on his partner. Suddenly her arm was seized and twisted up behind her back, while at the same time her assailant's other hand clamped firmly across her mouth. The leading man turned around and stepped close to her. In his hand there appeared a long, thin screwdriver which he held underneath her chin. She could feel it pricking the skin.

'Nice and quiet now,' said the man. He looked English and was well spoken. 'My partner is going to take his hand away. If you make a sound, I push upwards and you die.' The man increased the pressure. She tried to force her head back but the man behind held it. She felt a sharp sting as the skin broke.

The pressure on her mouth eased and she was able to speak. 'What do you want?' she whispered.

'We'll tell you in a moment,' said the man with the screwdriver. He seemed to be the leader. His companion had not yet said a word.

The second man's hand had been hovering a couple of inches from her mouth. Now he stepped back. As he did so the first man seized the back of Laura's head with his free hand and held it immobile, the screwdriver still pressed hard into her. For a split second Laura thought of screaming for help. He must have seen it in her eyes, for he increased the pressure on the screwdriver still further. 'Don't even think about it,' he said.

'Now then,' said the leader. 'You're going to walk over to the telephone, pick it up and dial your friend Mr Connick. You're going to tell him to come here and see you. If he asks why, tell him you have something urgent to discuss which can't wait. If you try to be clever I'll kill you without hesitation.'

Laura's eyes darted around the room, looking for some

way of escape. The man spoke again, savagely, urgently. 'Don't think about it, do it now.'

He took away the screwdriver and the other man propelled her from behind to the telephone. Laura thought of something. 'He's gone out. He said he was going out early this morning. He had to attend a meeting.'

'He's there,' said the leader. 'We checked. Now don't waste any more of my time or I'll stop being nice to you.'

The other man handed her the telephone. Reluctantly she dialled Bing's number. He answered immediately. His voice sounded ridiculously normal.

'Bing?' she said.

He said something but she could not speak. The silence stretched on for seconds. Too long. Surely he could tell something was wrong. Bing, as usual, let the silence hang. The leader put his arm around her, seized a handful of hair and held her head immobile. With the other he placed the tip of the screwdriver in her ear. He nodded to her.

'Bing. Can you come to my room right away?' She paused. Words failed her. She wanted to shout a warning, but she could feel the thin shaft pressing against her eardrum and hear the man breathing heavily, inches from her face. She stammered into the telephone, 'Something's come up, some news. Come straight away.'

The man seized the telephone from her and placed it back on the receiver. 'That was very good,' he said. 'Now, when he comes you're not going to go to the door, you're going to call out to him to step inside. That's all. No warnings, no tricky eye movements. Just do as you're told.'

'What's this all about?' said Laura.

'I can't tell you.'

'Are you telling me you don't know? What are you, just hired muscle?'

'No more questions. Just wait.'

The second man unlocked the door. They waited. Two

minutes later there was a knock. The man nodded to Laura. She tried to speak but her voice came out as a croak. She cleared her voice and tried again. 'Is that you Bing?'

'It's me, open up.'

'It's open,' she said. 'Come in.'

The door swung open and Bing stepped inside. He saw Laura standing in the middle of the room and said, 'What's up? You sounded strange on the phone.' He saw her eyes swivel in apprehension and started to turn in the direction she was looking. As he did he had an impression of a raised arm and something descending towards his head. He heard the thud as the sap caught him neatly behind the ear. The room swam and he crumpled to the floor.

Laura opened her mouth to cry out but one of the men, she didn't know which one, clamped his hand firmly over her mouth and again twisted her arm behind her back. She felt the other man rip her sleeve and the sharp jab of a needle. She tried to struggle but a warm feeling of peace began to spread through her body and it no longer seemed worth the effort. She was floating. She saw Bing on the floor, he seemed to be asleep, so peaceful. There was nothing to worry about any more. She felt the firm grip holding her up, had a vague sensation of being walked towards the bed where she lay down and drifted gently off to sleep.

'How long?' said the man who had held the screwdriver.

'Not sure. Gavaskar said maybe a couple of hours.' The leader sat down at the table and pulled out a pack of cards. 'Put out the do-not-disturb would you?' He began to shuffle. 'Rummy?'

Johnny Beard had worked for Madrid Laundry for fifteen years. He was happy with his lot, content to do a day's work, enjoy a pint afterwards and go to the footy on Saturday. He always looked forward to calling at the Athenaeum. The housekeeper was a plump West Indian woman who liked to flirt and he fancied he could do a bit of good there if he made the right moves.

The stop before was the Ritz. Johnny and his offsider, a pinch-faced young man with a mohawk and tattoos, arrived there in mid-morning and proceeded to unload the giant sacks of clean linen into the service elevator. From there they descended one level to the basement where they handed them over to the head housekeeper who checked briefly and signed for them. Johnny wished her a cheery good morning and headed back up in the elevator. 'Next stop the Athenaeum my son,' he said. 'I'm going to ask that Maria out today. I reckon she fancies me and it's about time I made me move.'

They climbed into the van and Johnny pressed the starter. Nothing happened. He tried again. 'Dead as a bleedin' doornail.' Sighing, he got out and went back into the elevator to look for a telephone.

It was an hour before the Madrid laundry could send out a new van and Johnny Beard was once more on his way. He headed up Piccadilly. As usual at this time of day it was choked with buses and taxis and it was another ten minutes before he turned into the lane beside the Athenaeum. The two men lugged in the big bags and Maria gave them a blowsy hello. 'They said you'd be late,' she told Johnny.

'Who's that my love,' he replied, giving her a grin.

'Your two mates. They came and picked up an hour ago. Said you'd be along later with the delivery.'

'Me mates, eh? Who were they then?'

'I don't know,' said Maria in her lilting voice. 'I didn't ask them their names.'

'Faithful to me are you?'

Maria squealed with laughter and slapped him playfully on the shoulder. 'Ooh you. You know you're the only man for me Johnny. These two fellers were such weakies, you should have seen them lugging out the bags. You'd have thought they had a bleedin' body in them or something.'

'Oh yeah, and what did they look like?'

'I dunno. One was a Pakistani or Indian maybe and the other was, just ordinary.'

'Come on Maria, you're 'avin' a lend of me. There ain't no Pakis working for Madrid.'

'Well there is now.'

Johnny shook his head. It was funny. The office had said nothing about sending a relief van. Oh well, it'd all become clear when he got back to the depot. He gave Maria a wink and said his goodbyes. With his mate in tow he got back in the van and continued on his way. It was only when he was a block away that he realised he had clean forgotten to ask her out.

Twenty-seven

Bing felt he was suffocating. His mouth was taped and his hands and feet were handcuffed. He was enveloped in something soft, pressing from all sides, smothering. Everything was black. No definition, no shape. His head was throbbing where he had been hit. He became aware of movement, then noise: the hum of tyres on a roadway, a horn honking, a motor accelerating and decelerating, gears changing up and down. In his soft cocoon he rolled from one side to the other as the vehicle, yes it was a vehicle, cornered, accelerated and braked.

Bing tried to wriggle his hands in their handcuffs. It was impossible. They were clamped painfully tight. He tried to force open his mouth. The tape was stuck fast, impossible to shift. Think, Bing. Your lack of judgment got us into this, now get us out. The fact that they were still alive indicated that they wanted to get them somewhere where they could be disposed of quietly. It was not easy to kill someone in a crowded city, so at least they had some breathing space. But how much?

The stops and starts seemed to be less frequent. They must be in the suburbs, or even out of London. He had no idea how long he had been unconscious. The gears ground and the vehicle swayed around several corners and stopped. It began to move backwards, stopped again.

He heard a door slam and then the clattering sound of a metal shutter opening. He noted irrelevantly that something needed oiling. The engine revved again and the van moved a few feet more. He heard the door squeak and then clang shut with a tinny sound. The engine was turned off and footsteps came towards him. Another door opening, in the vehicle this time. Hands pulling at the surrounding softness and, at last, light. He was in a bag of some sort surrounded by cloth.

He felt hands drag him out of the van and dump him on a hard floor. His blindfold was removed and he looked around for Laura. Two men were taking her out of a laundry bag. She was gagged with grey tape. They undid the handcuffs on her ankles and she kicked out, catching one of the men on the side of the head. His companion punched her and her head slammed against the side of the van. Bing fought against his bonds but could not move.

The man she had kicked put his hand to his head and examined the blood on his fingers. 'Bitch,' he said quietly and slapped her hard across the face.

They were in what looked like a suburban garage. A third man, a Pakistani, appeared and the three of them dragged Laura and Bing to a rear door which led through the kitchen to a lounge room. The floor was covered in a drab brown carpet and the furniture was cheap. Heavy curtains were drawn across the windows, leaving the room in semi-darkness. One of the men clicked on a light. Somewhere within the house a clock chimed the hour. One o'clock. He had been unconscious for four hours.

Laura and Bing were placed in two lounge chairs. Bing looked at his abductors. Three men: the Pakistani, who seemed to be the leader, and two Europeans, both fit-looking, with short military-style haircuts and wary eyes which missed nothing. The Europeans looked hard and tough. The Pakistani was slightly built, but had an economy of movement which suggested competence. No one had said a word. Now the Pakistani spoke. 'I apologise for the lack of comfort on your journey, but it was necessary I'm afraid. We're likely to be here for some hours yet. I would like to lessen the discomfort for you but I want to be assured of your cooperation.' Opening a slim black Porsche attaché case, he produced a syringe which he plunged into a vial, sucking up a clear liquid into the barrel. He held it upright and depressed the plunger until a tiny squirt emerged. 'I could simply drug you again, but if you give me an undertaking not to cry out I will remove the gags. Do I have that assurance?'

Bing and Laura nodded. The Pakistani laid the syringe carefully down on a coffee table and motioned to the man with the cut on his head. He stepped forward, caught hold of a corner of Laura's gag and ripped it off in one short, violent movement. She gasped with pain as the adhesive came away from her skin. Her lips were red and painful. 'That looks sore,' the man said. 'Can I kiss it better?' He grinned at his companion who tittered in reply.

'Don't you touch me,' hissed Laura.

The man walked over to Bing and ripped off his adhesive in one malicious swipe. Bing winced and tried not to cry out with pain. 'What about the handcuffs?' he said. 'We're obviously not going anywhere.'

The Pakistani considered this thoughtfully. 'Very well. He nodded again and one of the men produced a key with which he undid the cuffs. As he stepped back his coat fell open and Bing had a brief glimpse of a gun in a shoulder holster. Bing and Laura rubbed their wrists, trying to restore circulation.

'What about the feet?' said Bing.

'I'm afraid not,' replied the Pakistani.

'What happens now?' said Bing.

'We wait.'

'For what?'

'For darkness.'

Laura spoke, 'And what happens then?'

The Pakistani regarded her without expression. 'Please Mrs Bailey, I don't want to distress you. It would be better if you just made yourself comfortable and tried not to upset yourself.'

'What are you talking about?' Laura said. 'You're going to kill us aren't you?'

The Pakistani gave her a pained look. 'You think I am an uncivilised man don't you? I bear you no ill will at all,' he said reasonably. 'I'm merely a professional doing a job. I hope you understand that.'

Laura looked at him with loathing. 'Who are you working for? The KGB? Have they sent you to finish the job they tried to do in Kazakhstan?'

The Pakistani smiled, with conceit, not humour. 'It would be unprofessional of me to discuss my employer, Mrs Bailey, but I will tell you this much. No, it is not the KGB. They prefer to use their own people.'

'So who do you work for?' Bing asked.

'I work for anyone who requires the skills that I can provide and who can pay for them. And you would be surprised how many customers I have.'

'I'm sure,' said Bing drily. 'I'd like you to tell your employer that we have no intention of revealing anything about what we discovered in Russia.'

The Pakistani shook his head. 'And let you go? If you give that just a moment's thought you will see it is impossible. We have already passed the point of negotiation.'

'So you wait until it's dark and then you quietly bump us off and dispose of us, is that it?'

'I wouldn't put it as crudely as that.'

'How would you put it?'

'You are emotional, that's understandable, but I advise you to be calm and things will be much easier for everyone.'

Bing flared. 'You're a murderer. You can dress it up any fancy way you like, but you're no better than a common thug who kills for money.'

The Pakistani sighed, picked up the syringe and toyed with it. 'Mr Connick, if you insist on insulting me I will have to silence you. Do I make myself clear?'

Bing restrained himself with an effort. 'Perfectly.'

The Pakistani looked at his watch, opened his brief-case again and took out a thin mat which he laid out in a corner of the room. Taking off his shoes he knelt down and began to pray, bobbing his head to the floor now and then. Laura and Bing exchanged incredulous glances. Somehow this show of devotion, moments after so calmly discussing murder, seemed more frightening than any display of violence. The two muscle men began playing cards.

The Pakistani finished his devotions, got to his feet and neatly folded his prayer mat. He fastidiously placed it back in his case. 'Would you like tea, coffee?' he asked.

Bing and Laura shook their heads. The Pakistani continued, 'Such an unspiritual world we live in these days, don't you agree?' He looked from one to the other with interest. Neither of them replied. He went on, 'You don't follow the teachings of Mohammed. If you did you would feel much more calm. The Prophet tells us that whatever happens is written. Fate. I urge you to think about it.'

The Pakistani was gazing off into the distance somewhere. He continued speaking in a soft voice. 'Most people fail to see that our existence is an infinitesimal part of a grander plan.' He paused as if struck by a sudden thought. His eyes focused back on the two people sitting hobbled before him. 'But then only a true believer can understand this. How can I expect infidels to grasp the beauty of existence?'

One of the men looked up from his cards. 'Have we got any food here, boss? I'm kind of hungry.'

The Pakistani's gaze remained fixed thoughtfully on the two prisoners before him. This man could kill us at any moment, thought Bing. Who knows what's going on in that mind? Reluctantly, Gavaskar's gaze shifted to his assistant. 'Food? No, there is no food here.'

'What say I go out and get some?' suggested the man.

The Pakistani thought about it for some moments.

'We passed a deli down the road. I could get some stuff there,' the assistant suggested.

The Pakistani nodded. 'Yes. All right.'

Laura and Bing sat together in silence. Left without his partner, the second man sat down in a chair facing them, took out a handgun and placed it on a coffee table. He fumbled in his coat pocket and produced a silencer which he unhurriedly screwed on to the end of the barrel. The Pakistani also sat down. There seemed nothing to say. Bing could hear the clock ticking loudly in another room. The man with the gun was tapping the fingers of his left hand on the coffee table in a repetitive riff and whistling softly between his teeth. The Pakistani stared into space, his eyes unfocused, as if meditating.

I just can't sit here eating sandwiches waiting for these bastards to kill us, Bing thought. He judged the distance between him and the man with the gun. Even without his feet hobbled it would be too far. He would have the weapon levelled before he was halfway there and he didn't underestimate the Pakistani either, despite his slight build. He glanced at Laura, winked and gave a wry grimace. She clasped his hand, squeezed hard and held it. The sounds of suburbia filtered in from the street outside. A barking dog, a bicycle bell ringing, the occasional swish of a car passing along the street. Two children walked by, arguing about whose daddy was the richest. A few minutes later he heard two women, chatting as they approached the house. They stopped right outside and began discussing some television show or other. Bing felt Laura tense as though she might be about to cry out. The man with the gun took it up and casually pointed it at them, without bothering to rise from his seat. The Pakistani registered no sign of concern and continued to stare dreamily at nothing. Bing squeezed Laura's hand and shook his head. The man opposite nodded as if agreeing. Nobody spoke.

The women moved off at last and the man put the gun down. After some minutes there was a knock on the door. The man got up, murmured a question, waited for the answer and opened up. His associate walked in with two plastic bags full of parcels wrapped in white paper.

Laura wanted to talk to Bing and tell him it didn't matter, but she didn't want to say the words in front of their captors. It was as if they would be intruding on something intimate, like love. She continued to hold his hand in silence.

The man who had gone to the delicatessen was in the kitchen, whistling while he worked. After a time he emerged with plates of sandwiches. He and the other European began to eat hungrily. The Pakistani picked delicately at his but left most of it. Laura and Bing refused food.

The afternoon dragged on. The Pakistani asked one of his men to turn on the radio to check if there was a hue and cry about their disappearance, but there was nothing. Most of the news was international. Lithuania was mentioned, but it seemed irrelevant now. There was a report of a cricket Test being played in Australia. Bing tried to envisage his home near Sydney, sunshine dappling the gum trees, the birds on his verandah, the river flowing past at the bottom of the garden. He wanted to see them again, but he could think of no action he could take which would help them now.

The Pakistani got up and drew the curtains aside. Outside, it was beginning to get dark. He walked over to the syringe and picked it up, toying with it thoughtfully. Having reached some decision, he placed it back in its plastic container and put the container in his attaché case. He addressed the men. 'Gags and handcuffs please.' They got up and approached Bing warily. One of them bent towards his wrist with the handcuffs. Bing lashed out with his fist. Seated awkwardly as he was, he caught him a glancing blow on the side of the head. It wasn't good enough. The other man brought down the barrel of his gun onto Bing's wrist, causing him to cry out with pain. The one Bing had hit swung the handcuffs and caught him in the ear, drawing blood. Seconds later the two men had overpowered him. One of them walked out through the kitchen into the garage. They heard the van door slam and moments later he came back with a roll of grey tape. He unrolled a piece about nine inches long, tore it off and approached Bing. He attempted to squirm away but his associate walked around behind him, cuffed him across the back of the head with his open hand and then held him by the ears. They taped his mouth, then turned to Laura. She tried to struggle but was powerless to resist them. Within seconds she too had been rendered mute and immobile.

The Pakistani watched these goings-on patiently, as if waiting for a tiresome child to finish a tantrum. The two men first dragged Laura to the garage, each holding her under an armpit. They came back and did the same with Bing, rolling the two of them roughly into the back of the van. The door slammed shut and they eased out into the night.

Bing could see the backs of their captors' heads silhouetted against the windscreen in front of them. Looking back he could see the headlights of a car behind. It was raining and the beams shattered on the wet glass. In front, the driver cursed the car for leaving his lights on high. The van slowed at an intersection and came to a halt. Bing saw the lights swing out beside the van and disappear. He heard the car pull up beside them.

'Thank Christ for that, you prick,' said the the man in front. 'I've a good mind to get out and job him.'

His companion looked across and chuckled. 'Give him an earful.' The driver began to wind down his window, then shouted, 'Fuck, he's getting out.' The glass shattered with a roar and the driver was thrown across his companions. Something metallic thrust through the window, there was a flash and another deafening roar and the second muscle man reeled back, fragments of brain and skin and bone spattered on the window. The Pakistani, sitting between the bodies, was struggling to throw off their weight. Laura raised her cuffed hands and brought them down hard on his head once, twice. She felt the metal crack bone and the Pakistani lay still. There were footsteps running round to the rear doors and seconds later they were wrenched open. She and Bing were dragged out of the van door. One of the men lifted a pair of bolt cutters and in seconds severed the chains on their hands and feet. They were bundled into the back of the car beside them, where the driver was revving his engine impatiently. A man jumped into the front seat and the car accelerated away. The whole thing had taken less than a minute.

'What the hell's going on?' cried Bing.

The men did not turn round. 'Don't worry,' the man in the passenger seat said, 'you're in no danger. We're taking you somewhere safe.'

'Who the hell are you?' said Bing.

'Please, no more questions. You'll see shortly.'

It seemed to Bing that events had never been within his control. He was an observer caught up in a momentum he could not escape. What new revelation was about to occur he could not imagine. If the Pakistani and his two men were not in the pay of the KGB, as they had said, then who else wanted them dead?

He looked out the window trying to discern a sign or a shop front which might give him a clue where he was. They were in the suburbs somewhere, but there were no shops on this stretch of road, just rows of red-brick Victorian houses, anonymous as faces in a crowd. He had the feeling that this was London, although there was nothing he could see to support that assumption. It could just as easily have been any town in Britain.

The driver stayed carefully within the speed limit, obeying the road rules to the letter. Bing saw a shop sign advertising takeaway food, a dry-cleaners, a betting shop. They passed an entrance to an underground railway. There was the familiar British Rail sign but nothing to say what suburb the station was in. They passed through the shopping centre and entered another residential area. The car was slowing. It came to a halt outside a house like all the others. The driver turned off the engine and the two men got out. Laura and Bing glanced at one another without speaking and set off after them across the footpath. A wooden gate was open and they walked through it and up a short path to the front door. As they approached, it swung open revealing a bulky figure in the darkness. 'Come in,' said a voice they had heard somewhere before. The other two men stood aside for them to enter. The silhouette led them down a hallway into a well-lit lounge room. It was oddly chintzy; lace curtains on the windows and antimacassars on the seat backs. He turned and they saw his face for the first time. 'Laura, Bing, we meet again.' Bing's senses, already overloaded from the events of the night, reeled in confusion as he tried to remember the name. It came back to him. Pavel Rezchikova, the Russian businessman they had met in the dacha outside Moscow, stood before them smiling urbanely, as though welcoming them for dinner.

Rezchikova chuckled. 'Please excuse me, but you should see your faces.'

Bing found his voice. 'I think I'm going mad. Will someone please tell me what the hell is going on?'

'In a moment,' said Rezchikova. He indicated a lounge. 'Please make yourself comfortable. I must just ask my assistants to bring me up to date.'

Rezchikova addressed them in Russian and a rapid-fire conversation followed. After they had finished their briefing he turned to Laura and Bing. 'Everything seems to have gone well.' He chuckled again. 'I would not like to be Mr Gavaskar when the British police ask him to explain how he came to be in a van with two dead mercenaries. Now then, you look as if you could do with a drink. What would you like?'

Bing had a thousand questions but he didn't know where to start. 'Anything,' he said.

Laura nodded. 'Yes anything.'

'Vodka then.' I have some Stolichnaya here which should hit the spot, I think.'

Rezchikova poured out five vodkas into shot glasses and distributed them. 'Rudi and Oleg, well done. Laura and Bing, welcome to our house. I am sure you have heard the term safe house. That is what this is. You will be safe here.'

They drank. 'Where are we?' Laura asked.

'Shepherds Bush.'

'London?'

Rezchikova looked at her curiously, 'Yes of course, London.'

'It's just that I've lost track of time. We were drugged. I had no idea how far we'd travelled.'

'From the Athenaeum to Finchley. We have been watching Gavaskar all along, waiting for our chance.'

Bing said, 'Why were you watching him?'

'I'm sorry, Bing,' said the Russian. 'I can see this must be mystifying. Let me begin at the beginning.' He refilled the glasses and sat down in a chair opposite them. 'We have been keeping an eye on you ever since you arrived at the Athenaeum. When we saw Gavaskar check in we realised you were in danger, but before we could do anything he had already begun to make his move. We could only follow and hope for an opportunity to intervene.'

'Who's Gavaskar?' asked Bing.

'Gavaskar is a professional assassin. He has no political allegiance, but in the past he caused us considerable difficulty. I think it will be some time before he troubles us again.'

'Who was he working for this time?'

'Can't you guess?'

Laura broke in. 'In Kazakhstan there was an attempt on our lives by the KGB.'

'I know about Kazakhstan,' said Rezchikova. 'You're right, that was our people. There is only one other government who would have such an intense interest in your discoveries. Think about it.'

'So the CIA wants us dead too. Is that what you're saying?'

'Maybe not the CIA. But yes, someone in your government.'

'What are they afraid of?' Laura asked. 'What could

be so important about Dan Parkinson that they're prepared to kill to prevent it coming out?'

'He is not Dan Parkinson,' said Rezchikova. 'He has a different name now, a Russian name.'

Laura stared at him. 'He's alive? Dan's alive?'

'Alive and living in Lithuania.'

'So the trail does end there,' Laura said softly. 'Is he all right? Is he incarcerated?'

'No. He's free, living as a normal citizen.'

'And is he . . . is he alone?'

'No he's not alone, Laura. He's married with one child, a boy.'

Laura was silent. She supposed she should have been elated, but instead she felt oddly detached. She had known a young man, with an uncomplicated view of life, a man she understood and loved. They had planned a straightforward future together: marriage, a military career, a conventional American life. That man had obsessed her for twenty years. In some perverse way the knowledge that he was really alive made him seem more insubstantial than ever. The Dan she knew might just as well have died when his fighter crashed in Vietnam. This new Dan they were talking about, with a Russian name and a Russian past, was a stranger.

'I think you'd better tell us where you fit into the picture, Pavel,' Bing said. 'When we met in Moscow you said you were a businessman, looking for joint-venture partners. But I've never met a businessman who knows professional assassins and who has friends who can kill as efficiently as these two.'

Rezchikova smiled. 'It is true I travel abroad a lot,' he said, 'but not on business, at least not business in the conventional sense. I am employed by the same people who employ Blackwell.'

'In Kazakhstan the KGB wanted to kill us,' said Bing. 'Now you've just prevented someone else trying to kill us. What's going on?'

'To answer that question you need to understand the KGB,' said Rezchikova. 'The organisation is highly politicised. At the moment there are two factions, the hard-liners, who want it to be like it always was, and those who want change in the spirit of glasnost. We liberals believe that before there is a clean start all of the dirty tricks of the past have to be publicly acknowledged. The Soviet Union has always denied military involvement in Vietnam, but they were there. They have never admitted taking Americans back to Russia, but they did. Dan Parkinson is living proof of that. Unless we admit these things glasnost will be a sham.'

To Bing, some of what Rezchikova said made sense. He remembered Bellamy's briefing about the KGB factions. But he wondered how much to believe. Rezchikova portrayed himself as a patriot with high moral motives. While that might be true he suspected there was something more subtle behind his actions. 'So let me get this straight,' he said. 'The hard-liners wanted us killed and you're acting unilaterally, without official permission.'

'Exactly.'

'The KGB still wants us out of the way?'

'This is so.'

'And although you've managed to stop one attempt by the CIA or whoever it is, they're unlikely to just pack up their toys and go home either.'

'I would say not. It would certainly be uncharacteristic of them to retire at this stage.'

'So we really have no place to go that's safe.'

'Not at the moment, but you can change that.'

'How?'

'You're a journalist,' Rezchikova said. 'You began by looking for a story. Now you've found it. Write your story and the publicity will be so great that no one will dare touch you.'

Bing laughed mirthlessly. He shook his head. 'Pavel, I don't have a story. Forgive me for being blunt, but I have only your word that Parkinson is still alive. You say you have high motives, but how do I know what political games you're playing back in Moscow? I haven't seen Dan Parkinson with my own eyes. Unless

that can happen I have no story. And it's clearly impossible.'

'So if you could see him yourself you would be able
to write it?'

'Yes.'

'Very well then. Perhaps that can be arranged.'

Twenty-eight

Sergei was at home with Palmyra watching the news on television. The leading item on the bulletin concerned a visiting delegation of Bulgarian trade officials. There was shaky black and white film of men shaking hands and inspecting factories. The report ended with mute shots of a man making a speech, followed by shots of his audience silently clapping.

'Will you look at this, Palmyra. Lithuania declares independence and the first story in the news is a visit by a trade delegation. Censorship!'

Palmyra put a hand on his arm to quieten him. 'Look,' she said, pointing towards the screen.

The newsreader, wearing a dowdy suit and reading his copy on the desk with head bent, introduced a report from Lithuania. It showed Soviet Air Force planes dropping leaflets over Vilnius. The voice-over described the contents as informing the populace that the move towards independence did not represent the will of the people. The film cut to shots of President Ivashov in the Supreme Soviet. This time the camera crew had recorded sound. Ivashov told the deputies that unless the Lithuanian parliament came to its senses he would have to consider cutting off gas and oil supplies. The story ended and the newsreader introduced a report about a tractor factory which had exceeded its quota for the year.

Sergei snorted in amusement. The map of Europe was being redrawn and Moscow was treating the story as though it was a minor row. He had been watching the progress of the breakaway for days. Although the Moscow news bulletins did not show it, he knew that every day the streets were full of demonstrators voicing their support. He had thought of joining in but, heeding Timashov's warning, he had resisted the impulse.

The news ended and a variety show began. A solid-looking woman, bulging out of a cheap-looking sequinned dress, launched into a Petula Clark song. In the background, orange and brown mobiles waved lazily out of focus. The camera bumped and began a slow creep in to her face. 'Don't sleep in the subway darlin' . . .' she sang. Sergei leaned forward and switched off the set. He said to Palmyra, 'It's exciting. Independence! Just think of it. It's going to make a huge difference to our lives.'

'If Ivashov allows it to happen,' said Palmyra. 'I still can't believe that he will.'

Sergei's enthusiasm was not to be dampened. 'You know, people will be able to say what they like, go where they like, no more big brother controlling everything. Who knows, we might even be able to travel abroad one day.'

Palmyra smiled at the thought. 'Oh sure. We'll go to California for our holidays.'

'Don't laugh,' said Sergei. 'It may happen.' He continued enthusiastically, 'Imagine, seeing America again. Oh Palmyra, I'd love to show you what it's like.'

'You still miss America don't you, even after all this time?'

Sergei squeezed her shoulder affectionately. 'I love you and Alvidas. If I could transplant you to America my life would be perfect.'

'Would we drive a Cadillac with a roof that comes off?'

'A Caddy convertible, sure. And we'd eat hamburgers and sodas and you'd join the PTA and on Saturdays I'd coach Alvidas in the Little League.'

Palmyra looked affectionately at her husband. 'What on earth are the PTA and the Little League?'

'Don't worry.'

'Sergei?'

'Yes, my dove?'

'Do you still miss Laura?'

'Laura? What on earth made you think of her?'

'I don't know. We are talking about America and she was part of that life.'

'I never think about her,' lied Sergei. In fact he often wondered what had happened to Laura. It was an eerie feeling sometimes to think that she was out there in the world somewhere, living her American life. She undoubtedly thought that he was dead and would probably have all but forgotten about him by now. It had, after all, been twenty-three years since he had flown off to Vietnam. She would have mourned him for a while and then gotten on with her life. He sometimes fantasised about meeting her. These fantasies were romantic and tinged with eroticism. In them she was a young Laura, frozen in time in the America of the sixties. The practical side of him knew that these were only dreams, but he felt safe indulging himself. He knew that there was no chance he would ever see Laura again. The real world was here in Vilnius, but sometimes he felt he was only an observer, not a participant. 'I wish I could be part of what's happening,' he said to Palmyra. 'I hate sitting at home watching the news when I could be out there working for what I believe in.'

'Please don't say that,' Palmyra said. 'It frightens me. You can dream about Cadillacs and freedom, you know what these things are. But dreams frighten me. Dreams are dangerous.'

He hugged her. 'Don't be afraid. We've come too far to lose each other. If anything was going to happen to me it would have happened a long time ago.'

Palmyra pulled away from him angrily. 'Oh you! You've learned nothing have you? They torture you. They make you betray your country. Your friend Timashov watches you and writes his reports. The neighbours and people at work spy on you for Moscow. This is how it's always been. They're not going to allow this country to break away. Do you think that just because there's something called glasnost there are still no labour camps, no madhouses? Do you think you're immune from their bastardry? When they crack down it will be just as it always was, only worse. Anyone who was part of independence will be stamped on.'

Sergei put his arms around her and held her tightly. Even in his blackest moments he could never equal her cynicism. 'Hush, hush,' he said, like a parent consoling an upset child.

Palmyra started to cry, sobbing into his shoulder. 'I'm sorry, I don't want to shout at you, but I just couldn't bear to lose you.'

Sergei patted her and kissed her neck. 'And I couldn't bear to lose you either. If they tried to take me away now I don't know what I'd do. I'd kill them.'

Alvidas walked into the room and glanced curiously at his parents. It was hard to understand adults sometimes. They seemed to make life more complex than it needed to be. 'I've finished my homework,' he said. 'Can I watch TV for a while?'

Sergei looked at his son with love, his eyes avidly taking in the features which mirrored his own in so many ways. He had a sudden impulse to embrace him but he resisted it. 'Sure son. That variety show is on, the one with the pop music.'

'Thanks Daddy.' He switched on the set and sat down beside them. The woman was no longer singing. She had been replaced by a bearded man dressed in baggy pants and boots and a peasant's smock. He was the latest folk-singing rage in Russia and the cameras showed cut-aways of the young audience clapping adoringly in time to his music. Alvidas and Palmyra soon became absorbed in the screen, but Sergei could not concentrate. Beside him on the couch was his reason for living. His optimism was replaced by a more familiar emotion, a nagging worry; the fear of a loss too terrible to contemplate.

Twenty-nine

Igor Bakutin had been discussing the situation in Vilnius with President Ivashov for the last hour. The KGB had infiltrated deep within the Sajudis movement; they even counted a couple of deputies in the Lithuanian parliament among their informers. Bakutin had brought the President up to date on the latest intelligence about the rebels and was shuffling his papers back into his briefcase, preparing to leave, when the President had an afterthought. 'By the way, is there anything else to report on that defector in Vilnius, what's his name?'

'Sergei Bulak. His case officer paid him a visit and he also spoke to some informers. Bulak seems to have had a slight flirtation with Sajudis, attended a couple of rallies and so on, but nothing to indicate he's ready to do anything rash.'

The President had a new glass paperweight to replace the one he had smashed during one of their previous meetings. He picked it up from his desk and hefted it thoughtfully. 'I don't like loose ends,' he said.

'That is highly improbable,' Bakutin said. 'He's only a loose end if the Americans found something in Kazakhstan that leads them to Vilnius.'

The President put the paperweight carefully back on his desk. 'Let's just say that the journalist did find something. He writes a story for the American papers. He says an American was taken to Russia during the Vietnam War and is now living in Vilnius.'

'We would deny the story.'

'Say the American has the name, he names Bulak.'

'What proof could he have? None. Surely even an American newspaper would not be so irresponsible.'

'Really? Since when have the newspapers in America been responsible?'

'Yes, I see what you mean,' Bakutin said.

'Vilnius is swarming with Western journalists,' President Ivashov continued. 'If Bulak's name came out, they would all be looking for him.'

'You could admit everything and put it down to history. Nothing to do with you. You know, you're glad that this has come to light, you welcome the opportunity to reveal the truth about past misdeeds which happened before the new age of glasnost, that sort of thing.'

'Yes and what about the attempt, or more accurately your bungled attempt, on the two Americans in Saryshagan? That hardly looks like the work of an administration anxious to reveal the truth.'

Bakutin knew better than to respond to the barb. 'It is difficult,' he said.

'I know it's difficult,' retorted Ivashov. 'I would prefer some more constructive suggestions.' Bakutin said nothing. The President went on, 'Let us say this journalist writes his story. This wild allegation that there is an American living in Vilnius. He embellishes the tale with his adventures in Kazakhstan. He names Bulak. However, when others try to follow up this story they find that there is no Sergei Bulak in Vilnius. People begin to doubt the American's story. You said he was already outside the mainstream of journalism, some sort of eccentric. It would be easy to paint him as a hoaxer, trying to create a story for his own ends.'

'Bulak would have to be silenced,' said Bakutin thoughtfully.

'Yes.'

'These are troubled times in Vilnius. There are disturbances every day. Accidents can happen, especially to people who flirt with the politics of independence.'

'Quite,' said the President. 'Bulak might well be a dangerous radical, highly politicised, working against the legitimate sovereignty of the Soviet Union. It is not unexpected when such people come to grief.'

Bakutin had a thought which he hardly decreed worth mentioning. However, he decided he would speak out, as much out of interest in his leader's reaction as anything else. 'Bulak has a family, a wife and son.'

'That's regrettable, but the stability of the Soviet Union is more important than their fortunes.' Ivashov started fiddling with his paperweight again. He glanced towards the door. 'Is there anything else?'

'No, Comrade President.'

'Very well then, I have an appointment with the Foreign Minister. Let me know how you get on.'

Bakutin rose and went to the door. The President did not show him out personally.

Eight time zones away across the world in Washington, DC, the adventures of Laura Bailey and Bing Connick were also being discussed, in considerably less sanguine circumstances than in the Kremlin. President Blanchard was furious. If he had had a paperweight he would have thrown it, but he had to make do with stabbing a perfectly good Mont Blanc fountain pen nib-first into his blotter, staining his fingers with ink in the process. Dabbing his hand on the blotter he got up from his desk and paced over to the window. He swung round and faced his National Security Adviser, who had remained seated. 'Of all the screw-ups I've ever heard of, this takes the cake. It was supposed to be done without fuss and now you tell me that not only was it not done, but they've goddamn-well disappeared. How can this happen?'

'Well, Mr President, I'm not sure that you want to know all the details,' said Paine. In that he was correct. The President certainly would not want to hear about the deaths of two mercenaries and the questioning of a mysterious Pakistani found unconscious with them in a van in suburban London. Fortunately there had been no hint of a connection between these people and the government of the United States, but it had sent the crime reporters of Fleet Street into a frenzy. Their determination to get to the bottom of the story was matched only by that of the British authorities. The important thing in Paine's mind was to distance himself from the disaster. 'Hammond tells me that he hired the very best people,' he continued. 'People we've used before, but somehow things went wrong.'

'And they've disappeared, that's the bottom line.' The President looked around for something else to smash but nothing immediately caught his attention. 'Is any of this traceable, Brandon?'

'Absolutely not.' He hoped to God this was the truth.

'What are we doing about finding them?'

'Hammond thinks they've been snatched by some fringe political group. Either that or they may be in Russian hands. He says the operation was very professional.'

'Why would the damn Russians snatch them? It was in their interests as much as ours for them to disappear.'

'Don't ask me, Mr President. They may have some double-cross in mind is the only thing I can think of.'

The President resumed his seat, picked up the broken fountain pen and threw it into the wastepaper bin. 'Goddamned Ivashov, if he's got something cute planned I'll see that he never gets a cent of foreign aid.'

'Whoever it is, Hammond has contacts in various terrorist groups and even in the Russian intelligence community. He's got feelers out everywhere. He may be able to find out who's involved, but it'll take time.'

'Maybe I should get Langley involved. The CIA has the resources for this sort of stuff.'

'It widens the knowledge. Makes the whole thing less deniable,' cautioned Paine.

'Yeah you're probably right. And meanwhile, what?'

'Well about all we can do is wait.'

'Wait for them to cut my balls off, you mean,' said the President. 'All right, Brandon.'

Laura woke late, clinging to sleep. Last night she had been mentally exhausted and on going to bed her body had shut down into dreamless sleep. Curled in a foetal position, her hands between her thighs, the blankets pulled over her head, she felt as if she was floating and she was reluctant to leave the sanctuary of her semi-conscious state. It would be so pleasant just to close her eyes and slip back again into peace.

She hovered in a state of bliss for some minutes but oblivion would not return. In spite of herself her mind had begun to work, telling her that the world outside was still a dangerous place. Today she would have to decide how to deal with it. She drew back the blankets and got out of bed. The bedroom of the safe house was well appointed, with heavy, old-fashioned furniture, a wardrobe, a dressing table and a desk. There was an en-suite bathroom with a traditional enamelled bath with solid chromed fittings. She drew the curtains and looked out onto a suburban backyard with a clothes line and a tool shed. There were bars on the window, but in London there was nothing unusual about that. Like any big city, the citizens needed to protect themselves.

Laura ran a bath and poured in half a packet of salts. She immersed herself for half an hour, dried herself off and looked in the cupboard for her clothes from yesterday. There was a new skirt, blouse and jumper and half a dozen pairs of new underwear. Although they weren't what she would have chosen they fitted well enough. She had to admire Rezchikova's thoroughness.

She went out into the main room. Rezchikova, Bing, Rudi and Oleg were sitting around the remains of breakfast. 'Have you slept well?' enquired the Russian.

'I was exhausted. I can't remember when I slept so deeply.' She looked at her watch. She had been unconscious for fourteen hours. 'Thank you for the clothes.'

301

'I hope they fit all right, Rudi chose them.'

'They're fine, thank you.'

'Will you have some breakfast?'

'Just coffee, thanks.'

Rezchikova motioned to Rudi, who got up and went to the kitchen, returning with a pot of plunger coffee, which he poured for Laura.

After she had taken her first sip Bing said, 'Pavel and I have been discussing where to go from here.'

Laura felt her system come awake with the first jolt of caffeine. She was slowly coming back to life but she was still reluctant to grapple with the future. 'I'm afraid I haven't thought about it at all. I've been trying not to in fact.'

'Let me lay it out for you, Laura,' said Bing. 'Whoever's trying to kill us is desperate to prevent the story of Dan Parkinson from coming out. They don't know that we don't have enough information to publish, but while they think we have there'll be no place for us to hide. As long as we have only half a story we'll remain in danger. What Pavel said last night was right. We need all the ammunition. The whole story. Once it's made public we can't be touched. I have to go to Vilnius.'

'How can you possibly do that? You said yourself that you'd never get past the entry point.'

'The KGB is looking for someone with my passport details, that's right, but what if I had a different passport?'

Laura gave Bing a quizzical look. 'Hang on a minute. Haven't we got a role reversal here? I'm the one who always wants to take the stupid risks, you're the wise head, remember?'

'It's a risk, sure, but the alternative is to spend the rest of our lives hiding like rats.'

'And where would you propose getting a new passport?'

'That is not a problem Laura,' said Rezchikova. 'I can arrange whatever we need.'

'Vilnius is full of foreign newsmen at the moment,'

Bing said. 'I'd be just another face in the crowd. I could find Dan, confirm the story and get out. Write it here in London or maybe go to the States and do it and bingo, end of story.'

'And when are you suggesting we'd go?'

'Not we Laura,' Bing said. 'I'm going alone.'

Laura was about to take another sip of coffee. The cup stopped halfway to her lips. 'Pardon me?'

'I said I'm going alone. Two people just doubles the risk.'

Laura set her cup down carefully on the table. 'Now just a minute. You're forgetting what this is all about. It's not about a story. I hired you because I wanted to find Dan and as far as I'm concerned that's still my objective. If you think you can get into Lithuania then we can both get in.'

'And what about the risk of being caught?'

Laura stared at Bing in silence. Twice now within a couple of weeks she had been close to death. She had been more scared than she had imagined possible. She had seen people acting out terror in films and plays, but nothing could have prepared her for the real horror of the gun cocking in the still Kazakh night, the screwdriver in her ear in the hotel or that last ride in the van, handcuffed and awaiting execution. No she did not want to face more fear, but she could not just sit here and let the search go on without her.

'Isn't there another way?' she said.

'If there is I can't think of it. Stay here, Laura. I'll tell you everything you need to know when I get back.'

Laura shook her head slowly. 'No. I want to come. I've come this far and I'm going to see it through to the end.'

Bing slapped his hand on the table in frustration. 'Jesus Christ, you don't know when to give up do you?'

'That's right I don't. And I don't need you to tell me what I can or cannot do. I make my own decisions.'

'Can you? Where's the logic in this one? It just doesn't make sense for you to risk your life again.'

'If I was logical I would never have embarked on this in the first place, as you so kindly pointed out to me when we first met.'

'Yeah,' Bing said bitterly. 'And to think I could have stayed at home and gone fishing. Have you even thought about what you'd do if you found him?'

Laura had been staring him down defiantly. Now she lowered her gaze. Despite her obsession she had never thought through the moves she would make if she were to see Dan again. She had never really imagined it would happen. Now that the possibility was there, she was at a loss. Would she just walk up to him, tap him on the shoulder and say, 'Hi, remember me?' How would he react? Would he welcome being confronted by his past like that? Perhaps he would think it was a trick and just walk away. Or would he throw his arms around her and tell her he'd never forgotten her? The fact was she didn't have the slightest idea what she would do in Vilnius. 'To tell you the truth, Bing, I haven't a clue, I just don't know.'

'You don't really want to face him do you?'

'I don't know.'

'And you're determined to go anyway?'

'That's right.'

Bing sighed and turned to Rezchikova. 'How soon can we get the documentation?'

'Do you have passport photos?'

'They're back at the hotel,' Laura said.

'We can get them,' said Rezchikova.

'I've got a couple in my wallet,' Bing added.

'Give them to me. They should be ready in a couple of days.'

Pavel Rezchikova was pleased with the way things were going. It had been a high-risk strategy to snatch the two Americans in the hope of sending them back into Lithuania, but so far things were panning out well. If only the rest of it went as smoothly, he would be able to grasp the prize he had sought for more than a decade. He had enjoyed a brilliant career in the KGB, distinguishing himself in the field and managing to manoeuvre through the internal politics of the organisation with uncanny skill.

Bing's story, with all the details of the KGB's bungled attempt at murder, would be a worldwide sensation. When it broke, with Rezchikova's behind-the-scenes assistance, it would be enough to bring down the Director. Even if President Ivashov was prepared to forgive Bakutin, the Americans would demand his head. Then there would be nothing between him and the top job.

Rezchikova spent the next two days preparing the operation as if it were two of his own agents going under cover. He briefed Laura and Bing on their story. Bing was a journalist working for the *Des Moines Register*, come to cover the independence story. Laura was his photographer. He sent Rudi to a second-hand camera store to buy a well-used Nikon and a range of professional lenses, along with a worn-looking Billingham camera bag. Laura's new passport, in the name of Rosemary Tingle, was well thumbed and half-full of visas from exotic countries. Bing's, in the name of Jonathon Saffire, looked equally well travelled. To any immigration official they would appear to be exactly as they were described, a couple of newshounds flying in for a story. In addition he gave them each a handful of business cards to support their identities.

Bing flipped through his passport. 'The *Register*. Not a bad paper. Not quite the *Post* or the *Times*, but it'll do I guess.'

Rezchikova handed over a typewritten list to each of them. 'These are the names and addresses of the editor and senior staff. There are profiles of each of them. There are telephone and fax numbers, the address of the paper and a lot of other information you would be expected to know. I want you to memorise it all. I'll test you this afternoon.'

'I know nothing about newspapers or photography,' Laura said. 'I'd never stand up to real scrutiny.'

'I know that. There's enough here to get you through a cursory interrogation at the frontier. If the KGB gets hold of you . . .' he shrugged.

They studied for five hours and at the end of the day Rezchikova subjected them both to rigorous questioning. Neither of them could supply perfect answers to every question, but Pavel thought that with another day of study they would be good enough. That evening they all sat around the dining-room table eating plain stew, heavy with meat and potatoes, which Rudi had cooked. After dinner they watched the news on television. The story of the double murder in the van was one of the lead items. Police were questioning the Pakistani but no charges had been laid and they were still continuing their enquiries.

On the second day after breakfast, they again gathered around the dining-room table. Rezchikova told them what he knew about Sergei Bulak, his home address, where he worked, his daily movements, his family and work history. Laura listened intensely as she heard the details of his life as a Soviet citizen. Rezchikova imparted his information in dry professional tones, but nevertheless it painted a graphic picture: the cramped apartment, one of thousands of identical ones buried anonymously in a forest of high-rise buildings, the daily commute in public transport to his job in the factory, the dreary shortages, the lack of even the most basic comforts which Westerners would consider normal. Rezchikova described Palmyra and Alvidas in those same dry tones. For all its thoroughness, the briefing told Laura nothing about Sergei's mind. Was he happy or sad with his lot? Did he love his wife? Did he pine for his lover from the past or had his other life been erased forever from his memory? After the final briefing was over and Rezchikova had left them to make some telephone calls, she turned to Bing. 'It's so depressing, Bing. He was one of the Air Force's brightest electronics experts and he's working in a factory making TV sets. What a waste of a life. He must hate it.'

'At least he is alive, Laura. And who knows? Maybe

he's happy. He's probably pretty well off by Soviet standards.'

'By Soviet standards maybe. But I know Dan. He was so ambitious. He would never forget what it could have been like.'

'If it's true what Buggins said and they were killed if they didn't cooperate, then he had no choice. Dan is an accident of history, Laura. There are some things you can't influence. You just have to make the best of them.'

'They must have tortured him terribly,' mused Laura. 'He would never have turned otherwise. He believed in what he was doing.'

Rezchikova had finished his calls. He had no patience with this sentimentality, nevertheless he had to appear sympathetic in order to manipulate the two Americans. He handed them each a travel wallet with their passports, tickets and itinerary. 'I've booked you on the BA flight to Moscow tomorrow, transferring to Aeroflot flying direct to Vilnius. You're confirmed in a hotel in the centre of town. The details are all in the folder.'

'Is there any way we can get in touch with you if we need to?' Bing asked.

Rezchikova shook his head. 'Once you are there you will be on your own. I cannot help you inside the Soviet Union.'

At nine o'clock the following morning Rudi dropped Bing and Laura off at the BA terminal. The counter clerk gave their passports a cursory glance, checked that their visas were in order and they were whisked through immigration without so much as a second glance. They walked down the airbridge to the plane where a steward-ess was welcoming passengers at the door. As Laura handed her the boarding card there was a flash of recog-nition in the stewardess' eyes. 'Hello, I think we were on the same flight coming out of Moscow a couple of weeks ago weren't we? Mrs Bailey wasn't it?'

Laura was flustered. For a moment she panicked, then

she gathered her wits. 'No, I don't think so. I wasn't on a flight two weeks ago.'

The stewardess looked puzzled. 'Really, I could have sworn . . .' She glanced down at the boarding card and the name, Tingle R., Ms. She looked at Laura again and handed back the card. 'Amazing, you must have a double. Straight ahead, five rows down on the left. The window seat.'

Laura thanked her and took back her boarding card. Her ears were burning. When Bing had tried to dissuade her from going she had fought him instinctively, but now she wondered if perhaps he had been right after all, if she had the courage for this final step. During the last two days of briefings she had not really had time to contemplate the dangers ahead of them, or else she had subconsciously refused to face them. Now the enormity of what they were doing came home to her. If she was flustered by an encounter with an airline stewardess, how would she ever be able to bluff her way past Soviet officials? She had to admit that she was terrified at the prospect of being caught again. This was one fear, but there was another, the fear of seeing Dan. She didn't know which prospect scared her most.

Laura and Bing made their way down the aisle to their seats. When they were settled she glanced across at him, on the verge of confessing her doubts, but he was checking his travel documents. For one wild moment she thought of fleeing back down the aisle and away from the aeroplane, but she controlled herself. The door was closing and the stewardesses were fussing around preparing for the safety demonstration. For better or worse she was committed to a course of action which was now beyond her control.

Sitting beside Laura, Bing was thinking about what was to come. He wanted to get in and out as fast as possible. The first thing to do was establish that Dan Parkinson, alias Sergei Bulak, really did exist. He would have to get some positive identification, but he would not figure out how until the time came. The big decision was whether or not to approach him. An interview with the MIA would undoubtedly be the scoop of the decade, the centrepiece of a sensational story, but he wondered how Parkinson would react. He had no idea how thoroughly he had been indoctrinated. He might well consider Bing a threat and betray him to the authorities. Again he would have to play it by ear. The wild card was Laura. He couldn't tell how she was going to react and he doubted if she was any more certain now than when he'd asked the question two days ago. With his usual penchant for self-criticism, Bing laughed inwardly at himself. Some plan! They were doing what they had been doing all along, following their noses and making up the moves as they went.

The safety demonstration had taken place, but he hardly noticed it. Now the pilot came on the intercom and began to give them flight details. Rezchikova had assured them that there would be no problem with their travel documents, but Bing wondered. He knew nothing of Soviet immigration procedures. Perhaps the false names were no protection at all. Perhaps they had their descriptions in the computer. Perhaps they were under orders to give extra close scrutiny to reporters . . . perhaps, perhaps. He thought to himself, this is my last story ever, I'll do this one, then go home and go fishing. He glanced at his watch. In just over four hours they would face their first test.

Thirty

Ross Sellars picked up the telephone. His fingers strayed hesitantly towards the keypad, paused, wavered for a moment and returned to the desk. He put the handset down and began biting his nails. He had called Brandon Paine's secretary two days ago, seeking an appointment and she had not yet called back. He did not want to send a memo. What he had to say should be for Paine's ears only. He wanted to remind him of his promise. It had taken him days to get up the courage to call and while waiting for a reply he had worked himself into a state, firstly of nervous anticipation and then when no call came, anger. He was sick of people taking no notice of him and he was damn well going to do something about it. With a determined gesture he picked up the telephone and dialled the Director's office. His secretary came on with that snooty voice of hers. 'Director's office. Can I help you?'

'It's Ross Sellars here, I called two days ago asking to speak to Mr Paine, when he has a moment.'

'I remember the call, Mr Sellars.' He could detect the frost in her voice. 'I passed it on to the Director.'

'Ah, could you, er, perhaps give him a reminder? It's important.'

'He has your message already, Mr Sellars. I'm afraid I can do no more than I have done already.'

You goddamn ice queen, thought Sellars. His audible reply however sounded quavering even to his ears. 'Er, I'm sorry to bother you. I'll wait until he calls.'

The receiver clicked in his ear. This time he spoke his thoughts aloud. 'Fuck you, you bitch.' He thought of all the slights he had put up with for all these years, from his rivals in the office, from the hookers who laughed at him behind his back, from the failed computer dates. He thought of Brandon Paine slapping him on the back and swearing him to secrecy, making his empty politician's promises, knowing that he'd just lie down and take any crap they dished out, like he always did. He thought Paine had recognised the talent others failed to see, but Paine was just like all the rest. He slammed the receiver back down. 'And fuck you too Brandon Paine, I'm sick of being jerked around.'

In his office at KGB Headquarters in Moscow, the Head of Counterintelligence, Pasha Ponomaryov, was smarting with no less agitation over his treatment at the hands of his superior. Bakutin had summoned him to his office and rudely instructed him in the matter of one Sergei Bulak, a dissident Lithuanian who had been deemed an enemy of the state. Bakutin's manner, as on their last meeting, had been contemptuous and dismissive. Ponomaryov had to repress his urge to respond and had received his orders in passive silence. And what orders! Five years ago there would have been nothing remarkable about dealing harshly with dissidents. The mechanisms were there for that very purpose: the labour camp, the psychiatric ward, or in some cases more permanent solutions; Ponomaryov was familiar with them all. Now, with glasnost, it was no longer a crime to speak against the state, yet in Lithuania, where thousands were doing so every day with impunity, this one man apparently had to be silenced. It was curious. When he attempted to question the Director, Bakutin dismissed him with a flick of his fingers and handed him an armful of Manila folders. 'Read the files,' he said. 'You will see that there is a connection between your bungling in Kazakhstan and this. Read the files and this time do the job properly.'

Back in his office Ponomaryov finally learned the truth about the two Americans who he had assumed were intelligence agents. They were not spies at all, but civilians on an ill-conceived search for a former countryman, Parkinson, now Bulak. He shook his head at their suicidal foolishness. The file told him nothing of the politics behind the KGB's present interest but he could make a few guesses. The only question in his practical mind was why they had not disposed of Bulak twenty years ago when his usefulness as a weapons expert had run its course.

Turning the yellowing pages of badly typed files, Ponomaryov followed Bulak's fortunes with interest: his transfer from Saryshagan to Lithuania, his marriage and apparent assimilation into Soviet society. When he got to the more recent files, leafing through informers' reports and those of his case officer, he could still see no clue to the KGB's renewal of interest. Bulak, the fool, was flirting with the Sajudis movement. He had spoken openly of his support, something which would once have been enough in itself to condemn him to a labour camp, and had been seen attending at least one rally. The latest report by Timashov, just two weeks ago, indicated Bulak had retreated from this course and had apparently taken no part in the latest upheavals. It was as if he had suddenly realised the danger involvement might bring him. It was therefore all the more puzzling that Bakutin now wanted him silenced. Still, after the Kazakhstan debacle he could not afford the luxury of analysis. He needed to carry out this assignment well. Putting the files aside, Ponomaryov leaned back in his chair and thought. After a time he smiled as an idea came to him. He called his secretary. 'Get me Lazutkin.' Valery Lazutkin was the Head of the First Directorate, Timashov's superior and one of the old-guard KGB careerists still in a position of influence. Lazutkin and Ponomaryov understood one another.

In a moment Lazutkin came on the line. The two section heads exchanged polite greetings and Ponomaryov got quickly to the point. 'Valery, you have a Major Timashov who has been involved with a case which crosses over into counterintelligence. I wonder if I may borrow him for a few days? It's something the Director has taken a personal interest in.'

'Is this something I should know about?' said Lazutkin.

'I think not. It's a need-to-know thing.'

'Well if Bakutin sanctions it . . .'

'Yes Valery, you can trust me. It's just a small task I have for him but it's something that only Timashov can do.'

'Very well. Can you send me a memo to that effect?'

'It will be done. Thank you, Valery. Difficult times,' he added. 'I am in your debt.' Valery was one of the old ones, the good ones.

He clicked the receiver and buzzed his secretary again. 'There's a Major Timashov in the First Directorate. Call him and have him come and see me as soon as possible. If he asks what it's about tell him Lazutkin has cleared it.'

Ten minutes later Ponomaryov was regarding with dismay the elephantine bulk of Timashov overflowing one of his visitor's chairs. He tapped the pile of Manila folders he had been reading and said, 'Sergei Bulak, formerly Parkinson of the US Air Force. He's your case.'

Timashov was wheezing slightly from his journey through the corridors. The secretary had told him nothing of the reason for his summons except that it had been cleared with his own section chief. He patted the pocket over his labouring heart which contained his cigarettes. He craved nicotine but he would not presume to light up in the office of the Head of Counterintelligence. It was a reflex action to disguise the alarm he felt. 'Yes, that's right, I have handled Bulak from the beginning.'

'How well do you know him?'

'Quite well,' said Timashov cautiously.

'Do you know how he thinks?'

'About what, sir?'

The Head of Counterintelligence tapped the files again and said, 'These tell me Bulak's history. However, they puzzle me. He is a good Soviet citizen for twenty years and then suddenly he begins to behave foolishly. He shows interest in Sajudis, he speaks openly in support of the dissidents, then just as suddenly he backs away.' Ponomaryov stared directly into Timashov's eyes, a flat, dangerous stare. 'I find this curious. I cannot see the logic of his behaviour. The files tell me nothing about how he thinks. Perhaps you can explain it for me.'

Timashov returned the stare for a few moments and then averted his gaze. Sergei was in danger. He would have to be careful what he said, for Sergei's sake and for his own. 'When Bulak was first relocated to Vilnius, we were concerned that he might not adapt to the Soviet way of life. However, as you have read he did so very well. I think the Sajudis movement attracted the interest of a great many people in Vilnius who were not necessarily activists. In my opinion Bulak was curious, yes. He was interested but on reflection he decided against involvement. No more than that.'

Ponomaryov regarded Timashov for a moment without answering. 'You have told me nothing I did not know already.'

'I am sorry. I can't think of anything else which is relevant.'

'You write here that he has decided against involvement with Sajudis. How certain are you of that?'

Timashov knew there was a limit to how much he could endorse Sergei's actions. 'One cannot be completely certain about how another person is thinking,' he said carefully. 'May I ask, sir, what is the reason for this interest in Bulak?'

'You may not. What is your personal relationship with him?'

314

'Personal relationship? I don't know what you mean.'

Ponomaryov smiled. 'Come come, Timashov, don't dissemble. You practically lived with him at Saryshagan, you have seen him regularly, year after year, throughout half his life. You must have developed some sort of personal rapport.'

The alarm bells within Timashov's head were ringing loudly. In the early days he had taught Sergei the game of survival, now he needed to use those same skills himself. It was a matter of saying the right words. 'I have always maintained a professional relationship with Bulak, sir. It's the only way I can do my job properly.'

'So you have no personal feelings of affection for him?'

Timashov could see the trap now but he was powerless to avoid it. 'No, not particularly.'

Again the stare, this time accompanied by a wolfish smile. 'Good. A great deal depends on this operation being carried out successfully. The outcome is important to me. Director Bakutin is also personally interested.' He continued to gaze unblinkingly at Timashov. 'And I suggest, Major Timashov, that it will be especially important for you and your future career.'

Timashov again lowered his gaze. Ponomaryov continued. 'Listen carefully to what I have to say.'

Thirty-one

Rezchikova had picked the ideal cover for Laura and Bing. Vilnius was full of Western news correspondents and when they checked into the Riga Hotel in the centre of town they blended perfectly into their surroundings. They arrived in a taxi from the airport after passing through the entry controls without so much as a question being asked. Laura, at Rezchikova's insistence, had dressed down in clothes which she would not normally have chosen for herself. She was wearing jeans and flat-heeled loafers with a bulky jumper over which was a sleeveless vest with a multitude of pockets. Arriving with her battered camera bag she looked exactly like a news photographer. She and Bing entered the lobby just as an Italian television team was leaving to film the day's activity. At the reception desk a correspondent from the London *Times* was dictating a story into the hotel's one telephone. 'The streets of Vilnius were tense today,' he shouted. 'No no Vilnius, V-i-l-n-i-u-s, got it? Yes. Stop. New par. The head of the Sajudis freedom movement . . . yes Sajudis, I'll spell it for you . . .' Bing smiled at the familiar scene. Another camera crew was preparing to hit the streets, while men and women, with the trademark scruffiness of reporters the world over, milled about, chatting about the latest developments.

Bing had never understood how particular hotels became journalists' hangouts, but whenever he had covered an international crisis the media always gravitated to the same place. Herd instinct perhaps. He knew their location at the Riga and the crisis unfolding in the streets outside would be to their advantage. No one was likely to take notice of them poking about and asking unusual questions. The city was full of foreigners just like them, doing the same thing.

During the flight to Vilnius Laura and Bing had agreed on a rough plan of action, beginning with a preliminary reconnaissance of the area where Dan lived. There was no such thing as a car rental agency in Vilnius, but the hotel could arrange for a driver with a private car who spoke English. When he checked in, Bing ordered the vehicle to meet them at the front door in half an hour. It was two in the afternoon. Friday. Sergei, Dan—they could not agree on what to call their quarry—if he existed at all, was unlikely to be at home.

When they came down to the lobby, the receptionist beckoned to a middle-aged man with blond curly hair who introduced himself as Vytautis. Vytautis was dressed in corduroy trousers and a long green jumper which sagged to his thighs. As he approached he was preceded by a strong smell of sour body odour. According to Rezchikova's information, Sergei Bulak lived on the third floor of an apartment building in Karoliniskes, a suburb about three kilometres from the Riga Hotel. Bing told Vytautis the address and they set off.

The tension in the streets which the *Times* correspondent had been describing was not apparent to Laura and Bing. Vilnius had the appearance of a normal European city going about its business. If there were milling crowds and demonstrations they must have been elsewhere.

It took them only a few minutes to clear the centre of town and enter the residential suburbs. After they had been driving for about ten minutes more they passed a tower which the driver pointed out to them as the headquarters of Lithuanian Television. 'What suburb is this?' asked Bing.

'Karoliniskes. The street you want is just a little further on.'

Five minutes later they entered an area of high-rises, towering in row after dreary row above the tatty streets as far as they could see. The driver stopped and indicated a street off to their left like all the rest. Bing asked him to wait. They got out and, with Laura toting her camera bag, they began to walk.

Number 19, the number Rezchikova had given them, was exactly the same as the surrounding buildings. A glass door opened into a foyer with broken tiles on the floor and the paint peeling off the walls from rising damp. There was an elevator and a row of letterboxes. Bing quickly scanned the names. The name Bulak was beside apartment 312. It had been written in ink on a piece of paper and slipped inside a cracked glass cover. The ink was so faded with age as to be barely legible. While they were examining the names, the front door swung open and a woman with two small children heavily rugged up against the cold came in. The youngsters were chattering with excitement about something. The woman gave them a suspicious look and hurried her children along to the elevator. 'Come on, let's get out of here,' whispered Bing.

They left the building and walked back into the street. Opposite the entrance was a tiny park that the Soviet town planners had placed in a feeble attempt to relieve the monotony of the suburb. It was little more than a square of empty ground with a couple of benches and a small structure like a bus shelter, where people could get out of the weather. It would make a good position from which to observe the comings and goings at the apartment block.

Laura scanned the building. It looked as if it had never been painted and the grey concrete was streaked with rust where the reinforcing was breaking down. Each apartment had its own small balcony. Most of them were cluttered with unsightly junk and here and there washing flapped in the breeze. She counted up to the third floor. The windows of the apartments on this side were all tightly closed. The building looked stark, unfriendly, forbidding. She tried to comprehend what life could be like within that ugly monolith. Was Dan, or this Russian, Sergei, like those people she had seen on the streets of Moscow, pasty-faced and pudgy from bad diet, dressed in awful, low-quality clothing, their defeated faces reflecting joyless lives? He was unknowable. Despondency gripped her.

The street was practically deserted. There was the occasional pedestrian, but cars seemed to be a rarity. She assumed that most people would use public transport to go to and from work. While she watched, a vehicle pulled up outside the apartment building and an immensely fat man got out. He walked, or rather waddled in the front entrance. Laura could see him through the glass door writing something on a piece of paper which he then stuffed into one of the mailboxes. A minute later he returned to the car and motioned to the driver to move on.

She became aware of Bing beside her. 'Come on,' he said, 'we don't want to hang around here too long. Tomorrow's Saturday, we'll come back then and see if we can get a look at Sergei Bulak.'

They walked back up the street to their car. The driver was fast asleep with his head leaning against the window. They tapped on the glass to wake him and headed back to the hotel.

'The name's there on the mailbox,' said Bing. 'Sergei Bulak, in black and white. Well, faded blue anyway.'

Laura was looking out the window at the apartment blocks sliding by. 'I should be feeling elated or tearful, but instead I just feel sort of blank.'

'Did you expect the earth to move?'

'I don't honestly know what I expected, but something.'

Bing looked meaningfully at the driver. 'Perhaps we should talk about this later.'

The rest of the journey passed in silence. The hotel did not have a bar but there was a room with tables and chairs where coffee or beer was available. They ordered coffee which tasted as though it was made from burnt wood. The room was full of correspondents laughing and talking rowdily. Laura and Bing took a seat by themselves. At the table next to them the *Times* reporter was telling his colleagues about a meeting he had just had with some independence activists. 'Tomorrow's going to be a big one. They're planning a march to the TV station to demand the right to broadcast uncensored news programs. They tell me that the Army might turn up to try and stop them. There could be fireworks.'

' Let's hope so,' said a woman TV reporter. 'This story could do with a new twist. A decent riot is just what it needs right now.'

'Yes,' chimed in a young man with horn-rimmed glasses and over-long hair. 'A bit of bang bang, just the job.' There was a cynical chuckle of appreciation round the table.

Laura leaned towards Bing. 'I'm beginning to see why you quit journalism,' she said quietly. 'They're a pretty horrible lot aren't they?'

'The young ones always talk tough. Those who've seen a lot of action don't carry on with all that cynical bullshit.'

'Is it likely any of them will recognise you?'

'Not much chance. There's a new generation now. These guys would all have been in short pants when I was a correspondent. I guess there's a vague chance I might run into an old hand, but most of them are in desk jobs or retired. I didn't have a beard then either.'

'I wonder what they'd think if they knew what we were here for?'

'There's not one of them wouldn't kill his own mother for this story.'

'After seeing that mailbox today, do you believe we've found him?'

'I'll tell you when I see him walk out the door of that apartment block. Do you think you'd recognise Dan after all these years?'

'I don't know. I think so.'

'We'll go back tomorrow and stake out the place.'

'What if Dan Parkinson does walk out that door, what will we do?'

'See what he does, how he behaves, how he looks. I don't know. Play it by ear.'

'If it's him I want to talk to him.'

'That may not be a good idea. He might not want to be discovered.'

'I'll have to try. I'd never forgive myself if I walked away from here without trying to communicate.'

'Look let's just take it slowly,' Bing said. 'One step at a time. Tomorrow we'll check him out and then decide what to do? Agreed?'

Laura nodded her head. 'Agreed.'

It was dark when Sergei arrived home. The trolleybus had been particularly slow today. The driver had been the sort of bloody-minded product of the communist system who seemed to take delight in making things as difficult as possible for his fellow man. He had refused to give change to people who did not have the exact money. At three different stops there had been petty arguments. The fourth time an elderly woman, laden down with shopping bags, stepped on board, fumbled for her money and came up with a rouble note. The driver threw it back at her and demanded the correct fare. Watching this from halfway down the aisle, Sergei felt all his impatience of petty bastardry well up. Grabbing the driver by the collar he pulled his face close and snarled that if he did not give the lady change and get the bus moving he would punch him. The driver muttered and cursed and threatened official action, but he did as he was told. Although there was no more trouble for the rest of the journey, he drove deliberately slowly out of malice.

Sergei walked in the front door of his apartment building and checked his mailbox. The only thing it contained was a folded note with his name written on the outside. He recognised Timashov's handwriting. For once the elevator was working. As he ascended he opened the note and read it.

'Sergei, I find myself unexpectedly in Vilnius again, so soon after the last visit. I will call around this evening at eight in the hope that you and I can go out and eat together. Maybe we can go to the Estonian place again. It was good last time. Give my regards to Palmyra and I will see you tonight. Timashov.'

Odd that Timashov should be back so soon. Still, he was glad he was here. He always looked forward to meeting the fat man. He walked in his front door, kissed Palmyra and ruffled his son's hair. Seeing them helped put the unpleasant incident with the bus driver out of his mind. Frustrating as the system was, his family made his life worthwhile and besides, he was convinced that things were changing for the better. He said to Palmyra, 'There was a note from Timashov in the mail box, he wants to see me tonight for dinner.'

'Dinner eh? What Timashov wants to do is drink vodka.'

'Probably. Anyway, tomorrow's Saturday, I don't have to go to work.'

Palmyra gave him an affectionate peck on the cheek. 'Go and get drunk with your friend, Sergei. You work hard enough, you deserve it.'

An hour and a half later there was a knock on the door. Sergei opened it and there stood Timashov. 'Come in and say hello,' Sergei said.

Palmyra appeared at his side. 'Yes come in, Vladimir. Tell us how things are in Moscow.'

Timashov shook his head and his chins wobbled. 'Moscow is the same as always only worse. No I won't come in thank you, Sergei and I have a lot to talk about.'

322

'We do?' said Sergei, smiling.

Timashov gave him his mournful look but said nothing.

Palmyra smiled in defeat. 'All right, but see you get him home safe and sound.'

Palmyra thought she saw the trace of a grimace flit across Timashov's fat features. He mumbled goodbye and walked to the elevator. Sergei raised his eyebrows at Palmyra and shrugged his shoulders. He kissed her on the cheek and followed his friend.

Timashov had a driver waiting outside to take them to a little Estonian restaurant in the old part of town. They had been there before and they both enjoyed it. The food was plain, well cooked and, for a KGB officer travelling on expenses, affordable. Timashov's normal manner was that of a lugubrious philosopher, always ready to contribute a homily or two to any discussion, but during the car ride he was unusually silent. Over the years Sergei and Timashov had had many evenings of food and good conversation together. Their nights out tended to follow a typically Russian pattern. Early on Timashov would be cynical and witty, especially about politics. Later, when the vodka had done its work, he would become sentimental and maudlin. When they sat down at a small table in a far corner of the restaurant Sergei made several attempts to start a conversation, but each one petered out into silence. The fat man seemed distracted.

'What is it, Vladimir? Something's on your mind.'

Timashov lit one of his foul Russian cigarettes. He took a pull at it and flicked the ash nervously into a saucer. He threw down a glass of vodka with one gulp and looked not at Sergei but somewhere into the middle distance. 'I have done some terrible things in my life, Sergei. Terrible things.'

Sergei recognised this. It was Timashov in his maudlin mood, only it had started early. 'Come on, Vladimir, what have you done that's so terrible?'

'Do you remember Vietnam? Our first meeting when I tried to persuade you to defect?'

'Of course. How could I ever forget what happened there?'

'At first you refused. You were prepared to face execution rather than talk to a Russian.'

'Yes and if I had continued to do so I would not be alive today. I didn't feel good about that, but it's worked out all right. It's not perfect but at least I have a life.'

'In Vietnam I let them beat you so you would come over. That last time, remember? I pretended to you that I was shocked, but I let them know I wanted it done.'

'That was over twenty years ago, Vladimir, you were doing your job. I was the enemy.'

'Yes I was doing my job. I sometimes wonder about my job, Sergei. You know I have to write reports about you don't you?'

'Of course I do.'

'I work for the KGB. I was never meant to become your friend.'

'Hey come on,' Sergei said. 'We've talked about this before. I know you have to cover your arse. You've always advised me how to keep out of danger, so what's the problem? It's worked fine so far.'

Timashov poured another shot of vodka for them both. He sipped and put his glass down on the table. 'I want to tell you something I've never told anyone. I had a brother, two years younger than I. Back in the Breshnev era he was a dissident. He used to edit an underground newspaper which spoke out for freedom of speech, democracy; all the things that Ivashov speaks for today, only then they were considered treason.

'One day I was approached by a superior who said he wanted me to gather evidence against my brother. I could have refused and kissed my career goodbye, but I didn't. I spied on him, reported his movements, who his associates were and where the paper was printed. As a result of my information he was arrested and sent to a labour camp. He never returned.'

Timashov's eyes were glistening. He threw down his vodka at a gulp.

'Jesus, Vladimir, I don't know what to say.'

'I believed in communism then. I went through the Young Pioneers, joined the party, did all the right things. I thought I was being a patriot, betraying my own brother. I was weak. I should have said no, but I didn't.'

'We're all capable of betrayal if our own well-being requires it,' Sergei said thoughtfully. 'No one knows that better than I.'

Timashov dragged his gaze back to meet Sergei's eyes. 'Our own well-being. That's what it comes down to in the end isn't it?'

'That's right, Vladimir, we both know that.' He looked puzzled. 'Anyway what's brought this on all of a sudden?'

Timashov shook his head. 'Nothing my friend, nothing.'

'Well let's eat some food and talk about something else.'

The waiter was hovering. They had no need to look at a menu. They ordered quickly and a silence fell between them. The restaurant was a simple room with rough wooden tables and chairs and a minimum of decoration. It was clean and there were delicious smells coming from the kitchen. In a few moments the food arrived but Timashov seemed to take no pleasure in the sight of the steaming plate in front of him. Sergei attempted to break his mood. 'Vilnius is an interesting place these days,' he said. 'Demonstrations, threats by Ivashov, foreigners everywhere with cameras. It feels like a new beginning.'

'I can see the idea of independence still excites you,' said Timashov.

'Yes, but I've been following your advice. I haven't got involved.'

'Perhaps I was being over-cautious. On reflection I don't think it would matter so much. Not now.'

Sergei looked at him in amazement. 'Really? A while

ago you were predicting dire consequences if I even listened to a speech, now you say it doesn't matter.'

Timashov avoided his eyes. 'You said I was being over-cautious. I think now you were right.'

'There's a rally planned outside the TV station tomorrow.'

'Yes,' said Timashov. 'I heard about it this afternoon. Everyone in town is talking about it.'

'Are you telling me you think it would be all right to attend?'

Timashov was fiddling with his food. He had hardly eaten a thing, which was unusual. With his eyes downcast at the plate he replied, 'I don't see why not. In fact I might go with you. I'm quite interested myself.'

Sergei smiled. 'Great! That's great. You're not such a conservative after all, are you?'

Timashov's face creased into a stricken grin. 'No, we all change.' He was speaking automatically. He could not think clearly. Suddenly he could not bear to sit here with his friend any longer. He had to get away. With an effort he continued, 'I'm sorry, Sergei, I'm afraid I'm not very good company tonight. The truth is I don't feel well. Would you mind if we made an early night of it?'

'Of course not,' said Sergei with concern. 'Have an early night and I'm sure you'll feel OK in the morning. Come around at about eleven and we'll go to the rally together.'

Timashov dropped Sergei at his apartment and drove back to his accommodation in the centre of town. Dismissing the driver with orders to call around at ten-thirty the following morning, he entered his small room but did not immediately undress. Instead he sat at the dressing table staring blankly into space, thinking. It had been so easy. Too easy. Just like in Vietnam. He had tried to teach Sergei never to trust anyone, but he could not teach him that his own mentor would betray him. He had no idea how long he sat in his trance of self-loathing, but he was brought back to reality by a loud knock on the wall. A voice in the next room shouted angrily for quiet. He realised with surprise that he had been pounding his fist repeatedly on the table and cursing aloud his own evil genius.

Palmyra was still up when Sergei got home. She was sitting on the couch sewing buttons onto a shirt. 'You're home early,' she said. 'How's Timashov?'

Sergei sat down beside her. 'He's a bit strange as a matter of fact. He seems depressed about something. He said some odd things tonight, not just the usual homespun philosophy; dark stuff. I tried to change the conversation but he kept coming back to it.'

'What sort of stuff?'

'Oh all about the early days. How he tricked me into defecting, betrayal, stuff like that.'

'It sounds like Timashov when he's drunk.'

'Yes, but he wasn't drunk. I don't know, I guess he's having a hard time at work or something. He's a lonely old fellow you know. No family, no wife. About all he has to live for is his job.'

'I sometimes think you're the closest thing he has to family,' Palmyra said.

For an instant Sergei thought of telling her about Timashov's revelation, but she was already distrustful of his friend. He knew this would only disturb her further.

'How long is he staying in Vilnius?' said Palmyra.

'He didn't say. He wants me to go with him to the rally at the TV station tomorrow.'

Palmyra paused in her sewing. 'He what?'

'Yes I know, it's exactly what he was warning me against before. He says he thinks he was being over-cautious and I must say I agree with him.'

Palmyra put the shirt down and turned to Sergei. 'Don't go.'

'But I've already said I would.'

Palmyra took his hand in hers. 'Please, I'm afraid. Don't go.'

'My dove, it's just another rally like all the others. I'll

be all right. I just want to have a look, be part of it. This is my country too you know.'

Palmyra blinked with surprise. 'What did you say?'

Sergei was surprised himself. He reflected on his last remark and decided that it sounded right. 'I said this is my country too.'

'Oh Sergei, I never thought I would hear you say that.'

'No,' he said with wonder. 'Neither did I. I guess I've at last come to terms with it. I think it started at the rally the other day, when the choir sang. I was singing with them and for the first time since I was in the air force I felt like I was a part of something. I've never felt a part of Russia, but an independent Lithuania is different. It is my country now.'

Palmyra turned and embraced him tightly. She could not now ask him to stay home, not now that everyone was shouting for independence publicly, without fear of the consequences. Even so her instinct told her it was dangerous. 'I understand how you feel, but please don't decide until the morning. Promise me?'

Sergei was glad that he hadn't mentioned Timashov's brother. Palmyra would worry all night. 'All right. I promise. Let's go to bed.'

Thirty-two

At 8 a.m. Laura and Bing set off in the same hired car for Sergei's apartment. It was Saturday morning and the streets were quiet. There were no commuters about and hardly any traffic. Vytautis was dressed in the same baggy green jumper as the day before and his body odour, if anything, was worse. As they drove past closed shops and headed away from the city centre they each wound down their windows a crack, letting in freezing fresh air. They asked Vytautis to stop on the same corner as the day before and wait for them. Feeling conspicuous, they walked down the street to the park and sat inside the little shed. Hidden in the shadows there, they felt much safer. They could not easily be seen from the street and, for the moment at least, no one was using the park.

From this vantage point they watched the comings and goings at the apartment. A man came out with a grey German shepherd on a leash. He was about five feet eight inches. Too short. Two teenagers carrying skates left shortly afterwards and walked off down the street laughing at some joke. A few women, carrying shopping bags, emerged and trudged away, but there was no one who looked anything like Dan. Bing had the ability to sit immobile and silent, as if meditating, but Laura found it difficult to keep still. She wanted to be doing something.

They spoke little. After an hour and a half a car pulled up and the same fat man they had seen the night before got out and went inside. They saw through the glass door his huge form disappearing into the elevator. For another five minutes or so nothing happened and then the elevator door opened again and the man came out accompanied by another person wearing a blue anorak. They paused for a moment inside, talking, and then emerged into the open air. The second man had a shock of carrot-coloured hair.

As they began walking to the car Laura gasped and gripped Bing by the arm as if to stop herself falling. 'Oh sweet Jesus, it's him.'

'Are you sure?' said Bing.

'I've never been more sure of anything in my life. Look at his hair, his build, the way he walks. It's him. God I feel weak.'

'They're getting into the car,' said Bing.

The two men climbed in and closed the doors. As the car moved off Laura and Bing ran out of the park and sprinted the hundred yards to their own vehicle. The driver looked at them in surprise as they hastily climbed in and pointed to the other car just disappearing around a corner in the distance.

'Follow it,' gasped Bing.

Something of their excitement conveyed itself to Vytautis. He hurriedly turned the starter, put the car in gear and dropped the clutch so fast that he stalled. Laura drummed her fingers impatiently on the seat beside her. He started the engine again and this time moved off smoothly.

A few seconds later they turned the same corner. Dan's car had disappeared. Laura shouted with frustration, 'Quick Vytautis, drive!' They raced to the next intersection and looked urgently left and right. There he was in the distance, just turning another corner. They had him now. Their driver settled down to a steady speed, keeping a hundred yards back from the vehicle in front. After about five minutes they began to come across people all walking in the same direction. Some were carrying banners and placards. Bing asked the driver if this was the way to the television station.

'Yes that's right.'

The crowds were getting thicker, spilling out from the footpaths onto the road. Their driver was forced to slow to a walking pace as he threaded his way through them. The transmission tower was within sight now and Dan's car came to a halt. Dan and the fat man disembarked and began walking.

'Stop here,' urged Bing. The car pulled to a halt and the two of them got out. 'Wait for us here.'

Laura and Bing hurried through the crowd, fearful for a moment that they might lose their quarry. But it was impossible to miss the flame-haired man and his obese companion. The crowd was now shoulder to shoulder. They reached a point where the mass of people was locked solid. Dan and the fat man stopped. Everyone seemed to be waiting expectantly. Laura and Bing worked their way closer until they were only a few feet away. Laura could see Dan's face now as he talked with his companion. Dan looked relaxed but the fat man appeared nervous. He glanced about him now and then as if expecting something to happen. Dan had not changed that much. There was experience written in his face; some lines, maturity. He was a little heavier, but he still carried himself with the same erect military bearing she remembered. It was him.

A few policemen were hanging about on the edge of the crowd. They looked alert, but not particularly aggressive. Suddenly the murmur subsided. A man mounted the steps of the TV station and began to address them through a loudhailer.

Laura could not take her eyes off the red-haired man a few paces away from her. He was listening closely to what was being said, oblivious to anyone around him. So intense was his concentration she felt she could have stood beside him and he would not have noticed her. With an effort she tore her gaze away. She raised the

Nikon to her eye, focused on the speaker and clicked off two shots. No one took any notice. She swung the camera round and refocused on Dan. Through the 100 millimetre lens his face seemed so close she could touch it. He still had freckles on his nose. She squeezed the shutter release, wound on and squeezed again.

The crowd were becoming agitated now, responding to the speaker. Placards were hoisted into the air and a chant began. Later, when correspondents analysed the events of that day they would write that when they began calling for the occupation of the TV station was the turning point. She could understand nothing, but she could feel the anger running through them like a grassfire fast flaring out of control.

She could still not take her eyes off Dan. He was shouting along with the rest of them. The noise filled her mind. She became aware of another noise, the sound of heavy vehicles pulling up behind them. She looked over her shoulder and saw three truckloads of troops tumbling out with weapons at the ready. The crowd surged and swayed like a single living organism. Ahead she could see the first demonstrators running up the steps of the station and battering at the door. Behind her she heard the popping sound of shots being fired. A man went down and the crowd surged away from him in panic. The soldiers were moving into the crowd now, swinging their weapons savagely, clubbing people out of the way. More shots. She saw Dan turn towards the soldiers in alarm and the fat man move away from him. She couldn't take her eyes off him. Someone, not a soldier, was watching Dan too. Why wasn't he watching the troops? He wasn't part of the crowd, he was separate, not panicking like everyone else. Now he was moving up beside Dan. There was a glint of metal. Two more shots. Pop, pop. They sounded so harmless. Dan looked down at his chest in surprise at the red beginning to spread. He turned, looking for his friend, but the fat man had gone. He fell slowly to his knees and subsided sideways onto the ground. The crowd parted and rolled away. People were running, but Laura was rooted to the ground, staring at Dan. As if in a trance she moved forward against the flow. Bing shouted to her, 'No Laura,' but she did not hear him.

Laura came up to Dan and knelt down beside him. There was pink froth on his lips which bubbled as he breathed in and out. His eyes were closed. She bent close so that he could hear and told him, 'Dan, Dan, don't die now. Not now. You can't die now.'

Dan's eyes opened, staring with shock. She could not tell if he saw her or not. His lips parted as he tried to speak, but nothing came out. He tried again and Laura bent even closer to hear. Painfully, he whispered, 'Who are you?'

'Laura, Dan darling. I'm Laura. I'm here.' She could hear the blood bubbling in his lungs as he breathed.

He was trying to speak again. She could see the effort he was making. One last supreme effort. His lips opened and he said the single word, 'Laura'. Then as she watched in horror, the light went out of his eyes.

Bing was pulling at her urgently. The crowd had thinned and the soldiers were arresting the stragglers. 'Come on, Laura, we've got to get out of here.'

She shook off his hand. 'No,' she screamed. 'I'm not leaving.' She leaned down to Dan and hugged his body. 'Talk to me, Dan, Talk to me. You remember me don't you? I'm your lover, your friend. Laura.' She was oblivious to the blood staining her clothes.

Bing pulled her again. 'He's gone, Laura. And if we don't get out of here we're in deep shit.' Bing glanced nervously about. A soldier was looking at them curiously. He began to approach but just then a demonstrator rushed past, knocking him off balance. The demonstrator kept running and the soldier set off in pursuit.

Bing leaned down again and wrenched Laura to her feet. She was crying freely now, letting out the pain in great sobs of grief. She tried to fight him, but he gripped her by her arms and shook her. Suddenly she gave in and allowed him to lead her stumbling away. As they approached the car they could see three soldiers menacing the driver with their weapons, gesturing for him to move on. Vytautis was peering around anxiously, but had started his engine and begun to move off when Bing shouted for him to stop. The driver heard him and hesitated but the soldiers gestured angrily for him to keep going. He began to move again when Bing shouted one of the few Russian words he knew, 'Nyet, Nyet.' Panting, he ran up to the soldiers and fumbled for the press pass which Rezchikova had given him. For a few moments the soldiers argued. One of them was looking curiously at Laura's bloodstained blouse. With angry gestures, they stepped aside. Bing and Laura tumbled into the back seat and the car gave a lurch as Vytautis nervously let out the clutch. For a few moments the vehicle hopped up the road, then the revolutions settled down and they sped away.

The drive back passed in a blur. Laura was in shock. She lifted her hands and stared at the blood on her palms. Questions raced through her mind. Had Dan recognised her when he spoke her name the instant before he died? She would never know.

The hotel lobby was a madhouse of reporters and TV crews chattering excitedly to each other, high on the adrenalin of the massacre. There was a queue of people at the telephone waiting impatiently to file copy. Laura, her face streaked with tears, looked around her and took in the scene. 'Jesus!' she said in disgust. 'These people are getting off on this. They're actually glad about the shooting.'

Bing could not disagree with her. He had seen this media frenzy many times. 'Don't worry about them, they're just doing their job. Come on, I'm going to get you upstairs.'

Bing began to walk her through the crowd. She wrenched her arm free and cried out, 'You vultures! People died there today. Real people, not just names in a newspaper. Doesn't anyone care?'

The hubbub ceased. The journalists stopped talking and gave this wild-looking woman with the bloodstained clothing a surprised look. The young reporter with horn-rimmed glasses who had been hoping for action that morning, said, 'Hey lady, if you don't like the job, go shoot the social pages.'

There was a laugh and the news people resumed their chatter. It was not unheard of for people to become stressed around death and she looked a bit old to be covering stories like this. Perhaps she was another case of burn-out. They'd all seen it before.

Bing took Laura's elbow again and guided her through the lobby. When they got to her room she threw herself face down on the bed and closed her eyes, trying to shut out the horror she had just witnessed. Bing sat down beside her and gently stroked her back. Feeling inadequate, he said nothing. There were no words. Slowly the tears subsided to gulping sobs. She lay there silently for several minutes, then turned on her back and looked up at Bing with swollen eyes.

'I'm sorry,' said Bing.

Laura reached up and held his hand. 'I saw it, Bing. It wasn't the soldiers. It was a man in civilian clothing. He shot him twice. The fat man was with him but when the riot started he slipped away. The other man was waiting. It was a cold-blooded, planned assassination. Christ, what sort of people are they?'

'Very dangerous people, Laura. And they won't hesitate to kill us if they find out what we're here for. We should leave as soon as we can. There's nothing more we can do in Vilnius.'

'Yes, we've got what we came for,' she said bitterly. 'We found Dan. The only trouble is he's dead.'

'I'm going down to find out what's going on. Can I get you anything? A drink?'

'No thanks. I just need to be alone. I've got a lot to think about.'

'All right. I won't be far away if you need me.'

Bing leaned down and kissed her on the cheek. She

335

put her arms around his neck and hugged tight. He held her for a long moment then gently disengaged himself and walked to the door. 'Lock it behind me, Laura, and don't open up for anyone.'

Walking along the corridor he heard the chatter of recorded voices spooling at double speed coming from one of the rooms. A TV crew was in there editing their story. In the lobby, things had calmed down a little. Some of the journalists had gone back out. Bing knew they would be chasing up official sources for comment. While events were in this state of confusion he felt safe, but once things calmed down, he wondered how long it would take for people to start asking questions about the news photographer who had behaved so uncharacteristically. He knew their cover would not stand up to detailed scrutiny. If Dan's killers had an inkling of their knowledge, they would spare nothing to stop them.

Bing had no doubt that the murdered man was Dan Parkinson. Seeing him in the flesh was the final chapter of the story. He had it all now, complete with pictures. All he had to do was get out of Lithuania and find somewhere safe to write. He glanced around the lobby. There were still a few newsmen grouped around the telephone. He had a story which was bigger than anything they could dream about, so big that people were prepared to kill to prevent it being told. Yet he felt no elation.

Thirty-three

The attack on the demonstrators outside the television station was a turning point in the fight for independence. The international media reported that ten people died at the hands of the Russian soldiers. The local papers, in an uncensored outcry of rage, printed the names of the dead. They were mostly ordinary citizens who had gone along to the rally out of curiosity. Among them was one Sergei Bulak, a factory manager, married with one child. Like the others, they reported, he was shot by soldiers trying to prevent the demonstrators from storming the TV headquarters.

Three days after the killings, Ivashov and his KGB Director had their regular meeting in the President's office in the Kremlin. They reviewed the Lithuanian situation only briefly as it had moved beyond the KGB's area of interest. It was not until the end of their discussion that Igor Bakutin brought up the subject of the American defector. 'About that loose end in Vilnius,' he began.

The President looked up from the papers he had been tidying. 'Oh yes?'

'It's fixed.'

'Ah, I had forgotten. There's been no word about the MIA business at all. I daresay it's blown over.'

'Perhaps the Americans took care of those two,' suggested Bakutin.

'Hmm, probably. Anyway they can make all the fuss they like now can't they? The proof no longer exists.' Bakutin's intelligence was the one bright spot in a day that had been filled with crises. The Baltic states were not the only ones clamouring for independence and the economy was descending further into chaos. 'Well done,' the President said. 'You and your people have handled it well.'

'Are you going to tell Blanchard about Bulak?'

The President smiled. 'I don't think so. Let him stew.'

As Bakutin took his leave he thought to himself that he must congratulate those concerned. Ponomaryov had come good in the end, and a little flattery now would do no harm. When he returned to his own office he called his Head of Counterintelligence.

'I've just returned from seeing the President and he is pleased with the outcome of the Vilnius business.'

'Good,' said Ponomaryov warily. He was waiting for the 'but'.

'Well done.'

Ponomaryov took the receiver away from his ear and looked at it in surprise. He put it back and said, 'Thank you. Our people did well. I should mention in particular the work of the case officer, Major Timashov.'

'Yes I remember Timashov. The overweight fellow. Why, what part did he play?'

'He set it up. It was a delicate thing. He wouldn't admit it but he had, I think, some personal regard for Bulak.'

'But he did his duty.'

'Oh yes, there was never any question of that.'

'Perhaps he should be recognised in some way, a commendation of some sort.'

'I'll mention it to Lazutkin.'

'Yes, do that,' said Bakutin. He paused for a moment remembering a project which he had been considering for some time. 'Perhaps I'll speak to Timashov myself.'

Safe behind the anonymity of the telephone, Ponomaryov raised his eyebrows in surprise. 'Whatever you think, Comrade Director.' He replaced the receiver carefully. The Director personally congratulating a lowly major. He would never keep up with these changes. Perhaps it was time he thought about retiring.

Timashov spent the time since returning from Vilnius in a near-catatonic state. Each day he travelled like a zombie from his apartment to his office, where he sat all day motionless at the desk, smoking and toying occasionally with some papers, but incapable of work. During this time he thought of suicide, but he knew he would not have the courage to carry it out. He contemplated resigning, but that was impossible. People did not resign from his occupation, especially not at a time like this. He was sitting at his desk staring blindly into space when Bakutin's secretary called and told him the Director wished to see him in his office.

When Timashov lumbered in, Bakutin was surprised by his appearance. His clothes were even more rumpled than he remembered and there were food stains on his coat front which he had not bothered to remove. The collar of his shirt was dirty and there were dark shadows under his eyes. He looked like a man who had not slept for a week. For a moment he wondered if he had made the right choice. He had carefully reviewed Timashov's personal file. His career had been exemplary, the business with his brother and now Bulak had demonstrated his loyalty beyond doubt and the success of his latest assignment had shown that he was a lot more efficient than his appearance suggested. He decided to continue on the course he planned.

'Major Timashov, sit down. I want to congratulate you on your work in Vilnius. A distasteful task, but one which had to be done and you did it well.'

Timashov stared at him without speaking. Bakutin went on, 'I'm going to promote you to Colonel and I want to give you a new job. I've had the idea for some time that we need a new directorate, highly secret, which will concern itself with matters like the Vilnius affair. As you know the organisation is going through radical changes at the moment. In the new Soviet Union there is supposed to be no need for clandestine tasks like the Bulak matter. Unfortunately, you and I know that that is not the case. The world is a harsh place. There will always be delicate matters which will need someone of your experience to handle. You'll have your own staff and you'll receive orders from me alone.'

Timashov looked stricken. 'No no please,' he mumbled. 'I'm not the right person, you're making a mistake.'

Bakutin smiled at this modesty. 'Nonsense, Timashov, you're perfect. Now, go back and put your office in order and we'll meet again in a week to work out the details of your new appointment.' Bakutin got up from his desk and walked around as Timashov slowly rose from his seat. He was a strange one all right. He seemed to be in shock. Then again, you'd need to be pretty strange to perform the terrible deeds he seemed so good at. Suppressing a shudder, he clapped Timashov on the back as they walked to the door. 'Well done. We need people like you. People who aren't afraid to face the unpleasant tasks. Until next week.'

Timashov left without a word.

The feeling of satisfaction in the Kremlin was not reflected on the other side of the Atlantic. President Blanchard and Brandon Paine had heard nothing further about the disappearance of the two Americans in Britain. And the less they heard the less they liked it. Blanchard in particular was tortured by the spectre of the story appearing any day on the front page of the *Washington Post*. Logic and experience told him that he would hear about it well in advance of publication. They would call the White House for comment first. Even so, he opened his newspapers every morning with a feeling of dread.

Each time he met with Paine they discussed the matter, but there was never anything to report except that Hammond and his men were still trying every avenue at their disposal. They had feelers out all over Britain and Europe, even a man staking out Connick's home near Sydney, should they head back there. But Connick and the woman had vanished into thin air.

The President knew that Paine would tell him the moment he heard anything, nevertheless he couldn't help himself asking if there was anything new as they began their situation meeting in the Oval Office. Paine shook his head, 'Nothing, Mr President. Maybe no news is good news.'

'And maybe Connick is sitting down at the *Post* right now negotiating the rights to his story.' The President badly needed to hit out at someone. 'What about Hammond? He's screwed up all along the line here, why don't we fire him?'

'We can't fire Hammond. He knows too much. Besides, he doesn't officially exist.'

'Well retire him then, whatever it is you do with these people.'

'What we normally do is give them enough money to keep them safe and happy and out of mischief for the rest of their lives and ask them to quietly bury themselves somewhere out of the way.'

'Dammit, he makes a botch of things and he gets rewarded. Isn't there some way we can kick his ass?'

'No way that's safe, Mr President. Until Connick and Bailey turn up I think the best thing is to leave him doing what he's doing.'

The President wasn't happy. He was supposed to be the world's most powerful man and here he was waiting for the world to cave in on him. The worst of it was that he knew there was nothing he could do. 'OK,' he said grumpily. 'Keep me informed.'

Thirty-four

The day after the massacre Laura woke feeling listless and depressed. The curtains were closed and she lay in bed in semi-darkness trying to assemble her thoughts. She wondered if what she felt was grief. If so she should weep, but she had no tears. Seeing Dan die had been horrible, and yesterday, clutching him on the ground she had been overcome by unbearable emotion. Today she did not feel as though she had lost a lover. Perhaps if she had had time to talk to him, to rekindle that old spark she would have felt his death more keenly. As it was she felt nothing. Perhaps that was how her mind coped with grief. Maybe her mourning was still to come.

Questions. The same question she had asked herself for two decades. Who was he? And now new ones. Did he recognise her before he died? And why was he killed?

A devastating thought occurred to her and she sat bolt upright in bed with its impact. Dan had died because of her. Whoever had tried to prevent them finding him had tried to kill her and Bing, and when they failed they had killed Dan.

Laura covered her eyes as if she could physically shut out the thought. There was a knock on the door and Bing asked if she was awake. She called to him to wait, rose swiftly, put on a robe and ran a comb through her hair.

She went to the door and let him in and saw the concern in his eyes. Bing walked to the window and pulled the curtains. Outside it was a dull day with a light rain falling. The streets were practically deserted. Somewhere in the distance a church bell tolled. She remembered it was Sunday.

Bing turned away from the window. 'This afternoon we're on a flight to Moscow,' he told her. 'Then JAL to Tokyo. We'll think about where to go after that.'

'I killed him, Bing,' Laura said. 'If I hadn't tried to find him he'd still be alive. I killed him as surely as if I pulled the trigger.'

Bing shook his head. 'You didn't kill him, Laura. The Russians did that.'

'If I hadn't been so damned obsessive, so selfish about having to know what happened, he'd still be alive today.'

'You shouldn't blame yourself. Sometimes obsessions have to be followed no matter what the consequences. What was the alternative? Just forget him? You said yourself you could never do that.'

'I wish I had. God how I wish I had.'

Bing stepped up to her and took her in his arms. She rested her head on his shoulder. He said, 'You know, I told you when we first met you shouldn't get involved. I was wrong. Sometimes it's right to get involved. You were doing what you had to do.'

'Is that what you're going to write in your story? Follow your heart no matter what the price?'

'I haven't thought about it. Maybe something like that.'

'I don't know what to do. I feel as if I should be grieving, but I don't think what I feel is grief. It's more an awful disappointment, mixed up with guilt. I can't explain it.'

'Don't try. The tears will come later. Believe me, they'll come.'

Laura pulled back from his shoulder. 'You know about grief don't you?'

'Yes, I do.'

'Because of Phuong.'

'That's right, because of Phuong.'

'What should I do?'

'Start packing. We're leaving in three hours. It's almost over.'

It seemed that they had been travelling for ever. Australia to Thailand, Thailand to Moscow, Moscow to Kazakhstan, Kazakhstan to Moscow to London, London back to Moscow then to Vilnius. The weeks and the miles were like a weight pressing her down and now there was more air travel to be endured, half the world to traverse. They landed at the domestic airport in Moscow and caught a taxi to Sheremetyvo. Laura had hardly noticed the airport when she was here last, now she was struck by how run-down it looked. Most of the lights in the terminal were out, either because no one bothered to replace the bulbs, or as an economy measure. The pasengers moved around in a dim half-light, waiting in long queues to be processed. The immigration officers were as slow and meticulous as they had been the last time they left. Laura should have been jumping with nervousness, but she was beyond feeling. She stared back without expression as the uniformed officer studied her features with sullen intensity. He seemed as suspicious of people leaving Russia as entering, as he laboriously pecked at his computer keyboard and, after much pursing of lips and shaking of the head, let her go. When he followed Laura to the booth, Bing got the same painstaking examination. He hoped his expression did not give away the tenseness he felt. Again reluctantly, like a policeman forced to free a criminal on a technicality, the young officer handed back the false passport and waved him on.

They walked past the duty free shop and up some steps to a cafe where Bing ordered two coffees. It seemed to him that there was menace in everything around him: the sullen waitresses, the heavy-set Russian who followed them into the cafe and sat regarding them fixedly from a few tables away. The announcement of a half-hour delay in the departure time had the sound of a trap to Bing and even when they finally boarded and the plane left the runway, he could not let go the feeling that it had all been too easy. After all their troubles so far he could not believe that they were out of danger.

The flight took them through the Soviet night. After a few hours the sky outside the window began to lighten and Bing could see, six miles below, a barren landscape of bare, snow-covered hills. Mongolia perhaps. As they flew on over the sparsely occupied continent Bing got a sense of the vastness of the Soviet Union and his own insignificance. It was a country which would snuff out its enemies like a man swatting flies. They had escaped from Russia but he would not feel completely safe until his story was published. He was longing to return to his shack at Coaster's Retreat, but it was still too soon for that.

As the flight droned on he began thinking about the story. He would offer it to the *Washington Post* or the *New York Times*. Either of them would love it. He wondered if Dan Parkinson's parents, or perhaps a brother or sister, were still alive. The paper could put someone on to that. Once the story broke the repercussions would keep a team of reporters busy for months. He didn't want to know about any of the follow-up. He'd write his piece, get paid and let the vultures pick over the remains.

He turned and looked at Laura asleep beside him. Her chest was rising and falling regularly as she breathed. A few wisps of hair had fallen over her eyes and she twitched slightly in her sleep as they tickled her. Gently he lifted them out of the way. Laura stirred and murmured something but did not wake. Bing studied her for a long time, taking in every feature of her face. She had been through a lot, more than most people could cope with, and she needed time to heal. The search which had brought them together was over. In a few more days after he broke his story she would probably return home. He realised he did not want that to happen.

Laura shifted beside him and her eyes opened. 'How did you sleep?' he asked.

'Like I was dead. I felt exhausted.'

'You've been under a fair bit of stress lately, you're entitled.'

'And so are you.'

'Yes, I'll collapse soon, but not yet. My mind won't stop working.'

'What have you been thinking about?'

'The usual, what to do next.'

'I just want to stop moving, settle down somewhere and clear my mind.'

'Yeah? I know a good place for that.'

'You do, where?'

'Well there's this place I know on a river in Sydney. It's just a little shack, nothing fancy, but the weather's nice and the fishing's good.'

Laura managed a wan smile. 'Fishing eh? That's a real drawcard.'

'I thought that would swing it. You won't be disturbed there and you could stay as long as you like.'

'That's a nice offer,' Laura said. 'I'll have to think about it.'

'I forgot to add one thing. The company's fantastic.'

Laura was silent for a few minutes. Bing thought she might have gone back to sleep, then she spoke. 'We didn't make a very good start did we?'

'Not exactly. The thought was there if you remember, but events kept getting in the way.'

'I feel like I've come to the end of something. Maybe it's time for a new beginning.'

'I'd like to help you with that.'

'It'll take time, Bing. I'm not sure if it will work.'

'Me neither, but I'd like to try.'

'All right, let's try. Let's take it one day at a time and we'll see how it works out.'

'All right,' said Bing. 'One day at a time.'

Thirty-five

Larry Bebbington hated boats. He hated the way they moved all the time and threw spray in your face and left you exposed to the elements. His idea of surveillance was sitting in an air-conditioned room in a comfortable chair with a tripod-mounted telescope, coffee and sandwiches close to hand. Or maybe in a properly-appointed van. He'd used some nice vans in his day that were as comfortable as his own lounge room, with air-conditioning, refrigeration, the works. Unfortunately the only way to do this job was in a boat.

When he had first surveyed the area he noticed a sign saying 'Tom Grant's Boat Hire' right by the ferry terminus. The boats turned out to be a fleet of open runabouts used for fishing. He was damned if he was going to sit in one of those for hours on end and besides, if the job went on for more than a day or two Grant would start to get curious.

So, with Hammond's permission Larry Bebbington had bought a boat. It was twenty feet long with a big outboard motor, reasonably comfortable seats and a canopy to keep out the weather. For a week now he'd been going out every day at dawn, anchoring within sight of Connick's house at Coaster's Retreat and pretending to fish.

On his way to the surveillance spot each day he cruised past the ferry terminus and checked to see if Connick's commuter boat was still there. Apart from that there was nothing much else he could do. He knew he was conspicuous, and he'd told Hammond how unsatisfactory it was, but his orders were to stick it out until Connick turned up.

Today had been as bad as the rest. He didn't know which was worse, the boredom or the slight seasickness that he felt all the time he was on board. At dusk he gave it away, tied the boat up at the marina and phoned Hammond in London. 'Bebbington here,' he said testily. 'Nothing again. This is driving me crazy. I wish something would happen.'

Hamond replied with his braying salesman's laugh.

'Did I say something funny?'

'Funniest damn thing I've ever heard. Something's happened all right. We're too damn late. We've been chasing the wrong people.'

'What the hell are you talking about?'

'Have you watched the television news today?' Hammond said.

'I've been out in a goddamn boat, how would I watch TV?'

'Well go listen to the radio. I don't know what sort of news services they have down there but I guarantee this will be all over it.'

'What will be all over it? For Christ's sake, Hammond.'

Hammond was still laughing. 'Don't let me spoil it for you, just go listen.'

'What's going on? Do you want me to continue the surveillance?'

'The surveillance?' Hammond seemed close to hysteria now. Bebbington waited impatiently until Hammond got hold of himself. 'When you hear the news you'll understand.'

Bebbington turned on the radio. It was tuned to a music station, but normal programs had been replaced by a special news bulletin from Washington to which he listened in stunned amazement. When it finished he smiled with satisfaction. At least he wouldn't have to go out in that damn boat again.

Arnold Flashman was a wealthy man who loved art for its own, rather than investment's sake. He had discovered Brett Davey's work before he became fashionable and his paintings hung in several of his houses. He occasionally visited Brett at Coaster's Retreat and had become friendly with some of the other people who lived there. When Brett's neighbour Bing Connick called him and asked if he could rent his holiday house at Pearl Beach he agreed immediately. Gentleman that he was, he insisted he have it for nothing and stay as long as he liked.

Pearl Beach was a village on the coast about thirty miles north of Sydney. At its southern end there was a high, wooded headland and from there a crescent of yellow sand curved northwards. The houses, nestled in the sandhills behind the beach, used to be typically shabby weekenders until the place became trendy. Now they were architect-designed and sold for city prices.

Bing and Laura did not listen to the radio. Instead Bing put on a CD of a Schubert symphony, turned it down low and opened up the windows to let in the salty breeze from the ocean. The rich tones of the music mingled with the sound of the surf a hundred yards away.

Laura disappeared into the shower to wash away the grime of the long flight from Tokyo. She emerged twenty minutes later, wearing jeans, a blouse and no shoes. Her skin was shining and her blonde hair clung damply to her scalp. She smelt of steam and soap.

Bing followed her in and let the hot water do its work on the jetlag. By the time he emerged, wearing his old Hawaiian shirt and shorts, Laura had made a simple lunch of fresh bread rolls, tomatoes and avocados which they'd bought at the village store. Bing pulled a couple of cold beers out of the refrigerator and they sat on the verandah looking out at the waves as they ate.

Neither of them spoke much. Laura recalled that Bing's silences used to unnerve her. She'd regarded them as hostile and in that she had been partly right. Now she took comfort in them.

'When are you going to write the story?' Laura said.

'I should do it straight away. It's our insurance policy, but I think I'll leave it till a bit later. It's already written in my head. It won't take me long to bang it out.'

'I feel safe here for the first time in . . . how long has it been?'

'I don't know. Weeks since we left here to go to Bangkok.'

'Weeks? It feels like years. I feel like I've been travelling half a lifetime. I'll never be the same again.'

'Nor me,' said Bing. He got up and walked to where she was sitting. 'Your hair looks beautiful like that. The drowned look.'

'Thank you. It took a lot of work to get it this way.'

'You'll have to give me the name of your hairdresser.'

He leaned down towards her and she raised her face to meet him. They kissed tentatively at first, then with growing passion. Bing pulled her to her feet and led her to the bedroom. The restraints which held them back in the past were gone, the only thing that mattered now was their need.

Afterwards they slept, waking at dusk in each other's arms. They got up and Bing barbecued some lamb while Laura tossed some fresh lettuce into a salad. Bing opened a bottle of Hunter River red and they conversed without haste, lazy in their enjoyment of each other's company. Laura told him a little about her childhood in Nebraska, Bing told her about his life on the river and some of the odd characters who lived there whom she would meet in days to come. Neither of them mentioned the events of the last month. Bing thought of turning on the radio for some news, but he did not want to break the spell. Tired and relaxed, they went to bed and made love tenderly once more.

Next morning Bing woke first. He slipped on a pair of shorts and set off to walk to the store. His feet had gone soft from wearing shoes and he hobbled on the pebbles. They would harden up soon enough. He returned with the morning paper and carried it into the kitchen.

The headline covered half the front page. 'US, RUSSIAN PRESIDENTS ORDERED MIA MURDER—WITNESS TELLS.' Bing sat down at the kitchen table and quickly moved to the story. It was datelined Washington.

The US and Russian Presidents allegedly conspired together to murder two US citizens in an attempt to cover up revelations about an MIA, questioned and held in Russia during the Vietnam war.

The conspiracy has been revealed in a series of handwritten notes between Presidents Blanchard and Ivashov, advising each other of mutual efforts to silence the Americans.

The allegations were made by the *Washington Post*. The paper claims it was given copies of the secret communications by an employee of the National Security Agency, who translated them for President Blanchard.

The employee, Mr Ross Sellars, told the paper he was revealing the documents because his conscience troubled him.

Mr Sellars said the two Presidents conspired to murder the US citizens, a journalist, Mr Bing Connick and the former fiancée of the airman, Mrs Laura Bailey, after they began searching for the missing man in Russia . . .

Bing read on in amazement. The paper named Dan and said it was not known if he was alive or dead. It outlined President Blanchard's knowledge of the abduction dating back to the time he was Director of the CIA. The whistleblower, Ross Sellars, was in hiding and was speaking only to the *Post*.

There were separate stories detailing reaction from the White House and the Kremlin. Both Presidents had refused to comment so far. President Blanchard was expected to give a news conference at any moment.

Bing was sitting at the kitchen table reading when he felt Laura behind him. She kissed him and said, 'Hi. Ready to start work today?'

Bing kissed her back. 'I don't think I'll bother.' Silently he handed her the paper. 'It seems like someone else has done the job for me.'

Thirty-six

Bing guided the runabout slowly upriver. Laura was sitting in the bow with her back against a cushion, looking back at him as he described the occupants of each house they passed. He pointed to a weatherboard building almost hidden in the bush. That's Brett Davey's place. We might drop in and say hello on the way back.'

'First I want to catch one of these fish you've been talking about. You know I only came here because you promised.'

'Don't worry, we'll have bream for dinner tonight. I guarantee it.'

Bing guided the boat in close to the mangroves. The tide was high and the tree trunks grew straight up from the water. He took up a short fishing rod rigged with a light line and a lure. 'Do you know how to cast one of these?'

'My daddy used to take me trout fishing when I was a little girl. I haven't done it for a long time but I'll give it a try.'

'Cast as close to the roots as you can and wind in slowly.'

Laura swung the rod back with a practised action and flipped the lure to within a foot of the trees. She began to retrieve slowly and the rod suddenly bent downwards.

The reel screamed as the line ran out against the drag and she gave a whoop of excitement.

Bing watched her with pleasure as she skilfully played the fish. Her eyes were shining and her cheeks were flush with excitement. She knew what she was doing. When she had it exhausted and flapping on the surface next to the boat he slipped the net under and lifted it clear. It was a fine two-pound bream.

After half an hour they had six good fish. Bing started the motor and headed back down the river. As they approached Brett Davey's pontoon they saw him waiting for them. He was dressed in his usual summer attire of paint-spattered sarong and nothing else.

'Hey Bing, you're famous.'

Bing scowled. 'I know. Brett Davey, meet Laura Bailey.'

Brett said, 'Hello Laura, I've been reading about you.'

Laura grimaced and held out her hand. 'Pleased to meeet you Brett.'

Brett sensed that now was not the time to ask them about their adventures. He shook Laura's hand and moved on to more immediate concerns. 'What have you got?'

'Six bream,' said Laura.

'Laura caught them all,' Bing added.

Brett whistled in appreciation. 'Impressive. I netted a few prawns last night and got some blue swimmer crabs in the trap this morning. Want to come over for dinner? You supply the fish, we'll supply the rest.'

Bing looked at Laura. 'I'd love to,' she said.

They arrived back at Brett's place just as the sun was going down. Brett took charge of cooking and showed Laura how to use the fish heads and prawn shells for stock. He chopped the fish into chunks, cleaned and quartered the crabs and threw them, along with the prawns, some tomato puree and herbs, into a huge pot.

Kath served the stew directly from the pot at a great hardwood table in the main room of the house. Children and adults all sat down together to eat. It was a noisy family meal, which made Laura think of childhood meals in warm farm kitchens in Nebraska. She felt safe.

They told Kath and Brett about the events of the last few weeks, starting from the time they left Australia; the meeting with Buggins in Bangkok, Bing's escape in Moscow, the execution attempt in Kazakhstan, their adventures in London and the final terrible scene outside the TV station in Vilnius.

They listened in open-mouthed silence. When the narrative was over Brett said, 'My God, you're lucky to be alive.' Instinct told them not to enquire too deeply about Dan.

'You're going to need some time to get over all that,' Kath said to Laura. 'Are you planning to stay a while?'

She took Bing's hand and squeezed it. 'I'd like to stay for a long time, but I'll have to at least go back and visit soon. I run a ranch.'

'Do you miss it?'

Laura thought for a moment. 'I don't miss the business of ranching, but I miss the country.'

'I can understand that. My people live in the Northern Territory. To us the land is not just something you own, it's part of us and we're part of it, like the rocks and the trees and the animals.'

'Yes, I know exactly what you mean.'

The two women smiled at each other.

When they said their goodbyes at midnight the river was still and glassy. The wind had died to nothing and the air was warm. They slipped smoothly along in the little boat, the phosphorescence glittering in the wake. Occasionally a mullet threw itself clear of the water, falling back with a splash of light.

They undressed and got into bed. Laura lay back and sighed with contentment. 'I like your friends. I think I'm going to like Kath a lot.'

'That's good.'

'I've never heard you talk so much about yourself. They must be pretty close.'

'Yeah they are. We get on.'

Laura rolled onto her side to face him. 'I think I love you Bing Connick.'

He kissed her gently. I don't know what I'd do without you, he thought, but did not dare say it aloud.

Laura and Bing quickly lost their European pallor. After a week at Coaster's Retreat their muscles had toned and their skin was brown and healthy again. They could not get enough of each other. They were as passionate as teenagers, making love in the most unexpected places and at any time of the day and night.

Bing slept deeply, untroubled by the nightmare. One night he was woken by a strange sound. In the half-conscious moment between sleep and wakefulness he wondered if perhaps it was some animal crying in the bush, then his mind cleared and he realised it was Laura sobbing quietly beside him.

'What is it?' he whispered.

'It's Dan. I dreamed about Vilnius. It was so vivid it was like I was there again.'

'It'll go away. It just takes time.'

'I'm so happy here, Bing, but every now and then it comes back like a shock. I keep seeing his blood on my hands and I realise that he died because of me. I can't get over the guilt.'

'Come here.' He put his arm around her and she rested her head on his chest. He could feel her tears wetting his skin. He stroked her hair and held her. After a time she slept.

Winter came and with it log fires and nights spent with friends eating and drinking, talking, laughing and arguing. The news told of President Blanchard's resignation. The Soviet President was deposed to make way for another, more reformist leader. Some reporters tracked Laura and Bing to Coaster's Retreat, but they sent them away with no comment other than to confirm that they were the ones who had sought out the MIA. Other reporters tried in vain to find the missing Dan Parkinson in the Soviet Union, but in the chaos of the collapsing

356

empire it was an impossible task. The new Russian President pledged to open the KGB files and solve the mystery once and for all, but it seemed the files could not be found. Some experts speculated that he might still be alive, but in the end the fate of Dan Parkinson remained a mystery. Eventually, as always, the story ran out of impetus and the media turned their attention to other things.

Summer. Laura began to think that she might go home for a visit. The land pulled her. She asked Bing if he would come with her, but the thought of America appalled him.

One morning she woke early and padded naked to the kitchen for a glass of fresh orange juice. She sat at the table as the morning sun streamed in and looked about her at the place she had grown to love and which she knew would never be home. She finished the juice and walked back to the bedroom. Bing was awake. He gazed with admiration at her and smilingly pulled the bedsheet aside. She went to him and mounted him and they loved with a passion which was the more intense because she knew it was the last time.

When they were spent she lay beside him, afraid to speak. She had no need.

'When?' Bing asked.

'As soon as I can get a flight. I'll call today.'

'And will you come back? No, don't answer that. Remember what we said?'

'One day at a time.'

'Right. One day at a time.'

Later, Laura walked alone to the end of the jetty and stood gazing out over the river. For minutes she remained motionless, trance-like. Then, with a decisive movement, she reached into her pocket and pulled out a small cylindrical container. Shaking out the roll of undeveloped film, she unhesitatingly drew back her arm and tossed it far out into the water. She turned, walked away and did not look back.

Afterword

The headline in the *New York Times* of 8 December 1991 was typically bald. 'SOVIETS SAY THEY QUESTIONED US POWs HELD BY HANOI.'

The article quoted a former KGB General, Oleg Kalugin, saying that he had personally supervised the interrogation of three US servicemen in Hanoi in 1978, three years after the Paris peace accords had been signed and all Americans were supposed to have come home. One was an air force pilot, one was a high-ranking naval officer and the third was a CIA agent.

The *Times* was not the first news outlet to report Kalugin's assertions, although it was the first to be taken seriously. Two months earlier, in October, he had made the same statement to an Australian television program, *60 Minutes,* and to a feature writer working for the *Los Angeles Times*. The story had a roundabout journey to prominence. It was followed up by a columnist on the *San Diego Union* and finally caught the attention of the influential Eastern States media. It was only then that Washington began to take notice.

While these claims of Russian involvement were not new, what was new was that a high-ranking Soviet official was prepared to state categorically that interrogations took place.

Major General Kalugin was an interesting man. During the Cold War he headed the counterintelligence arm of the KGB. Between 1975 and 1978 he was in charge of the team in Vietnam which, if his story was true, would have interrogated Americans. He himself never visited Vietnam. He said he controlled the interrogations from Moscow. In 1990 Kalugin retired from the KGB and was elected to the Soviet Parliament, which was later disbanded.

After his statements were published in 1991, in the US he was invited to testify before the Senate Committee on POW/MIA affairs. In January 1992, amid a flurry of publicity, Kalugin arrived in Washington. It was the first time a member of the KGB had appeared before a Senate Committee and his testimony received wide media coverage. Kalugin was a convincing witness. Dressed immaculately and speaking confidently in flawless English, he repeated his story to the senators and named the officer who carried out the interrogations, Colonel Oleg Nechiporenko.

Naturally enough the news media were keen to speak to Nechiporenko and in the new open Russia, where former KGB officers spoke to newsmen with impunity and appeared before the US Senate, it was now possible for them to do so. By 1992 the KGB had been renamed the Russian Intelligence Service and it was anxious to display an attitude of openness and cooperation with the West. In Moscow, the Intelligence Service invited news representatives to a press conference to meet Colonel Nechiporenko. Dapperly dressed and sporting a white goatee, he denied Kalugin's story. He had interrogated a CIA agent, he said, but it was in 1973, not 1978.

Who was lying? Was Kalugin making up his story for reasons of his own? Or was the Russian Intelligence Service trying to discredit it through Nechiporenko?

At about the same time as the Kalugin story broke in America a Russian journalist, Yuri Pankov, published a piece in the Moscow weekly *Kommersant,* quoting an anonymous KGB source who had interviewed US POWs in Vietnam. According to this source, five POWs had been interrogated and afterwards executed by the North Vietnamese. Pankov also spoke to Russian Air Force pilots who had carried American POWs within Vietnam and Laos. His story supported Kalugin's assertions of Russian involvement, but it went further. According to Pankov, a US airman had been taken from Vietnam to the Soviet republic of Kazakhstan in September 1967.

For years, the flawed history of American investigations into the MIAs had abounded with rumours of Russian involvement. Certain intelligence analysts had deduced that one and possibly as many as ten POWs were taken to Russia. They had a word for them. They called them MBs, Moscow-bound. Pankov's inquiries appeared to give credence to these allegations. As a result of Pankov's story, two officers from the US Embassy in Moscow travelled to the town of Saryshagan in Kazakhstan, where there is an air defence research establishment. Not surprisingly, they found nothing.

Both the former Soviet President, Mikhail Gorbachev, and the Russian President Boris Yeltsin have publicly pledged to do all they can to find out if the stories of Americans being taken to Russia are true. It is reasonable to suppose that such information would be easily accessed through the KGB archives. However, despite their pledges, no evidence has been forthcoming either to support or deny the allegations. In the absence of hard facts, investigators have been left to speculate on what might have happened. Such speculation, while tantalising, should of course be treated as fiction.